DREW

BOOK ONE OF THE PERFECTLY INDEPENDENT SERIES

AMANDA SHELLEY

Copyright © 2020 by Amanda Shelley
All rights reserved.
ISBN
E-book: 978-1-951947-12-5
Paperback: 978-1-951947-13-2

Editor: Renita McKinney
A Book A Day
www.abookaday.biz
Editor: Sue Soares
SJS Editorial Services
https://www.facebook.com/sue.soares71
Proof Reader: Julie Deaton
Deaton Author Services
http://jdproofs.wixsite.com/jddeaton
Cover Design: Amy Queau
Q Design Covers and
https://www.qcoverdesign.com

No part of this book may be reproduced in any form or by any electronic or mechanical means, including information storage and retrieval systems, without written permission from the author, except for the use of brief quotations in a book review.
This is a work of fiction. Names, characters, organizations, places, events, and incidents are either products of the author's imagination or are used fictitiously. Any resemblance to actual persons, living or dead, events, or locales is entirely coincidental. The author acknowledges the trademarked status and trademark owners of various products referenced in this work of fiction, which have been used without permission. The publication/use of these trademarks isn't authorized, associated with, or sponsored by the trademark owners.

Visit my website at
www.amandashelley.com

CONNECT WITH AMANDA SHELLEY

Want to be the first to know about upcoming sales and new releases? Make sure you sign up for my newsletter as well as connect with me on social media and your favorite retail store.

Website:
www.amandashelley.com
Newsletter:
https://bit.ly/3iyENe6
Facebook:
https://www.facebook.com/authoramandashelley/
Instagram:
https://www.instagram.com/authoramandashelley/
Twitter:
https://twitter.com/AmandShelley
Reader's Group:
https://www.facebook.com/groups/AmandasArmyofReaders/
Amazon:

https://www.amazon.com/author/amandashelley
Goodreads:
https://www.goodreads.com/author/show/19713563.Amanda_Shelley
Book Bub:
https://www.bookbub.com/profile/amanda-shelley

ABOUT THE BOOK

Abby

My heart races, palms sweat and knees go weak.

I've never seen anyone like Drew in a science lab. He's made me a firm believer in chemistry existing outside a textbook. Until his ego shows up. Nope – No thank you. Moving on. I mean… who has an entourage in college?

When our professor announces we'll be stuck as lab partners, I nearly lose my mind – I'm certain my dreams of becoming a doctor will go up in smoke with a distraction like him around.

Drew

I don't date during the season.

The number of trolls who venture into the arena simply to chase jerseys is unbelievable. In fact, I typically distance myself from the social side of being a college athlete because I have my eye on something bigger than our next D-1 championship.

I've taken painstaking measures to avoid distractions – at all costs. This plan has worked perfectly until Abby shows up at my door.

Gone is the *plain studious girl* I left in lab the day before. Left in her place is the intriguing woman I want to know better. Here I thought she wouldn't be a distraction – yeah right... I am so screwed.

Abby's gorgeous and there's nothing plain about her.

I am this close to having it all. If I let Abby in, will my perfectly laid out plans disappear?

1

DREW

DAMMIT, I'm late.

I hate being late.

Glancing at my watch, I know class hasn't started yet, and I still have some time, but it's been ingrained into me since I can remember—always show up early. Being on time is late—and today of all days, I need to be early.

I inwardly growl and readjust my backpack to pick up my pace.

From the moment I've walked into this building, I've been bombarded with fans. Sure, this is a D-1 school. I'm the captain of the basketball team and the lead scorer, so it's to be expected. But enough is enough. Of course, I'm noticed. It's not like I can help it. Being nearly six foot five is something I'm using to my advantage. I need to keep this scholarship and graduate with honors to get into med school. I know playing ball will only get me so far, and my dreams are bigger than that.

I like basketball, and I happen to be great at it. But ever since my sister died of Hodgkin's when she was twelve, I've had my heart set on becoming a doctor. I want to treat kids like her, with hopes of different outcomes. With her illness, my parents were up to their ears in debt. I've had to use my height and athleticism to get me where I am today—And I'm not taking any chances.

I've heard to choose my seat wisely on the first day of class. I need to get there to scout out the room. Not wanting another person to stop and discuss my last game, I keep my eyes trained on the floor, until I make it to the door.

Once inside, I'm relieved there are plenty of vacant seats still available. As I stop to look it over, I immediately notice a guy's face light with recognition, and I quickly dart my eyes away.

Nope. Not a chance.

Unfortunately, I've learned the hard way some fans can't get past my stats when I'm off the court. I need a partner who's focused. So, without a second's hesitation, I continue to survey the room for the person least likely to be a distraction.

Then I spot her.

From behind, she's non-descript. Her brown hair is tied into a ponytail, and she wears a plain white t-shirt, jeans, and Chuck Taylors. She isn't socializing with anyone, and with her large-framed glasses, she fits the bill for being the stereotype of studious.

As I approach, I find her focus unyielding. With her eyes locked onto the textbook in front of her, I can't help but smile. I need someone like her. When I pull out my stool and sit beside her, she doesn't even glance my way. It isn't until I greet her with, "Hey," she looks in my direction for the first time.

I smile and nod in greeting.

No recognition.

But her eyes lock with mine, and we stare at one another for a long moment.

Great. Maybe she does recognize me.

Should I look for somewhere else to sit? I glance around and find the tables around us are filling up.

But she grabs my attention when she finally mumbles, "Hey, I'm Abby."

I nod and grin in her direction. She clearly already knows my name.

A flicker of annoyance crosses her features before her expression turns blank, and she quickly returns her focus on her book. The corner of my lips pull up without my consent, but the moment I recognize it, I quickly school my features. She's just what I need her to be.

While we sit here, a guy I don't recognize stops by our table and high-fives me as he gushes, "Great game, man. You had me on the edge of my seat."

Not wanting to be rude, I shrug and accept the compliment. "Thanks. We were on fire last night. That's for sure." Then I make an exaggerated effort to pull out my notebook from my backpack.

I exhale heavily as he takes the hint and says, "You sure were. I'll see ya around." He looks in the direction of a vacant seat a few tables down, then returns a smile back at me. "Good luck next week."

"Thanks, man."

Abby continues reading her book in silence. But when a string of people stop and congratulate me on our latest win, I notice when she balls her hands into fists a few times. I try to keep my conversations short, but as soon as a person leaves, I'm greeted by another. It's not like I can help it. I'm not about to be rude to fans, and it's not like class has started yet.

When another person approaches, I hear a loud huff from my side. But I do my best to ignore it. *She's obviously annoyed and just as focused as I need her to be.* I grin in amusement. My gut has never steered me wrong.

As this new guy greets me, the professor walks into the room, and relief washes through me. At least with class in session, people will leave me alone, and I can focus on why I'm here.

The professor stands in the center of the room for just a moment before clearing his throat. Everyone scatters to their seats as the aging man in the tweed jacket gathers some papers to put onto a podium. Once everyone's settled, the professor stands in front of the room and announces, "Good afternoon, ladies and gentlemen. Look to the person next to you. This is your permanent lab partner. There's no switching unless you want a ten percent reduction of your grade."

Gasps are heard around the room, and a light chuckle escapes from me as I glance to the girl next to me. Her jaw practically lands on the table, and it's all I can do to contain my amusement.

I manage to mumble, "It's a good thing I chose you for a

partner then, isn't it?" as the professor launches into discussing the syllabus as well as his expectations for the semester.

Somehow, Abby manages to regain her composure, and the two of us spend the remainder of class taking copious notes. Abby's diligent, and that's just what I need with the season getting started and my full course load to stay on track for graduation.

Typically, athletes take fewer credits during the season, but if I'm to graduate on time and get into the school of my dreams, I can't afford to slow my pace. As it is, I'm already busting my butt and have had to take summer classes to get the extra classes necessary for admissions.

When class ends, Abby quickly gathers her things and abruptly stands. She won't even look in my direction as she makes her way out of the room. I can't help but stare after her and wonder what our next class will bring.

2
ABBY

WHEN I RETURN to lab the following Tuesday, I'm quickly reminded of how I left. To avoid any conversation with my extremely popular lab partner, I stormed out of the classroom, wondering how I'll get through this semester.

He might not be that bad, but the string of people who kept stopping by... No, thank you.

Unfortunately, I remember the professor's words all too well. I can't afford a drop in my grade, especially this early in the semester.

It's only one semester, Abby. You can do this.

Of all the places he could sit, why did he choose my table? When he mumbled something about specifically choosing me, what the hell did he mean by that?

Shit, is he planning on using me like Toby did my sophomore year?

Christ. I can't go through that again. There's no way in hell, I'd survive. I'm already taking twenty credits and working as many hours as I can at the library. I can't afford to pull someone along to maintain the grade I deserve. Don't even get me started on how it felt to be used emotionally either. Been there, done that. Don't need the t-shirt.

When I walk in, I'm relieved to find my table empty. I sit and unpack my things to settle in for class. I'm reviewing this week's reading assignment to make sure it's fresh in my mind when the hair on the back of my neck pricks. As if my body knows he's here before I consciously do, I'm alerted to the scrape of a stool next to me.

I smile a greeting in his direction.

Maybe today will be different?

He nods once, then digs into his backpack, and for the most part, ignores me.

The smell of his cologne permeates the air, and my stomach does a small involuntary flip. I take a moment to take him in, realizing I might not have given him a fair chance the last time we met.

Okay, I'll admit it, the man's hotter than anyone I've ever laid eyes on in a science lab. His dark hair makes his blue eyes pop and smolder. His large frame fills out the black shirt he's wearing, as if it's been tailor made for his well-defined chest underneath. His square jaw with just the right amount of scruff and perfect lips are set in a straight line. When my gaze finally returns to his eyes, I find him staring expectantly. *Holy hell! Get it together, Abby. He's just a guy. But why did he choose to sit by me?*

To regain control over my body's reaction to the mysterious man sitting next to me, I quickly return my attention to my book. Though let's be honest, I've hardly read more than a page since he made his presence known.

My ability to focus is thwarted by his sexy masculine scent and the unpacking of his materials for class. From the corner of my eye, I can't help but watch his every move. As he pulls out a notebook, his muscular arms flex, and his elbow slightly brushes my arm, sending shivers down my spine.

Just like last time, people continue to stop and chat with him before class begins. My mind drifts to our last encounter, and I grimace.

I'm quickly reminded of how he thought he was too important to be bothered to mention his name... *and how my instant crush ended*. The man may be hot as hell, but he's one of the cockiest people I've ever met, and that's a major turnoff. Hell, I don't have time to date, even if he wasn't so arrogant, so it's a moot point.

As our professor gets lab started, I'm relieved to find the guy next to me may be a jock, but at least he isn't a dumb jock. He's able to hold his own when it comes to our chemistry lab. We work solidly together until the professor announces we can take a short break and leave when we're through.

"Do you mind if we work through the break? I have someplace I have to be after class," Mr. No Name asks.

I'd ask his name but after working with him for the past hour, it's just beyond weird to ask now. Maybe he'll get called something other than Dude, or Man and I can figure it out, when the time comes.

Knowing I have work later, I eagerly agree but keep our extraneous conversation to a minimum. "Sounds great."

We work diligently until a steady stream of people flock over to converse again about the latest game. Mr. Socialite is all smiles as he greets them. I try not to let it bother me, but after the fourth interruption, I finally lose it and feel the need to remind him of the commitment he's made.

In an attempt to regain control of my emotions and not sound like a complete bitch, I take a deep breath, but it comes out as a huff instead. This immediately gets the attention of Mr. Blue Eyes, who's now staring in my direction. I almost lose my nerve when I see the smile form on his perfectly shaped lips. *Who the hell is this guy?*

"Okay, *partner*," I spit out. "Are we doing this, or what?" I look pointedly at the lab in front of us. "You said we needed to get done early because you had places to be. You're too busy being Mr. Socialite to get anything done."

Instead of his smile fading, it grows into a smirk. "I knew you'd keep me on track." I glance around, and everyone has dispersed. "I just might keep you around."

"Keep me around?" There's no way I heard him correctly. "What do you mean by that?"

"I made the right choice by sitting here. You won't let distractions stop us, and you can pull your weight on the labs." He shrugs his shoulders, as if that should explain everything.

How should I respond to that?

Thankfully, my irritated vibe must project throughout the room because we're no longer bothered by any unwelcome guests. A sense of satisfaction spreads over me as we finally delve back into our project.

When our work is finished, we make use of the remaining

time going over required assignments. Blue Eyes (yes, that's what I'm calling him since I still don't know his name) and I decide we'll need to meet outside of class to get a few things done.

When I suggest meeting at the library or local coffee shop, he hesitates and looks around.

"What?" I ask, not understanding his reaction.

"Well..." His chagrin look surprises me. He glances around the room once again. *What is it that makes him think everyone is watching?* "Can you think of anywhere less... public?"

How big of him to not want to be seen with the likes of me. *What a cocky-ass!* "If you'd rather do this on your own, go ahead. We'll just split up the work." After spending time working with him today, I'm confident he'd do the quality of work I expect from myself.

"Um..." His expression is unreadable for a split second before he continues, "I want to complete it together."

"So, you want to collaborate but not be seen with me in public? Exactly how am I supposed to take that?" My defenses are up. If this douche canoe wants my help but doesn't want to be seen with me, he's got another thing coming.

"Ohmigod, no," he quickly replies. He suddenly looks apologetic, which catches me off guard. "This has nothing to do with being seen with you. It's just... me..."

"Oh, so the 'it's not you, it's me' speech." I shake my head in disgust. I thought we'd gotten along fine for our lab, but this takes the cake. "Wow. That's rich." I pack up my things. I'm not putting up with his crap. I have better things to do this afternoon.

I stand to leave, but he captures my wrist as I do. There's a spark of electricity pulsing between us, holding me in place.

"Abby, let me explain," he pleads. His blue eyes pierce through me as if he's searching for the words, as I remain frozen in place.

"Go for it, Blue Eyes," I say without any thought.

"It's Drew." His lashes lower as he looks somewhat humble—sort of. The jury's still out until I hear what he has to say. I shake my head at his statement, wondering what the hell he's talking about.

"My name. It's Drew. There's no problem being seen with you. Before you jumped to conclusions, I'm trying to explain how public places tend to get hectic. You've only seen a glimpse of what it's like." He looks around the room as if that's an explanation. "I think it would be best to meet somewhere out of the public eye, for your sake... So we won't have as many distractions."

"Oh." What can I say to that?

"Come to my place. We can avoid groupies," he suggests with a shrug.

"You want me... to come to your place?" I stare at him, surprised. Then another thought hits me. "You have... groupies?"

Drew looks as if he's unsure of himself. As I look into his eyes, trying to read his expression, I suddenly realize how tall he is. My neck hurts to look up at him. How tall is he? I'm five-eight, and I'm a dwarf to him in comparison.

He shakes his head, breaking my internal inquiry about the giant before me. "Christ, this is more difficult than it has to be."

He looks around before whispering, "I promise nothing will happen to you at my house. I'm on a tight schedule with practice, and I don't have time to traipse all over campus trying to find a private place to work."

"Well, this is unexpected," I mumble. A thousand questions come to mind, but not knowing where to start, I just stare.

He takes my silence as needing further explanation. He spends the next few minutes quickly explaining how his popularity has risen since their championship game last season. He tells me it's hard for him to blend in as a typical guy on campus. I have no doubts of that because come on... look at him. He may be arrogant as hell, but he's ultimately a beautiful giant. Though I'd never admit that part to him aloud.

Drew's voice is low and deep when I finally concede to his request. "You mentioned having to work tonight. What about tomorrow night? We need to get the first assignment done before I leave Friday morning with the team. It's due on Monday, and I won't be back until Sunday afternoon."

Shit! Of course, he chooses tomorrow night. It's my only night off this week, and I already have plans. Though... my plans won't happen until later. Maybe I can squeeze in a study session to finish this assignment. Knowing it's our only option, I sigh in defeat. "Okay. Tomorrow will work. Can we make it early because I have plans later?"

Drew's blue eyes widen for a fraction of a second, but it's quickly replaced with relief. "Sure. Give me your phone number, and I'll text my address. Practice ends at six, would seven work for you?"

I'll have to figure out dinner on my own. Not sure my

friends will understand, but they'll get over it—hopefully. We weren't planning to leave until eight, so it should be fine. I nod in agreement and give him my number. Within seconds, a notification arrives on my phone. Knowing it's likely him, I keep it in my pocket.

"Thanks." Drew sighs with relief as he gathers his things. "I gotta get to practice. But I'll see you then."

I let out a heavy sigh, knowing my friends might kill me for changing our dinner plans. "Sounds good. I'll have to leave as soon as we finish. My friends will be expecting me."

"Hey, Abby?" Drew asks hesitantly. "Would you mind keeping my number between us? I'd rather not share it with everyone."

"There go my plans for writing it on the bathroom stall," I mumble sarcastically. Drew just stares. His dark eyebrows pinched. Apparently, my humor's lost on him. I quickly put him at ease. "Just kidding," I assure him, and his perfect lips quirk into a smile. With that, he leaves our table, leaving me to stare after him.

WHEN I GET to my apartment after work that evening, I throw my backpack onto the couch and plop down beside it. My roommate Chloe looks up from the kitchen table where she's studying and asks, "That bad?"

"Yes," I say in a groan. "I have the worst lab partner this term."

"Tell me more," she prompts. Chloe's a psychology major

and has been one of my best friends since summer camp in seventh grade. She likes to use what she's learning in class on me, so I stick my tongue out at her to let her know I can see she's up to her usual antics. She bursts out with laughter. *Great. Just what I need.* "Seriously, Abs, tell me what's going on. There must be more to this than a crappy lab partner. This is so unlike you."

"Uggh," I groan in frustration. It would've been so simple if only he'd chosen a different seat.

When I don't say anything, Chloe merely lifts a perfectly sculpted eyebrow and waits.

"Well..." I start, not knowing where to begin. Taking a deep breath, I let it all out, knowing I might as well start from the beginning. "It all started on the first day of class. This *guy*..." I say with disdain, causing Chloe to smirk, but I ignore her. "Plopped down next to me and didn't say anything but 'hey.' Then as if he's Mr. Popularity himself, he has a constant string of people stopping by to talk about his latest game. It was soooo frustrating. They wouldn't go away. As soon as one person left, it was like it signaled another to drop by. *Just when I think it couldn't get any worse*, the professor walks in and makes an announcement that was like a bomb detonating. The person next to us has just become a permanent partner for the term, unless we want a ten percent reduction in grade... You know I can't have that. I need straight As or med school's no longer an option." I inhale sharply and take a breath. But I can't help but cringe when I think of what I must tell her next.

"But that's not even the worst part. We must finish up a

project before Friday, and the only night the almighty Drew is available, is tomorrow night. Can you believe that?"

"Um..." Chloe puts her index finger on her chin and pretends to think something over. "What part of this is supposed to be bad enough to put you into such a pissy mood?"

My eyes nearly pop out of my head as it snaps in her direction. "That's how you're going to handle clients one day?" I ask in disbelief. Chloe's known for her zero BS policy, but this is a bit over the top, even for her.

"You're going to miss me next year, and you know it. It's all your fault, you're a Brainiac and will graduate earlier than the rest of us."

Yeah, I came into CRU with enough credits to graduate a year early, but she's known that since—forever—so I simply roll my eyes and wait for a real response.

"Well, since you know me *too* well, you'll never be my client, but... I think there's more than what you've just told me at play here. What's really going on?" Her brown eyes widen as she waits expectantly.

I shake my head and stare at my feet, now propped up on the coffee table. "I... Uh... have to cancel our dinner plans tomorrow night. I must study with *him*, at seven. It shouldn't take long to finish our project, but I won't be able to meet you until afterward."

"Girl, you're *not* bailing on us tomorrow night." Chloe steps up from the table, and her oversized scoop-neck top slips off one shoulder. She comes to stand in front of me at the couch as she eyes me suspiciously. "We all coordinated our schedules to celebrate *you*. This is a once in a lifetime thing. You can't ditch us. Syd will be pissed."

I shake my head, knowing she's right but trying to make her see she's not hearing me correctly. "I'll be there. There's no doubt about that. I'll just have to meet you after dinner. That's all. I looked over the assignment, and it really shouldn't take Drew and me too long to complete."

As if she doesn't believe me, Chloe cocks her head to the side and eyes me suspiciously. "Are you sure you're not trying to ditch us? I know you didn't want to go out. But this is a big deal. You *have* to go with us."

Internally I groan, though I keep that thought to myself. "Chloe, I won't miss this. I promise."

"If you do, Sydney will kick your ass." Chloe tries to keep a serious face but completely fails, causing both of us to break into laughter.

Sydney's our other roommate. She's been one of my closest friends since freshman year. She lived across the hall from us in the dorms. She's taking tomorrow night off, which is rare for her. I know she needs the money. I also know they want to celebrate together. This only comes along once in a lifetime.

"I know it's important. I'll be there," I promise.

3
DREW

ABBY'S STUBBORN. But she's also tenacious. She remembers facts and numbers like nobody I've ever met. It's almost as if she has a photographic memory. I can only wish my mind worked as well as hers. For the most part, Abby sticks to business, and I get little in terms of reading her personality beyond having an amazing work ethic.

As I contemplate our conversation in class, I can't help but smile. It took me a while to explain that I play basketball, and since we won the championship game last season, my popularity's skyrocketed. I can't be a random guy on campus anymore. Her feisty attitude and unwillingness to take my shit is quite intriguing. I couldn't help but laugh when she asked, "How do you expect to blend in as a giant?"

I've been a starter here at Columbia River University since freshman year. I didn't redshirt because I don't intend to play in the NBA. I'm here to get my degree. However, the fame that comes with winning is a double-edged sword. It opens doors for me, but being unable to be a regular guy on campus is unnerving.

I don't usually date during the season to avoid distractions. The number of trolls who venture into the arena to simply chase jerseys is unbelievable. I distance myself from the social side of being a college athlete by keeping my head in the game and focusing on my studies. Besides, this keeps the girls away who aren't interested in getting to know the *real* Drew Jacobs.

When there's a knock at my door, promptly at seven, I rush to greet Abby. I'm blown away by how different she looks. Standing before me is a beautiful girl with long, wavy, brown hair and brown eyes I can see. She's wearing a fitted blue sweater that accentuates her curves and a faded pair of denim jeans that are worn in just the right places. The only resemblance to my nerdy lab partner is her Chuck Taylors.

"Abby?" I state, but it comes out like a question. *So much for not being a distraction. I'm so fucking screwed.* Of course, my cock chooses this moment to spring to attention. I've never been more thankful for wearing jeans, as my basketball shorts leave little to the imagination.

"Drew?" She stares for a moment. "Planning on letting me in?"

"Um... sure." I step aside as I swing the door open wide to let her pass. I point to the couch where I've set up my homework and gesture for her to take a seat. As she walks by, the scent of her coconut shampoo and something that's entirely her has my senses on overload. Unfortunately, this also leaves me having to inconspicuously adjust myself before I make it to the couch beside her.

She catches me staring and self-consciously pats down her hair as she asks, "What?"

"It's just... you look... nice tonight. Special occasion?"

"Oh," she groans, catching me off guard. "It's my twenty-first birthday, and my friends *insist* on going out." She rolls her eyes and shrugs as if it's not a big deal. Interesting.

"Why the hell did you agree to study on your birthday?" I ask in disbelief.

She shrugs... again. "I take my classes seriously. Besides, you said this was the only time you're available."

Holy shit. I'm an ass. I hadn't given her a choice when I suggested the time, I threw one out there, and she agreed. I have to rectify this. I can't force her to study tonight of all nights. We only get so many birthdays, and I'm not about to ruin one of hers.

I may be hardcore when it comes to staying focused for school, but I'm not a complete monster. "Are you busy tomorrow night?"

"I work in the early evening. Why?" she asks speculatively, apprehension clearly written across her features.

Realizing she'll be drinking later, another thought hits me, and I blurt out, "Have you eaten?" With as serious as she is, I'd almost bet my favorite pair of sneakers that she hasn't had much experience with alcohol. She needs to eat a decent meal.

"Not yet. I'm picking something up after we finish our assignment." She sets her backpack down next to the coffee table and sits on the couch next to where I've laid out my things.

"Don't unpack," I say as I pick up my notebooks and books.

There's no way I'm making her stick to our plans. I know firsthand just how short life can be.

"Drew? What's going on?" She looks at me as if I've lost my mind. *Hell, maybe I have.* But I'm not a complete selfish asshat, and I won't ruin her birthday.

"Can we study tomorrow night?" I ask, giving her an option this time.

"That shouldn't be a problem. But what are you doing?" A perfectly arched eyebrow cocks over her beautiful golden-brown eyes. *How had I not noticed them earlier?* I draw in a deep breath and steady my thoughts.

"I'm taking you to dinner. Since it's your twenty-first birthday, there's no way I'm forcing you to study, let alone go out without a proper meal." Thinking about my twenty-one-run, I add, "You need food and lots of it."

"Why?" she almost stutters. "Why would you do this?"

"Well..." *Why am I doing this?* "Birthdays are important. You're only given so many, so you have to make them count."

4

ABBY

I WATCH in disbelief as Drew gathers his things like his ass is on fire and takes them into what I assume is a bedroom. When he returns a few minutes later, he's wearing a nice black sweater, dressier jeans, and dress shoes. Compared to the faded jeans and t-shirt he was wearing when I arrived, I can't help but appreciate his effort. He grabs his wallet, keys from his kitchen counter, and stops to ask, "Are you ready?"

"For what?"

"I told you. We're getting dinner."

Cocky much?

Leaving no room for argument, he places a hand on the small of my back and leads me to his black SUV. He surprises me by opening my door and waiting for me to get in to buckle, before closing it. *Maybe he can be a gentleman?*

To my surprise, the ride's filled with comfortable conversation on the way to God only knows where. He's yet to fill me in on our where we're going, but fills the time by making small talk about life on campus. Even though we've never met apparently, we lived in the same dorm our freshman year. *How could I not notice the likes of him?*

It's not long until we arrive at the restaurant. That's when I realize he's taken me to a nice place. I mentally count my cash on hand, knowing I don't have a lot to spare in my minuscule bank account. Working for the college as a library assistant, I only get paid twice a month, and payday's still a week away.

"Um, Drew? I'm not sure we should go here." I try to think of a way to suggest a fast food restaurant I can afford.

"Why not? It's your birthday. You deserve a special treat."

"Yeah... but... um..." *How the hell do I say this?*

"Relax, Abby, it's my treat. It's your special day." *Does he have special mind-reading abilities?*

"Are you sure?" I feel weird. It's almost date-like. Not that I go on many of those.

"Absolutely. Let's go inside and celebrate."

He grabs my hand and walks me to the door. My body trembles with the warmth of his hand in mine. Shivers race up my spine, and butterflies flip in my belly. I'm not sure what to make of Drew. Where did the cocky, self-absorbed jock go?

When we get inside, the hostess tells us she has a table available. We follow her in and are promptly seated at a cozy table in the back corner. It's not easily seen from the rest of the restaurant, and I wonder if Drew had anything to do with the choice of seating.

The hostess hands us our menus and asks if we'd like to have anything to drink while we decide. Drew orders a Coke, and I settle with water for now. My friends and I have plans later, and I don't want to get ahead of myself. I've heard plenty of horror stories of twenty-one-runs, and I have no intentions of being a statistic. Hell, I wouldn't even be going out if Chloe and Sydney didn't threaten to drag me out, kicking and screaming. They've been planning this for months.

When Drew immediately sets his menu down, I feel a bit self-conscious. Having never been here before, I'm unsure of what to order. Though he said he's paying, I want to feel out what he orders, so I can get something similar in price. "Have you already decided?" I ask as I continue perusing the menu with what I hope is nonchalance.

"Yeah, I'm getting the asparagus-stuffed chicken breast and a baked potato. Do you know what you'd like?"

I peruse over the menu, and everything looks delicious. But the thought of asparagus has my mouth watering. Hmmm... another thing we have in common, how odd. I didn't think there would be much after our encounters in class. "I think... I'll go with that as well."

Drew raises an eyebrow but doesn't say anything.

As soon as the waitress takes our order and leaves, Drew asks, "So... what made you choose CRU?"

"Well..." I say as I finish a drink of water. "I've wanted to come here since I was little. My parents encouraged me to tour many campuses, but I had my heart set on CRU. When I came to visit my sophomore year in high school, for summer camp, I was determined to make this my college."

"You came to summer camp at Columbia River University?"

"Yeah, it was a science camp. Geared toward girls in math and science. We got to stay in the dorms for a week and see what college life was like. It was inspiring, to say the least."

"Wow... I spent my summers in high school focusing on one basketball camp or the next. I knew I had to get a scholarship to get into college, and thankfully, it worked out for me. But you were already focused on your career." He looks at me with wonder in his eyes and something else I can't quite describe. As I replay his words in my mind, and I try to figure him out, a thought springs to mind.

Crap. He's here on scholarship. There's no way he should pay for my dinner tonight. Thankfully, I can afford what I've ordered, so relief washes through me. But how do I bring it up to him?

"Everything okay?" Drew asks, pulling me out of my thoughts.

I shake my head and force my worries away. "Yeah. I'm fine."

He grimaces for a split second, then his features clear as if he doesn't believe me. But for now, he lets it go when he asks, "So... what's the plan for tonight?"

"I'm meeting my best friends Chloe and Sydney, and I'm sure we'll end up at Sherman's, since that's where Syd works. They know I'm not much of a partier, but they still insist on making sure I have a birthday I'll never forget."

Drew chuckles a deep laugh, and the butterflies are back in my belly.

"Does that mean you will *all* be drinking?" Drew asks in

curiosity, but there's something else there, too. Protectiveness? Why would he feel protective over me? We just met.

"I'm pretty sure one of them will be the DD." Most likely, it'll be Sydney. For being a bartender, she mysteriously never drinks. Maybe she sees the effects of alcohol on a regular basis and doesn't want to live it. Who knows?

"But you're not sure?" Drew asks with concern.

"Oh, I'm sure. Sydney wouldn't let us drive home with anyone who wasn't safe. She's a stickler about things like that. I'm sure she's got it all planned out anyway." I tuck a loose strand of hair behind my ear and take a drink of water. "It's not like her to do anything unplanned."

Drew leans forward on the table, resting on his forearms with interest. "What do you mean?"

We're interrupted by a waiter bringing our food. As he sets the food down, my mouth waters, and I let out a small moan in appreciation. Glancing at Drew, I say, "This looks amazing. I'm so glad you suggested it."

Drew's perfect lips form a smile, and my breath catches. "Thanks, it's one of my favorites. I found this place my sophomore year. I try to come back as often as I can." He takes a bite of asparagus and grins in appreciation, then looks to me questioningly. "You were telling me about your friend..."

"Oh, right, Sydney..." I laugh at his determination to stay on topic. "Syd and I met our freshman year of college, the day we moved into the dorms. She lived across the hall from me, and we've been friends ever since."

Drew nods, and an appreciative grin turns up his lips. "I have a few friends like that, though most of them are on the team. It makes it a lot easier when you have people in your corner."

I let out a deep sigh in agreement. "No kidding. I don't know what I'd do without Chloe or Syd in my life. We've lived together since sophomore year, in an apartment off campus. Though all of us have great families of our own, we've become our own family." As Drew takes another bite, I continue with, "Chloe and I have been friends since seventh grade. We met at summer camp one year and have been friends ever since."

Drew cocks his head to the side and asks, "Did you grow up in the same town?"

"Unfortunately, no," I sigh. "But we lived about an hour apart. I lived in the north end of Seattle, and Chloe lived near Tacoma. As soon as we started driving, we saw each other as often as possible. When we found out we were both attending Columbia River University, we knew we had to live together. Once we met Sydney, we've been like the Three Musketeers." I smile at the memory, then change the topic to him. "Where did you grow up?"

Drew shrugs. "I'm from Spokane. But I spent a lot of time growing up in Seattle." Something dark crosses his features, but it's gone before I can figure it out.

I realize we have another thing in common. "I've only been to Spokane a few times as we drove through to meet family in Coeur d'Alene. I loved visiting my cousins in the summer. They had a cabin on the lake. We'd spend hours waterskiing, tubing, and knee boarding as kids."

"It's a great town. That's for sure," Drew agrees.

When we're nearly done with our meal, Drew excuses

himself to use the restroom. I take this time to enjoy what's left of my delicious meal but mostly ponder over Drew. He sure is a lot different from the guy I met in class. I thought for sure I'd hate this semester, having him as a partner. But I think I might be wrong.

When he returns, he leans back in his chair, crossing his muscular arms over his chest. "Will there be any guys joining the Three Musketeers tonight?" Drew's question completely catches me off guard.

"Uh..." Where did that come from? "Not that I know of."

Surprise fills Drew's features. "So... is it just a girls' night out thing?"

I shake my head. "Not intentionally. As far as I know, we're all single. Chloe and Jeff broke up this summer, and Syd's... well, she's a bit picky. I doubt she's seeing anyone new."

"What about you? Are you hoping someone will be there tonight?" Drew's question rolls off his tongue with ease.

Laughter erupts from me. "Nope." I pop the p for emphasis. "I'm definitely not. I don't have time to date. Between work and school, I have my eye on the prize, and I'm not letting anything get in my way."

"Sounds like you have a story to tell..." Drew probes.

Shaking my head, I reply, "No. Not really. I dated someone most of sophomore year, but he ended up just wanting to use me to get through bio-chem. He was more concerned with the chemistry in our textbook than what we might've had together. So... No, thank you. I'm fine being on my own."

Drew's mouth hangs open, and his eyes widen. Before he can say anything, we're interrupted by what appears to be the entire waitstaff arriving at our table.

I eye Drew suspiciously. But his focus remains on the waitress.

"Excuse me... Ladies and Gentlemen..." a girl about my age announces, "can we please have your attention. It seems we have a birthday girl in our midst who wanted to let her birthday skip by. Please join us in wishing Abby a happy *twenty-first birthday*." She places a large red-velvet cupcake in front of me with a candle burning bright.

Hoots and hollers erupt around the restaurant. My eyes dart to Drew, who shrugs sheepishly as a wide grin forms on his perfect lips, then he joins in and sings.

I want to crawl under the table and die. It's so embarrassing being the center of attention. My cheeks flush, and it's all I can do not to cover my face. No one has ever done anything like this for me. When Drew pulls out his phone, I try to glare at him, but it's useless. He smirks and has a look that says there's nothing I can do about it, so I break out into laughter. *If I can't beat him, I might as well join him.* By the end of the song, we're both laughing.

When it's time to blow out the candle, I regain my composure and make a wish.

I hope I don't regret meeting Drew.

5
DREW

AS I GET to know Abby, there's no way I want her going out tonight without me. First, I'm completely enamored by her. She's not only smart but the more I get to know her, she's beautiful from the inside out. I'm just not ready for my time with her to end.

When she tells me she's never drank before, or had a serious boyfriend, I suddenly feel protective. Sure, she's safe going out with her girlfriends, but for some inexplicable reason, I feel like I need to be there, too.

I know I should probably examine this further, but I'll save that for another day.

Tonight, we're celebrating.

Hmmm... I wonder what I can say to not look like a complete ass by inserting myself into her evening?

When inspiration finally hits, I can barely contain the grin spreading across my face. Of course, I'm not able to share this brilliant thought with Abby because we've just arrived at her place. So, I let it go for now.

As we enter her apartment, Chloe and Sydney's wide eyes and gasps tell me they weren't expecting me. I smile and do my best to roll with the punches. Sydney and Chloe greet Abby with drinks in hand as they open the door, making me feel even more grateful I forced her to eat first.

I've never met Chloe, but I know Sydney's a bartender. I've seen her around. My buddies from the team have hit on her, and I've watched her shoot them down, one by one. From an outsider, it's been comical to watch. But I wonder if there will be a guy that turns her head at some point.

Before Abby can take a second sip of her drink, Sydney asks, "Have you eaten yet?"

"Yes, Mom," Abby exaggerates. She looks to me, throwing her index finger in my direction. "Drew here already made sure I had dinner. Apparently, his twenty-one-run was memorable and insists I eat lots tonight."

"You play basketball, right, Drew?" Sydney asks with suspicion. Great. Here it comes. *There goes just being me for the entire evening.*

"Uh, Yes. I do," I admit. Because what else am I supposed to say?

"I thought that was you, but it's hard to recognize you without your Bears gear on and being close up. I'm a huge fan and have been to every home game since arriving as a freshman." Her smile is genuine, until she smirks ruefully. "Though, my favorite player is DeShawn Miller. He has a jump shot that can't be beat from back court."

I chuckle. She's right. "I'll tell him you said that."

"Please don't. He already has enough ego to fill up the arena. But I truly see why people applaud his skills. He's a damn fine baller, and I appreciate him—for his skills only." She shrugs and turns her attention to Chloe. "Chloe, are you ready yet?"

Interesting. Not what I'd expect from a single coed. But I see her point. DeShawn's a fantastic baller, but he's got quite the reputation for playing off the court just as hard. From what I've seen about Sydney and my teammates at the bar, she's not into guys who are full of themselves. *Maybe tonight won't be so bad after all.*

If I can get them to consider my idea.

I might as well seize this opportunity.

When Sydney and Chloe appear to be ready, I offer to the room, "Would you like me to be your designated driver? I have plenty of room in my SUV, and I don't drink during the season." Sydney looks skeptical, but when I add, "This way, you'd be able to celebrate Abby tonight without having to worry." When a relief crosses her features for the briefest of seconds, I know I've hooked her.

Chloe's mouth hangs open, and Sydney just stares. They look back and forth between Abby and me, trying to determine if I mean what I've just said and if Abby is okay with my offer.

Please be okay with my offer.

Relief washes through me when Abby grabs Syd and Chloe's hands and comes to my rescue. "Sure, we'd love it. I can't wait to get with my girls and dance to real music."

Dancing. Great. I'd forgotten about that part of the experience. Sherman's is known to have a DJ as well as live music. I wonder what we'll be getting ourselves into tonight. The place is usually packed on the weekend, but for a school night, I doubt it'll be full.

As I get to know her throughout the evening, I quickly find Sydney's a great friend to have. I still don't know Chloe that well, but if she's hanging with these two, she must be a good person. Thankfully, Abby paces herself, having only one drink before leaving for the bar. We all pile into my SUV, Abby sits up front, and I can't help but smile with her as she anticipates her evening.

When we arrive, I spot a booth against one wall of the dance floor and suggest we take it before anyone else steals the prime real estate. For a Wednesday night, the place is hopping, and the DJ keeps a steady beat flowing. Sydney excuses herself, and she makes her way to the bar to order some drinks for the girls. From the short ride, I can tell she has her heart set on sharing some of her favorites with Abby tonight. She offers to get me a soda, and I nod in appreciation. Chloe goes with her to help carry everything back.

"I'll need to pick up my car from your place at some point tomorrow," Abby states as she watches a few couples out on the dance floor.

"I can make sure it's there in the morning. I work out at five thirty, but I'm usually done by seven. Will you need it before then?" I ask, wondering how I can make this work for her. She shouldn't be put out just because I hijacked her evening.

"Uh, that will be fine. My first class isn't until nine."

Before either of us can say anything, Sydney and Chloe return with some drinks for Abby to sample. After she's taken a sip of the pink concoction, she moans in appreciation. "Oh... this is so yummy," Abby cries over the music. "What is it?"

"Pink vodka lemonade," Sydney replies. They each take another drink in appreciation. It must taste good if the expressions on their faces are anything to go by. They close their eyes and slowly sip the drink they've been handed.

"You can't even taste the alcohol," Abby gushes. "I think I finally found a drink I like." The smile on her face is infectious, and I find myself grinning at her enthusiasm.

"That only makes it dangerous," Chloe teases. "Be sure to pace yourself. I remember one night when these snuck up on me." The look of disgust tells me there's quite a story there, that doesn't have a happy ending.

The song changes to one the girls must recognize because suddenly, they're screaming and jumping out of the booth to dance in the center of the floor. I remain in the booth, watching over their drinks. Of course, my attention is focused on my lab partner and her friends as well. Her long, wavy hair flows in rhythm to the music as she dances gracefully. Each sway of her hips, each bop with the beat, has me looking at Abby in a whole new light. Gone is the plain, studious girl I left in the lab the day before. Left in her place is the intriguing woman I want to know better. Here I thought she wouldn't be a distraction. *I am so screwed.* Abby's gorgeous, and there's nothing plain about her.

At one point, a slow song comes on, and both Sydney and Chloe are quickly asked to dance by a couple of guys who'd been watching them all night. Before Abby has a chance to be asked, she comes back to the booth and plops down.

"Whew! This is fun." Her cheeks are rosy, and her eyes are bright with enthusiasm. "I totally get why people love going out to bars now."

"Does that mean you'll be doing this more often?" I ask teasingly.

"Every once in a while, sure. But I'm not turning into a barfly or anything. I don't have *that* much time on my hands." She sips the last of her drink as she stares at her friends dancing with their partners.

The longing on her face makes me react before I have time to think of the ramifications. I snap to my feet and extend a hand. It's the first time I've moved most of the night, not wanting to draw more attention to myself than necessary, but my intent is clear. I want to dance with her.

She shakes her head and looks around as if I should be asking someone else. But I assure her she's the only one on my dance card for the evening when I state, "Come on. Let's go have some fun!"

We make our way to the dance floor, and I draw her body close to mine. Taking one hand in mine, I place my other on her hip. Her free arm wraps naturally around my neck. I feel a slight tremble from Abby when my palm reaches the base of her back, but she relaxes when I guide her around the dance floor with ease.

I take a bit of pride in the fact I don't allow Abby to just stand and sway to the music, like many of the couples out here on the dance floor. My freshman year, I was among the many men who signed up for American social dance as an elective. It might have started as a joke, but it's left me with many skills and I have no regrets. I lead her around the dance floor like a pro, guiding her through spins, dips, as I shuffle to the music in sync with the beat. Abby dances effortlessly in my arms and has no problem keeping up. As the song ends, I spin her around once more, and she giggles. I just might have to keep her out here, so I can keep the euphoric grin on her face. I've never seen anyone look so free or beautiful for that matter, just by dancing.

Now that I'm out on the dance floor, Abby, Sydney, and Chloe don't let me leave. At one point, I excuse myself to use the restroom. Unfortunately, a couple of jersey chasers try to corner me in the hallway on my return. I'm just about to say something to get them to back off when Abby shocks the shit out of me by appearing out of nowhere to rescue me.

"Excuse me, ladies." She pushes between us as if she's done this type of thing before. "Drew's helping me celebrate my birthday." Abby wraps an arm around me and gives them a pointed stare, showing their attention is unwelcomed. Then before I can take my next breath, she looks innocently up at me. "Syd and Chloe are waiting for us."

I can't help but be impressed. The jersey chasers back off without another word.

Abby's the perfect combination of assertive and innocence wrapped into one.

As we walk to our table, Abby pulls my head down so she can whisper into my ear. The action alone has me burning with desire. "Are you ever going to tell me what all the fuss is about?"

What the hell is she talking about? "Fuss?"

"You know. Why people fawn over you and you can't go out in public without causing a scene?" She rolls her eyes as if I should already know this.

"I play basketball." I shrug.

She cocks her head, not buying it. "Are you any good?"

"You could say that."

"You seem to be something special," she whispers. Then she grazes my cheek with a kiss. I'm not usually a touchy-feely guy, but I crave contact with her.

What is it about this girl that has me wanting to spend more time with her?

After a few more dances and a couple more drinks, the girls decide to call it quits, and I take everyone home. I make a point to walk Abby to her door. Chloe and Sydney make themselves scarce as soon as we get to their apartment.

As much as I'm dying to kiss her, I won't take advantage of her. From the look in her eyes, she wants more, too. Instead of making a move, I whisper the first thing to pop into my mind, "I hope you've had a happy birthday."

"Thanks for everything." She looks up into my eyes and rocks from her heels to her toes. I'm not sure if it's the alcohol or nerves, but that bit of wobble reminds me I need to tread carefully. There's been an undercurrent of chemistry zinging between us all night.

"If you give me your keys, I'll bring your car over in the morning," I offer, to stay just a moment longer with Abby.

She digs out her keys from her pocket and hands them over. "Thanks. It's a blue Honda Accord. I parked right in front of your place."

"Sounds good. I'll see you in the morning." It takes everything in my power to only kiss her cheek and say goodbye.

6
DREW

THE NEXT MORNING, a little after seven, I knock on Abby's door. Hoping I'm not waking her too early, I rock on my heels as I wait for what seems like forever for her to answer. Eventually, I hear a bit of a commotion from the other side, so I wait patiently, instead of knocking again. When the door opens, Abby sounds as if she's out of breath as she greets me with a mischievous smile, "Hello."

"Hey, Abby." I grin down at her and ask, "How are ya feeling?"

"Oddly enough, just fine," she admits. "Syd and Chloe insisted I drink a full glass of water and eat again when we got home. They also had me take some ibuprofen, just to be safe. I kept a good buzz going last night, but I never tipped over the edge of being drunk... ya know?"

She looks adorable as she meets my gaze. Her hair's in one of those messy buns girls do to keep it up and out of their face.

She's wearing an oversized CRU sweatshirt that falls off one of her shoulders and a pair of black yoga pants. She may have just rolled out of bed, but she couldn't look more gorgeous if she tried. My body instantly tightens, and the electric sparks that flowed between us last night quickly return.

When my brain catches up to my body's reaction to Abby, I scold myself. *Christ. Get it together, Jacobs. You don't have time for distractions like this. Even if you did, you've kept a strict no-dating during the season policy since freshman year. It's kept you on a winning streak, and you're not about to change it up now. Calm the fuck down.*

When I don't respond to Abby's comment, her cheeks darken, and she averts her eyes. Shit. Now I've embarrassed her. Hell. I can't win for losing with this situation. I quickly rush to assure her I understand. "I get it..." I swallow, trying to remember what I should be saying, but her golden-brown eyes turn my brain to liquid mush.

"You do?" she asks in disbelief. "I thought you didn't drink?" She sucks her bottom lip and chews on it, making my dick go hard and my pants go tight. *Why'd she have to go and do a thing like that? Geez, I can't catch a break here.*

I quickly clear my throat and mentally kick myself for letting my brain drift into the gutter. "I may not drink during the season. But I've had my share of booze. Trust me. There's a fine line between a good buzz and being drunk. I don't particularly like to lose control of my functions, but I can't say it's never happened." I shrug in defense. I've been an athlete for as long as I can remember. Alcohol was always at the ready, to celebrate our wins or commiserate our losses. Sure, most of my partying days were in high school, but it's a feeling you don't soon forget.

After losing Summer, I went a little wild in the off season. But once I realized I'm all my parents have left, I knew I couldn't do that to them. So, before it ever got out of hand, I straightened up my act and became the disciplined athlete I am today.

Before I let myself go down the rabbit hole of my past, I quickly change the subject. "Have you had breakfast?"

Abby's eyes widen in my sudden change of subject. "Um... No. I just got out of bed. All I've managed to do is get dressed."

"I typically eat after practice, and I'm starving. Wanna grab a bite to eat before our first class?" As if on cue, my stomach snarls, causing Abby to erupt with laughter.

"Sure," she says through an adorable giggle. "Let me get my things, and we can head out." Abby pivots and leaves the door open for me to enter their apartment. It's quiet, and I'm not sure if Syd and Chloe are already at class or still sleeping.

Abby strides over to her couch and picks up her backpack. She grabs her wallet from the coffee table and stuffs it into her bag. Then she walks to where I'm standing and slides her feet into a pair of sneakers by the door.

"I could've waited for you, if you needed to do more to get ready," I offer, not wanting her to feel rushed.

"I was ready. Besides, after last night, I'm starving. The thought of not having to cook breakfast is a treat I'm willing to give myself. Besides... if you haven't figured it out by now, I'm more of a what you see is what you get kind of girl. I don't spend a lot of time primping, as I have no one to impress." *Oh, you impress people, Abby. Trust me. How is it merely days ago, I thought the beautiful woman before me was plain?* Thankfully, I'm able to keep my thoughts to myself as we walk to her car.

As she unlocks the door, I head to the passenger side. When I get inside, she simply sits there and stares at her outstretched hands and feet. She moves them around as if she's doing stretching exercises and starts laughing.

Confused, I ask, "Mind filling me in on the joke? Or do you need me to drive?" Maybe she's had more to drink last night than she realizes.

"How tall are you?" she asks in wonder. She looks me over from head to toe, as I've jammed my body into the passenger seat. To give my knees some relief from the dashboard, I release the seat and sigh with relief as I glide it back to its furthest position.

"Six-five. Why?"

Abby smirks, and another chortle escapes. "Well, I'm not." And it's then I really look at her. She can't reach the wheel or the pedals beneath her feet and her arms and legs are stretched to prove it. Christ, she's adorable.

"Sorry," I say through the laughter I hold in. She doesn't seem that small next to me, but when I look at her flailing about, it's downright comical. "I couldn't fit otherwise," I try to explain.

"No worries. I just wasn't expecting to feel like a toddler

taking the wheel for the first time." She quickly adjusts her seat and the rearview mirror, and turns on the ignition. As she puts the car in gear and pulls onto the road, she asks, "Where do you want to eat?"

"Let's hit that diner down off Franklin Street. There's a full menu, so you can pick anything you'd like." The thought alone makes my stomach rumble... again, earning me a smirk from Abby.

"You sure you can make it?" Abby teases.

"You'd better step on it, to make sure," I quickly respond, earning a beautiful laugh. "I'm wasting away over here. I was running late this morning and only had time for a protein shake before my workout."

"Oh." Abby visibly cringes as she sneaks a peek in my direction. Concern fills her features. "I didn't make you late by staying out celebrating, did I?"

I shake my head, but since her eyes are on the road, I follow it with, "Nope. I just let myself sleep in a bit longer than usual. I was there on time, no worries."

Within a few minutes, we pull into the diner. Thankfully, there's not a line, and we're told to take an open booth of our choice. I lead Abby to the closest booth and hand her a menu that's permanently held on a stand at the back of the table.

Vanessa, one of the regular waitresses, walks up and introduces herself to Abby. "Hi! I'm Vanessa. Can I get you some coffee, tea, or anything to drink while you decide? Drew, would you like your regular coffee?"

I nod in appreciation as Abby eyes me suspiciously, then shakes her head and says, "I'll have an orange juice."

"Coming right up." Vanessa smiles and leaves to get our drinks.

Abby cocks her head to the side and juts out her chin. "So... you come here often?"

I shrug. There's no point in denying it. "Yeah. College kids usually hang out closer to campus, and this is a great place to study, so no one pays me any attention. The food's amazing and can't be beat with the prices. I... uh... usually come once or twice a week."

"Does Vanessa attend CRU?" Abby's eyes follow Vanessa around the restaurant as she asks.

"Yeah. She's a senior, I think. She's been working here since I found the place, freshman year. I needed a break from the dorms and ventured out one morning after practice. It's a hidden gem, as far as I'm concerned. This place keeps pretty steady with customers but over the years, we've made small talk, but I can't say I've seen her much outside these walls, aside from randomly bumping into her on campus now and again." I'm not sure why I add that last bit into my explanation. I guess I don't want Abby to think there's anything going on with Vanessa. She's pretty, don't get me wrong, but neither of us have shown an interest beyond casual friendship. Very casual at that.

"Oh," Abby states quietly as she focuses intently on the menu before her. I wish she'd look up, so I could read her hidden expression. I'm not sure why, but for some reason, I don't want her to get the wrong impression about me.

When she sets her menu down, I attempt to break her silence. "Decide what you want?"

"Yep." Abby grins with delight. "The bacon and Tillamook cheese omelet has my name written all over it."

"I'm going with the grilled chicken, mushroom, and asparagus egg-white omelet."

Abby's mouth drops wide. "That's a mouth full." Then her eyes narrow. "Wait, are you a health nut?"

What the hell does that mean? "I... uh... eat healthy. But I'm not a nut by any means. You saw me drink soda last night." I can't help but roll my eyes and shake my head at her assumption, before adding, "Obviously, I eat a variety of foods."

"I guess I'm just feeling a bit self-conscious," Abby shyly admits. "You've already risen before the crack of dawn, worked out, showered, and are choosing the egg-white option for breakfast. Whereas, I've barely hauled my butt out of bed. Sure, I showered last night, but I've done nothing but drive to the restaurant to eat. I'm such a slacker in comparison."

The way she scrunches up her nose at the end has me shaking my head in laughter. "You're not a slacker. Trust me. If it wasn't basketball season, I probably would've done the same thing and waited to work out this afternoon. But I don't exactly get to choose my schedule most days, so I'm stuck with what I've got. Those are the breaks for being a Division-One athlete and trying to graduate on time. It's all about time management." When Abby cocks an eyebrow and opens her mouth to say something, I cut her off, "Don't get me wrong. I'm not complaining about my circumstances. I'm just sayin' that in the off season, my schedule's a bit different."

Before Abby can respond, Vanessa comes to take our

order. By the time she's gone, Abby changes the subject. "I work tonight at the library until eight. Will you be able to work on our project after that? I can come to your place or reserve a private study room for us to avoid distractions. Doesn't matter either way."

Since she's already on campus that late, I offer, "Let's meet on campus. Text me. If you can't get a study room, I'll just meet you at your place. Since I hijacked your plans last night, no need to put you out any further."

Abby's face fills with humor. "You definitely made my birthday memorable, but I wouldn't say it was hijacked."

"Well..." I take in a deep breath and try to make light of things. "I was an ass in assuming your plans weren't important. I'll try not to do that again. But next time, just be straight with me, okay?"

"I think I can handle that," she says with a hint of sarcasm, which makes me smile. "Do you have practice again later?"

I typically get asked a lot of questions, but the way Abby seems genuinely interested in my schedule is endearing. Instead of being guarded, I easily explain how we usually condition on our own in the morning, then have full practices in the early afternoons and evenings.

"When do you find time to study?" she asks in disbelief when I tell her we play multiple games a week during the season. She had no idea how crazy my schedule is when it comes to traveling.

"I study *a lot* on the bus," I admit. "I'm shit for being a regular study partner with set times and dates, but I promise...

I'll pull my weight in this class. I can't afford anything less than an A, so you shouldn't worry. We can even video conference if need be," I offer as a solution to any potential problems we may encounter.

"Okay..." I hear the doubt loud and clear.

"Abby." I wait until I have her full attention. "I *have* to ace this class, or I can't get into med school. It isn't an option for me. So... trust me when I say, *I'll make the time.*"

A strange expression morphs onto her face. A cross somewhere between shock and admiration. I'm not sure which wins out as she simply stares at me in disbelief. Her jaw drops as if this tidbit of news apparently has rendered her speechless.

Ten seconds pass. Twenty. When things move past the point of her silence turning awkward, I end the torture with, "Abby? Everything okay?"

"But... you're... here on an athletic scholarship."

Great. She thinks I'm just a dumb jock. Perfect. "Uh... last I checked, doctors can play sports, too," flies out of my mouth acidly.

She pulls back and blinks as if my words have slapped her across the face. "No... that's not what I meant," she responds, and her eyes fill with regret. Fuck. I probably should listen to her explanation before jumping to anymore conclusions. No sense in making a complete ass out of myself.

Abby takes in a deep breath and continues, "I'm trying to process how you're doing it all?" It comes out as both a statement and question. I can't help the smirk that comes out.

"Trust me. It hasn't been easy."

Before I can say anything, she continues, "I'm busting my

ass to get into med school, and I'm not playing basketball... at a Division-One school for that matter... How the heck are you keeping your scholarship and acing your classes? Do you have a magical Time-Turner I have yet to discover?"

I feel my lips quirk, and I know without a doubt, Abby didn't have any malice in her words from before. "Uh... No, as far as I know, only Hermione's been able to have one of those. I just keep my nose to the ground and do it the old-fashioned way... lots of hard work and studying."

"That would be pretty awesome though, wouldn't it?" Abby looks to the sky in awe. "Not having to worry about time management as strictly as I'm sure you do."

"No kidding. J.K. Rowling's mind sure is diabolical. The things she comes up with are beyond brilliant. I devoured the *Harry Potter* series once I was old enough to read them on my own." I chuckle at the memory. "It was the first fiction series I'd ever been interested in reading. My mom wouldn't let me watch any of the movies until I'd read the books. It was a huge motivator."

"Mine were the same way," Abby commiserates. "But as soon as I started book one, I was glad I didn't have to wait for the next. Can you believe when they were originally released, people had to wait a year for the next one? I can't imagine that kind of dedication and agony. I read the entire series in weeks."

"Me, too," I admit.

Vanessa stops to check if we need anything else. When both of us claim we're full, she lays the check on the table. Abby's reflexes are as quick as a snake. I can't even process it's hit the table before she whisks it away in her hand. "My treat. You bought dinner last night. It's the least I can do."

"Abby." I attempt to sound firm. "No one should pay on their birthday. Besides, I asked you." I reach out for the check, but Abby isn't having it.

"Too bad." She juts out her chin in a 'don't mess with me' way.

Realizing she won't concede, I shake my head and give in. "Okay. You can pay... but I'll leave the tip. Deal?" I suggest as a compromise.

"Deal." Abby's face lights up like she's just won the world championship, and all I can do is smile in return. She sure is competitive.

AS I WALK into the locker room to change into my practice gear, I'm greeted by DeShawn Miller. His sly smile tells me he's up to something. Since his locker's next to mine, I set into changing, knowing he'll say what's on his mind soon enough.

Just as I'm tying my shoes, DeShawn doesn't disappoint. "So... Are the rumors true? Did Mr. 'I Don't Date During the Season' shake his tail on the dance floor last night and stay out past curfew?"

Instead of dignifying his assumption, I just stare blankly in his direction. No sense in getting caught up in gossip, even if it's true.

DeShawn cocks an eyebrow and waits patiently. We've been friends since I arrived at CRU. Between him and Grey

Gibbons, they probably know me best. Grey chooses this time to take a seat on the other side of me as I tie my shoes on the bench near my locker.

"Dude, I saw you myself. There's no point in denying it. You might as well be straight with us." He looks to DeShawn and back to me before asking, "So, who is she?"

I go with the truth as I have nothing to hide. "It was Abby, my lab partner's birthday. I inadvertently asked her to finish a project last night and didn't know it was her birthday until she arrived at my place. So... I rectified it."

"Dude." Grey's eyes go so wide, it's almost comical. "That's what you're calling it these days?" Then he turns to DeShawn. "Where can I get a lab partner like that? She was h—o—t—hot! I'm telling you, man. Jacobs was shaking it, like it was 1999. I never thought I'd see the day." He shakes his head like he still can't believe the thought I'd have a life. What a dick. Sure, I typically don't go out during the season, but it's not like I've never been out with the guys. He fucking knows this, too.

"Andrew Jacobs," DeShawn mocks in a voice that could pass as his mother's. "Is that the type of studying you're into these days? I thought you only knew about chemistry in books... maybe you have game after all."

"Seriously." I could cut Grey in half with the daggers I'm sending his way. "Show some respect. I simply made sure Abby was safe for her twenty-one-run. Don't make it any bigger than it is. I was their DD and wasn't out too late either, so you can shut your traps about spreading rumors," I warn.

Knowing these guys are among my best friends, I don't

have to worry too much. The fact that Grey was out after curfew is something I'm about to ask about, but Coach bellows, "Two minutes," and we quickly get our gear on and rush out to the court without discussing it further. I know this won't be the end of their inquisition, but for now, it's time to focus on practice. As I walk to the court, I can't help but wonder, *what is it about Abby that I can't seem to walk away from?*

7

ABBY

DREW WASN'T KIDDING when he said he was determined to be a good lab partner. We've met up a few times and even video chatted while he was in a hotel room outside of Eugene, just to get our assignment completed in a joint effort. He's adamant about doing his fair share and if it weren't so damn annoying, it'd almost be admirable.

Two weeks later, as I drag myself into my apartment one evening after working all afternoon at the library, Sydney ambushes me as soon as I enter the door.

"Good, you're home!" She's decked out in CRU gear, and even has our school's logo temporarily tattooed to her cheek.

"What's going on?" I ask. *Crap, have I missed something?* Chloe's nowhere to be seen, but the crazed look in Sydney's eyes has me on alert.

"Chloe's working late, and you're going to the game with me. We have thirty minutes to tip-off, and I didn't think you'd get here on time." Sydney takes my hand and drags me into her bedroom. "Here. You can wear this." She throws me a black basketball jersey with our school logo and the number twenty-four in red across the back. "I have an extra tattoo in my bathroom for your face and some pom-poms you can use."

I stare at her as if I've entered an alternate reality. *Since when do I attend basketball games, dressed as a crazed fan, eager to cheer them on?* Sure, I've gone to a few games in the past, but I'm a come as you are type of fan. No need to get all riled up. "Uh, when did I say I was going to the game?"

As far as I'm concerned, I have a date with my textbook and loads of reading to endure to be ready for class tomorrow. Basketball is the furthest thing from my mind. Syd should know this.

"Come on!" she begs. "It's one of the biggest games of the season. We're playing Washington, and we can't miss this. Chloe had to pull a double shift, and I don't want to go alone," Sydney practically pleads at the end and then goes for my Achilles heel. "Abs... If you go, I'll bake cinnamon rolls tomorrow. I'll even make a special pan, just for you..." She bats her eyes, then adds her ace in the hole. "With as much glaze as you want." She waggles an eyebrow in my direction as she eagerly awaits my response.

Shit, she knows I have an affection for her freaking cinnamon rolls. For some reason, I can never make the glaze as perfect as her. It's almost like she's beaten down some poor person at Cinnabon for their special ingredients. Unfortunately, that means I typically eat most of the pan when I can get away with it, but let's be real, her pastries are pure perfection and worth every ounce of extra padding they've added to me over the years.

I sigh heavily as I know there's only one answer I'll give her. "Just give me a minute, and I'll be ready."

Syd squeals loud enough for the neighbors down the street to hear and throws her arms around me. "You're the best, Abs. Drew's been on fire these past few weeks, and I'm sure he'll appreciate you being there to cheer him on."

"Uh... I hate to point it out to you, Syd, but Drew's just my lab partner. Besides, there's no way he'll know I'm there with an arena full of fans."

"Oh, Abby." Sydney shakes her head. "Trust me. He'll know you're there."

"I highly doubt it," I mumble as I switch out my shirt for the jersey and take the two minutes necessary to run a brush through my hair before declaring I'm ready to leave.

When we get to the arena, it's packed, and the air buzzes with anticipation for the big game. We each show our sports pass and make our way to find a seat among the cheering crowd. Evidently, we haven't missed tip-off because the opposing team's being announced as we walk down the stairs to find our seats. Instead of heading to the student section, as I presumed we'd sit, Sydney takes us closer to the court and shows her phone to the attendant. Before I know it, we're ushered to seats only three rows up from the center of the court.

"Uh... since when do we no longer sit in the student

section?" I ask with the realization that she must've done something extra to get these seats.

"Since my boss offered me his season tickets for tonight when he found out I was going. He's out of town and wasn't using them. There's no way I'd pass up a chance to get this close to the action, Abs. I may be a work-a-holic, but even my boss knows I'm a huge basketball fan. Of course, I jumped at the chance." Sydney's eyes dance in anticipation as she scopes out the players entering the court. Her love of the game is evident in her appraisal of the players. Knowing Sydney, she's likely mentally calculating their stats as they're introduced. She has such a knack at remembering the most trivial things sports related.

We take our seats as the stadium lights dim. The spotlight goes wild, and music blasts to welcome CRU's team to the arena. Fanatic fans scream as each player's introduced and their position announced. I'm up on my feet, cheering right along with the crowd, when Drew's introduced at the end of the lineup. The announcer draws out his name as if Drew Jacobs is the most exciting person in the room. Apparently, Drew's beaten many school records, and the announcer feels the need to share it with the room. As my eyes dart to Drew, he appears humble in his reaction. His face has a plastered-on smile but when the accolades are announced, his eyes dart to the floor, almost in disbelief. *Interesting.* He's *so* not the jock I thought I met on our first day of classes. There's much more to Drew Jacobs than most know. I'm sure.

Once the National Anthem is sung, the ball is brought out

to center court to be tipped. Drew's not in the center of the action for this moment, but once CRU wins the ball, it's quickly taken by our point guard and dribbled hard for our net. At the last moment, he passes the ball to Drew for an assist, and SWISH! It's nothing but net. Drew has a bounce in his step as he celebrates the score but is quickly back on defense as a member of Washington's team returns the ball to their side of the court.

I may not come to many games, but I've spent plenty of time on a basketball court watching my older brother Travis play as we grew up. As I watch the ball zoom down the court and baskets be made by both teams, I cheer right along with Sydney and the rest of the crowd.

My heart beats quicker each time CRU takes possession of the ball. When it's passed to Drew, it nearly rockets out of my chest. A sense of pride soars through me as I watch Drew handle the basketball. As if the ball's an extension of himself, he maneuvers it through the defense with ease and scores nearly every time he touches the ball. His muscles flex, and his face fills with such intensity, it's hard not to stare at him in awe. Drew Jacobs is a God on the court. The other players pale in comparison. Though the other team keeps pace with us as far as scoring is concerned, no one on the court handles the ball with such precision as Drew. Other players are rotated in and out of the game as the coach sees fit, but Drew's like a workhorse, unyielding until he finishes his task.

Just as the buzzer signals for halftime, Drew's gaze locks onto mine. An involuntary shudder rolls through my body as he looks me over from head to toe. It's as if there's an electric current directly connected to my spinal cord, and I feel every spot his eyes roam as they take me in, cheering him on from the stands. *What the hell is he doing to me?* I've never had such an intense reaction to anyone like this.

Drew's smile spreads wide when his eyes return to mine. He tips his head to the side and nods once with a quick wink before DeShawn Miller claps him on the back, and he's ushered to the locker room. It happens so fast, I thought I'd imagined it. But when Sydney giggles and brushes her shoulder to mine, I'm not so sure I did.

"What the hell is that?" she teases as she continues watching Drew run off court.

"What do you mean?" I ask in confusion while keeping my eyes on Drew until he and the rest of the team are no longer visible, then turn to face her.

"Uh..." Sydney's green eyes are wide, and her strawberry-blond ponytail swishes behind her as she whips her head in my direction. "The guy clearly winked at you..." she accuses.

"Are you sure? Sweat was rolling off his forehead. He could've had something in his eye..."

"Abby," she chides, holding my gaze.

"I'm sure you're mistaken," I casually dismiss. "Why would he wink at me? That makes no sense."

"Abby, you have to be kidding me. Obviously, Drew was focused on you. His entire face lit up when he found you. There's no sense in arguing with me." Syd eyes me pointedly as she brushes a strand of stray hair behind her ear.

"What do you want me to say?" I sound defensive, even to

me. I don't know why he looked at me that way. He could've been looking at the person behind me, for all I know. *Why on earth did she have to notice?*

"I just want you to be honest. I know he's your lab partner. But maybe there's something more."

"Syd," I groan in frustration. "You know it's not like that."

"But it could be like that..." she sing-songs playfully.

I scoff. "You're one to talk. You won't give anyone the time of day." Maybe if I turn the table on her, she'll back off and leave me alone. "When was the last time you went out on a date?"

Sydney rolls her eyes and shakes her head. "I've probably been out on a date more recently than you. I date. I'm just picky and if they're not worth mentioning, I haven't."

I stare at her in disbelief. "Are you telling me you've actually been on a date and not told me about it?"

"Of course I have." She lifts her chin indignantly. "For your information, I went on one last week." She almost sounds convincing. If it weren't for the involuntary shiver of her entire body at the end, I'd almost believe her.

"What aren't you telling me, Syd?" I probe, knowing there must be more. Her lips purse, and her eyebrows squint together. Irritation fills her features, and her sudden grimace tells me she'd rather keep it to herself. Not wanting to give up, I simply stare.

She shrugs. "It was just a typical date. He seemed different, but..." she sighs heavily. "He was just like everyone else I've been out with lately. At the end of the night, he leaned in to kiss me... his intent, of things being more obvious... and I just wasn't feeling it. No spark. No chemistry, ya know?"

"Boy, I can relate." It's been forever since someone lit me up from the inside out. After the last few flops, I decided it wasn't worth the effort. Besides, now that I only have a few classes left to go until I find out if I've been accepted to med school, my priorities need to be elsewhere.

Syd shakes her head in commiseration. "I'm not looking for a Mr. Forever or anything..." She trails off then bursts out giggling. "Hell, I'd settle for a Mr. Right Now... if you know what I mean... But there has to at least be a spark." She waggles her eyebrow seductively, and I burst into laughter.

"Syd..." I chastise her bluntness and look around to see if anyone's paying us attention.

"What?" She laughs off my reaction. "I have needs, too. Maybe you've been out of the game so long you've forgotten yours, but I certainly haven't forgotten mine."

"Okay, whatever you say." I laugh it off. Knowing Sydney as I do, I know most of this is all bravado. She's had some short-term relationships and when they're no longer mutually beneficial, she's moved on. But she's not into casual flings. She gets irritated when guys assume that just because she bartends, she'll go home with them after last call. Hence, the reason she's picky. Some might even say a bit jaded because she hardly lets her heart get attached. Hell, I don't even blame her. If I had guys treat me the way she's been treated, I'd be skeptical, too.

Thankfully, I don't have to say more to Sydney. The players come back onto the court to warm up before the second half of the game. Like a moth to a flame, my eyes follow

Drew around the court as if they have a mind of their own. If Sydney notices, she doesn't say anything.

Drew's focus is entirely on the game for the second half. He's unstoppable when it comes to offense. I can probably count on one hand the amount of shots he hasn't made when he's gone to the basket. As the score volleys for who takes the lead, I'm on pins and needles. With each shot made, the other team returns to their net and scores. My heart races with anticipation as I watch each player leave their heart out on the court.

When there's only twenty seconds left in the game, CRU's down by two and Washington has the ball. Washington makes a fast break for the basket, but CRU blocks it. Relief floods me as our point guard quickly takes control of the ball. He dribbles hard for the basket and at the last second, passes it off to Drew. My heart freezes when I realize Drew doesn't have the shot once the ball's in his hands. With cat-like reflexes, Drew arcs the ball wide across the court into the capable hands of DeShawn, who's wide open behind the three-point line. With three seconds left to go on the clock and the crowd counting down, DeShawn dribbles once, squares his shoulders, and jumps into the air, releasing the ball at his full height.

I swear the entire arena sucks in a deep breath as they anxiously await the result. It's as if the ball's in slow motion, as it arcs slowly through the air. I'm on my tippy toes wishing it to make it into the basket.

It hits the rim, at the backboard.

It bounces once into the air, landing on the rim again.

Then SWISH, it falls into the basket, and the arena goes wild as the sound of the buzzer goes off.

"We did it!" Sydney screams as she jumps up and down with joy. "We beat Washington." She rushes in to squeeze me tight in a hug. "Holy shit. I didn't think DeShawn would pull that off. But he did it!"

"It was freaking amazing!" I holler in agreement to be heard over the crowd. We pull apart and high-five the fans erupting in celebration around us. The enthusiasm in the crowd is almost palpable. My skin tingles with excitement, and I can't help but watch Drew as he celebrates CRU's win with his teammates.

After rushing over to greet DeShawn with a chest bump, Drew and DeShawn hug each other intensely. As if they'd practiced that pass countless times, it was orchestrated to perfection. Their other teammates join in the celebration before their coach calls them over for a team celebration.

Eventually, CRU calms down, and each team shakes each other's hand as a show of respect to one another. I'm surprised how many of them seem to know one another off the court because they stop to say something and seem genuine in their greetings. By the time they've finished, the crowd around us disperses.

When Sydney suggests we get going, I can't help but give one last glance to Drew. As if he senses me watching, his eyes dart to mine, and a shit-eating grin explodes across his face. I can't help but laugh in return. I'm so friggin' happy for him. I know this was a huge game, and he was pivotal in making this a win for CRU. Drew holds my gaze for a long moment then nods once in my direction as if to say, "*See you tomorrow.*" Though I know I'm probably making that part up in my mind. He's excited and just pulled off a big win.

Sydney pulls on my arm, and I drop my focus from Drew. As we get to the top of the stairs, I glance back once more. He's still looking in my direction. *Maybe I'm not so off after all.*

8
DREW

I BREEZE through my classes the next morning after our big win. By pulling off that pass at the last minute, I helped lead CRU to victory. Not only did it allow for major bragging rights against our biggest rival in the division, but when I looked up, Abby and Sydney were in the stands watching it all happen. I'm not sure why it mattered so much. Maybe it's because I haven't had anyone close in the stands to watch me in a while, but for some reason, just knowing Abby was there, made me want to show her just what I could do.

As I make my way from class to class, people stop and congratulate me. I'm happy to have fans, but it takes longer to go anywhere when this happens. Typically, I avoid crowds but for some reason, I can't get away from them today. As the season progresses, I'm sure it'll just get worse if our winning streak continues. I wouldn't trade the win for the world, but it gets old being bombarded by fans and their constant interruption.

I slink onto my stool and plop my bag down just as the professor begins. I quickly greet Abby with a smile as I pull out my notebook and materials needed to start.

While listening to what our assignment is for today, I can't help but notice Abby's her typical self for class. It's adorable the way her big dark glasses perch on her nose as she hunches over her notebook, taking furious notes about our expectations. Her hair is pulled back from her face, and she rests one hand on her notebook to keep it in place. We've sat in class several times together over the past couple of weeks, but for some reason today, is the first I'm noticing. Who the hell knows what's changed? She even smells good, for crying out loud. Without a conscious thought, I lean closer to determine the exact scent that keeps intriguing my senses. Trying not to be obvious, I pull in a deep breath. Hmmm... Is it citrus or pear? A combination of both? Damn, whatever it is, it smells delicious. There's also something uniquely Abby floating in the air, and my senses are on high alert.

Abby's body moves and when my eyes find hers, she looks pointedly at me, forcing me out of my revelry.

"What?" she defensively whispers and looks herself over with care, checking if anything's out of place.

I quickly shake my head and dismiss her concern as I silently mouth, *"It's nothing, don't worry about it."*

Christ, Jacobs. Concentrate on the lab, not your lab partner. Get it the fuck together. Feeling like a dumbass for being caught, I shake all thoughts of Abby and her mouthwatering scent away from the forefront of my mind.

Thankfully, I read over today's chapters to better prepare

myself last night after the game. It was hard concentrating with adrenaline from winning coursing through my veins, but after a while, I was disciplined enough to get the job done. Glancing at Abby, I wonder if she did the same. Knowing her, she'd already read everything a couple of days ago at best, so I don't feel bad she was there to watch us win last night. Just the thought of seeing her cheering in the stands has my heart beating faster.

When the professor suggests we get to work, Abby opens our conversation with, "Great game last night. I was on the edge of my seat the entire last half. You and DeShawn were so in sync with one another, it's almost scary."

"Well, I do spend more time with him than just about anyone else on the team," I say, rolling off my tongue sarcastically.

Abby shakes her head. "That's obvious. It's almost as if you knew he'd be there to make the shot."

"Well, he and Grey are probably my closest friends off the court, so we're bound to be in sync from time to time," I say to keep things light, but when Abby's eyes narrow and her lips purse, I'm not sure that was the message delivered.

She stares and pulls in her lower lip as if she's contemplating her next words. "Why do you do that?" Barely above a whisper, her question leaves me to wonder if she spoke her thoughts aloud, or if she wants an answer.

"Do what?" I finally ask when she doesn't release her gaze.

"Downplay everything."

What the hell am I supposed to do? Act like a cocky ass and strut around as if I think my shit doesn't stink. I don't think so. Abby scrutinizes my reaction and when I realize she's not letting this go, I ask, "Would you rather I be a cocky ass?"

Abby laughs, and it's a beautiful sight to see. "No. Been there, done that—on the first day of class. I'd rather not see that side of you. Thank you very much."

Wait, I was an ass the first day we met?

Before I can defend myself, she places a palm on my bicep. "Don't worry. Your secret's safe with me."

Not entirely following her train of thought, I ask, "And what secret would that be?"

"That underneath the cocky exterior you use to keep people out, you're really a decent guy."

"Uh..." I start, but I'm clueless how to respond.

"Forget I said anything..." Abby shakes her head dismissively. "Let's get this lab done. I have to work, and you have practice."

I shake my head, relieved to let the subject drop. I'm obviously not the only task master here.

AS WE EXIT the science building after lab, I pat my rumbling stomach. "Wanna grab a bite to eat?"

Abby's eyes nearly reach her hairline as she glances at her watch. "Uh... I guess so. I have about an hour before work. Mind if it's near the library?"

Knowing that the crowds are thinning out at this time of day, I make a split-second decision to break my typical rule about eating on campus. Hoping people will mind their own business, I reply with, "Sure. I'm short on time, too."

As we make our way to the center of campus, Abby suggests, "Thai sound good?"

Placing my thumb on my chin, I mull over the possibilities of healthy menu choices. "Sure. Thai works," and we turn toward the Student Union Building.

Abby may be a full head shorter, but damn, the girl can eat up the pavement as she walks across campus. *Is she a professional speed walker?* Leaving no opportunities for talking, I quicken my pace, and we're at the restaurant in no time. Thankfully, there's no wait, and the waitress seats us right away. She quickly takes our order, after bringing glasses of water to drink.

As soon as the waitress leaves, Abby takes a long drink of her water. As I watch, it dawns on me, she's not making eye contact. She's looking anywhere but at me. *What the hell? Is something wrong with me?*

I clear my throat to get her attention. When her golden-brown eyes land on mine, she slowly places her glass down and lets her forearms rest on the table. I wouldn't say she's at ease; something still seems off. Through her large-rimmed glasses, her eyes look into mine as if she's searching for answers.

"Everything okay?" Even though I just cleared my throat, it comes out raspy.

"Why wouldn't it be?" Abby's chin pulls back defensively.

"I don't know... you just seem off," I suggest as I look her over with care.

Abby's eyes shoot to the ceiling, and her cheeks darken as

she pulls her bottom lip into her mouth to chew on it. What the hell is going on? *Is she embarrassed?* She's hardly said a word since we left class. Instead of asking one of the thousands of questions flying through my mind, I lean back in my seat and attempt to be patient as I await her answer.

She nervously brushes back a strand of hair behind her ear as she shrugs. "I don't know... I guess I'm trying to figure out why I'm here."

"You're hungry?" I flippantly state, though it comes out as a question.

She lets out a loud huff. "That's not what I meant."

"What *did* you mean?" I pointedly ask. Because I don't have a clue. We're usually pretty at ease with one another, and her behavior makes no sense.

As if she's suddenly in the hot seat, Abby fidgets before looking me in the eye again. If I weren't trying to figure out what was wrong, she'd almost be adorable. Each new train of thought brings an entirely different expression. I can't help the smile that forms on my face as I await her response. Abby's not usually so indecisive.

"I guess..." She pauses as if she's holding onto her thought by pressing her forefinger to her chin. "I'm wondering what this means."

I raise an eyebrow in her direction. "We're eating," I deadpan.

She rolls her eyes as if I should know better. "What I mean is, what made you ask me to join you?"

"This isn't rocket science. I was hungry. Thought you

might be, too. It's as simple as that," I quickly explain, though it should be obvious.

She shakes her head and rolls her eyes as if I'm being dense. "Drew," she sighs but suddenly shakes her head and changes her tone. "For the last few weeks, other than my birthday, you've kept things very business-like when it comes to our time together. Don't get me wrong, I'm all for that. I don't have time for messing around, either. But what I don't understand is why you've invited me to dinner when we don't have work to do?"

Whoa? Where is this coming from? Have I been that much of an ass to her? I thought I'd been somewhat personable since we've met. "Am I allowed to enjoy your company?"

This earns me a stare. Her mouth drops open, then shuts, then opens once more, but nothing comes out. She's freaking adorable. Her blush reaches down her neck to the V of her mostly zipped hoodie.

"It's just dinner, Abby." Though, as I get to know her more, I can see myself asking to do this again. She's a bit of a riot to watch as she processes her thoughts, and she certainly keeps me on my toes.

Her cheeks tint a beautiful shade of pink, and she looks to her hands. "I'm such a dork. I... uh... didn't mean to make this into anything. Forget I said anything," she tacks on the end, earning a light chuckle from me.

"You have nothing to worry about, Abby. If I've given you the impression that I'm a complete douche, sorry. I love the fact that you work just as hard as me and take things seriously."

"Speaking of working hard... I've tried not to ask, but I'm dying to know... which medical schools have you applied to?"

Caught off guard because everyone typically sticks to basketball, I grin at her elephant-like memory. I think I mentioned med school once in her presence, and she never asked about it again. "I'm waiting to hear from Johns Hopkins, University of Colorado, and the University of Pennsylvania." Abby's eyes widen as I prattle off my top three schools. I've applied to a few others, but if I get into any of these, I'll jump at the chance. "I want to specialize in pediatric oncology."

"Is Johns Hopkins your first choice?" she asks, almost in disbelief.

"Um... yeah," I whisper. I've dreamed of going there since Summer was diagnosed. One of her best doctors had graduated from there, and it gave me hope for others. Just the thought of Summer alone makes my heart pang, so I quickly tamp that thought down and focus my attention back to Abby.

"Wow... I can't believe it," Abby whispers almost to herself.

What. The. Hell?

Does she think I can't get in?

"Why can't you believe it?" I respond, cold.

She blinks a few times at my change of tone and pulls a face that tells me I've just offended her.

Then she shakes her head as if to regain her thoughts.

"Well, *hotshot*." Suddenly, I wonder if she's about to rip me a new one. "For your information, out of all the schools you *could* apply to, you just chose three of my top five."

Wait. What is she talking about? I stare and wait for her to continue.

"Add Stanford and Baylor, and you've just mentioned the schools I've applied to. Though I just want to focus on pediatrics, not oncology."

"Why haven't you mentioned this before?"

Am I that unapproachable?

Hell. We likely have much more in common than I realize.

What else don't I know about her? When I stop and think about it, I don't know jack shit. Looking into her golden-brown eyes, I know I need to rectify this.

"Well, it's not like we've given each other our life stories. Other than my birthday, we've focused on class. You're not really forthcoming when it comes to divulging information about yourself, so I haven't brought it up."

Fuck. She has a point. I'm tight-lipped when it comes to revealing my personal life. But then again... no one's ever taken the time to get to know the real Drew Jacobs. Could Abby be the first? With a sly smile, I simply state, "Well, if we're going to be friends, I need to know one thing."

"Oh, yeah, what's that?" She smirks.

"Your last name."

9
ABBY

I STARE at Drew in disbelief. He's kidding, right? We've worked together for weeks. We've celebrated my birthday together. Hell, we've even danced together, and I've been wrapped in his arms. And the one thing he wants to know before he'll divulge any information about his past is my last name?

Have I never told him?

Thinking back over our conversations, maybe it's never come up. Instead of giving it to him right away, I raise an eyebrow and smirk. "Is this so you can run a full background check and look for references before giving up anything about yourself?"

"Well, you might be sketchy," he teases, and the smile that spreads across his perfect lips makes my belly flip and my spine tingle.

He shouldn't unleash his full potency on unexpecting co-eds. Damn. Drew even has a small dimple on his right cheek.

His eyes crinkle at the corners, causing the blueness of them to pop.

"So, I've been told," I deadpan. "You've gotta watch out for those chemistry majors who want to go into pediatrics. We're a real sketchy bunch."

This earns me a deep belly laugh from Drew. "Abby—with no last name—you're killing me." With that, I lose my battle at keeping a straight face and join him. I'm such a brat.

When our laughter settles, I put him at ease. "It's Angelos."

"Angelos... Like Angel." He glances up to meet my eyes and shakes his head. "Sorry." Drew's cheeks darken, and he rushes to explain, "It's how I remember names. I associate it with words the person reminds me of, and I'm much better at recall. I'm great with faces. Names—not so much. But it's not like I'll be forgetting either of yours anytime soon."

"And why is that?" I chuckle as I roll my eyes in anticipation to his response. Cue cheesy line now, I'm sure. *You must've fallen from heaven... Can I borrow your phone? God's missing an angel?* With a last name like Angelos, I've heard it all. Trust me.

With a smirk, he flippantly replies, "Let's just say—You've made quite an impression." Then almost under his breath, he adds, "For someone who I thought would keep me free of distraction, you've been anything but."

My mouth flies open, and all my air leaves with it. A huff escapes as my palms hit the table in front of me. He didn't just say that. "What the hell is that supposed to mean? How am I a distraction?"

"Oh, Angel..." He laughs. "You're adorable when you get worked up." He rolls his eyes. "Calm down. I didn't mean anything by it."

He called me Angel. I'm about to correct him, but the way he said it with the quirk of his perfect lips and the pop of his delicious dimple, makes me think twice. I'll let it slide for now. But if it gets out of hand, I'll squash that train of thought like a menacing mosquito.

The waitress delivers our food. Drew picks up his fork and inhales half of his plate, leaving me to ponder why I'm suddenly okay with his endearment. When I realize he has dropped the subject, I dig into my cashew nut chicken. Damn, this tastes delicious. It's not long before I hear Drew clear his throat and wipe his mouth with a napkin.

"Now that we're *friends,* can I ask if you're coming to Monday night's game?"

Shit. I wasn't planning on it. Is it rude to say no? Sydney's going to the game. I'm sure she'd love the company, but can I afford the break from studying?

Clearly, he reads this on my face because before I can say anything, he blurts out, "How can you miss the game? We're playing the Spartans, and it's bound to be just as good as last night's."

Christ. Last night had me on pins and needles, dying to know what would happen next. I loved every moment, but my heart beat a thousand miles a minute. "I'm not sure I can handle the excitement," I admit sarcastically. Sydney screamed her ass off, and I was right there with her.

Drew's mouth turns up at the corners, and his perfectly

chiseled chin juts out to the side. "Oh, come on," he practically pleads. "You know you had fun."

Yes. I did. But there's no way I'm admitting he was a big part in my entertainment for the evening.

Damn.

Just thinking of his corded forearms, his bulging biceps, and the way he filled out his CRU uniform perfectly has me squirming in my seat.

Who knew I was into arm porn?

Geesh. Get it together, Abby.

When his dark-blue eyes penetrate my train of thought, I realize he's waiting for an answer from me. To distract myself, I reveal my regularly scheduled plans for Monday nights. "I'd planned on studying."

"Oh. Come on, Angel." His deep voice turns gravelly, making my belly flip. Holy shit... I'd do just about anything if he keeps talking like that. I brace myself for what's coming, hoping what he asks is at least legal. Because at this point, if he asked me to commit a felony, I'd go to jail with a smile on my face.

Before I have a chance to respond, Drew's phone must've vibrated in his pocket because suddenly, he pulls it out as he keeps his lazy smile on me, making my heart race. He greets the caller with a friendly, "Hello."

He's silent for a moment then in an apprehensive tone validates who he is. "Speaking."

His eyes bore into mine, so I clearly witness his expression instantly morph from carefree and relaxed to rigid and... holy fuck, frightened. Clearly the person on the other line isn't delivering good news.

A chill runs up my spine as pain radiates through Drew's features. He immediately bolts from his chair and stands as he states barely above a whisper, "Yes, they are."

Drew's silent and his complexion pales. His bottom lip trembles, and he bites on his lip, trying to regain control. His free hand that dangles, fists then releases several times as he listens. Finally, after what seems like forever, I release the breath I didn't realize I'd been holding as he speaks once again. "No..." he says in a whispered cry, sending me immediately to my feet. His cracking voice alone has my heart breaking for the news that's being delivered, as he continues, "I... I... No, I can't."

Whatever is being said on the other end of the line has Drew on the verge of breaking and me on full alert.

He wobbles in front of me. Taking his hand, I guide him back to the chair across from me because I'm afraid he'll fall over at any moment.

I don't give a fuck if we're causing a scene. The message he's receiving is clearly fucking with his mind, and he needs help. When my hand reaches his, his eyes lock on mine once again. Instead of the cocky playfulness I've come to expect, he has the most grief-stricken expression I've ever seen.

"Please," he begs, and I'm not sure if it's to me or to the person on the phone, but instinctually, I step closer and place my free hand on his bicep to guide him into a sitting position.

"Do whatever it takes." Drew is nearly breathless, and my gut clenches. "They're all I've got. Shit..." He's silent as he places an elbow on the table and drags a hand almost painfully through his hair. He stares at a spot on the table and shakes his head, as if he's in denial before his breath hitches, and he practically begs, "I can't lose them."

Holy fuck. What's going on? He repeats practically to himself, "I can't lose them," until I realize the person on the other end of the phone is raising their voice to get his attention.

Through the phone, I hear, "Drew... Drew... Are you all right? Can you hear me, Drew? Please respond."

In a state of shock, Drew simply continues to stare at the table and mutter. My heart aches for him, and I fear the news I will encounter as I reach for the phone in his hand. He can easily overpower me and keep his phone with ease, but when he feels me gently tug it, it's released instantly.

With as much strength as I can muster, I take control of this situation. "Hello. This is Abby Angelos. I'm a friend of Drew."

"Hello, Abby. I'm a nurse at Spokane Valley Hospital. Is Drew okay?" Holy shit. A hospital. This must be bad. Did someone die? I'm brought out of my worries when the woman asks, "Abby?"

"Yes, I'm here," I assure her as I focus my attention to Drew. I squeeze Drew's hand as I ask, "Drew, are you okay?"

It takes him a moment before his watery eyes find mine. He stares for a moment and doesn't say anything, but he nods.

His blue eyes look hollow, and his face ashen, but no other physical signs are present. "Yes... he's okay. He seems to be in shock," I relay to the nurse, hoping she'll fill me in.

"Is Drew able to talk with me?" the woman calmly asks on the other line.

Squeezing Drew's hand to get his attention, his eyes slowly find mine. "Drew?" I wait until I know he's listening. "Can you talk to the woman on the phone?"

Drew's head shakes as his eyes squeeze shut. Then he inhales deeply, as if to steady himself and regain what little control he's holding onto. When they reopen, it's clear he asking me to do it for him. To keep him from having to summon the strength that's clearly left his body, I ask, "Would you like me to get the information you need?"

An infinitesimal amount of relief washes over Drew's handsome features as he nods. "Please."

I'll do anything to take the obvious pain in Drew's eyes away, I offer to the woman on the phone, "Is there a way you can tell me the information he needs? I'm not sure he's able to talk now."

Drew squeezes my hand and defeatedly whispers, "Thank you." Whatever this woman is about to tell me, I know in this instant, I won't let Drew go through this alone.

She takes in a quick breath and releases into my ear. "Well... due to HIPAA laws, I'll need Drew's verbal consent to continue."

I want to reach through the phone and rip her friggin' tongue out. How can she do this to Drew? Her call alone has turned him from a boisterous guy to the ghost of a man before me. Though at this instant, he looks more like a lost little boy than a man who's on top of his world about to graduate from college. Knowing she's only doing her job, I take a deep breath to steady myself before getting Drew's attention.

"She needs verbal consent to share the information."

I hand Drew the phone and can hear the nurse on the other end speaking, but her actual words are unclear. Drew simply nods and gravely gives his consent before handing the phone back to me.

"Hello?" I offer out of habit when receiving a phone.

"Hello, Abby. I'm sorry to be the one to relay this information, but both of Drew's parents have been involved in a car accident."

I gasp, even though I knew her news would be horrific. This unfortunately catches Drew's attention, and I fortify myself to be strong for Drew when she tells me the inevitable news. "They were both brought in via ambulance to Spokane Valley Hospital." Fuck. Fuck. Fuck. Here it comes. I brace myself for the bomb she's about to drop.

"They were unconscious at the time but stable." Relief washes through me. Thank the fucking Lord they're alive. Stable means good, right? I'm about to clarify my thoughts but never get the chance. The nurse keeps prattling on—to get her explanation out. "Upon further examination, they each were diagnosed as being critical and in need of emergency surgery. His mother has a ruptured spleen and has a broken radius. Mostly likely, it is from her bracing on impact. Drew's father had his lung collapse as well as a fractured tibia as he was trapped in the car and had to have the jaws of life retrieve him. They each have concussions as well as minor bumps and bruises throughout their bodies."

Holy shit. Both sound serious, but something they *should* be able to recover from. "Are they..." I hesitate to ask, because God knows I don't want to have to break even more bad news to Drew. Drew comes out of his shock and locks his eyes to mine with both interest and eagerness to know the answer to my unasked question.

I clear my throat and force myself to begin again, "Are they expected to recover?"

The nurse lets out what I hope is a positive breath. "We hope that's the case. Of course, with any surgery, there are always risks. As the doctors proceed, they might find more things wrong with them. We'll know more as time progresses." I've watched enough shows on TV, that I know this is standard protocol to not promise anything.

But hope returns, where it had once been lost, and I give Drew a reassuring squeeze with my hand.

"How long will they be in surgery?" I ask, trying to get as much information as possible to relay to Drew.

"I'm not sure at this time. I'm simply trying to relay the message to Drew, so he can get here should he choose."

"We're both at Columbia River University, just outside of Portland, so I'll see what I can do to look into flights or figure out a way to get him there. When he arrives, where should he go?"

"If you stop at any information desk, they'll be able to locate his parents. If you want status updates until you can arrive, I just came on shift. I'll be here for the next twelve hours. Just call and ask for Janice." She proceeds to give me a number where I quickly pull out my phone and type it in and quickly call before hanging up immediately, so it will be stored to my recent calls. We talk for a few more minutes about logistics, and I tell her that Drew will be there as soon as he can before hanging up.

When I get off the phone, Drew looks to me as if his life depends on what I'm about to say. My heart breaks for his uncertainty, but I'm thankful I get to share better news than what I'd feared.

"They're... gonna be okay?" Drew asks, deep and broken between fortifying breaths.

Knowing this isn't the time to sugar coat anything, I go with honesty. Pulling my chair closer to his, I sit and remain holding his hand. "They're both stable. That's the best we can hope for now. We'll know more once they come out of surgery." I go into further detail about what type of surgery each of his parents need.

When I finish, Drew stands and throws some bills on the table before blatantly stating, "I need to get there." He quickly gathers his backpack and hands me mine as he pulls me out of the restaurant.

Once outside, Drew's hand runs through his hair as he paces a few feet in one direction, before turning and heading in the other.

"Is there anyone I should call?" I offer, making his pacing end abruptly.

With a hand raised to his chin, he contemplates my question. "Uh... probably just Coach. He'll contact my professors and explain everything." Drew hesitates and squeezes his eyes tight.

"Fuck. I don't think I can do this," he whispers so I barely hear it. I reach out to take his hand, to calm him. When he squeezes mine like a lifeline, I quickly come to the rescue.

Since I'm still holding his phone, I guide him to a nearby bench and simply ask, "What's his number?"

"It's under, Coach B. His name's Ted Bradford."

Without a second of hesitation, I quickly pull up the contact and press the button to make the call. Thankfully, he answers on the second ring.

"Jacobs. To what do I owe the pleasure?" His voice is kind and filled with genuine like for Drew, which makes it easier to relay the information I'm about to dump on him.

"Hello, sir. I'm Abby Angelos, a friend of Drew's."

Immediately, I can tell Coach B's on high alert. "Is Drew all right?"

"Yes, sir. He's fine, but his parents aren't." I quickly explain what's going on and that Drew's unable to talk at this time. I don't go into quite as much detail as the nurse explained, but I clearly express Drew's need to go home as soon as possible. After double checking Drew's okay, Coach B wholeheartedly agrees.

Before we end the call, Coach offers to look into flights and tells me he'll call Drew's phone when he has an update. When he asks if I'll accompany Drew to his parents, I don't even blink. "Of course I am, sir." There's no way I'll let Drew go alone. Just looking at his pained face has me confident in my answer. Once Drew's settled, if he wants me to leave him alone, I will. But until then, he's stuck with me.

Coach suggests I give him my class information and

assures me he'll take care of things on his end, by letting each of our professors know there's been an emergency. While we wait for him to call us back with details for our flight, he suggests we pack and get ready to leave on the next flight out. Knowing Drew's tenacious study habits, he also reminds me to pack his books since we don't know how long he'll need to be gone.

When I finish the call, Drew stands and pulls me into him. His gigantic arms envelop me as he hugs me fiercely. I return his bear hug and just stand here breathing with him as he processes this life-changing information. Not knowing what to say or wanting to break the connection between us, I simply hold on for all I'm worth and let him squeeze the crap out of me. His sexy masculine scent invades my senses, causing me to relax into him.

As time goes on, his grip loosens but doesn't let up. His arms stay around me as he rests his chin on my head. I feel his words rumble out of his chest as he speaks, "Thank you so much, Abby. I don't know what I'd do without you."

"Why don't we walk to my apartment? I'll pick up some things and drive you to your place while we wait for your coach to return our call. If there's a flight available soon, we may be able to catch it."

He presses his head to the top of mine and squeezes once more. "I'm so glad you're with me," he mumbles.

He releases his hold, but it's as if he can't let go completely. He reaches for my hand, and we walk quickly to my apartment.

Once inside, I suggest Drew take a seat on the couch while

I rush to my room to pack. Sydney's gone, but Chloe's there when we arrive.

Shocked by our sudden presence, she follows me as I rush to my room like my ass is on fire and quickly pull out a small suitcase that'll easily pass as a carry-on.

"Can you call the library and tell them I won't be able to make my shift?"

Chloe's eyebrows lift to her hairline, knowing something must be seriously wrong. I'd never miss work if I can help it. I'll go in on my deathbed before calling in. "Uh... what should I say happened?" Clearly, she wants to know the details herself as she eyes me up and down with care.

"Tell them I've had a family emergency. I'll let them know when I have more information. Be sure to talk with Tarrin. She's my immediate supervisor." I walk to my dresser and pull out as many pairs of underwear as I have clean and multiple pairs of socks. Thank God for small miracles I did laundry this week.

I quickly open my drawers and pull out the first things I can put my hands on. I pack a few pairs of jeans, yoga pants, and some t-shirts that will go with any of the pants I've stuffed into my suitcase.

"I'll grab your things from your bathroom. Tell me what's going on?" Chloe says as she disappears into the bathroom off my bedroom. She knows I'm not high maintenance, so I'm sure whatever she packs will be fine.

I give her the CliffsNotes version, and I can hear her gasp from the bathroom. Within a few minutes, she's brought back my travel bag and puts it in my suitcase.

"I have your toothbrush, toothpaste, deodorant, and a few samples of shampoo and conditioner. I also packed your brush and tossed in a few hair ties for you."

I throw open my arms and embrace her in a hug. "You are the best."

"Just keep me posted. I'm happy to do anything you need," she says as she releases me, then gasps. "Do you have cash?"

"I... uh... usually just use my debit card," I admit honestly.

Before I can say another word, Chloe rushes out of the room. Not having time to guess what she's doing, I finish putting a few more things into my carry-on. She returns with a fist full of cash and stuffs it into my hand. "Here. It's the tip money I've been saving."

"Chloe, you don't have to do this." I start pushing it back in her direction, and she gives me a look that tells me not to mess with her.

"You'll pay me back. I insist. It's only about two hundred dollars."

Not knowing what I'll need in terms of money for a place to stay or a ride home, I stuff it into my purse. "You're the best," I whisper with one last squeeze. "I'll let you know when I know more."

I gather the textbooks I'll need for the remainder of my classes and squeeze those into my suitcase. I return to the living room where Drew hasn't budged from the couch. My heart breaks at how distraught he looks. He's so lost in thought he doesn't even look up when Chloe and I approach. God. *What's going on in that brilliant mind of his?*

I drop my bags and approach him carefully, so I don't

startle him. When I reach out to take his hand, he turns his attention to me. "Have you heard back from Coach?"

I pull out his phone from my pocket and see that it shows no notifications. Shaking my head, I sigh. "Not yet. Let's get you to your place, so we'll be ready when he calls. Hopefully, he'll get us on a flight in a few hours." I squeeze his hand in reassurance to let him know he's not going through this alone.

Drew pulls in a fortifying breath as he stands, his hand still linked in mine. "You ready?" He looks around the room and spots my suitcase next to my backpack.

"Yeah." I nod as we walk toward my things.

Chloe reaches out and pats Drew on the shoulder as we pass. "Please let me know if you need anything..." She looks from me to him. "I'm only a phone call away."

Drew thanks her, and I stop to pull her in for a hug. "Thanks for all your help," I whisper. "I'll be in touch."

When we get to Drew's apartment, it's still as if he's on auto pilot. He unlocks the door and together, we walk to his living room. At first, I'm hesitant, not knowing what he needs. But when he asks, "Will you help me?" I jump into action.

I quickly follow him to his bedroom, which mainly consists of a king-sized bed that's neatly made, a desk, and a dresser. There are textbooks on a bookshelf as well as scattered across his desk. "What books do you need to keep on top of your classes?" I ask to give myself something to do.

"Just the ones on my desk. Everything else, along with my laptop, is already in my backpack." He walks to his closet and gets what looks like a team-issued travel bag. It's a large duffel bag with the team's logo as well as Jacobs embroidered into the end. He plops onto his bed and turns to his dresser to grab some clothes for himself.

As soon as I get what textbooks he pointed out into his bag, I ask, "What else can I do to help?"

"Just be here... please." He sounds broken as if he's still fighting for control of his emotions.

I notice he stuffs shirts, jeans, sweats, basketball shorts as well as a team hoodie into his bag. When I notice he's missing some essentials, I remind him, "Uh... what about socks and underwear?" As soon as the words come out, heat floods my cheeks.

Did I just ask him that?

But when I see his numb expression, the heat quickly disperses because there's nothing to be embarrassed about.

"Oh, right. I forgot." He nods in agreement as he opens his top drawer and stuffs several pairs of each into his bag.

When he stops and just stares at the bag on his bed, I prompt, "Toiletries?"

Without a word, he walks to what I assume is a bathroom off his bedroom and disappears.

I look around his tidy room and realize Drew's almost obsessively clean. I'm not sure what I expected, but a pristine room wasn't it. As I take in the simplicity, a phone buzzes in my pocket.

Hoping it's not the hospital to tell us bad news, I pull it from my pocket and see Coach B's name flash across the screen.

"Hello?"

"Abby?" Coach B greets.

"Yes. It's me. Any word on a flight for Drew?"

Coach takes in a deep breath, that doesn't sound promising. Shit, please don't let there be a problem. "The earliest I could get is six tomorrow morning."

Fuck. "We can drive there in less time than that," I voice my thoughts aloud, with barely any filter.

"I was thinking the same thing. Are you sure you're up to taking him? He doesn't need to be alone at a time like this. After everything with his sister, he can't be in the greatest head space."

What happened to his sister?

I look to Drew who's just returning with his travel bag in hand.

Cutting to the chase, I tell Drew the news. "We can't get a flight until tomorrow morning. Would you rather drive?"

Drew's muscular jaw clenches as he processes my words. Simultaneously, he shakes his head and says, "No. I can't wait. I need to get there."

I knew he'd feel that way. If I were in his shoes, I don't think I would've had the fortitude to even pack.

From the phone, I hear Coach B ask, "Does that mean you'll drive?"

"I'll drive," I tell them. Drew's shoulders relax a fraction, and I know I've made the right decision.

To his coach, I say, "I'll let you know as I know more."

"Please do. You can call or text to let me know you've made it? Please tell Drew not to worry about anything but being with his family. I'll be in touch." With that, he hangs up the phone.

When I reach out to hand Drew his phone, he shoves it in his pocket. "I just filled up my car last night. It's more comfortable than yours for a long trip, so let's take mine."

Remembering how he filled up every square inch of my car, and how roomy his SUV was, I wholeheartedly agree. "Sure, no problem."

"Can you do me one more favor?" Drew asks hesitantly.

"Anything."

"I'm not in the right frame of mind for driving. Will you take the first leg of our trip? I'm too wound up to be on the road, I'd likely break about a thousand traffic laws getting to my parents." He sucks in a deep breath, but his breath catches upon release. "I can't fucking lose them."

10

DREW

EVER SINCE I got that fucking call, everything's been a blur. Through it all, Abby's been a rock at my side. I'd be in a fucking ball, bawling on the floor, if she hadn't taken charge. She's thought of everything, including making sure I grab some water bottles and snacks, so we wouldn't have to stop for anything along the way.

I can't fucking lose them, plays on a loop through my mind as Abby leads me through the motions of packing and getting on the road.

I can't lose them.

I can't.

Losing Summer was fucking tragic—and I was able to prepare myself the best I could before she lost her battle with cancer. But having both my parents here one day and not the next, rips me to shreds. Chills run up my spine, and all I can do is stare out the window in front of me.

As if she can sense I need more support, Abby reaches

across the console and squeezes my thigh. "We'll get there as soon as we can. Your parents are getting the help they need. If anything changes, we'd be notified."

Feeling the warmth flow from her, my hand reflexively moves to hold hers in place. Her simple touch and confidence isn't something I'm willing to let go of.

Fuck. She's right. Get it together, Jacobs. They'll be okay. They have to. Other than my mom's sister, they're the only family I have left. Fuck. I'm so not ready to lose them, too. They will survive this. They must.

Abby squeezes my thigh once more, and offers, "You can talk to me, Drew. I can only imagine what you're feeling right now. But staying stuck in your head won't help anything."

Fuck. Where do I even begin? My mind's racing like leaves blowing in a hurricane, and I can't catch a hold of a thought long enough to voice it aloud.

I must take too long because Abby quietly assures me, "It's okay." She takes in a deep breath, then releases it slowly. "Just know that I'm here for you when you're ready."

Needing to get my mind on anything but my parents and their impending news, I force myself to ask the first question that sticks in my head, "What's the craziest thing you've ever done?"

Though the sun has set, and the car is dark, from the dashboard lights, I see her eyebrows raise as her face darts to mine. "Seriously? That's what you're going with?"

"Humor me," I urge. "I need a distraction."

"Hmmmm... let's see..." She tilts her head from side to side as if weighing her decision carefully. "Well... when I was little... I once went to church in my brother's underwear. Does that count as crazy?"

It does the trick. A chuckle escapes, and I must know. "Why?"

She shakes her head. "My aunt was teaching me a lesson. I always went to her house to spend the night on the weekends, but I typically forgot some essential or another. You know... like a toothbrush, socks... or underwear."

She pauses for a moment. So, I prompt, "Go on..."

I feel the hand that I've yet to release tense as her body squirms. "Well, I told her I couldn't take a bath before church because I didn't have any clean underwear."

"Okay..." I know there must be more to this story, so I wait. And wait... for further explanation.

Finally, she gives in, "You see... I was eight years old. I hated washing my hair because I'd have to sit long enough to have it brushed. I thought if I didn't have underwear, she wouldn't torture me. It was the third time I'd come unprepared for church, and she wasn't having it." She chuckles and shakes her head. "Years later, she told me she was sure I'd been lying about not having underwear. So when she threatened to make me wear Travis's tighty-whities to church, she'd thought I'd run and grab mine. But nope. It was me in a fluffy dress—which I hated by the way because I was a tomboy through and through at that age—and a pair of tighty-whities."

"I'm sure it wasn't that bad," I offer. "No one knew but you and your aunt, right?"

"I wish," she groans. "Prior to that day, I thought the worse offense I could do in church was fart or laugh inappropriately.

Nope—wearing Travis's undies and having him smile and wink through the entire service at me, made me feel as if I would burst into flames. To this day, underwear is the first thing I pack when traveling."

A chuckle escapes, and I can't help but wonder what kind of underwear she sports these days. "I can imagine. But I have plenty of boxers, should you need to borrow any."

What the fuck? Why the hell did I just offer her my underwear? The last thing I need to be thinking about is what kind of underwear Abby has on.

"Thanks. I'm glad you're willing to make such sacrifices." She shakes her head. "Okay... your turn, buddy. Tell me the craziest thing you've done."

"Well, it's nothing that would cause me to go up in flames at church..." I attempt to tease. Why did I ask her this question?

What the hell have I done that's crazy?

Ever since Summer died, I've had my nose to the grindstone to make something of my life. To live the life she never had. But when I see Abby raise an eyebrow in my direction, I know I need to respond. "I guess... I'd have to say... it was probably the time I helped pull a prank on DeShawn. Since we're roommates, I know plenty of his habits. Before each game, he always loads his pockets with condoms as well as the essentials... like his phone, wallet, keys... ya know?"

"Oookay?" she draws out, clearly not seeing where I'm going with this.

"Well, after the game, he was finally going out on a date with a girl he really liked. While he was in the shower, I snuck over to his locker and saw his dress pants laid out. I took a pair of scissors and cut his pockets partially open. Not big enough so his wallet would fall out, but plenty big enough for condoms and other small things.

"Our other roommate Grey and I followed him. Ya know... to see if anything would happen. At first, we thought nothing exciting would ever come of it. But then the girl he was meeting drags him over to meet her parents, of all people."

"No way!" Abby shakes her head, and I can't help but laugh at the memory.

"Just as he reaches out to shake her father's hand, a condom drops from his pants leg."

Abby gasps, "You're kidding me." She shakes her head in disbelief and joins me in laughing at the memory.

"I can't make this up—seriously. It fell... right there on the ground between them as he stepped back from their handshake. The poor girl's dad just blinked and stared at the foil wrapper."

"Ohmigod!" Abby gasps.

"But you haven't heard the best part yet..."

A chuckle escapes from the memory, as Abby asks, "And what's that?"

"Her mother didn't miss a beat. She stepped forward to DeShawn, shook his hand, and states clear enough for us to hear from twenty feet away, 'Thank heavens you're not going to make me a grandma at such a young age. Like my husband, who's an ex-SEAL, it's good to see you're always prepared.'"

"No way." Abby shakes her head in disbelief. "Her dad was an ex-SEAL?"

"Apparently. The dude was as tall as me and fit. I would've pissed myself if I were DeShawn. That's definitely an introduction that'll go down in the books as 'What not to do.'"

"How did DeShawn handle it?" Abby asks with genuine concern.

"Well..." Trying to remember his exact words, I rub my chin and look out the window. "I believe he said something along the lines of, 'I have no idea where that condom came from, but since this is only our first date, I doubt we'll be using it.'"

"Oh. My. God. He didn't say that." Abby's jaw hangs as she waits for my response.

"Yep. He sure did. Everyone burst into laughter, including Grey and me. Of course, all DeShawn had to do was look at us and realize we were behind the condom fiasco. He's yet to get even, but I'm sure it will only be a matter of time before he does."

"Wow. Did you know he was going to meet her parents?"

"Nope. Not a clue. Fate just intervened." I shake my head and relax into the car seat once again as I chortle at the memory.

After a short period of silence, Abby states quietly, "You have a great laugh."

God. I've been laughing. And it feels good. Going with the assumption that no news is good news about my parents, it's a relief to feel the tension lighten up. Apparently, Abby's more of a distraction than I realized. "Thanks," I whisper.

"How are you really doing?" Her voice is laced with genuine concern.

I'm about to lie and say I'm fine, but she interrupts with, "Seriously. You've hardly spoken since you got the news, and it's not good to keep things bottled up."

"Sorry about freaking out," I say sheepishly. Fuck. Here I am wanting to be a doctor and at the first sight of bad news, I freak the fuck out. I shake my head, disappointed in myself.

"You were in shock, Drew. There's nothing to apologize for. I would've probably started bawling, so you handled it way better than me." She squeezes my thigh in assurance. And I pick up her hand to hold between mine.

"Yeah, but I probably could've handled it better," I admit.

Abby side-eyes me with a grimace that levels me as she shakes her head. She can see through my shit from a mile away. I might as well tell her the real reason I freaked the fuck out.

I take a deep breath, and let it all out. "My sister died when I was sixteen. If I lose my parents, other than my aunt, I have no family left."

Abby takes in a measured breath and slowly releases it. Her hand on the wheel tightens, as she squeezes my hand in reassurance. "I'm sorry for your loss."

"Thanks." I've heard that phrase a million times, and it still reminds me of my numbness when Summer passed. Shaking my head to rid myself of the dark memories after her funeral, I realize I'd rather tell Abby what happened than make her ask what always follows that statement.

To keep my emotions at bay, I stick with the basic facts as I explain Summer's death. "When Summer was eight years old, she was diagnosed with Hodgkin's. By the time she was ten, she was in remission, and my family couldn't have been happier. But it returned with a vengeance shortly after she turned twelve, and she didn't survive."

"Oh, Drew." Abby's voice sounds gravelly, as if she's holding back her emotions. "That must've been so hard."

My chest aches, and the muscle in my throat squeezes tight. I force myself to clear the lump in my throat before I can acknowledge her words and admit, "It was."

We ride for a few miles in silence as I get lost in my head. Fuck. I still remember vividly when my parents sat me down to tell me the news that her cancer had returned. My heart aches at the memories of Summer going through her treatments. She was so small and weak at the end, but her personality was bigger than life.

Abby's quiet for a few more moments, but when she breaks the silence, her voice is filled with compassion and interest. "Tell me about Summer."

Where do I begin? "Summer was the type of girl whose personality would light up the room. No matter what was going on in her life, she always stayed positive." A memory of her trying to hang out with me and my friends flashes through my mind, and I can't help but share. "Sure, she was a pesky little sister and was annoying as any little sister can be. She wanted to be one of the big kids. When she was learning to ride a bike... gosh, she must've been four at the time, she insisted my dad take off her training wheels. She pointed her finger right at his face and said in the sassiest voice you can imagine, *'I just like Drew. I don't need training wheels. Drew doesn't have training wheels, I ride with him.'*"

"So, what did your dad do?"

I shake my head and left the memory. "He gave into her. She'd been riding a balance bike for a couple of days well on her own. It took her a couple of hours, but she was determined. The next thing I knew, she was screaming down the street, 'Drew! Drew, look at me. I'm big like you.'" I smile at the memory and notice Abby doing the same.

"She must've been excited," Abby guesses.

"Yeah, it was an incredible day. She rode her bike everywhere. For weeks, she made me take her around the block as often as possible. My buddies liked to jump their bikes off ramps we had built, so I usually found a way to ditch her to go with them. One day, she followed me, and the next thing I knew, she was jumping off the ramps like a pro."

"I'll bet your mom was excited about that."

"Nope. Can't say she was." I chuckle at the memory. "Mom just about had a heart attack when she saw Summer go off a two-foot ramp and fly through the air, landing it with grace."

Abby cringes. "Holy crap. Your sister was four?"

A light laugh escapes at Abby's reaction. "Yeah. Summer was as tough as nails. There was no stopping her once she got something in her mind."

"Your poor mom." Abby laughs and shakes her head in commiseration with my mom.

"That's why it was so hard on my family when she got the diagnosis. She was a bad-ass through and through, and she wouldn't let anything get her down. One day, while she was in remission, we were talking about our dreams and goals for the future. I told her I wanted to be a doctor and help little girls like her. She told me she wanted to be a scientist, so she could invent a cure for all cancers. She was wicked smart and if she'd survived, I'm sure she would've done just that."

"Wow. Summer's an inspiration."

"I know." I suck in a deep breath and prepare myself for what I have to say next. "Unfortunately, she caught a simple cold right after one of her first chemo treatments after being re-diagnosed. It caused an infection, and she never recovered."

"Oh my God, I'm so sorry. I can't imagine a loss like that."

I sigh heavily. "It's been hard, that's for sure."

"But you're still following the dream you shared with her. That's amazing. I can't imagine how you manage your coursework and play basketball at a D1 school."

"It's not always easy, but I've managed." I've worked my ass off to get where I am, but there's no reason to go into that detail with Abby. She knows what it's like to maintain the GPA that's required for admissions.

Abby keeps her attention focused on the road for a few minutes before she asks, "You're really good at basketball. Have you ever considered the NBA?"

"When I was twelve, maybe," I say a bit sarcastically. "I knew my parents were broke and had to find a way to get into college. I took the gift God gave me, and I made the most of it. I may be good, but I'm not good enough for the NBA. I'm focusing my time and energy on something I know I can do for myself, not a pipe dream."

"Why would that be a pipe dream?"

"Um... roughly two percent of the NCAA, play ball

professionally. I knew going in, the odds weren't in my favor. But I was guaranteed an education, so I chose the school that gave me the highest chance of getting into the graduate school of my choice."

"Wow. I don't even know what to say."

"The best part is when I finish, my only debt will be med school. Hopefully, I can score a scholarship, so the amount of debt I have will be even less. My parents help with what they can, but they didn't qualify for loans, since they basically had to file for bankruptcy from Summer's medical bills."

"Wow. I can't imagine going through that."

Shit.

Is that pity I hear in her voice?

"Don't feel sorry for me," I say more forceful than I intend. It may be harsh, but I don't need her looking at me any different or think any less of me because of the hardships my family has gone through. We got through it, and that's all that matters.

"I... I wasn't," she whispers, and she pulls her hand away to place it on the wheel. This simple act makes my heart sink, and my stomach turns to lead. I've fucking hurt her feelings.

Fuck. I didn't mean to do that. She's been nothing but kind to me. Hell, she even took charge in my fucked-up state and is driving me across the state to see my parents in a godforsaken hospital.

Great, Jacobs. Way to go.

Douche of the Year—goes to me.

"Look..." I start but don't know where to begin. When she doesn't say anything, I go with the truth. "I'm sorry. Few people know about my past because I don't want them to think any different of me. You've been nothing but kind, and I'm a complete douche for reacting like this. Please, forgive me."

I look to her with pleading eyes, hoping she won't hold my knee-jerk reaction against me. She sighs heavily and readjusts her hands on the wheel.

"You're not a douche, Drew. Prideful, maybe. But you've just been put into a situation where circumstances were stacked against you. You're a fighter, just like Summer. I won't hold that against you. And by the way—I don't feel sorry for you. In fact, if anything, I feel admiration. You've been through so much, and you don't give yourself enough credit. There's no way I would've picked myself up as you have, and still manage to reach your goal. Am I sad you had to go through this? Yes. But I don't feel sorry for you. I feel empathy and compassion. Pity is for someone who you feel is beneath you. If anything, I look up to you."

Abby gives me a sly smile, and reaches out to pat my hand once more. Instead of letting her pull back, I clasp my hand in hers and squeeze it tight. Her simple touch brings me a sense of peace.

11
ABBY

BY THE TIME we arrive at the hospital, I'm exhausted and stiff from hours of being in the car. I park in the closest parking lot to the emergency room. As soon as we've exited the car and walk to the emergency room doors, Drew grabs my hand, as if it's the most natural thing in the world. He's hardly let go of it since I made it clear I never felt sorry for him.

Tension rolls off him in waves as we enter the emergency room door. His grip remains firm. He quickly asks the woman behind the desk where to find his parents.

After tapping his information into her computer, she tells us we'll need to go to the seventh floor to meet with Dr. Reagan's team. She asks us to go through some locked doors, where a nurse will show us where to go.

The entire ride up the elevator, I can tell Drew's barely hanging on. His clasp on my hand tightens, while his other hand fists and releases, as if he's preparing himself for the worse. His breathing is slow and steady, almost as if it's calculated. My heart aches for the pain this is causing him. The fear of the unknown is always greater to deal with.

I lean closer to him and whisper so only he can hear, "It's okay. It's gonna be okay."

Drew remains silent, but when I feel him squeeze my hand twice, I know he's heard me. From the look on his face, I doubt he can say anything, even if he wanted. His pale complexion lets me know his nerves have taken over.

When we exit the elevator, the nurse introduces herself as Janice. She has us stay in a waiting area, assuring us she'll send someone out soon with an update. We sit next to one another on the couch and wait.

It feels like forever before a woman in blue scrubs approaches. "Drew Jacobs?"

Drew immediately stands. "That's me."

The doctor looks from him to me and back. Drew gives her a quick nod, and she proceeds by reaching out her hand to shake his. "Hi, I'm Dr. Reagan. I've worked on your dad's case. He's out of surgery and is expected to make a full recovery. We'll keep him in the hospital for a few days to monitor the progress of his lungs, and he'll be on crutches until his leg completely heals. We had to put some pins in, which will be removed in about eight weeks. I've just spoken with your mother's surgeon, and she's out of surgery, as well. She's still in recovery but will be transported to share a room with your father when she's ready."

Drew's deep voice cracks when he asks, "Can I..." He clears his throat and repeats himself. "Can we see him?"

Dr. Reagan nods. "Follow me, and I'll take you to his room."

As we approach the door, I wonder if I should go in. The doctor walks in ahead of us, but I stop at the entry. Drew looks to me with concern, and I whisper, "Do you need time alone?"

Drew pins me with his deep blue eyes and pleads silently for me to not make him do this alone. "Please?"

The look of sheer desperation on his face as his eyes bore into mine, make my decision for me. I know I'd follow him anywhere. I take in a deep breath and prepare myself for what's on the other side, as I follow him through the door.

When we walk in, a man is lying in a hospital bed, with his face turned away. From where I stand, it's evident he's tall as he takes up most of the bed. The bed's adjusted so that both his chest and legs are raised. The doctor walks immediately to him and checks his vitals, as well as reading the machines.

Without letting go of my hand, Drew walks to stand beside his father. Wordlessly, Drew places his free hand on his father's shoulder, causing him to stir. When his head slowly turns in our direction, I'm shocked to see an older version of Drew staring back at us. He has the same dark hair and shade of eyes as his son. The only difference between the two men is that the man in the bed has a few wrinkles around his eyes and has started to gray at his temples. He also has a few cuts and scrapes and slight bruising from the accident. But other than that, I'm staring at what Drew will likely be in thirty years.

The moment he recognizes Drew, his face lights up. With a weak smile, he croaks, "Drew... You're here."

"I'm here, Dad." Drew pats his shoulder softly, and a

matching smile mirrors his dad's. Drew's rigid posture eases as he lets out a low chuckle. "There was no need to go to quite the theatrics. If you wanted me to visit, you could've just asked."

His dad shakes his head and ignores his smart-ass comment as he explains, "I... I didn't see the other car coming until the last minute. I swerved, and we must've hit a patch of ice. They said your mom's still in surgery. Have you heard anything?"

Drew nods. "Yeah. She's out now. They say she'll make a full recovery. You guys were damn lucky."

Drew's dad takes a labored breath and winces when it causes him pain. It's all I can do just to sit back and watch. "I'm... I'm so glad she's okay. I don't know what I would do without her."

"You and me both, Dad. You and me both." Drew lets out a deep breath, and I feel his body relax next to mine. My heart aches at the stress he must be under. I can't imagine what I'd be like if my parents were in this situation.

The doctor turns her attention from the monitors to us and says, "Mrs. Jacobs should be back in the room anytime. Mr. Jacobs, don't you worry about a thing. We have you taken care of. Is there anything I can get the two of you? I know you've traveled quite the distance to get here."

"We're good, thanks," Drew answers for both of us, and I nod in agreement. I can get whatever I need after we know Drew's parents are okay.

"Well... if you need anything," she looks between the three of us, "just ask for the nurses. I'll be back in a bit to check on him." With that, she leaves the room.

Before I can return my attention to Drew's dad, I hear his deep voice. "Well, son... who've you got here?"

Drew releases my hand and gestures from his dad to me. "Dad, this is Abby."

Mr. Jacobs nods in my direction and says, "Nice to meet you."

I reach out and touch the hand laying in front of me and give it a gentle squeeze. "It's nice to meet you, too." Mr. Jacobs gives me a warm smile, but confusion flits across his features as he takes me in. Knowing he's likely wondering what I'm doing in his hospital room, I say the first thing that comes to mind. "I'm really glad you're out of surgery and doing better."

"You can say that again." Drew reaches out to hold his dad's hand. His dad gives Drew's hand a squeeze, but neither of them let go.

Mr. Jacobs' head relaxes into his pillow, and his eyes blink but remain closed for longer than normal. Exhaustion or maybe it's the effects of the medicine from surgery that make him drowsy. His eyes spring open when Drew releases his hold on him. Drew pats his dad's arm reassuringly, and Mr. Jacobs' tension fades.

"Get some rest, Dad. We'll be right here." Mr. Jacobs sighs and nods sleepily in acknowledgement.

After a few moments, it's evident Mr. Jacobs will be out of it for a while. Drew turns to me and states just above a whisper, "Want to sit with me for a while and wait for my mom?"

There's only one chair in the room, and Drew looks like he could use it more than me. If I sit down and get too comfortable, I'll likely pass out. I quickly offer, "Why don't I ask the nurse for an extra chair? I don't know about you, but I could use some caffeine. Want me to get you anything?"

"Why don't I come with you. We haven't eaten anything in hours and now that I know my parents are on the mend, I'm finally hungry."

After running into Janice in the hall, she reaffirms Drew's mother won't be out of recovery for some time yet. She also encourages us to grab some food and lets us know she'll bring in a chair to the room when she points us in the direction of the cafeteria. On the way to the cafeteria, I spot a restroom and quickly excuse myself, and Drew does the same, telling me he'll meet in the hall.

Once I've done my business and wash my hands, I notice my reflection. Exhaustion has overtaken me. My eyes are puffy, and my hair is lifeless. I quickly pull my hands through my hair, making it look more presentable as well as splash some water on my face. The cool water is refreshing and makes me look less sleepy. Taking a paper towel, I dry off my face and hope that it doesn't appear as if I've spent time primping in the bathroom.

Drew's long body leans against the hall outside the women's room. His dark hair looks as if his fingers had just run through it, as well. The moment I exit, he steps off the wall and greets me with a smile that makes my spine tingle and my nerve endings on hyperdrive. *How can he look so good after driving countless hours and being under tremendous amounts of stress?* As I walk toward him, he steps off the wall and effortlessly reaches his hand out to mine. When he takes my hand once again and holds it, like we belong together, I remind myself I'm only here for support. This doesn't mean anything.

Though the main part of the cafeteria is closed at this hour, we each manage to grab a few things to tide us over until breakfast tomorrow. Drew suggests eating in the cafeteria, so I follow him to a table by the window.

Not realizing how hungry I am, I take my first bite only to discover I'm ravenous. My mouth waters as I eat my chicken salad sandwich. Neither of us had much of an appetite on the way to Spokane, so the snacks I suggested we pack were left untouched. Apparently, both of our appetites have returned with a vengeance. When finally I look up, Drew's tray is half empty.

When Drew's eyes meet mine, they soften, making me wonder what's going on in that head of his. It's the most relaxed I've seen him since we got the news, and I feel a smile form on my lips.

Drew wipes his mouth with a napkin and clears his throat. "In case I've forgotten to mention this, thank you for today. I don't know what I would've done without you."

"It's no problem," I pass off dismissively, but his facial expression tells me that's not an option. "Seriously, Drew. I'm glad I can be here for you."

"I'm glad you're here, too. After we make sure my mom's stable, and I've seen her with my own eyes, what do you say we head to my parents' house to get some sleep for a few hours? You have to be exhausted after driving all this way."

"I could sleep," I admit and as if my body knows there's rest in sight, I stifle a big yawn, causing Drew's dimple to show.

"Hopefully, Mom will be out of recovery soon."

By the time we return to his parents' room, there's another bed in the once open space. Janice is putting the IV drip on the pole and greets us with, "Did you find something good to eat?"

"We grabbed a few sandwiches and a couple of drinks," Drew offers. "How's my mom doing?"

"She'll be in and out of it for a while. When she woke up, she asked about you. I told her you were grabbing a bite to eat." Janice shakes her head. "I'm not sure she'll even remember our conversation. She'll likely be sleeping heavily for the next few hours."

Relieved everyone's no longer in severe danger, the tension I'd been holding on to releases from my body. I look to Drew, and he's nodding eagerly.

"That's great."

"If the two of you want to take off and get some rest, we'll be here taking care of everything. If anything changes, I'll be sure to give you a call. I leave at seven tomorrow morning, but I'll let the person who's replacing me know where you can be reached."

"Thank you. We'll stay for a while, then head home to get some sleep."

Janice nods in approval, then reassures us with, "I seriously doubt they will wake anytime soon. Take your time and get some rest." She looks between the two of us, and her face fills with concern. "You both look exhausted. Do you have far to drive?"

"We live here in the valley, so only about twenty minutes from here."

Janice gives a knowing nod. "Well, since It's nearly two in the morning, make sure you drive safe. There's no need to make this entirely a family affair." It may come off as sarcastic, but there's no malice to her tone. She simply cares. Her smile is wide as she pats Drew once on the arm as she stands near him.

"We'll be safe," Drew assures her. "I think there's more than enough of us taking up beds in this place. I promise we won't add to the count."

"You do that. You need to remember to take care of you, too. Or you'll be of no help to them." With that, Drew nods, and she exits the room.

Drew makes my heart melt when he walks to his mom and brushes the hair from her forehead. She isn't as bruised as his father, but her cast and IVs still attached show that she's been through a lot. Drew simply leans over and kisses her as he whispers, "I love you, Mom."

My heart pangs with emotion. If it were my mom lying in a hospital bed, hooked up to an IV, I'd feel completely helpless. My mom and I have always been close, and if it weren't nearly two in the morning, I'd call her to tell her how much I love her. But calling at this time would cause a heart attack. After she recovered, she'd likely come through the phone to rip my arms off and beat me with them for the unnecessary worry I'd put her through.

Drew says something so quietly, I can't make out the words then turns to sit next to me. Reaching out his hand, he pulls me close. The only thing I can do is rest my head on his chest and listen to his steady heartbeat as he holds me against him. After a few moments, he inhales deeply, squeezing me tighter. I know without a doubt, he appreciates me being here. I thought it would feel awkward being here with him, but knowing I can give him this moment of solace, I'd sit here all night if necessary.

I sigh heavily as I relax into his masculine body and process the events of the day. I can't believe only hours ago, we were in lab together, and everything was so different. I remember feeling nervous when he asked me to dinner, but my nerves have completely disappeared when it comes to Drew. He needed a friend, and I'm happy to be here for him. If our roles were reversed, I'm sure he'd do the same for me. The moment I fully relax into him, I feel him do the same. The constant strum of beeps from the machines and the steady breaths from his parents are all that can be heard while Drew and I watch his parents sleep in silence.

I'm not sure how long we sit here like this, but eventually, Drew's deep gravelly voice comes out just above a whisper. "There's nothing we can do for them now. Let's go home and come back when they're awake in the morning."

I sit up and yawn heavily. "Sure." Drew chuckles.

"You're exhausted. Give me the keys. I'll drive us home."

"Are you sure you have room? I don't have a lot of money, but I'm sure I could find a hotel."

Drew pins me with his dark blue eyes as he deadpans. "No. I thought you'd be sleeping in the car. Or better yet—maybe I could see if there's room at the youth hostel in town." He shakes his head as if he's clearing his thoughts. "Seriously,

Abby, you're coming home with me. It's ridiculous to think anything else."

Before I can utter another word, he grabs my hand and practically drags me out of the building.

12

DREW

AS IF I'D let her stay anywhere but at my place. It may not be much, but it's home. Abby's traipsed across the friggin' state for me. I'm not about to let her leave now. Besides, it's late, and we're both running on fumes. From the way she felt heavier the longer she leaned against me, I doubt she'll hold out much longer.

Abby's quiet on the ride home. I have no idea if it's because she's nervous or about to pass out from sheer exhaustion. While we're waiting at a light about five miles from my house, I see her eyelids finally give up the fight they've been diligently battling since we entered my darkened SUV.

Selfish as I am, I've hardly let her hand go, since the whole ordeal began at dinner.

Has it only been a few hours? God, it feels like months have passed.

Abby's a true miracle. She's been a solid rock. Her unwavering support means the world to me. I seriously don't know what I would've done without her.

I hit the button to open the garage as I pull into the driveway. Once the door opens, my heart squeezes, and the reality of today's events set in. Only Dad's truck is inside. A shiver runs up my spine, knowing I could've lost them both today.

Don't even go there. I scold myself.

Mom and Dad are okay. Don't borrow trouble.

I quickly force my mind to focus on the simple task of driving.

Instead of parking in my usual spot on the driveway, I pull into the garage. It feels strange parking in Mom's spot, but it also means I won't be spending time scraping the windows tomorrow morning, when we return to the hospital.

Living in eastern Washington means you get to experience four distinct seasons throughout the year. My SUV hadn't had a chance to freeze over completely while we visited my parents, but as we left, I noticed plenty of other cars in the lot were well on their way. Knowing Abby's asleep also made my decision easier to keep her from slipping on our sloped driveway.

When I turn off the engine, Abby stirs. At first, she startles, but when I squeeze her hand in reassurance, a beautiful smile forms. "Hey," she whispers. Her voice, thick with sleep.

"Hey yourself, Angel. We're here. Want me to get your bag? I'll give you a quick tour and let you get some rest. You look exhausted."

"Sounds great," she says in a yawn as she unbuckles and

stretches before opening the door. Her dark-brown hair has fallen out of the ponytail she'd secured it in at the beginning of our trip, and she couldn't look more adorable if she tried.

We make quick work of gathering our things and getting into the house. Once inside, another wave of emotion from the day hits me like a ton of bricks. Not having them here to greet me is beyond surreal. My throat tightens, and my eyes prick as I blink away my emotions. Of course, Abby picks up on my shift in mood. She's like a lifeline I never knew I needed as she instinctively wraps her arms around me in a hug. The strength and solace I feel from her helps me relax into her.

"They're fine. You've seen it for yourself," she assures me. As if she knows exactly what I need, Abby squeezes harder to prove her confidence. "If anything changes, you'll be the first to know. Let's get you settled, so you can finally get some rest."

I chuckle at her sudden protectiveness. "I thought that was supposed to be my line."

Abby pulls back but doesn't release her hold on me and smirks. "Give me the CliffsNotes version of a tour. All I need for tonight are the essentials—bathroom and where I'll be sleeping. I'm sure I can figure out everything else in the morning."

I walk her to what used to be my sister's room, which my parents have long ago turned into a guest bedroom/office space for themselves. Since money was tight with Summer's medical bills, we downgraded our home after she was in remission. Summer only stayed in the room less than a year before returning to the hospital. For the longest time, it just sat empty but eventually they chose to move forward. One summer, I returned home to find it renovated into what it is today.

"Here's your room. My parents just redecorated this, so you should be comfortable." We walk in, and she looks around at the queen-sized bed and the desk that takes up the entire wall to the left of it. "They still use it as an office, so excuse the mess."

"This is perfect, thanks." Abby spots the pocket door to the bathroom she and I will share and arches a brow.

Before she can ask, I offer, "Through there, you'll find a Jack and Jill bathroom. My room's off the other side. When my parents bought the house, Summer used to joke about having a bathroom like the Brady Bunch. Apparently, while in the hospital, one of the late-night networks had all the reruns in syndication, and she was a huge fan," I offer in explanation and smile at the memory.

"Sounds good. I won't need but a few minutes, then it'll be all yours."

Not knowing what to do or say next, I roll on the balls of my feet back and forth a few times, as Abby pulls the things she needs out of her carry-on suitcase. She retrieves a small black bag and a wad of clothes that I assume are her pajamas. "I... I'll... just be in my room should you need anything," I hastily say before bolting out of the room.

Instead of walking through the bathroom, I exit out into the main hall, in search of a glass of water and my own bag from the family room.

By the time I enter my room, I hear the water running and

the toilet flush. I quickly pull out a pair of basketball shorts to sleep in. Usually I sleep in only my boxers, but with company, I'd rather not chance it. I quickly shuck off my shirt and grab my toiletry bag to use the bathroom when she finishes.

A soft knock at the door, and Abby's voice startles me, even though I know she's there. "I'm finished. The bathroom's all yours."

Instinctually, I stride over to open the door. "Thanks. I'll only be a few minutes..." I start to say but stop as I watch Abby's mouth drop open, and her eyes roam over every inch of my body.

Hmmm. Interesting. Apparently, I'm not the only one affected.

I'm a guy. Of course, I look her over, too. Though I won't act upon it. I do have some self-control. Unfortunately, as I take in her sexy sleep shorts... my body gets other ideas.

Damn—she's beautiful. Her long, toned legs tell me she must work out regularly.

Wait... is that... cats I see on her sexy sleep shorts? And does her black tank really say *Feline Warm and Cozy*?

"Boy, Angel..." I chuckle. "Should I worry about you turning into a crazy cat lady, later in life? Just how many cats do you have?"

Abby lets out a loud huff, as if she's irritated that I forced her to lose concentration.

It's adorable.

Her eyes narrow, and frustration leaks through in her tone. "No... thank you very much. They happen to be a gift from

Chloe. Since she helped pack, I'm sure she had something to do with these being in here."

I hold up my hands in defense. "Hey... No judgement here. I happen to think the whole ensemble's adorable. Though I'll never understand the whole matching pajamas thing. I'm a 'sleep in my boxers' type of guy—though I settle for gym shorts in the presence of company."

What the hell? Why did I just tell her I sleep in my underwear?

I watch Abby's eyes widen as she blatantly looks me over from head to toe. Her eyes linger on my pecs and my biceps as her lips part. She obviously likes what she sees, and I'm only human when I grin with pride.

Don't get me wrong, I'm proud of my body. But with her appreciation, I need to think dark and depressing thoughts to keep my body in check. Basketball shorts leave nothing to the imagination, and I'm not about to show her firsthand the effects of her perusal.

"I... Uh... will have to take your word for it." She suddenly looks everywhere but at me. It's almost comical. Apparently, my Angel's a shy one. I could get used to that.

What? My Angel? Where did that come from?

To keep from making a fool of myself, I step to the sink and put some toothpaste on my toothbrush. "I'll just brush my teeth and be on my way to bed." I turn on the water and begin brushing, like it's my only job in life. She quickly excuses herself, shutting the door behind her.

Once I'm finished in the bathroom, my gut tells me I

should make sure she's all right. Through the mirror, I saw her face flush.

God, I hope I didn't just make things awkward.

Hell. Who am I kidding? I'd give just about anything to see her again. And I'm not too proud to use this weak excuse.

I knock quietly on the door and wait for her reply.

I faintly hear her say, "Come in." So, I do.

She's already in bed and has the main light off. A bedside lamp illuminates her beautiful skin. Her dark-brown hair looks mussed as it flows around her shoulders. Damn. She's beautiful. As my eyes roam over her body, I notice she's removed her bra. Her boobs are fucking gorgeous. Full, round, with perfect tips poking through her shirt.

Instantly, my dick's begging to salute and have her full attention.

Fuck, I inwardly groan. *Why did I have to notice?*

Get it together, Jacobs, I scold myself as I look anywhere but at her perfect breasts.

"Drew?" She stares in my direction.

Fuck. What did I come in here for?

Or what am I willing to admit to her, is the better question.

"I... Um... Just... Want to make sure you didn't need anything."

"I'm good, thanks," she says as she scoots further down the bed, adjusting the pillow behind her.

Well, this just got awkward.

I sigh at my ridiculousness and lean against the door frame, to keep from joining her in the guest bed. "Since I can't work out in a gym, I'm going for a run when I wake up. If I'm not here, just make yourself at home. I can't imagine Mom doesn't have the fridge stocked. If you don't find anything you like, there's bound to be something in the pantry."

"Uh... how far do you typically run?" she asks, throwing me off guard even further.

"Just a couple of miles, but I'll throw in sprints along the way."

"Would you be up for some company? I'm not much of a sprinter, but I'm good for a few miles." She shrugs as she fans out her dark-brown hair on the pillow, which makes my dick twitch again.

Damn, Abby's beautiful.

"Sure... uh... no problem," I practically stammer. *What am I, twelve?* I don't even remember the last time I was remotely tongue tied around a girl. Fuck, Jacobs—Get it together.

"Just wake me when you get up."

"Will do," I quickly agree. Needing to get out of this room before I do or say anything stupid, I quickly add, "Have a good night. Sleep well, Angel."

With my endearment, I swear I hear a faint gasp as Abby's eyes widen, then quickly return to normal. If I hadn't been watching her every move, I would've missed it. "Night, Drew. See you in the morning."

WHEN I CALL the hospital first thing in the morning, the nurse who's replaced Janice encourages me to take my time, as both my parents are still resting soundly, but on the mend. My rigid body loosens at this news, and I finally take the breath I didn't know I'd been holding.

Abby must've heard me talking because the next thing I know, she's standing before me in yoga pants, a sweatshirt, and a pair of sneakers, ready to run. Just as I hang up the phone, her knowing grin calms me as she states, "You look like you're ready to get out of here."

When I meet her expectant eyes, it's clear she gets my need to work off this nervous energy. We take a few minutes to stretch, and I fill her in on the state of my parents. It gives me unexpected comfort when she lets out an audible sigh of her own. She visibly relaxes as if she's been shouldering this burden with me all along.

I must stare at her in wonder for longer than socially acceptable because she's suddenly cocking her head to the side as her features fill with concern. "Drew? Everything okay?"

"Uh... Yeah..." I shake my head to clear my thoughts and focus on the task at hand. "You ready to run?"

She beams in my direction a smile that lights up her entire face. "Ready if you are."

AS WE FINISH OUR WORKOUT, I almost feel bad. She goes through my full regimen because she insists on keeping to my normal routine. When I reach the end of the block before her and turn to see her struggling, I feel the need to cheer her on in support.

"Come on! You can do it, only fifty more feet," I holler encouragingly as she finishes the sprint. When she reaches me, she bends over and sucks in air heavily, trying to catch her breath.

She's a fucking trooper to endure this, without building up to it. I admire and am in awe of her strength.

"Is your trainer pure evil?" she says between deep pants. "Do you really do this type of thing daily? I thought for sure I'd easily be able to keep up with you, but you can kick my ass from here to Sunday with those legs." More deep pants. Then a sigh as she wipes the sweat from her forehead. "Not all of us are freaking giants, ya know."

Great. She thinks I'm a sadist.

I laugh and shake my head at the notion, then do my best to explain, "I've been at this for years. Don't be too hard on yourself. You're doing great," I encourage.

"Let's just finish, so we can visit your parents," she pants out as her breathing returns closer to normal.

"Just another couple of blocks," I assure her as we slowly jog the rest of the way.

"Good," she says between deep breaths. "I may run regularly, but I should know better than to go against a giant D-1 athlete. Your leg span alone is three times mine."

"Hey, I can't help it if you're short," I tease, hoping to get a rise out of her.

She doesn't disappoint. "Hey, for your information, five-eight is a respectable height. You're the one with the giant genes, Jacobs."

She earns a deep belly laugh with that. Damn, this girl is something else.

When we reach my house, an unfamiliar car's in the driveway, which pulls Abby and me up short.

Before Abby can ask the question clearly written across her features, I quickly explain, "It seems my mom's sister has arrived."

As soon as she sees us coming up the sidewalk, Kathy rushes out of her car and pulls me into a hug. I try to keep my distance, knowing I stink, but she won't have it. "Come here, you," she practically commands, so I bend down and hug her fiercely. As I pull back, she brushes her palm along my face. "I'm so glad they're all right. I don't know what I'd do without them."

"Me neither," I agree. Kathy looks to Abby, and I quickly make introductions.

"Kathy, this is Abby. She was gracious enough to drive me home yesterday. We called the hospital this morning and found Mom and Dad are still out of it but on the mend. If you give us a chance to clean up, I'd be happy to drive you to see them."

Kathy reaches out to Abby and pulls her in for a hug as well. "It's so nice of you to bring our dear Andrew home. I can't imagine what went through his head when he got the news. No one could reach me until they were out of surgery—and even then—knowing they were okay, it still scared the life out me." She looks to me. "I was so worried. I came straight here, figuring you might be sleeping…" She shakes her head, then mumbles, "I should've known better."

"I'm fine," I assure her, with a side-arm hug before ushering her inside. Feeling Kathy relax in my arms shows me the stress she's been under. I love her even more for coming to check on me first, though I know neither of us will completely relax until this entire mess is behind us. She's the only family I have left.

13
DREW

WHEN ABBY, Kathy, and I enter my parents' hospital room, I'm relieved to see both of my parents alert and most importantly, alive. Even though I was assured they were okay, I've been preparing for the other shoe to drop. My heart soars when their faces light up with smiles to greet us.

"Drew," Mom gasps as an arm reaches for me. My heart aches at the possibility of never being able to hold her again. I reach out and squeeze the hand she's extended, then lean down and kiss her cheek.

"I love you, Mom," I greet her, my voice gruff. Even though I know she's all right, I'm assaulted with an unexpected wave of emotion. My throat tightens and tears prick at the back of my eyes, as I take her in.

Thank God, she's all right.

Her bright blue eyes have dark circles under them, though I'm not sure if it's from the accident or exhaustion. Her normally straight brown hair, is in disarray from the events of the past twenty-four hours. Her other arm rests across at her waist and has a cast up to her elbow. She must've broken her radius closer to her wrist, than elbow—or it would be a full-arm cast.

"Love you, too, Drew. I'm sorry we worried you. You must've been a wreck when you got the call." Her eyes shine as if she's on the verge of crying, and my gut twists.

I do my best to put her at ease. "I've had better days, that's for sure. But I'm much better knowing you're both all right. Besides, Abby took charge and made all the arrangements to get here. I hardly had anything to worry about."

"Abby?" Mom looks in her direction, her face fills with gratitude. "Your dad mentioned a friend being with you. Is this her?"

Abby steps forward, with one hand grasping her other elbow and a nervous expression on her face. Her eyes had been downcast toward the floor before Mom mentioned her name, as if she didn't want any accolades for helping. "Yes, ma'am. But it was no problem. Drew would've done the same for me. I'm glad you're okay."

Mom lets go of me and reaches her good hand out to Abby. "Thank you so much for taking care of our Drew. He's good under pressure, but I'd been worried about the hospital being too much for him."

Geesh, Mom. Way to lay it all out there.

"Uh... I'm standing right here," I remind them, but it lands on deaf ears.

Abby squeezes Mom's hand and quickly comes to my defense. "He's a trooper. Sure... There was some initial shock, but when it was all said and done, his only concern was to get here to you." That's not how I recall the last twenty-four hours, but who am I to argue?

"I'm just thankful you're both okay," I say to get the focus off me as I look to Dad. "How are you feeling?"

"Oh..." He releases a breath slowly. "I'm still a bit winded, but I'll heal in time."

"What about your leg?" I ask and all eyes go to the leg that's laying out of the covers on his bed. There's a cast to just below his knee, and a sock over the end, most likely to keep his toes warm.

"Right now, my lungs hurt way worse than my leg," he surprisingly admits. "Though..." he lets out a breathy sigh, "when I'm no longer on pain meds, that may change."

"I'm sorry I couldn't get here sooner," Kathy says as she squeezes my dad's hand. "I didn't get the message until nearly midnight, when I got off the plane."

"How was the conference in Tallahassee? I hope you went sightseeing, while you were there." Mom shakes her head and grimaces. "I'm just glad you didn't have to cut your trip short."

Kathy lets out a huff at my mother's selflessness. "I would've come the minute I found out either way. There's only so much you can learn at an agricultural conference after being so many years in the business."

Kathy's been working for the same food transportation company, for as long as I can remember. Mom says she's close to retiring. But I'll believe it when I see it. Ever since her husband died about fifteen years ago, she's thrown herself into her work and never lets up.

"Did you get to the coast like you wanted?" Mom dismisses her worries and focuses on her burning question.

Kathy sighs and walks over to Mom. "Yes, I got to spend a day there. I made the drive to St. George Island, and it lived up to the hype. The white sandy beaches were unlike any I've ever experienced. I'd highly recommend you and Marty take a trip there when you retire."

"Maybe we can go once Drew's out of school," Mom suggests casually to Dad.

And with one comment alone, the guilt pours in.

Being on a D-1 scholarship means I can only work during the summer, and I can't have a part-time job during the school year. My parents are at the prime of their lives and should be close to enjoying a retirement. But with Summer's sickness and me in school, they've been financially strapped for as long as I can remember.

"Sounds like a great plan," Dad agrees and by the look he gives Mom, I can tell he's going to find a way to make that happen. There's nothing Dad won't do to make Mom live life to the fullest, now that Summer's gone. We've all taken that mentality and work our asses off to reach the goals we want to accomplish. They've nearly recovered from their bankruptcy and once I'm out of school, or at least no longer playing ball, they'll have a lot more financial freedom.

"So... Abby..." Mom says in that tone that tells me she's on her way to her version of the Spanish Inquisition. "How'd you meet Drew?"

Huh. That's simple enough. Knowing Mom, there'll be

loaded questions embedded into her version of a casual conversation.

"We're lab partners," Abby offers.

"You're a chemistry major, too?" Dad asks as he looks Abby over critically.

"Yes. I've applied to med school and will find out if I've been accepted later this spring."

"Interesting," Mom murmurs so that only I can hear, then speaks louder to Abby. "Which schools have you applied to?"

"You won't believe it, but she's applied to a lot of the same schools I have—except Stanford and Baylor are in her top five schools."

This time, Dad pipes in as he looks to Mom with an unreadable expression. "Interesting, indeed."

"What does that mean?" I rush out defensively. They're obviously having a silent conversation, and it's only fair to share it with the room.

Mom pats my arm. "It's nothing, Drew. Don't get your undies in a twist."

Could she be anymore patronizing?

Obviously, she and Dad think something as their expressions have turned smug, but they remain tightlipped. *I love my parents, but really?*

"Well," Kathy gushes. "I think it's wonderful. You'll both be doctors someday."

Okay, captain obvious.

"How long are you staying?" Dad asks, all sense of smugness evaporated.

I look to Abby, who simply shrugs. "Uh... as long as you need me."

Dad clears his throat. "Well, since you're missing class today and have a game Monday, I think it's best you travel back tomorrow or Sunday."

My brows raise in disbelief. "Are you trying to get rid of me?"

"No. Of course not." Mom comes to Dad's rescue. "We know you have your studies and an important game to get back to... Now that we're out of the woods, so to speak, there's no need for you to stay around for us."

Uh. They're still in the fucking hospital. I'm not leaving.

As if Dad's a friggin' mind-reader, he states, "Drew, we're not invalids. Now that we're okay, there's no need for you to fall behind in your studies or miss any game time."

Before I can respond, Aunt Kathy interrupts, "I'm off for the next two weeks on vacation. I'll stay here with them, so you won't have to worry."

I look between the three of them, and it's obvious they're a united front. They all have determined looks on their faces, to convince me I'm being ridiculous. "You've both just had surgery," I remind them.

"Drew," Mom says in a softer tone. "We understand you'd rather be here to see for yourself, but it's foolish to sit here and watch us, when we're perfectly capable of taking care of ourselves. We're not leaving the hospital, until we're good and ready—so there's plenty of people to care for us." Then she looks to Kathy. "I doubt my sister will leave anytime soon, either. There's seriously *no* reason for you to sit and do the same."

"But..." I start to protest.

"No buts, Andrew," Dad says in finality. "We know you love us and are worried..." He trails off as he takes a breath before continuing, "We're in perfectly good hands, and your aunt will stick around to make sure we can manage on our own once we're released. You can stay tomorrow and leave Sunday."

I glance to Abby, who only shrugs as if to say, *this is between you and your parents.*

When I look around the rest of the room, I can see I've met my match. I let out a deep sigh in defeat. "Okay. But if *anything* changes, and I mean *anything* at all, you call me, and I'm coming right back."

Mom pats my hand in reassurance. "You know we will, son. We love you, too."

14

ABBY

I SPEND the rest of the weekend getting to know Drew's family. When we weren't with his parents, Drew and I did our best to catch up on the classes we missed. With a ten-page paper due next week, I made use of my time away from the hospital. I also shopped with Kathy to get a few of the things his parents will need once they return home, while Drew keeps his parents company.

Thankfully, by the time we leave, both are up and slowly moving around in their hospital room. We're all relieved when we're told they could go home as early as Monday, should they keep progressing. With Kathy insistent that she'll call if anything changes, Drew's stress level lowers about returning to school.

As Drew leisurely drives us back to school, we've kept up casual conversation. One thing that's changed is that he hasn't touched me or held my hand. I must admit, I miss the way his skin feels against mine as well as the comfort of being in his arms. He must have just been an emotional wreck and trying to hold it together earlier—nothing more.

Not wanting to make things awkward, I'm doing my best to pretend what we shared hasn't completely changed the way my body reacts when he enters the room. It's almost as if I now have a super Spidey sense when it comes to Drew. Instinctively, I feel him enter a room without even seeing him. I recognize his scent from afar, and my spine tingles when he brushes against me casually.

Yeah. It's not awkward at all.

If I just keep telling myself he doesn't affect me in that way, maybe I'll eventually believe it.

"Abby?" Hearing my name pulls me out of my head. "So... are you?"

"Wha... I'm sorry. I must've spaced out. Can you repeat that?" I risk a glance to Drew and see him shake his head, but his lips tip up into the most perfect smile.

He clears his throat and looks out at the road. "I asked... If you're coming to the game tomorrow night?"

Crap. He asked me this before the call from the hospital. I didn't know how to turn him down before and now that I've gotten to know the real Drew Jacobs, it's hard to disappoint him. As much as I'd love to see him play again, I force myself to go with the ugly truth.

"We have that huge exam next week," I remind him but look anywhere but him. One glimpse of those beautiful eyes will be my kryptonite. Add in a smile on those perfect lips, and I'll combust on the spot. Not to mention, lose my ground.

Drew remains quiet for an uncomfortable amount of time.

When I can't take the silence any longer, I sneak a peek. Yep. I should've known better.

With a sly grin, he quietly states, "I have to study, too."

When his lips quirk, and his eyes make full contact with mine, I may hyperventilate.

Is it hot in here?

I pull on the collar of my shirt, then push up my sleeves. It doesn't help.

He takes my silence as an opportunity to continue, "Why don't we study together? You can come to my place. I'll even provide snacks. We'll study until we feel confident we'll ace the test. If you're feeling behind in any other class, we can study for that, too."

Why would he do that? It makes no sense. "We can study together, but you don't need to study unnecessarily."

Drew's eyes light up like I've just given him a puppy for his birthday. "So... you'll come?"

"Drew, we can study, with or without me watching your game," I point out the obvious.

"Angel... you're killing me." His tone almost makes me feel sorry for him. Almost.

"Why?" I whisper.

"Just say you'll come," he practically pleads.

Why is this so important to him?

"Drew..." I draw out. "You have thousands of fans—literally—all cheering for you in the stands. You'll never even know I'm there."

He cocks an eyebrow and blanches, as if what I've just said is completely ludicrous.

Drew reaches across the console between us and takes my hand in his, sending electric pulses up my spine. He squeezes my hand lightly and locks his eyes with mine briefly before returning them to the road. "Obviously, I'm asking because I want YOU at my game. Trust me. You could sit in the nosebleeds, and I'd know you're there... though why you'd choose to sit that far from the action is beyond me." Rolling his eyes, he shakes his head in disbelief.

I chuckle at his antics. "I can't say Sydney would let me sit in no-man's land."

"I knew I liked Sydney." He grins as if he's already won the game.

"This still doesn't mean I'm going," I attempt to protest. But damn. He and I both know, I'll be at the game tomorrow night.

WHEN WE GET to my place, Drew parks and carries my bag to the door for me. He mentions having an early class tomorrow morning, so I know he's not staying. But when he sets my bag down, he stuffs his hands into his pockets and rocks back on his feet.

When his eyes focus on his suddenly interesting shoes, I feel uncomfortable. Not knowing what I should say or do, I fiddle with my keys and look anywhere but at him. *Should I ask him in?* Crap. I have no idea what to do, and my stomach flips as my palms sweat.

Drew clears his throat, drawing my attention. I stare into

his beautiful blue eyes for an immeasurable amount of time. Well, until he clears his throat again.

Shit. Did he say something?

I look him over for any signs. No, I don't think I missed anything.

Damn. Those perfect lips quirk and form the most perfect smile. Energy zings throughout my entire body, like a live wire that will detonate on touch.

"Thanks for everything this weekend, Abby. I seriously don't know what I would've done if you hadn't taken charge. That was..." He stops and takes a big breath before trying again. "That was the first time I'd stepped foot in a hospital..." He shakes his head as if he's trying to rid himself of his thoughts. "And... I just want you to know how much it meant for you to be there for me."

"Drew," I say dismissively. "It's fine... really. I'm glad I could be there for you. Once we knew your parents were okay, I had a lot of fun. Who knew you used to like dressing up as superhero characters and wore your costumes in public for days on end?" I add the tidbit of information from his aunt Kathy at the end, in hopes of lightening the mood.

It does the trick.

Drew's eyes widen, and his mouth forms the perfect O. When he finds his voice, he shakes his head in disbelief. "Uh... who do I have to kill for divulging that bit of information?"

I smile sheepishly and shake my head in denial. "My lips are sealed." Thank God, I close my mouth before *'But I'd love to see you dressed up now'* pops out. I bite my lower lip to keep from saying more.

Thankfully, he doesn't sense my mind plummeting into the gutter. He rests his one finger on his lips and pretends to think hard about something, then cracks a smile. "Now I'm curious as to what other dark secrets my family shared with you."

I narrow my eyes and school my features to be as serious as possible before I deadpan, "You should be afraid, Drew. Very afraid."

This earns a deep belly laugh from Drew. "Honestly, you already know more about me than most. I highly doubt anyone had much else to reveal."

"If you say so." I keep up with my teasing. But I'm sure he can see right through my efforts since he lets the subject drop.

Drew glances at his watch and shakes his head. Then he pins me with his now dark-blue eyes, nearly taking my breath away. "I... uh better get going." I see him peruse my face once more, and I could've sworn his gaze focused on my lips longer than the rest of me. But when I blink, his focus has returned to my eyes.

Now it's my turn to rock. My keys jingle between us as I fidget. "Okay, then..." I draw out. "I'll see you later."

He stares for a moment longer then pivots to walk away, causing whatever breath I'd been holding to release. After a few steps, he looks back. "I'll see you at the game tomorrow, 'kay?"

Instinctively, I manage to nod.

Did I just agree to go to the basketball game?

Once Drew leaves, I head into my bedroom to change into pajamas. When I return to the living room, I flop onto the couch and put my feet on the coffee table. Sydney's in the kitchen getting a snack, and Chloe's curled up on the loveseat next to me.

"How was your trip?" Syd asks as she enters the room to sit next to me. She hands me a spoon and asks, "Strawberry cheesecake?" as she holds out my own pint of my favorite ice cream and another in her hand for herself. Thank God for great friends and delicious ice cream. They can be counted on to take my stress away.

I pop the lid and scoop out a healthy glob, then slowly taste my efforts. Ice cream is to be savored, not devoured. Just the taste of sweet strawberry melts my troubles away. "Better than I expected." I sigh heavily as exhaustion creeps over me. It was quite the opposite. "Drew's parents are on the mend, and it was nice to get to know his family."

My mind lingers on the last of my conversation with Drew. *Why would he want me at his game?*

Sydney takes another bite from her spoon and stops midlick. She eyes me curiously then shakes her head and returns her attention to the TV.

But Chloe pipes in, "Are you sure you're all right? Something seems off."

I could lie and pass it off as just being tired. But these girls are the closest people in the world to me. I take a heavy breath and draw out. "So... Drew asked me to go to the basketball game tomorrow night."

"Really?" Chloe asks in surprise. "He asked you to go to the game?"

Um... I just said that. I stare at her as if she's missing a brain cell or a million.

"What's wrong with going to the basketball game?" Sydney asks in a tone that clearly states I should tread lightly and not feed her any of the BS I'm about to flop her way.

"It's... It's just... weird? I mean..." I try to regain my thoughts as they've scattered like bugs on a windshield. None of them make sense and lead me to dead ends. "Why would it matter if I'm there or not?" I look to each of my friends, hoping for a better insight on the situation.

They each stare at me with their mouths agape. They look to each other slowly, then back to me. Then back to each other, before Sydney speaks up, "Oh... you're serious."

"Why wouldn't I be serious?" My pitch creeps higher, almost defensively.

"Holy shit. For being one of the smartest people I know, you sure can be dense," Chloe teases. Well, at least I hope she's teasing. I look back and forth between my two best friends in the world, and they both have the same mirrored expression, as they roll their eyes.

"What?" I practically yell when they remain quiet.

"Abby." Sydney's voice is stern, like when she must cut off a drunk frat guy, or threaten to call the cops. "He obviously likes you."

"We're just lab partners, and I helped him with his family emergency. That's all," I say as quick as the thought forms. "He's never indicated anything otherwise."

But then... there was the hand holding...and the hugging.

But that was just because he needed comfort, right?

"If you say so..." Chloe shakes her head. "Sydney knows more about the basketball players than me, but I'm sure he wouldn't have asked you if he didn't like you. You can live in the land of denial all you want, but I'd bet a pint of Ben & Jerry's that the guy is into you."

I roll my disbelieving eyes because there's no way a guy who's got his sights set on a championship—not to mention getting into med school—would think twice about dating someone at this point in the game. His plate's practically overflowing between basketball and graduating with honors. There must be something else going on. He did say he wanted to be friends. Maybe this is his idea of what friends do?

"You're going to the game," Sydney says with conviction, and I give her a sideeye glare.

So you say...

When Syd doesn't relent with her stare, my shoulders slump in defeat.

I suck in a deep breath and let it out slowly, as another thought hits me. Seeing Drew in his element is a sight to behold. I won't even go into how the thought alone has my body lighting on fire. Before the accident, he'd claimed he wanted to be friends. *Who am I to deny a friend's request?*

15

DREW

BEFORE HEADING to the arena for the game, I do something uncharacteristic. Well, for me. I whip out my phone and send a quick text.

Me: You coming tonight?

I see my message is instantly read, and I wait for what feels like forever to see those three little dots to tell me she's replying.

Abby: I'll be there. Sydney will kill me if I back out now. It had better be worth all the hype. Lol

Her sharp tongue has me smiling uncontrollably. I can picture her eyes narrowing and her expression serious.

Me: It'll be a great game. If we win, will you come to the next home game?

Her response is instant.

Abby: What happens if you don't?

Me: Bite your tongue, woman. You're gonna jinx us. Just for that, you owe me.

Abby: For what?

Me: For having such little faith.

Abby: Sorry. No harm meant. How can I make it up to you and your precious ego?

I can picture her chin jutting out and her eyes rolling. But I'm almost certain she's not backing out.

Me: When we win—which we will—I'll think of something. So be ready.

I see the dots appear, then disappear, and repeat this pattern for a few agonizing moments. When I can't take it any longer, I quickly tap a question into the text field.

Me: What time do you want to study tomorrow?

Abby: I work until noon. But I'm free afterward.

Me: Want me to pick you up from the library at noon?

Abby: Sure. BTW—good luck tonight.

Me: Thanks. Gotta run. See you there.

Abby: Sure—It'll be like finding Waldo in the crowd. Lol

I laugh aloud, earning a questioning look from DeShawn as he enters my room wearing a suit and CRU color for his shirt and tie. We're each wearing a variation of this for game day. Instead of paying him any attention, I send my last text to Abby.

Me: If we win tonight, I'll be at your place an hour after the game ends to celebrate. If I don't, I'll be there to commiserate.

I cringe when it hits me that I might be overstepping a boundary. We haven't talked about any of this. But I'm a go with your gut type of guy.
I just hope I didn't fuck up royally.
Instead of waiting for a response, I quickly shove my

phone into my pocket. Looking to DeShawn, who's adjusting his tie in my mirror, I ask, "Ready to go?"

"Sure thing, man. Let's go kick some ass." He fist-bumps me, and we head out to find Grey. Of course, the sports fanatic he is, we find him in his usual spot on the couch, dressed and ready to go, watching highlights on SportsCenter. He immediately stands, and we leave for the arena.

IT ISN'T until after the National Anthem has been sung that I notice Abby in the stands. It's almost as if my body sensed her before my eyes can. She's flanked by Chloe and Sydney on both sides as she shimmies her way to a seat in the student section. She's not as close to the court as the last game, but she's easy to spot. They're decked out in CRU gear and appear eager to watch the game. I can't help the smile that forms when Sydney spots me staring and bumps Abby in the shoulder to point me out. Not wanting to make a scene, I nod and wink in her direction, letting her know that I did indeed find Waldo in this sea of red and black.

Abby rolls her eyes and shrugs, sending the message of *yes, you found me,* from across the arena.

What is it about this girl that makes her so special? It's not like me to be this distracted before a game. But the moment I find her, I feel the calm I need wash over me.

I don't have time to consider this because Coach calls us into a huddle. After giving a team cheer, the game begins, and my focus switches entirely to the court. There's no way I'm going to let Colorado win, if I can help it.

By the time the buzzer for halftime sounds, CRU's in the lead by ten points. As we make our way off the court to the locker room, I spot Abby still watching my every move. I raise an eyebrow and shrug in her direction, "Having fun?"

Somehow, she reads my lips through the crowd, and she smiles and nods, making my heart rate soar. DeShawn slaps me on the back as he joins me, switching my focus back to the team. We jog off the court to the locker room, and I take my usual place for Coach's words of wisdom.

CRU's pumped when we hit the floor to warm up again. As much as I want to glance at Abby, I keep my head in the game and my thoughts controlled. We practice a few drills and before I know it, the game has resumed. We keep our lead through the second half, thanks to DeShawn's jump shot from the back court, and my stats stay consistent. The rest of the team is on fire, and Colorado just can't catch a break.

When the final buzzer sounds, the crowd is on its feet, showing their appreciation. I finally let myself glance to Abby. Even from across the room, her infectious smile lights me up from the inside. I can't wait to celebrate with her this evening. I have something planned, but it's been so long since I've tried anything like this with a girl. I'm afraid to admit, I'm a bit out of practice, and just pray it won't be a flop.

Unfortunately, by the time I get to Abby's, it's been well over an hour since the game ended. I was pulled into the conference room to conduct a live interview and couldn't leave the arena as soon as I'd hoped.

God, I hope she'll understand; some things are beyond my control when it comes to my time after a game.

I knock on her door and wait hesitantly.

I'm still riding the high from our win. But the longer I wait, an unusual feeling settles over me. A tingle races up my spine, and my palms sweat as I wonder if she's still willing to help me celebrate.

I grip the necessary supplies loaded in my arms tighter, as I take in a deep breath to calm myself.

God, I freaking hope I didn't read her wrong.

When the door opens, Abby takes my breath away. Her long brown hair flows over her shoulders in waves. Her oversized CRU basketball jersey somehow looks sexy, and her dark skinny jeans make her legs look as if they go on for miles. But that's not what does it for me. Nope—it's the way she slowly peruses me up and down—almost subconsciously. Hmmm. Maybe I have a similar effect on her.

When I went home to pick up everything for tonight, I changed into a pair of jeans and dark-fitted henley. Showing up to her place in a suit would've been a bit much for what I have planned.

When her eyes finally drag up my body to meet mine, she pulls in her lower lip and chews it nervously.

Fuck, if that doesn't make my cock stir.

Ignoring my body's natural reaction, I force myself to string coherent thoughts together. "Hey."

Yeah. I'm rockin' this.

Shit, Jacobs, pull your head out of your ass and speak in

full sentences. "Sorry I'm late. There was a press conference after the game."

"I know. Sydney made us watch as soon as we got home. I figured you'd be later than expected." She suddenly notices the bag in my hand and opens the door wider. "Wanna come in?"

"Sure. Thanks." I step through the door, and she shuts it behind us. Instead of stopping in the living room, I walk directly to her kitchen and pull out items from my bag.

"Do you like cinnamon rolls?" I ask innocently.

Her eyes widen in surprise. "Um, yeah. How'd you know?"

I know I've hit my mark when she eagerly looks to the bag in my hands. I may have done some social media stalking—but I won't confirm or deny it, if ever asked.

"Just a guess. I picked up Cinnabon from the mall after class. I even managed to snag some extra frosting." I attempt to sound as if this is something I'd ordinarily do. "Mind if I warm this up in the microwave?"

"No, I most certainly don't mind." She sounds almost giddy, and I know I hit the mark. But then her eyes narrow, and she pointedly asks, "Did Sydney tell you cinnamon rolls are my kryptonite?" She looks down the hall to where I assume Sydney is.

"I haven't spoken a word to Sydney." That I can say with honesty.

"Chloe? Did you talk to Chloe?" Abby asks again, her voice filled with suspicion.

"Nope. Haven't talk with her either."

Abby stares at me in disbelief. "Then how did you know these are my favorite?"

Not wanting to admit my blatant stalking, I shrug dismissively. "Lucky guess?"

"Hmmm..." Abby ponders, but when the microwave dings, she's like a kid on Christmas morning, waiting for her treat as she jumps to the microwave and practically claps her hands together in delight. Her smile's so infectious, I'd bring her cinnamon rolls every day if I get to see this expression. Damn, she's beautiful.

She hands me silverware, and I plate our gooey perfection onto the dishes she places on the counter.

Abby doesn't wait for me to get my cinnamon roll onto my plate. She takes one of the extra toppings and pops the lid to spread some of its creamy goodness on top of her cinnamon roll.

Before she says another word, she slices a fork through the gooey concoction and lifts a piece to her beautiful mouth. The guttural moan she lets out makes me wonder what other type of sounds she makes in pleasure.

With her mouth still full, she covers it and practically moans. "God, I love these."

And all the blood in my body decides to head south at this exact moment.

Holy hell. Kill. Me. Now.

With the few brain cells I have firing, I quickly close my eyes and will my body to regain control. To focus my attention elsewhere, I take a bite of my own cinnamon roll.

She isn't lying. This is amazing. I manage to finish chewing before I agree wholeheartedly. "Damn. These are good. I haven't had one in forever."

She looks at me in mock horror. "You don't get one every time you go near their store?" She pulls a face and suddenly, she looks serious. "I'm not sure we can be friends."

I roll my eyes at her theatrics. "Well, we can't have that. Does this mean if we ever venture to the mall, this is a required stop?"

She takes another bite and savors the taste before replying, "The only time I don't stop is when Sydney bribes me with a whole pan at home. I swear she must've stolen their recipe because hers are almost better than this, if you can imagine." She takes another bite and groans in appreciation.

Seriously? Kill. Me. Now.

Holy hell! Abby's breathtaking when she loses her inhibitions and allows pleasure to take over.

Wonder what she would do if I made her feel that good?
Jesus! Don't go there.
I don't have time for the type of relationship she deserves, I scold myself. *Focus!*

Drawing my eyes back to my cinnamon roll, I take another delicious bite to further distract myself. I manage to keep my tone casual in response to her last statement. "Wow. That's impressive. I can't imagine anyone beating these. They were Summer's favorite, too." Remembering how she got excited when we got her one brings a smile to my face.

"She had good taste." Abby smiles widely and scrapes more frosting onto her cinnamon roll. The girl sure has a sweet tooth.

"Yeah, she did." Then I cringe, remembering Summer's eccentric tastes before she got sick. "Except, she also liked peanut butter and pickle sandwiches with Doritos smashed inside them."

"Ewww..." Abby wrinkles her nose in disgust, and I don't blame her one bit. YUCK!

"Exactly. She used to make them for me and because of our 'No Thank You' rule, the brat knew I had to take at least one bite before I could politely decline her concoctions. I swear she used that rule to her advantage each time. Since she knew I'd do almost anything for her, if I didn't have to eat some of her culinary delights." I shiver at the grossness of some of her 'experiments' as she liked to call them. Sure, some were decent. But most were inedible.

"I would've loved to have met her. She sounds amazing. Though, I've never been brave when it comes to trying new things with food."

As we finish our rolls, I ask, "I know we have early classes tomorrow, but I'm too keyed up from the game. Wanna go for a walk and help me burn off some of this energy?"

"Not to mention the sugar rush," she teases.

"That, too," I agree. "Let's walk around campus. I know it's dark, but it's a clear night for a change. Let's take advantage of the unusually mild winter in the Pacific Northwest."

Abby hops up from her chair at the table. "Sure, just let me get my jacket." She starts taking her plate to the sink, but I reach for it instead. "How about I clean these while you do that?"

Damn. Her grateful smile has my pulse picking up a beat.

Thankfully, she exits the room quickly. I swear if her eyes lock on mine any longer, I would have followed her into the other room in only a matter of a heartbeat.

Geez, what the hell has gotten into me?

Not wanting to make an ass of myself as soon as she's out of sight, I quickly turn my attention to the plate in my hand and have our mess cleaned up in no time.

Unfortunately, as we make our way onto campus, there's an unspoken electric pulse that flows between us. I swear, I'm acutely aware of her every movement. It takes everything in me not to reach out and hold her hand. Somehow, I manage to refrain. It also helps when she talks with her hands animatedly about how she and Chloe tried to replicate Sydney's cinnamon roll recipe, which led to an epic fail, and the opportunity passes. Apparently, they forgot to put yeast in the dough, and it ended up being a gooey mess.

When we get to the cobblestone courtyard in the center of campus, I'm pleased to find it empty. During the day, the outlining benches are filled with people mingling. But for now, we have it to ourselves. The brick buildings are lit from the ground, making it almost magical.

"I love it here at night," Abby sighs as she spins around in a circle with her arms wide. The glow from the lights shine on Abby, making her even more beautiful. Her hair is now almost black as it flows out from her twirl. My hands itch to touch her.

Then she makes a second twirl as she takes in the beauty of the campus.

Without another thought, I reach out and take her hand. I guide her through a series of twirls to keep her moving, so we can stay in this moment. Her light laughter warms my heart, the look of pure abandon on her face makes me wish I could pause this moment to live in it forever. We dance effortlessly around the center of campus without a care in the world before we're interrupted by a group of people coming around the corner.

Without any prompting, Abby stops dancing and pulls me down a path in the opposite direction. Once we're out of sight, she lets go of my hand and shrugs. "Sorry. After pulling off that win, I doubt they wouldn't recognize you. And I'm being selfish; I don't feel like sharing you now with your fans."

Holy shit. She knows me better than I thought. Don't get me wrong. I love my fans, but right now, I just want to be with her. Could she be anymore perfect? I practically stutter in both shock and awe. "I... Um... Don't want to be shared."

"That's what I thought." Abby smirks, and I want nothing more than to pull her in and kiss that expression off her face. But I refrain. Just barely.

Before I get a chance to respond, Abby turns on her heels and practically speed walks back toward her place.

How the hell can someone her size eat up the pavement so fast?

Seriously, was she a competitive speed walker?

But being a few paces behind her leaves a fantastic view. Her jeans are worn in just the right places, making me wonder even more what it'd be like to get them off her.

"What's the rush?" I finally ask when I force myself to stop staring at her perfect ass.

Abby stops and turns to me. "I didn't think you wanted to be bombarded?"

"It doesn't mean I want to rush my time with you," I point out. "Wanna slow your roll?" I tease.

This earns me an eye roll and a breathtaking smile. "I'm not walking *that* fast," she insists as she places a hand on her hip.

"Um, I'm six-five, and you were pulling away from me—and I was walking my normal pace. Do you always walk like your ass is on fire?" I quirk an eyebrow, trying to make my point, though I hope she doesn't accuse me of staring at her ass. I'm a guy. But that's beside the point.

She scoffs. "I like to be efficient. You know that," she says defensively.

"Uh... have I done something to offend you and now you want to end our evening?"

"Uh," she huffs. "No." She looks anywhere but at me for a long moment. But when I don't say anything, she mutters, "I'm just embarrassed because I let myself get carried away back there."

So... she walks like a speeding freight train when she's uncomfortable.

Interesting.

I file that piece of information away and get back to the point at hand. Shrugging, I act as casual as I can. "You have nothing to be embarrassed about. *I'm* the one who saw you twirl and had to dance with you. So, if anyone got carried away, I'd say it was me. I'm not ashamed I enjoyed our moment, are you?"

She sighs heavily, and her shoulders visibly relax, and I feel my heartbeat relax with hers. "No, I'm not ashamed. I just don't let myself get carried away like that."

"Ever hear all work and no play makes one cranky all day?" I tease.

This time I get an eye roll with a shaking of her head. "I don't think I've heard it like *that* before, but something along those lines. You might be paraphrasing."

"Well, Angel... it's time to let your hair down and relax. You're far too young for worry lines and premature gray hair. Don't get me wrong, I work hard, but I also see the benefit of letting loose when the time's right. If losing Summer has taught me anything, it's that each moment is precious—and if you can't find something to smile about each day, there's not a lot to live for."

Abby's mouth gapes open, and she stares for an immeasurable moment.

"Are you sure you're not a philosophy major? Besides, I'm sure I'm a long way from getting any wrinkles or gray hair." She takes a deep breath as if to steady herself, then challenges, "Okay, Mr. Blue Eyes, when was the last time you did something fun that wasn't playing basketball or related to school?"

Shit. She's got me there. My schedule's tight as it is, and extracurricular activities aren't on the top of my priority list. "Well, I hijacked your evening, brought you Cinnabon, and danced with you to no music." I shrug as if that should explain everything.

This earns another eye roll. "Before that," she accuses, and she waits expectantly.

Fuck. She's right. With the season starting, I haven't had time to do much other than to study and go to practice. I shrug and shake my head. "Honestly, I have no idea. But let's rectify that right now. What's one thing you love to do and haven't had the chance since starting CRU?"

She places a hand on her chin and looks to the sky. She must have just as much life as me, for as long as she takes to answer the question. "Um, I haven't been bowling in a long time."

"Okay." I take a deep breath, trying to figure out how to make this happen. "I'm traveling out of town for a game Friday night. I don't know when I'll return Saturday, since we're riding on a bus from Boise. Let's go bowling Sunday. I'll let you pick this time, but I'm choosing next time."

"And what makes you think I want to do these things with you?"

My Angel is saucy. The fire in her eyes makes my blood race and heart soar.

"Call it a hunch." I smirk. "If you don't want to go, you can always back out. But I'm going with or without you. I think you might like a break from the constant studying and worrying about med school. Besides, we've already applied—it's up to the universe if we get in at this point. So that your GPA doesn't drop—we'll study, too."

Abby's mouth hangs open as she stares at me as if I've just lost my ever-loving mind. Hell, maybe I have. But if I end up spending more time with my Angel—what a way to go.

I give her a grin I'm sure she can't resist and finally ask, "What do you say, Angel? Wanna bowl with me?"

16

ABBY

BOWLING. He wants to go bowling with me. Drew Jacobs, star athlete at CRU, the guy that's had his nose to the grindstone to get into the right med school is proposing to take me bowling? I only chose bowling because I thought he'd laugh, and that'd be the end of it. Sure, I like to bowl. But I wasn't expecting him to want to go with me.

With me. Abby Angelos—the most boring person on the planet.

Did he hit his head and get a concussion during that game, and I didn't notice?

"Uhhh..." I manage to get out. Great. Real coherent, Abby. Get it together.

Drew puts his hands together in a prayer and pleads, "Come on... Angel. Don't make me do this alone. Since neither of us do much outside of school, or work... and in my case basketball, maybe we can do one thing a week out of the ordinary to mix things up. I promise it won't take up too much of your time, as I don't have a lot to spare either... And we'll keep up with our studies."

When his blue eyes darken, and his perfect lips turn into a shy smile, I. Am. Done for. Seriously, I don't know how anyone can resist the full force of Drew Jacobs. Thank God, he typically uses his power for good and not evil. Hell, if he keeps smiling at me like that, I'd streak across the center of campus in my undies if he were waiting for me at the finish line.

"Okay," I whisper as I stare at his beautiful face.

"Okay?" he asks for clarification. "Okay, as in you'll do it or okay, Drew's lost his last marble, and I need to get away from him?"

I can't control the burst of laughter that flows out of me. Damn, he's freaking adorable when he wants something. I shake my head and do my best to regain my thoughts. "Okay... as in I'll go bowling with you. But consider yourself warned, I'm a bit competitive. So, you'd better choose the items on your list carefully."

Without a word, Drew closes the distance between us in two strides. He bends down and wraps me in the biggest bear hug, lifting me off the ground as he spins us around in a circle. When he sets me down, I swear I hear, "God, I knew I'd chosen the right partner the day I walked into lab."

What the hell is that supposed to mean?

From the way he just hugged me, I could've sworn he was feeling the same as I was. Was I just imagining the hunger I saw in his eyes? Does he just want to be friends? Lab partners? Something more?

He sets me down and reaches for my hand to walk toward my apartment.

Maybe Drew's just a touchy-feely type of guy?

Wait... Does he hold hands with everyone he considers just his friend?

I'm completely lost in my head, contemplating Drew's comment as he guides me home. Neither of us say anything. Or if he does, I don't hear him, and he never bothers repeating it.

When we get to my door, Drew stops and turns to me. "I've had a great time tonight, Angel. Thanks for coming to my game."

Now that I can look him straight in the eyes, I take this moment to study his features, hoping he'll give anything away about his thoughts or feelings.

Nope. Not a chance.

He genuinely looks as if it's what you see is what you get. Which is nothing... gah, this is so frustrating. But I force myself to focus.

"You're welcome. I had a great time," I admit honestly. I may be confused as fuck, but until his last comment, I'd thoroughly enjoyed myself. Maybe a little too much.

"I'll see you tomorrow at noon." He bends down and embraces me in a hug. Not wanting to let this opportunity pass me by, I inhale his delicious scent and return his hug with equal force. Drew may just be my lab partner, but the man gives a great hug.

"Okay. See you tomorrow."

And with that, he turns and walks away, leaving me to question... well, everything.

The next day as I exit the library, I quickly find Drew in the parking lot nearby. His face widens into a delicious smile when he spots me approaching, sending tingles down my spine. Before I can get to his SUV, he jumps out and runs around to open my door.

"Hey, Angel. How was work?" He reaches in and hugs me before I can respond. Damn. He smells delicious. I let myself linger by taking a deep breath to savor the moment before he releases me to grab my backpack and place it in the back seat.

Is Drew just a serial hugger? I didn't think he'd be the type, but who knows.

My eyes lock onto his delicious form as he rounds the front of the vehicle. When he gets settled, instead of asking the thousands of questions spinning in my head, I force myself to answer his.

"It was fine. I had a few freshmen who'd likely never stepped into the library before. They didn't know how to research anything without it being digital. It was almost comical trying to explain the Dewey Decimal System to them, so they could find the physical book they need."

Drew pulls out of the spot as he shakes his head and chuckles. "I can't imagine. Isn't it pretty late in the year to be figuring this out?"

"Um, yeah. Hopefully, the poor kid isn't on the verge of flunking out." I shake my head, remembering his desperation.

"That would suck." He shakes off the thought, then

changes the subject. "I have things for sandwiches, is that okay? Or would you like to stop and pick up something?"

"That'll be fine. As long as there's no peanut butter and pickles," I clarify at the end. I'm a college student who's learned not to be picky when it comes to food, but there are some lines my stomach won't allow me to cross.

Drew's chuckle fills his SUV, and I can't help but join in. "I'm right there with ya. Don't worry, there's a variety of lunch meats to choose from. Between me and my roommates, a couple of different types of bread."

"I'm sure it's fine. Will they be joining us?"

"Uh... I have no idea. Usually DeShawn has class, and I have no idea what Grey's up to. They won't bug us too much though. They know I don't like distractions when studying."

"Are you the taskmaster of the house?" I ask in surprise. I can't imagine three athletes living in one house and keeping their distance from one another. On the court, their personalities look larger than life.

"No. Believe it or not, they use our place to chill and get away from it all. They each have heavy loads and like to work hard, so they can play harder when the time comes."

"Not to sound stereotypical, but don't athletes have a reputation for partying and what not?"

"Sorry to disappoint, but we've learned not to bring the parties to our place. Sure, we'll have a good time when we get together, but we'd rather keep the chaos away. It's kind of an unspoken rule..." He opens his mouth to say something but apparently changes his mind.

"Too many wild parties as underclassmen?" I tease, hoping

he'll relax and say what else is on his mind. He's obviously keeping something from me.

"Well, when we moved out of the dorms our freshman year, we were determined to keep our place private. You wouldn't believe the lengths some would go to as jersey chasers." Drew winces, and my curiosity's piqued.

I expect him to say more, but Drew remains tight-lipped. *What is he not telling me?* From the look on his face, clearly there's a lot more to the story.

I clear my throat, pondering how to satisfy my curiosity. When I finally find my voice, it comes out a bit strange and uneven. "Uh... are you speaking from firsthand experience?"

Drew groans, and I have my answer.

He's quiet for a minute as he parallel parks. For as long as he's silent, I'm almost certain he's going to change the subject. But once we're parked like a pro, his cheeks darken as he tells me more than I need to know.

"Well, my freshman year, there was this girl..."

Great. Just how all good stories start.

My gut clenches at an onslaught of possibilities, while I wait for him to continue.

I can tell Drew really doesn't want to finish his thought, and by the unpleasant look on his face, I'm not so sure I want to know either. To let him off the hook, I offer, "It's okay, Drew. You don't have to say anything."

Drew lets out a huge sigh, then surprises me by continuing, "It's actually better you know." He shakes his head and has a look of disgust for a fleeting moment before his features clear. "You see, when I was a freshman, I was already a starter and getting a big name on campus. A couple of girls in the dorms made it their mission to be *with* me..." Drew looks up to the sky as if the rest of the story is written there and takes a deep breath.

"Okay..." I draw out. And I'm suddenly positive I would rather not know what happened. My stomach lurches, and my heart accelerates to a staccato. *God, please don't let it be that bad.*

Drew's low voice finally breaks the silence, "One night, I came back to the dorm and found one of the girls who'd been following me around, naked in my bed."

"Seriously?" I ask in disbelief. Holy shit. What the hell is wrong with people?

Drew rolls his eyes. "Seriously. Now, don't get me wrong. I'm all for having naked girls in my bed because... well... I'm a guy." He shrugs as if that should explain everything. "But—trust me when I say, I prefer to be there when it happens. Or at least have invited them there in the first place."

No shit. I think I'd freak out if someone showed up in my bed unexpected. "What did you do?"

Ohmigod, do I even want to know?

Duh, Abby, most guys would usually join her. I wince, hoping I don't regret asking Drew this question.

Drew swallows slowly as he watches me like a hawk to gauge my reaction. "I politely asked her to leave, and when that didn't work, I went to sleep somewhere else."

Huh. Wasn't expecting that.

My jaw drops. As much as I didn't want to hear about any

sexcapades, I find it hard to believe him entirely. "Are you kidding me?"

"Unfortunately, no. I saw more than my share of her body as she tried to make a move. She was beautiful, but there's something about respect that holds my attention more." He shakes his head then. His voice sounds more forceful when he continues, "Clearly, she had none for me. Hell, I didn't even know her name. Listen... I'm not a prude, and I enjoy sex as much as the next guy... But it needs to be consensual, ya know?"

No shit.

He takes in a deep breath and slowly releases it, shaking his head. "After that experience, I made a point to move out of the dorm as soon as possible. There was no way I wanted *that* to happen again... And that's how I ended up with this place."

"Wow. I can't even imagine."

"Trust me, neither could I. I'd heard stories about it happening, but I never thought in a million years, I'd experience it."

"Drew, you're a star athlete at a D-1 school. Don't women flock to you?" I'm genuinely curious, but my question sounds more accusatory. I know my first reaction to him, and I didn't even know he played basketball. But then again, seconds later, I thought he was a cocky ass... so there's that.

Drew makes a sound between a strangled laugh and a cough. "Umm... I wouldn't say flock."

Maybe it's best that I don't know the answer to this question. You know the whole curiosity killed the cat and all.

Unfortunately, I can't help but roll my eyes in his attempt

at modesty. "It's really none of my business. Seriously, Drew. I don't need to know."

"I'm neither a saint nor a virgin, but I'm not a player off the court either, Angel. Yeah, I've used my popularity to my advantage from time to time. But that comes with a double-edged sword. It's a constant wonder of whether they're with me—the athlete, or me—the real Drew Jacobs."

Drew's nothing like I expected. There's so much more to him than my first impression. But when I look at the sincerity in his eyes, my heart plummets to my stomach.

"Ugg, I'd hate that," I admit. I guess that's one advantage to not being an athlete. I have enough problems of my own, thank you very much.

"On that—we'll both agree." Drew grins. "Let's get inside and get something to eat. I'm starving."

Drew's back to business as usual once we finish lunch. He sits on one end of the couch, and I sit on the other. I've taken off my shoes and made myself comfortable by curling into the corner, so I can face him. We quiz each other until we both feel ready to ace this test. I admire his tenacious work ethic, and I feel prepared. Sure, it takes me a minute to get my head in the game, but once I focus on only the chemistry in the books, everything flows together.

By the time we finish a couple of hours later, Drew asks if I want to grab a bite before we head back to campus. When he offers to make creamy chicken pasta with broccoli, there's no way I'm going to object. Not only do I want to know if he can cook, but I'm hungry after spending hours studying.

I glance at the clock and ask, "Do you have time before practice?"

Drew gives me a knowing look and stares blatantly at me until I get his point. "I've gotta eat, too."

I offer to help, but Drew dismisses me quickly. "I have this." Since his kitchen is small, he suggests I stay in the living room and relax. But me being me, I read a book on my phone for pleasure.

Before I know it, I'm deep into Brittney Sahin's latest romantic suspense novel. God, I love how she creates a world. I never want to leave. It's like I'm on the edge of my seat waiting to find out what happens next as I flip through the pages. I don't even notice Drew standing over me, until he says, "Abby? You okay? I've called your name a few times. Whatever you're reading must be good."

Embarrassment rushes through me for being so caught up in the story. I seriously didn't hear him. But instead of giving excuses, I go with the truth. "Sorry, got stuck in a book." I quickly shove my phone into my pocket and follow him to the dining room where I find he's set and filled two plates for us.

"Oh my God, Drew. This is delicious." I practically moan as I devour my first bite. Damn. The man can cook.

Drew grins wide in appreciation of my suddenly ravenous appetite. "Thanks. My mom used to make it all the time growing up."

"I love it. Your mom taught you to cook?"

"When Summer was sick, I tried to help out as much as I could. She taught me how to make my favorites, so Dad and I could still eat while she was at the hospital. My dad's an amazing cook, too. But sometimes, he had to work."

I can't imagine going through the loss of a sibling. I love my brother to death. Even though we fought like cats and dogs growing up, I'd be lost without him. I don't feel sorry for Drew because I know it's not necessary, but my heart aches for what his family went through.

Drew must be a mind reader because he reaches out to hold my hand as he quietly says, "It's okay, Abby. My mom would've taught me how to cook anyway. I was a growing boy and needed to eat. I knew how to cook long before Summer was diagnosed."

His touch alone sends shivers down my spine. My body heats, and I'm unsure what to say. Once again, I go with the truth. "Have I told you how amazing your family is?"

This earns me a sheepish grin. "They are pretty great. What do you say we finish up so I can get to practice on time?"

Later that night, just as I'm nodding off to sleep, my phone vibrates with a text notification. Expecting it to be from my mom or roommates, I'm surprised to find Drew's name flash across the screen.

Drew: You awake?

Me: Yeah, everything okay?

The three little dots appear then disappear as if he's written something, then deleted it all—just to start over again. Finally, a new message appears.

Drew: We still on for Sunday?

Why is he asking about Sunday? We'll see each other in class before he leaves for his road trip. Does he not want to go?

Me: That's the plan.

Drew: Are you busy tomorrow night?

Well, this is unexpected.

Me: I'm working until ten. Why?

Drew: Never mind. I'll see you in class tomorrow. Have a good night.

What the hell? Even for Drew, this is vague. I want to say something but don't even know where to begin.
 I start to type something, and then stop.
 Delete every word, then do it all over again.
 Finally, I stick with simple.

Me: You, too. See you tomorrow.

I roll over to get comfortable. But the vagueness of our conversation rolls through my mind on a loop, leaving me more confused than ever.

17

ABBY

THE REST of the week flies by. Sure, I see Drew during class, and we text. Each night, he manages to message me right before bed. Nothing comes of our conversations, but they make my day complete.

Is it weird that I like his attention? I mean, we're just lab partners... but I'd like to think we're becoming friends, too.

What shocks me the most is when Drew texts right before his game.

Drew: How was your day, Angel?

Yes, he typically starts each text like that, making my heart race and stomach flutter.

Me: Good. Ready for the game?

Drew: As ready as I'll ever be. It sucked being on

the road for so long, but I finished a paper and studied a bit. Though Grey snoring next to me proved to be a challenge. That man can sleep through anything.

I laugh at a picture of Grey snoring next to Drew on the bus. I can only imagine what road trips with the team must be like.

Me: How are your parents?

Drew: Good. Kathy's taking good care of them at home. She's a godsend.

Me: Tell them I say hi, next time you talk to them.

Drew: Will do. Since the game's not televised, what are you doing tonight?

I laugh aloud, knowing I wouldn't be watching the game either way. I'm not that big of a fan.
Though if it meant I'd get to see his sexy form running up and down the court, I could be persuaded
But I'd never admit it to anyone, especially him.

Drew: I gotta run. Need to warm up. I'll let you know how we do.

Abby: Knock 'em dead. Talk soon.

Smiling, I shake my head and shove my phone into my pocket. Since I'm done studying for the night, I head to the living room to see if Chloe's home. I find her in the kitchen making a snack. Just as she reaches into the freezer, she asks, "Want a pint?"

I don't even care what flavor. This is Ben & Jerry's we're talking about. "Duh! Like you have to ask."

I hear her chuckle as I grab spoons for the two of us and head for the couch. "What do you feel like watching?" I ask as I plop down and get comfortable.

"I don't really care. What looks good on Netflix?" She flops herself down next to me and hands me my pint of Ben & Jerry's. Then she picks up the remote on her side of the couch.

Yum. It's one of my favorites, Salted Caramel. "You can choose. I have no idea what's showing these days," I offer as I take a bite of delicious ice cream.

Chloe settles on a romantic comedy I'd never heard of before. As the opening credits start, she asks, "So... what's going on with Drew?"

Instantly, my hackles rise. "What do you mean?"

Chloe just stares at me expectantly, so I feel the need to explain the obvious. "We're friends." I shrug dismissively, though even I can tell I sound a bit defensive. But it's the truth, so why deny it.

I huff out a sigh at that realization. *Pathetic, right?*

Chloe eyes me suspiciously and remains quiet. I can tell her wheels are turning, and I may not like what's on her mind.

"You want more," she eventually says as a statement, rather than a question.

I exhale heavily and roll my eyes, as I practically whine, "I don't know…"

I clear my throat, so I can gather my thoughts and continue in a normal voice. "At first, I thought we were only friends. When everything happened with his parents… I could've sworn there was something more. Then, when we returned to school… there was that romantic evening on campus… but at the end of the night, nothing changed." I shrug as if that should explain everything.

"Is he the one who's been texting you at night?"

How does Chloe know about that? I've been tight-lipped about Drew since returning from Spokane.

"Yeah," I admit.

Chloe drops her chin and stares at me as if she knows I'm holding out on her. Damn, she'd make a good warden. With that look alone, I'm ready to confess just about anything.

"Okay… Okay." I hold my hands up in defense. "Yes, Drew and I've been texting. But so far… it's stayed completely in the friend zone."

Chloe's eyebrows shoot to her forehead. "You… want out of the friend zone? I mean… Drew's hot as hell. If he were paying attention to me, like he is to you, I'd jumped all over that."

"Chloe," I chastise.

"What?" She throws her arms up, then continues, "Why don't you just tell him how you feel? It's not that difficult. I know you're out of practice since you dated that douche canoe.

But communication is key in relationships. You do want a relationship with him, right?"

I bury my head in my hands. "I don't know what I want. I mean... I know I'm attracted to Drew. But is he worth the risk?"

"What risk are you talking about?" Chloe asks, her voice sincere.

I take in a deep breath and slowly exhale. "I guess... after my fiasco with the douche canoe, I've been focused on getting into med school. I don't even know where I'll be living next year. Is it worth getting involved with someone, knowing I'll be moving in a matter of months?"

Chloe reaches out her hand and pats my leg. "That's something only you can decide. But for what it's worth, I think Drew's a great guy."

"I know," I groan.

"Why not think of it this way... What if..." Chloe cocks her head to the side and stares at the ceiling for a moment, deep in thought. "Ask yourself, what you'd be thinking a year from now if you *don't* tell Drew how you feel?"

I take a moment to consider my feelings. If I'm being honest, I know there's more going on between Drew and me than just a friendship. Instantly, I recall the electric current that flows in his presence.

But do I want to act upon it?

As if sensing my thoughts, Chloe places a hand on my thigh as she solemnly states, "You know, Abby... More people regret the things they don't do, rather than the ones they do. Only you can make this decision, but I don't want you to wake up a year from now, wishing you'd said something to him. There's a long time between now and next fall. Think of all the time you could enjoy together until then."

"But what if..." I stop myself from revealing my deepest fear.

Fuck, if I voice it aloud, it could become reality.

Before Chloe or I can say anything more, Sydney walks into the room and drops her purse onto the coffee table. "But what if what?" she asks the room.

Chloe looks to Sydney with a slight grin. "Abby..." She looks pointedly at me. "Has feelings for Drew but is afraid to voice them."

"He's made it very clear..." I look to them to clarify. "All he wants to be is friends."

Sydney shakes her head in disagreement. "I don't think so, Abs."

"Did you ever stop to think that maybe he thinks you've *friend-zoned* him?" Chloe points out. "I mean, you're so focused on school that you never even notice the guys around you."

"But why would he be interested in *me* that way?"

There. I've finally voiced my biggest fear aloud.

I close my eyes for a moment as the next words tumble out of my mouth. "I mean, he can have anyone he wants. Why me?"

"Why not you?" As I finally open my eyes, I see Sydney shaking her head. "You're smart, funny, beautiful..."

Chloe cuts her off, "Trust me. I've seen the way he looks at you; it's not in a friend-zone way, Abs. I'd be willing to bet he'd like something more."

"He says he never dates during the season," I quickly spew out. "And he's made this weird comment more than once about being glad he's chosen me for a lab partner." Suddenly, I gasp at the realization. Shit. "You don't think he's going to turn out like the douche canoe, do you?"

"I'm pretty sure no one is like douche canoe." Sydney shakes her head in laughter. "Drew pulls his weight in class, right?"

Rolling my eyes at the effort he's gone to do his share, I know without a doubt he's nothing like my ex. "Yes. Drew does. In fact, I've never had a better lab partner. So... he's definitely not like him."

"Thank God!" Chloe shouts out to the room and flops back on the couch.

"No kidding." Sydney laughs at Chloe's theatrics.

"Seriously, Abs. You just need to relax and let whatever's supposed to happen between the two of you, happen. And for God's sake, just tell the guy you like him."

I shake my head dismissively as I contemplate their points.

Before I can say anything further, Sydney interrupts my thoughts.

"Well..." Sydney draws out. "Since he's on a road trip and won't be home until late tomorrow, let's go out tomorrow night to get your mind off things. It's my first Saturday off since your birthday, and I want to dance. What do you say?" Sydney looks to both of us before continuing. "Wanna go?"

There's something about the way Sydney invites us that

makes me think there's more going on. Usually, she's the last person who'd be at a bar on her night off. Maybe she's had a stressful week and just wants to let off steam. I keep my opinions to myself, knowing Sydney will reveal what's bothering her in her own due time.

Chloe never being one to turn down a night out with the girls, shouts, "I know just the place."

EVEN THOUGH THE place is crowded for a Saturday night, Chloe, Sydney, and I don't have to wait long. Chloe marches us to the front of the line, and we're let in within minutes. Chloe and I spot a table against the wall, while Syd makes a beeline to the bar. She returns with shots for all of us. Apparently, Syd's not messing around when it comes to letting loose. Chloe and I each look at each other, eyebrows raised before looking back at the shots. Hopefully, the alcohol will loosen Sydney's lips, and she'll reveal what's bothering her. Because this is unusual, even for her.

On the outside, Sydney looks as if she's having the time of her life. "These are B-52s. Let's drink up, ladies." She hands us each a shot glass, then lifts hers to the air. Chloe and I quickly join her for a toast. "Here's to taking what we want and never settling for less." The look of determination in Sydney's eyes tells a different story but for now, she throws back her drink like a pro, and Chloe and I do the same.

Having never taken a shot before, I'm surprised I'm able to drink it all at once. It tastes better than expected as the alcohol flows down my throat. I might just have to try another one before the night's through.

Before either Chloe or I set our glasses on the table, Sydney heads back to the bar for more drinks. I give Chloe an apprehensive look, but when Sydney returns with a smile on her face and says, "I couldn't carry both the drinks and the shots. Here... I got us all White Russians. Be sure you stick with Kahlua tonight, or you'll regret it in the morning."

"Everything all right?" I ask Sydney as I watch for her tells. She and I can't hide much from each other, and if something is bothering her, I'll know.

"I just need to unwind. It's been a long week, and I want to shake my ass on the dance floor. Drink up, so we can get out there."

We each reach for our drinks from Sydney, and I do as I'm told. It goes down easy. Maybe too easy, and I realize... I need to pace myself if we're staying out all night.

Just as we're finishing our drinks, my phone buzzes in my pocket. I pull it out to check my notifications. I can't help the smile that spreads across my face when I see Drew's name flash across the screen. Is he back in town?

Of course, my two best friends notice and laugh at me.

"Guuurrrlll," Chloe drags out. "You have it so bad." I hear as I rush to unlock my phone.

Drew: Just got back, you busy?

"It's Drew. He wants to know what I'm doing!" I yell above the music to Chloe and Syd, in hopes that they won't mind my answering his text.

Before I can type a reply, Chloe grabs my phone and quickly types something into it. She waits for a reply then types something again. Just as I reach to get it back, she shoves my phone down her bra, pivots, and leaves for the dance floor.

Not knowing what she has said, I panic. She could've told him to get lost, or worse, that I like him. Total honesty, both options are equally horrifying at this moment.

"What the hell did you say to him?" I scream over the music as I follow her out to the dance floor.

Chloe shimmies and sashays her way to the middle of the dance floor. She throws her arms up and dances without a care in the world. When she finally makes eye contact, she says, "You'll just have to trust me."

Trust her? How the hell am I supposed to trust her? I'm not even sure I like her now. She just stole my phone and said God knows what to Drew. She knows how I feel about him, so I doubt she'll do much harm. But I don't ever do well with the unknown.

"Dance with me," she pleads. "I promise it'll work out."

I stare at her for a long moment, contemplating what to do next. I should just reach down her shirt to get my phone. But do I really want to make a scene?

No. Not really.

Throwing my arms in the air, I let the music flow through my body and get caught up in the moment. I'm still irritated, but I'm not mad. The smile on Chloe's face shows she's got my number, and I just nod foolishly in agreement.

Yeah. I still like her.

Barely.

A few beats later, Sydney's dancing on the other side of us. As the music pulses through my veins, I feel the effects of the alcohol. My body's warm, and my muscles loosen as I shake my ass on the dance floor, without a care in the world.

A few songs later, I feel two large hands grip my hips from behind. At first, I tense, not wanting to dance with a stranger, the way Sydney's doing now. Not that I'm judging. I just wish it were Drew.

Before I can look in his direction, the stranger bends to speak in my ear, "Mind if I dance with you?" My body lights on fire. His touch, his scent, and the possessive way he guides my body on the dance floor has an effect greater than the alcohol in my system. My heart races, my nerve endings explode, and I get lost in the moment. The entire room could burst into flames, and I wouldn't notice.

With his chest to my back, his body grinds into me in the sexiest of ways. He has one hand in the air like mine, while the other guides my hips. We bop, dip, and sway in sync with the music. I've never felt more exhilarated in my life.

When the song turns to a slow one, my partner spins me to face him. His beautiful face and perfect lips take my breath away. Did he get even better looking in just a few days? Is that even possible? "Hi," I say, breathless.

"Hi yourself, Angel." He grins devilishly, and my heart skyrockets nearly out of my chest.

I force myself to remember to breathe.

18

DREW

I'VE SPENT all day on a bus, riding back to CRU. What would've taken a five-hour trip in a car, turned into seven hours on a bus. I love my teammates, but I just wanted to get the fuck off the bus. With any luck, Abby won't be busy tonight, and we'll get to hang out. I've tried all week to do the right thing and just see her as a friend. But let's face it—at this point, it would be like trying to survive without air. Somehow, she has managed to work her way under my skin, and I'm not sure I want to let her go.

Oddly enough, it took Mom pointing it out for me to realize just how important Abby's become. My parents came to the game in Spokane. It was their first outing since leaving the hospital.

After the game, I spent a few minutes with them before I returned to the team's hotel. I'm sure if I'd asked Coach, he would've let me stay at home, but since we had a volunteer clinic early this morning, I thought it best to stay with the team.

After pulling off another win, my parents wait in their seats for me. They are in the ADA section since Dad doesn't have the full strength to travel far on crutches. I feel their sense of pride as I approach.

With Mom being more mobile, she stands to greet me. Throwing her good arm out and extending her cast for me to embrace her in a hug. "Oh, Drew, it's so good to see you. You had an amazing game. Well done, honey."

"It's good to see you, too, Mom." I pick her up off her feet, like I've done since I became taller than she, then set her down before turning to Dad. "How's the leg?" I ask as I give him a side arm hug.

"As good as expected," Dad downplays with a shrug. "My lungs still give me hell from time to time, but they're getting better every day."

I hug Kathy in greeting, but before any of us can say anything, we're interrupted.

"Great to see you all out and about. You gave all of us quite the scare last week." Coach Bradford walks over to Dad and shakes his hand. "Nice to see you again."

"Thanks, we're glad to be here." Dad smiles then shakes his head. "It could've been a hell of a lot worse."

"No kidding." Coach nods in agreement. "I'm glad you're on the road to recovery. It was sure nice of Drew's friend to take charge and get him home safely. If she hadn't done it, I would've driven him over myself. There's no way I'd let him travel all this way alone."

"Abby sure is something," Kathy agrees. "She'll always have a special place in my heart."

"Well..." Coach looks around at the three of us, "I have yet to meet her in person, but when I do, I'll pass along my gratitude."

Mom looks pointedly at me, as a smile forms on her face. "I hope Drew plans to bring her around soon."

"Mom..." I start to protest. This isn't the time nor the place to talk about my personal life. I look around the crowd, realizing no one heard. "I'm sure Abby has more important things to do than hang around with us."

Mom shakes her head, and her eyes roll. "Drew, I love you, honey. But you're clueless when it comes to girls."

This causes laughter to erupt from everyone, including Coach. Great. Now he thinks I'm an idiot off the court.

Not liking to be the butt end of a joke, I scowl at my mom. But she just pats me on the arm and dismisses it. "You may think you're '*just friends...*'" Yes. She friggin' uses air quotes in front of my coach and the whole world to see. "But trust me, I doubt you'll just stay that way for long. I've seen the way you look at her. It's the same look your dad gave me when we met."

"Now I can't wait to meet Abby." Coach grins widely at me, then notices something off in the distance. "Look, I have an interview. I'll catch up with you later." He looks to my parents. "I'm really glad you're on the mend."

"Us, too." Dad smiles, and I get the false sense of being let off the hook from my family.

I should've known better.

Dad turns to me and claps me on the shoulder. "Your

mom's right, Drew. Life is precious, so choose who you spend it with wisely." Then he chuckles. "Hell... I was ass over end in love with your mom before I even knew what hit me." He looks lovingly to her, then continues. "Your mom was a little quicker on the uptake, so I'd take her advice."

Wow. Just wow.

What the hell do I say after that?

"Drew, honey..." She waits until she has my attention. "You're gonna catch flies with your mouth hanging open like that. Give us some love and get back with your team. Call to let us know you're home safe." She steps up and wraps her arm tight around me for another hug. Then she whispers in my ear, "I love you so much. You do what's right for you. Don't forget to tell Abby hello for us."

I nod in agreement then say goodbye to the rest of my family.

Our conversation runs on a loop through my mind my entire ride home. Sure, I manage to get some work done. But one thing is certain—I need to see Abby.

AS SOON AS I get back to my apartment, I take a quick shower to wash the day of travel off. I rush through getting dressed in a button down and a pair of jeans. Then I pull out my phone, hoping she's around.

Me: Just got back, are you busy?

I wait anxiously for a reply. I know I'm being presumptuous, I really want to see her tonight. Though I was never prepared for her text.

Abby: Hey, sexy, I can't stop thinking about you. I'm out at Jack's getting my groove on.

Sexy?
Is Abby drunk?
This is so unlike her, but a part of me hopes this isn't a joke. I quickly rush out another text.

Me: Have you been drinking?

Abby: Maybe? You'll have to come join me if you wanna know for sure.

Yeah. This might not be Abby on the other end. But there's no fucking way I'm passing up the opportunity to see her. I just hope she's not so drunk she regrets this text in the morning.

Within seconds, I grab the keys and slip on my shoes. DeShawn stops me at the door. "Dude, what's the rush?"

I smile and shrug. "Gotta meet up with Abby!"

DeShawn groans. "You're studying on Saturday night?"

I'm sure my grin is wolfish as I quickly reply, "Not if I can help it."

Without waiting for a reply, I bolt out the door and head to my SUV. Maybe I'm reading this wrong, but I sure as hell hope

I'm not. Abby clearly invited me, and drunk or not, I'm going to be there for her.

It doesn't take long to drive across town to Jack's. I snag one of the last spots in the lot and rush to get inside. The place is packed, and it takes me a few minutes to find Abby. She's with Chloe and Sydney out on the dance floor. Her body moves freely to the beat of the music. Her long hair flows down her back as her arms flow above her head as if she doesn't have a care in the world. With her back to me, I take a few moments and watch.

Damn. She's beautiful.

When I notice a guy dancing with Sydney, instinctively my body closes the distance between us. I may enjoy the view, but there's no way I'm going to sit back and watch another man ask Abby to dance.

Now standing behind her, I reach out to grab her hip, as I bend down to whisper, "Mind if I dance with you?" To let her know it's me.

I feel her body tremble then melt into mine. Her back presses against me. Of course, this also brings my dick straight to attention. I adjust Abby so she won't feel the effect she has on me, and I let my body flow with hers to the music. I get lost in the rhythm as I feel Abby's voluptuous curves move with me. Damn. She's sexy as hell as she dips and sways.

When a slow song starts, I spin her around to face me. Sure, I'm able to tell what she's feeling by the way her body moves, but I'm dying to see her facial expression to see if they match what I'm conjuring in my mind.

When she turns around, her eyes roam over my body.

When her beautiful brown eyes meet mine, they widen in appreciation as the sexiest smile forms. "Hi," she says, breathless, and my heart stutters.

"Hi yourself, Angel," I say deep and huskier than I anticipate. I take her hand in mine, leading her around the dance floor effortlessly.

Having an excuse to hold her, I pull her body close to mine. My blood races, and my heart soars, as I see my feelings mirrored in her face. I could get drunk on her expression alone without having to touch a drop of alcohol. Abby's something special, and I hope before the night is through, I'll be able to tell her just exactly what I'm thinking.

When the song comes to an end, Abby asks, "Mind if we get another drink? I'm dying of thirst."

"Sure." I take her hand in mine as I lead her off the dance floor. We spot Chloe taking a break at a table and decide to join her.

"What can I get you ladies to drink?" I offer to the two of them once Abby settles at the table.

Abby's wide eyes as she looks to Chloe remind me she's inexperienced with ordering at the bar. Just when I'm about to suggest something, Chloe shouts out above the music, "Anything with Kahlua." They both break out into giggles.

Have I missed some inside joke?

"Okay," I draw out. "I'll be right back." They each reach into their pockets and offer some cash, but I shake my head, and turn to head to the bar, contemplating what exactly to get them. Shit. There's a ton of drinks with that in it. What would they like? Hopefully, the bartender can help because as someone who sticks to soda or beer, I'm clearly out of my element.

I must wait in line before the bartender asks for my order. "What would you recommend with Kahlua?"

"Do you want shots or mixed drinks?"

I look to the table where the girls are before giving my answer. Shots go down fast and if they're thirsty, they might want something that will last. "Let's stick with mixed drinks."

"Mudslide?" the bartender suggests.

Hell. I have no idea what's in it, but I've heard girls love them. "Sure. Sounds great. Give me two and a glass of water, while you're at it."

"Coming right up." The guy behind the bar turns and gets to work on my order. While I wait, my eyes naturally wander to Abby. Her discussion with Chloe appears quite serious, and I'd love to know what they're talking about. When Abby glances nervously to me, it doesn't take a rocket scientist to guess I have something to do with it.

After paying for the drinks, I make my way back to the table to join the girls. When they go quiet as I approach, I can't help but feel self-conscious.

"The bartender suggested mudslides, is that okay?" I offer to break the uncomfortable silence.

"This is great. Thank you." Abby reaches out to take her drink from my hand, while Chloe does the same.

"Thank you so much, Drew. Are you sure we can't repay you?" Abby pulls her lip into her teeth as she fiddles with her straw.

"Nope. This one's on me," I offer, then address the

elephant in the room. "So, did I interrupt something?" I look from Abby to Chloe to see which one will break first.

They each look anywhere but at me. Eventually, Abby breaks the silence. "I'm just trying to get my phone back from Chloe. I'm not sure what she texted you, but I'm sorry if you feel you're here under false pretenses."

Well, that explains the texts.

Wait... does that mean Abby doesn't want me here? I look to her and remember our interactions—and I quickly have my answer.

No. I don't think so. The way her body responded to mine on the dance floor alone tells me she is happy I arrived.

I turn to Chloe and go with the truth. "Thanks for the invite, Chloe. I'm having a great time."

Then I reach for Abby's hand that lays on the table and give it a squeeze to let her know in no uncertain terms, I mean every word I just said. "It's nice to see Abby let her hair down and enjoy herself. I'm glad I crashed your party."

"You didn't crash anything," Chloe assures me, then turns to Abby with a knowing grin. "I'm glad I could help."

Chloe takes a long sip of her drink, then reaches into her shirt. Somehow, she had an entire phone stuffed in there. She quickly hands it to Abby.

"Remember, I was doing you a favor. You can thank me later." After that, she takes another long pull on her drink, nearly finishing it. She hops out of her chair and points to the dance floor. "If you need me, I'll be out there. I need to see a man about a dance."

Both Abby and I watch Chloe strut onto the dance floor

and dance with a guy who's eager to welcome her into his arms. I'm not sure if they know one another, but then again—you don't need words to enjoy the music.

When Abby starts to unlock her phone, I reach out and place a hand over it, and she looks at me expectantly. I shake my head and once again, go for the truth. "It doesn't matter what she said. I'm here. Let's just enjoy our time together. Can we do that—just for tonight?"

19

ABBY

WHEN DREW REACHES for my hand, I could care less what Chloe said to get him here. The point is this sexy man is sitting across the table from me and more importantly, wants to spend time with me—Abby Angelos. And I'm certain it has nothing to do with being friends at this moment.

"Yeah, I think I can do that." I grin as shivers run up my spine from the pulsing currents between us.

For the next few minutes, we sit in silence and watch the crowd as he sips his water, and I enjoy my mudslide. This drink is stronger than the others I've had tonight, and I'm not sure if I'm reacting to the fact that Drew's holding my hand, or the effects of the alcohol. But either way—I hope this feeling doesn't end.

When I'm close to finishing my drink, Drew suggests returning to the dance floor. Any excuse to feel his muscular body against mine is an emphatic—YES—in my book. There must be a God, because when we get to the center of the dance floor next to Chloe and Sydney, the song changes to a slow one, and he pulls me into him.

As I wrap my arms around his neck, I can't help but inhale slowly. His sensual masculine scent seriously makes my mouth water. I feel like I'm drifting on a cloud, as I lay my head against what feels like a perfectly sculpted chest. One hand drifts to his chest, as if it has a mind of its own. It instinctually outlines the defined muscles hidden under his dark-blue button down. Damn. This man has muscles on top of muscles hidden under here. I can only imagine what he looks like without any clothes on.

Fuck. The thought alone has my temperature rising. If we weren't in public, I might be bold enough to make an actual move. Right here in this moment, I don't care that we're supposed to be *just* friends. I don't care that neither of us know where we'll be living in a year from now. Right now, the only thing that matters is being here in his arms.

I'm not sure how long we dance. It could be minutes or hours. Being wrapped in Drew's arms feels like heaven. When the song changes from slow to fast, he keeps me close and moves to the beat of the music with me. The man knows just how to spin, dip, and sway to the music, so that I'm unable to think about anything but enjoying him.

It's the most freeing feeling to turn off your mind and just react. All I focus on is the pulsing of the beats and the flow of the currents between us as he guides me around the floor.

I'm brought to reality when Sydney interrupts my blissful cocoon. "Hey, Chloe and I are about to take off. I have an Uber on the way. Do you want a ride?" She looks between

Drew and me, then back at him. "Or can you get her home safely?"

I look to Drew before I respond, and the smile that forms on his perfect lips makes my heart skip a beat. I'm not ready to leave yet, but I don't want to put him out.

As if Drew can read my mind, he jumps in before I have a chance to respond. "I've been drinking water all night. I'll get her home, Syd." Then he turns to me. "Are you okay with that?"

I grin widely and wrap my arms around his neck once again. "I'm more than okay with that." I glance to Sydney. "Text me to let me know you've made it home. I'll see you later."

"Okay, Mom," she teases. "Don't do anything I wouldn't do." And with that, she leans in and whispers, "I want details tomorrow," causing me to laugh.

She leaves just as another slow song comes on. Drew steps closer and wraps his arms around me. I know, without a doubt, there's no place I'd rather be.

Eventually, all good things must come to an end. When the DJ calls for the last song, Drew and I take it as our cue to leave. We're still in our blissful bubble as we walk hand in hand to his car. He opens the door for me like a gentleman and gets me settled. I can't help but check out his fine ass when he walks around the car. Damn, the man can fill out a pair of jeans. At one point, he glances into the car and catches me. His only response is a perfect smirk, which makes my heart rate spike.

Being the gracious guy Drew is, when he enters the car, he

simply reaches for my hand and starts the engine. As I relax into his cool leather seats, I stare out the window, recalling my favorite moments of the evening. I still haven't pulled out my phone to see what it is that Chloe said to get him here, but when I look at the gorgeous man beside me, I must ask myself, *do I really care?*

When we get to my apartment, Drew parks and walks me up to the door. Instead of being the confident man he's been all night, I notice a bit of nerves setting in as he rocks back and forth on his heels and fiddles with the keys in his hands.

His voice comes out rough and low when he finally speaks. "I had a great time tonight. Are you still up for bowling tomorrow?"

"Yeah, I am," I say barely above a whisper as my eyes lock with his. My heart skips a beat, and I feel the need to moisten my suddenly dry lips.

His perfect lips quirk, and a hint of his delicious dimple shows. "That's great." Almost as if he doesn't know what to do with his hands, he suddenly shoves them both into his pockets.

We stare at each other for a countless moment, and I wonder if he's finally going to kiss me.

One hand is released from the confines of his pocket as he reaches out to place a strand of wayward hair behind my ear. His touch alone makes my skin burn with desire.

"Well... I guess I'll see you then," he barely whispers.

He steps in and pulls me into an embrace.

Okay, here it is.

Butterflies soar in my stomach, my breathing quickens, and

my heart races as Drew tilts his head to the side and studies me intently.

Damn, his blue eyes smolder, and I lean closer instinctually.

Instead of kissing me, he pulls me in for a hug.

My heart sputters, and the contents of my stomach morph into concrete, as our perfect moment is destroyed.

Don't get me wrong, being in Drew's arms is wonderful. But my entire body anticipated the kiss of a lifetime, and disappointment fills me faster than I could have imagined.

"I had an amazing time tonight," Drew says while he still holds me tight. "I can't wait to see you tomorrow."

With that, he releases me and steps back.

Words don't form, as I stare at him in disbelief.

This is how he's going to end our perfect night?

"Good night, Abby."

And he turns and walks down the steps, putting some distance between us.

Somehow, I manage to get my brain firing on all cylinders again. "Night. Drew." And before I can do or say anything stupid, I dig my key out of my pocket and walk into my apartment and close the door.

Without a word to my roommates, I walk straight to my bedroom and close the door. I flop myself down on my bed—face first—and scream into the pillow.

What the hell is wrong with me?

20

DREW

I MUST BE the stupidest dumb fuck on the planet. Abby and I were having the perfect night. And I fucking blew it by ending it—with a hug—for Christ's sake. I wanted to kiss her until the sun came up. Hell, after having her sexy as hell body rub against me all night, I wanted to fuck her right there for the world so see.

But I'm not an exhibitionist... And she'd been drinking.

And from what I could tell, she'd kept a decent buzz going. I wasn't about to take advantage of her. But, God, do I wish she'd been sober.

Those doe eyes she gave me as she stared expectantly at her doorstep? They'll be forever etched in my brain as a constant reminder of what a dumb fuck I am.

Why the fuck didn't I just kiss her?

She'd been sending me the signals all night.

Hell, it's not like a kiss must lead to sex.

I need to rectify this.

Unable to sleep, I get up early and punish myself some more by enduring a grueling workout. Knowing I can't show up at her place until a decent time, I push things to the limit, and every muscle in my body knows just how much I fucking hate what I didn't do to Abby last night. Then I rush home to shower and shave.

Now as I drum on the steering wheel of my SUV, I'm second-guessing my need to rush to Abby's. Shit. It's only eight twenty-one—there's no way I can knock on her door at an ungodly hour after she's been up late drinking.

Nine o'clock is a respectable time.

I'll wait until then.

Yeah—that's so much easier said than done. I pull out my phone, but it holds no interest. I'd text my parents, but I'm not in the mood to explain why I suddenly feel so freaking nervous. I don't share much with my parents, but texting early on a Sunday morning will bring on more questions than necessary.

Thinking back on last night, I seriously let the perfect moment slip away. Of course, I had good intentions. But let's face it—doing the right thing left me with a bad case of blue balls—not that I would've let it go that far. Holding her tight little body against mine on the dance floor felt incredible. Our bodies were in perfect sync as we moved. I can only imagine what would happen if we were together behind closed doors.

I glance to the clock. Only freaking twelve minutes have passed. How the hell is this possible? Is time slowing down?

Fuck, this is torture!

I take a deep breath to calm my nerves as I run my hands down my jeans. The minute I'm calm, my mind goes back to Abby. There's no way this is a one-way street. She's been sending distinct vibes in my direction.

Abby's not one to mince words or string someone along. Neither am I, for that matter. It's time to fish or cut bait as my grandfather used to say. What's the worst that can happen?

She just wants to be friends.

Shit. That would suck.

But if I don't tell her how I feel, I'll never know.

My instincts have never led me wrong. I'm certain she feels something toward me.

I'm just not sure what.

I mentally prep myself for what I'll tell her, much in the same way I do before each game. I shake out my hands and release any built-up tension.

You have this, Jacobs. Just walk up to her and tell her how you feel.

The answer will always be no if I never ask.

When the clock finally reads nine, I let myself get out of the car I've been parked in for the last thirty minutes and practically run up Abby's stairs. I quickly knock on the door with three solid raps.

I hear movement from the other side, and I impatiently wait for the door to answer. Hell, I don't even know what I'm going to say, but I know with every fiber of my being, I need to see her.

When the door cracks open, I'm relieved as fuck to find Abby on the other side. She's fresh out of the shower with her long hair dripping wet. Her face is free of any makeup, and she's wearing an oversized sweatshirt and yoga pants. Even with her shocked expression, she's beyond beautiful.

Disbelief registers on her face, as I step toward her and practically growl, "Abby, you look gorgeous."

My hand instinctively reaches out to settle at the base of her neck, and the pad of my thumb traces the bottom lip she's trying to tuck under her teeth. I want to free that lip with my teeth, but I refrain and say what I came here for. "I told myself I couldn't do this last night while you were drinking, but now, I don't have to stop myself."

Without wasting another second, my hand envelops her waist, and her head naturally tilts. Her minty breath saturates my senses, and I close the gap between us.

Our lips touch, flames ignite, and I draw her closer to me. Our difference in height has me lifting her as she wraps her legs around my waist. Sweeping my tongue across her lips, she opens for me, and her taste is nothing I've ever experienced.

She. Is. Everything.

Everything I've ever hoped for.

Everything I've dreamed of, and everything I never knew I wanted.

I can't control my sudden rush of emotions. I'm sure I've fallen for the woman in my arms. That realization alone makes me completely lose myself in her and get consumed with our kiss.

Eventually, a car door slams in the distance, and I'm brought back to reality. I slow our kiss and when I completely regain control of myself, I place her back on her feet. We hold each other as our breaths even out.

When she pulls back, Abby rocks my world even further when she smirks and says, "Took you long enough," causing us both to burst out in laughter.

Damn. Is there anything I don't like about her?

"I've been dying to do that for so long," I hungrily admit as I reach out to brush her hair from her face, so I can fully read her expressions. Her beautiful brown eyes are the color of honey in this light.

"You and me both, mister," she teases, then she reaches for my hand. "Wanna come inside or are we going to continue giving the neighbors a show?"

Shaking my head, I follow her inside. I may have gotten lost in the moment, but I'm not an exhibitionist. "Have you eaten breakfast?" I ask when I hear movement from down the hall.

"No. I just got out of the shower. Do you want anything?"

Knowing if I stay here in this apartment much longer, the only thing I'm going to want for breakfast—is her, I suggest, "Wanna go to the diner?"

Abby looks to the kitchen, then back at me. "Uh. Sure. Give me a second, and I'll just grab my purse."

Before she can step away, I grab her by the waist and pull her close. Now that I've had a taste, I'm a greedy bastard and want more. I press my lips to hers and what starts out as a light and feathery kiss, quickly turns to an inferno. I could kiss Abby for days. Her hands wrap around my neck, and her fingers run through my hair. She feels amazing. Eventually, the clearing of a throat registers in the background, and I force myself to pull away.

Sydney cringes in our direction as we make eye contact with her. "Sorry." She scratches the back of her head and looks extremely uncomfortable. "I... uh... was already in the hallway when you started, and since I'm not into voyeurism... And I need to get to my study group, I'd rather let you know I was here. Besides, you're blocking my only exit, unless I want to crawl out my bedroom window."

Abby shakes her head and chuckles. "Well, that'd be difficult, since we're on the second floor." She reaches for my hand and pulls me into the kitchen with her, so Sydney can pass by. "Drew and I were just on our way to the diner for some breakfast, have time to join us?"

Sydney's cheeks darken. "Uh, I'm not sure you'd even notice I was there. I'll just take a raincheck. Besides..." She looks pointedly between the two of us. "I think you might have some unfinished business."

When I glance to Abby, I almost groan. She's chewing on that damn lip again. But I force my attention to stay on Sydney. "You're more than welcome. I'm sure we can manage to behave if you'd like to join us." This causes Abby's face to blush for the first time since I arrived.

"Yeah," she agrees. "Please come."

Sydney grumbles something under her breath I don't quite catch, but I could swear it was, "I don't think I'll be the only one coming..." Then she clears her throat and continues, "Thanks for the offer, but I've gotta pass." With that, she grabs her backpack next to the couch and says, "I'll see you later."

Nabbing her keys from the hook on the wall, Sydney exits the apartment like a bat out of hell.

Sydney doesn't seem like the type who gets shocked easily, so I ask, "Did we make her uncomfortable?"

Abby rolls her eyes. "Please... I'm sure she's seen a lot worse by working at the bar. Let me get my things, and we'll grab some food. I'm starving."

As Abby and I settle into a corner booth at my favorite diner, I reach out and hold her hand in mine across the table. I won't bother denying it took us longer to leave her apartment because I can't keep my hands, or lips for that matter, off her. I'm not sure what's come over me, maybe I'm just trying to make up for lost time, but now that she'll let me kiss her, I don't want to stop.

Vanessa, my usual waitress, leaves menus for us to peruse. After my strenuous workout this morning, I feel like I could eat half the menu and still be hungry. I settle on a large stack of pancakes, eggs, and sausage links, while Abby orders French toast and bacon.

When Vanessa leaves, it hits me that I might've hijacked Abby's day. I force myself to ask, "Did you have anything other than bowling planned for today?"

She looks to the sky as if she's contemplating. Crap. Maybe I did overstep things. But when she says, "Other than laundry, no," my heart soars.

"So..." I drag out. "You won't mind me hanging around?"

When she reaches out and pats me on the forearm playfully, my heart skips a beat. "No. I rather like your plans so far."

While we wait for our food, I find myself fascinated with every nuance about Abby. The way her hair curls at the ends when it's wet. The way she bites on her lower lip when she's thinking, and the way she glances at me when she thinks I'm not looking, sends my body into hyperdrive. Add the fact that I can finally touch her, and I think I might be in heaven.

I don't know what kind of spell she's put on me, but my need to touch her every chance I get is all-consuming. Whether it's to brush a wayward lock of hair from her face, to reach for her fingers from across the booth, or to press my long legs against hers under the table. I don't think a minute goes by where I'm not touching her in one form or another.

My pulse races, and my pride soars now that I finally know she likes me, too. Her smile's infectious as her cheeks occasionally turn a beautiful shade of pink when I take her by surprise by reaching out to touch her or hold her gaze.

Once the food arrives, there's little room for conversation. We're both ravenous and devour what's on our plates. Note to self—drinking makes Abby hungry.

When she's nearly finished half her plate, she finally makes eye contact. She suddenly bites on her lower lip, and I stop eating to see what's the matter.

"Everything okay?" I ask as soon as my mouth is empty.

"I'm just... well... I didn't realize I was that hungry," she whispers.

I chuckle and try to make light of it. "Well... drinking has a tendency to do that to you."

"I didn't drink that much," she protests.

Shaking my head, I clarify, "I was joking—albeit a bad joke. Sorry, Angel, I wasn't implying anything."

Her eyes soften, and a smile forms as she reaches out to take my hand across the table. She squeezes my hand as she says, "I didn't take it that way. I'm not one to party. You've actually been with me *both* times I've been out."

Just remembering her birthday makes my body come alive. It's the day Abby became *my Angel*. If I hadn't bulldozed my way into taking her to dinner, I wouldn't be here right now in this moment. "It's not like I go out often either, Angel. Though I'd like to be a part of your future... If you'll let me."

Abby lowers her chin and pushes a strand of hair behind her ear. She takes in a deep breath, and I hear her slowly release it. I carefully watch her as she gives her sole attention to the tabletop. It's almost as if she's trying to process my meaning.

Didn't I make my feelings clear?

I replay my words in my mind, to ensure I didn't come off as a pretentious ass.

Shit. Did I misread her and make the wrong assumptions?

Relief washes over me when she peers out from under her dark lashes, and her golden-brown eyes pin me in place. A slight smile forms on her beautiful pink lips, and my breath catches in my chest. "I think that can be arranged."

Thank fuck.

"Good," I say before I can stop myself or use a filter. "I have a lot more plans in mind for you."

Her perfectly manicured brow lifts in disbelief. "And just what type of plans to you have in mind, Drew?"

Not wanting to get ahead of myself, I simply smirk and playfully tease, "Some things are better left unsaid. I wouldn't want to give my entire game away."

This earns me an eye roll and a smirk. She's fucking adorable. "So... this is just a game to you... I see."

I shake my head emphatically, making sure she completely understands. "No. It's not a game at all."

21

ABBY

WHEN DREW REACHES out and squeezes my hand once more, he draws my attention back to him. The look in his dark-blue eyes tells me he isn't playing a game. The zing of electricity that travels from the base of my neck to the tips of my toes makes me want to at least see where this goes.

To sound unaffected by the beautiful man before me, I flippantly state, "Good. I'm not into games either." Then I add a bit more of a truth, "Besides, I don't play games I can't win."

This makes Drew's perfect lips twitch, and my pulse race. "Oh, Angel. You have no idea."

Before either of us can say anything further, Vanessa interrupts us, "Is there anything else I can get the two of you?"

Drew looks to me, and I shake my head. My eyes were way bigger than my stomach, and there's no way I can eat another bite. But instead of answering for myself, he simply states, "No. I think we're good here. Thanks."

Vanessa gives each of us a friendly smile. "Great. I'll be right back with your check."

"Why don't we hit the bowling alley early? It should be open any time," Drew suggests when she leaves. "I have to tell you, Angel, I don't think I've bowled since I was a kid." His expression turns doubtful, and I almost laugh aloud.

Holy hell, is Drew nervous? No. I must be mistaken. I cock my head to the side to study his features. "Is this your way of telling me you suck at something?" I tease. The man seems to do everything with ease. Surely, he can throw a ball down the lane and knock a few pins down.

"Just keeping it real." He rolls his eyes as a low chuckle escapes. "I'm sure it'll be entertaining, to say the least," he says with a shrug.

This will be good. I highly doubt the most competitive guy on the planet doesn't know how to bowl. "Don't worry, if it gets too bad, we can put bumpers on the lanes," I offer as a joke—but also as a way out. I haven't bowled in ages, either.

DREW MAY BE A D-1 BALLER, but he most definitely isn't a bowler. If there is an A for effort, the man would be raking in the points, but knocking pins down? Nope. He's not doing well.

"I swear there must be glue on the bottom of the pins," he grumbles when he bowls yet another split and only knocks down four pins. We're only in the middle of our fourth frame, but already I can tell bowling's not his sport.

I'd like to offer him advice, but I'm not doing much better. I get lucky and hit a strike in the first frame and pick up a spare nearly every frame since, so my score is considerably higher, but I can't say I have actual skill. The poor guy is averaging six to eight pins a frame. A couple of times, he throws a wicked curve ball, but it only ended up in the gutter.

At least he's a good sport and celebrates with me when I do well. When I get another strike, he stands and wraps me in a hug. "Congratulations, Angel," he whispers in my ear, and my body tingles with desire as he sets me on my feet.

"If you're gonna celebrate like that, you're only encouraging me to do it again," I tease.

Drew's blue eyes darken as a smile spreads across his face, making my belly flop. Damn, he's sexy. "Maybe your talents will rub off on me, and you can be my good-luck charm."

Once the pins reset themselves, Drew walks to the ball return and picks up his ball. He shifts his weight from foot to foot, and I can't help but check out his ass. His jeans are sexy. It's almost as if they were tailor made to fit him. They stretch over his muscles perfectly. Maybe he should model for that brand. Women everywhere would be purchasing that brand in hopes their spouses would look that good. My mouth goes dry, just watching his every move.

I'm so focused on his perfect form, I barely notice Drew finally rolls a strike. The moment all the pins go down, Drew spins around like a kid who's just been told he's going to Disneyland and pumps a fist in the air. "Yes!" His smile is infectious, and my heart soars with excitement for him.

In three fluid steps, he's standing in front of me. His long arms wrap me into a hug and lifts me as he spins me around. "It's about damn time." He chuckles in my ear. "Maybe you *are* my good luck charm."

When he sets me down, I shake my head as I roll my eyes. *Me? A good-luck charm? Yeah, right.*

"Uh... I highly doubt that. If I were, you would've been doing that all day. Don't you know, you make your own luck, silly," I tease.

But the way he stares into my eyes makes me wonder if he believes in good-luck charms. I mean... I've heard of athletes being superstitious. But I had nothing to do with him rolling that strike.

Drew looks like he's about to say something but decides against it. He shakes his head slowly, then pats me on the ass, like you would a teammate. "You're up, Angel." I have no clue how to take that, so I do the only thing I can.

I roll another strike.

By the time we leave the bowling alley after a few more games, Drew's convinced I bowl more frequently than I let on. I try to tell him otherwise, but he won't have it. I didn't even beat my personal record. But if we're looking at the numbers... my score practically doubles his at one-forty.

At least Drew's a graceful loser. He celebrates my success as well as his. Sure... he teases me, but he doesn't make it into an issue. Overall, I'd say we had a great first date.

As we get into his SUV, Drew turns to me and asks, "So, what's next on our list?"

"Uh..." I'm totally unprepared for what to say. I'd been having such a good time, I hadn't thought about what we can do for the next item on the list. "Well..." I drive out. "Since I picked this one, it's only fair you get the next."

This earns me a devilish grin. His perfect lips perk up, making me want to kiss the cocky expression right off his face. *Oh, who am I kidding? Now that I've had a taste of him, I can't wait to kiss him again.*

Drew places a finger on his chin, and his eyebrows pull together. His expression morphs from cocky to concentration in an instant, and I can't help wondering what he's thinking about so heavily.

Finally, he breaks the silence. "What do you think about geocaching? I used to love going all the time when I was younger, but I don't think I've gone since Summer was re-diagnosed. It was something we used to do together when I babysat her."

"Are you sure?" I don't want to do anything to cause him pain.

He nods enthusiastically. "Yeah, I'm sure. She'd kick my ass if she knew I'd stopped going because it reminds me of her. I don't think that's the reason I stopped; I haven't had the chance since I started college. What do you say to doing that, then it's your turn to choose?"

"Won't you be tired of me by then?" I tease. Because seriously, he's talking about a couple more dates, and this is only date one.

Drew stares at me in disbelief, his jaw slack. "Not gonna happen, Angel."

When we get back to my place, Drew parks the car and walks me to my door. This time thankfully, there's no awkwardness between us. It's natural when I offer, "Wanna come in?"

He surprises me with his brutal honesty. "I don't want to hijack your day, but I'm not ready to leave either." Then he rocks back on his feet as he awaits my response.

Wanting to put him out of his misery as fast as possible, I suggest, "Let's go inside, and I'll start a load of laundry. I'm caught up with studying for the week. Maybe we can watch a movie?"

Drew's instant smile causes my heart to skip a beat. *Seriously, how does anyone get anything done around this man?* His dimple pops, and I know in this instance, I'd do practically anything to keep him looking at me in this way. "Only if you let me pick," he teases.

Yep. He can watch whatever the heck he wants, with a smile like that. "I think I can manage letting you choose. But be warned, I'm picking the next one."

"Sounds like a plan." Drew nods in agreement as he walks inside.

22

DREW

AFTER FINDING we have the apartment to ourselves, Abby suggests watching the movie in the living room. While she attends to her laundry, I scroll through the options to watch. Not having time to watch anything current, I pick the first thing that looks interesting—the latest Avengers movie.

Abby's eyes light up when she sees my selection. "Oooh... I haven't seen this yet." I stretch out my arm to suggest she sit next to me. My heart soars when she doesn't hesitate. Pulling her close, my arm wraps around her with ease. Instinctually, I kiss the top of her head and let out a deep sigh as her body relaxes into mine. Normally, I'm not what you'd say a touchy-feely type, but with Abby, I can't stop myself. *The girl must have some sort of spell on me.*

The smell of her shampoo's intoxicating. I take in a deep breath and savor the scent as Abby snuggles closer and rests her head against my chest. Before the opening credits roll, my body zings to life, and I suddenly have the urge to do a hell of a lot more than just hold her. Since this is only our first date, I manage to contain my urges—just barely.

My concentration's shit. About twenty minutes into the movie, I realize I don't have a fucking clue as to what it's about. But I can tell you Abby has natural highlights in her hair, there are six freckles on her arm, her breathing is slow and even, and she smiles when either of the Chrises make an appearance on screen. I'd almost be jealous, but when she glances in my direction, I see more heat directed at me than at them—so I let it slide.

When something funny happens on the screen, and I don't laugh, Abby turns to me and catches me studying her. Her cheeks darken as she asks, "Are you not interested in the movie?"

"The movie's fine," I reply in a deeper tone than normal. I clear my throat as I brush a lock of hair from her face. My thumb lingers on the corner of her lip when it makes contact. Suddenly, I have the urge to taste her again.

"We can watch something else," she suggests as her eyes carefully flit back and forth to watch mine.

Even though I have no idea what the plot is, I offer, "No. This is fine." She could put on my favorite movie in the world, and I'd still rather watch her instead. Her lips purse, and I lean in to kiss the confusion off her face.

To my surprise, her hand instantly cups the back of my neck and pulls me closer to deepen the kiss. She feels amazing. Her tongue darts out to meet mine, and I know I need more. But sitting like this, I can't get close enough to kiss her the way she deserves. I guide her to change positions so that she's straddling my lap. Somehow, we manage without breaking our all-consuming kiss. Knowing she wants this just as much, my dick strains against my jeans when she places her knees outside my thighs to get better leverage.

Damn. The woman can kiss.

I love how her heat radiates through the fabric of her clothes, and her body perfectly aligns with mine. When Abby lets out a quiet moan, my senses go into overdrive.

Now that she's right where I want her, I allow my free hand to roam the hem of her shirt. The feel of her smooth skin, the taste of her soft lips, and the smell of her intoxicating body isn't enough. I need more. I run my hand along her spine under her shirt. Her body hums with desire to match mine.

When I feel like I can no longer breathe because she's completely consumed me, I force myself to break our kiss. Not wanting to break contact with her skin, I kiss along her jawline to her neck. When her breath hitches as I reach a sensitive spot, I know she's just as turned on as me. Her hands run through my hair as her body shifts to find a release against my straining cock. She rubs herself along my ridge, as her fingers fist my hair.

"Angel," I groan as I reach her earlobe, and her movements become more intentional. My hand cups her perfect breast, and I roll her nipple through the fabric of her silky bra. Her body bucks on my lap, letting me know I should continue.

"Oh... Drew..." she moans as I push the fabric aside and kiss my way down her bare skin. When I pull her darkened nipple into my mouth and flick it with my tongue, she writhes almost out of control.

Could she come, just like this?

The thought alone has my dick turning to steel, and my mind wanders with possibilities. She's so responsive. With every nip, suck, and lick, her body comes more alive. Our bodies are so in tune with one another, I can't believe this is our first experience together.

Abby's hands roam down my chest and reach under the hem of my shirt. Her fingers feather their way across the muscles of my abdomen and instinctually, my abs tighten. Her light grazing sends shivers up my spine because—fuck—I'm ticklish. I let out a stifled groan, well, more like a cross between a laugh and a moan. Why, of all things, is my body betraying me at this moment? Hell, I've never been this ticklish before. As much as I enjoy her touching me, I can't let this continue.

Not wanting to ruin the mood, I reach out and lace my fingers through the offending hand. Abby doesn't seem to notice my intent because she only intensifies our kiss. Holy shit. I could get lost in this.

Abby's other hand locks me in place as she once again maneuvers her body along the ridge of my cock. Whether it is intentional or not doesn't matter. If she doesn't stop soon, I'll blow my entire load like a prepubescent teen—And that just can't happen.

"Angel," I practically pant as I shift her back just a fraction of an inch, in hopes of some relief. "You're killing me."

Abby raises a brow as a smirk forms. "In a good or bad way?"

The vixen.

I reposition her to let her form her own opinion.

"What do you think?" I reply, almost feral.

From the sly grin on her swollen lips, she rolls out, "I can't say that's a bad thing."

Before she can say anymore, I flip us so that she's lying on her back, and I hover over the top of her. "Angel, unless you plan on following through with that thought, I suggest you watch your words very carefully."

Her eyes gleam, and her smile widens. Holy shit, I think I've met my match with Abby Angelos. When her legs wrap around me, her intention is clear.

Not wanting to disappoint, I close the distance between us and continue kissing her senseless. Her body writhes and moans escape as she gets lost in us. I still feel as if my cock is made of steel, but in this new position, I manage to maintain control of myself.

Abby's hands pull at the hem of my shirt and the next thing I know, her warm fingers trace up my spine. I rest my entire body weight on one elbow as my other hand slides along Abby's rib cage. By the way she arches into me and the purr that escapes from her lips, I know I'm on the right track. Her skin feels smooth and soft against my fingertips. Trailing my lips along her jaw to her collarbone, Abby makes the sexiest moan imaginable. By the time I reach that soft spot behind her ear, she's practically clawing at me to take off my shirt.

I pull back to see for myself if that's what she really wants, and not just a figment of my imagination. Nope—The desire in Abby's eyes is undeniable.

"Need to feel your skin on mine," she practically begs as she nods in reassurance to my unanswered question.

As her hands snake up my back to remove my shirt, her front door flies open, banging against the wall. I nearly jump out of my skin as I clamber off Abby to put myself between her and the intruder.

As soon as my eyes land on Sydney's, she shouts, "Oh—Shit. Sorry. Had to pee. And couldn't get the door to release my key." She glances at the wall behind the door and sees a small dent from the handle. Maybe it was already there; she shrugs at Abby, then bolts to what I presume is the bathroom.

Abby bursts out laughing as Sydney shuts the door. "Doesn't she have impeccable timing."

That's for damn sure. I want to mutter as I adjust myself before turning to face Abby. But her infectious laugh has me changing my tune in a heartbeat. "Guess she really had to go..."

This causes us both to laugh harder.

Abby reaches out her hand to me and pulls me back to her side. "Thanks for being willing to take one for the team. I don't think I've ever seen anyone move so fast to protect me. I was almost afraid for who was coming through the door. You were in total beast mode."

"Glad I can be your entertainment, too," I deadpan, and this earns me a smack on the arm. It doesn't hurt, but the scowl on Abby's face is adorable.

"You know what I mean." Her eyebrows narrow in her attempt to sound stern.

"I'll always protect you," I tease, and she shakes her head. "Do you often have people breaking down your door to pee?"

Abby shakes her head. "I've gotta say, this was a first."

Sydney interrupts our conversation when she opens the door and steps out with a loud huff. When her eyes meet mine, she shakes her head as if to clear her thoughts. "I am sooo sorry. Today seems to be my day for cock blocking you, Abs. You just can't catch a break with me around."

Cock blocking? Seriously. She thinks we were about to have sex. *On the couch of all places?* I have way too much respect for Abby to even have considered that. A good make-out session—Yeah, I'll give her that. But I had no intentions of taking things much further. Not wanting her to get the wrong impression, I stop her in her tracks with, "Not that it's any of your business, but we weren't having sex, so there was no 'cock blocking' involved."

"Ohmigod." Abby covers her mouth to contain a giggle. "No—We were definitely *not* having sex. You know as well as I do, Syd, that I don't roll that way. I'm not an exhibitionist and have no desire to flaunt my bits in public."

I'll keep her *bits* for myself—thank you very much. There's no way I want her on display for the world to see—or even her roommates for that matter.

Whoa. When did I get so possessive?

Before I can give it another thought, Sydney draws my attention to her. "Gah... you are so adorable when you get embarrassed, Abs. You know I'm just teasing you. I'm happy you found a guy worthy of dating. Sorry if I made it sound like you were just his conquest. I've known from the start, it isn't like that with the two of you, and I shouldn't have opened my big fat mouth. Seriously, I was joking—you know—since I walked in on you this morning and just now. I felt bad for interrupting, and to be truthful, I was a bit scared when someone came charging at me as I entered the door. It was a knee-jerk reaction to make light of the situation."

"Please stop," Abby begs. "It's not a big deal. It's not like I have company over often—well, the kind that would have *you* of all people stammering."

What the hell does that mean?

Instead of getting an answer, Sydney turns to me. "I'm sorry if I came across rude. I was teasing Abby and didn't realize you might have taken it the wrong way."

To shrug it off and *completely* change the subject away from this slippery slope, I ask, "Would you like to watch the rest of our movie with us?"

Sydney looks between Abby and me a few times, then glances to the screen before she replies, "Are you sure?"

Abby scoots over, so that she's in the center of the couch, as she grabs my hand. "Absolutely. Who else am I going to enjoy Chris with? No offense, Drew, but I don't think you appreciate him as much as I do."

"Got it—It's a good thing I'm up for some competition." I grin as I hunker down to watch the movie.

Honestly, I don't care what I'm doing. As long as I get to do it next to Abby.

23

ABBY

AFTER SPENDING the day with Drew last Sunday, I've hardly seen hide nor hair of him. Not that I'll admit it to anyone, but I've missed him. Just thinking about his smile, the way he reaches out to hold my hand as if it's the most natural thing in the world, and his sexy masculine scent brings a smile to my face. I'm not sure how I've grown accustomed to him in my everyday life in such a short period of time, but somehow, he's managed to worm his way in, and I'm not sure what to make of it.

I can't fault him for being gone though. He's had away games and traveled most of the week. He wasn't even in class, though he managed to do what he could of our assignment from a hotel room—since our professor had given him the assignment early. We worked on it before class over the phone.

I'm sprawled out over the couch. Books and papers everywhere as I study for an upcoming exam the following Friday night. Suddenly, there's a knock on my front door. Knowing

Sydney's at work and Chloe is with her parents for the weekend, I holler, "Just a minute," as I scramble to my feet to answer the door.

I tug on my holey sweatshirt and adjust my sleep shorts as I hear another impatient knock.

"Hold your horses," I grumble as I open the door, preparing the words I'm about to unleash on my unexpected guest, to show them just what I think of their impatience.

Instead of unleashing my irritation, I'm blown away by the sight of Drew. Standing there in a dark gray henley, faded jeans, and a pair of Chucks, his blue eyes crinkle at the corners when a smile forms on his perfect lips. His hair is still wet from a shower, and it doesn't look like he's shaved in days. He looks almost edible.

He isn't supposed to be back until later tonight, so we'd made plans for tomorrow. I look down at my battered and worn-out sleep clothes and shyly glance in his direction. I quickly pat down the messy bun I'd thrown my hair into in my haste to make it stay out of my way while studying.

Drew rocks back on his heels as he looks me over from head to toe. I can only imagine what he's thinking. I look worse than a three a.m. shopper at Wally World. I'm not ready to impress anyone. My cheeks heat as I feel his stare glide over me.

"Um... am I interrupting?" he asks, unsure of himself.

"No." I shake my head and bat my hand in the air. "Not at all, come in."

"I couldn't wait to see you," he practically growls as he reaches out to wrap me in his arms. Tugging me closer, he slants his head and presses his lips to mine. The second our lips meet, a zing of electricity ignites, short circuiting my brain. The next thing I know, he lifts me with ease, and my legs dangle in the air as I kiss him for all I'm worth.

Eventually, he breaks our kiss and practically pants, "Damn, I've missed you."

As he steps inside and shuts the door behind us, he slowly releases me to my feet. "Uh—good to see you, too," I tease as I inhale his fresh out of the shower scent. Damn. He smells edible. I want to lick him from head to toe. My mouth waters as my mind fills with possibilities.

When I feel his eyes roaming my body, I give myself another once-over and immediately apologize for my state of disarray. "Sorry, I wasn't expecting anyone."

Drew's eyes turn mischievous as his smile widens. "If this is how you dress when I'm not around, I'll have to stop by more often. You're beautiful, Angel. Please," he almost begs, "don't ever change on my account."

Okay, then.

"When did you get back?"

"Around seven, then I dropped off Grey and showered before coming over. I know we didn't have plans until tomorrow, but I just couldn't wait to see you. It's been one hell of a week."

If only he knew. But as I cock my head to the side and examine Drew's face further, there's something beyond the surface I can't quite put my finger on. "Everything okay?"

"Yeah." Drew lets out a long, drawn-out sigh. "We managed to pull off both wins, but traveling has taken its toll on me. Don't get me wrong, I love basketball, but back-to-back games out of town and keeping up on my classes is no easy feat."

Taking Drew's hand in mine, I lead him to the couch, and he chuckles when he takes in the mountain of papers around where I had been working. "Obviously, I'm interrupting."

"Are you kidding? I've been at it all night, and I'm due for a break. My brain's nearly fried," I say as I hastily gather things into a pile. "Besides, now that you're here, I'm pretty sure I can find better things to do."

Drew's deep laughter sends butterflies flittering through my belly.

"Oh," he says through a chortle, "I might be able to help you with that." He reaches out to brush a piece of hair behind my ear.

When I get the couch cleared, Drew plops down. Before I can process what's happening, I'm pulled onto his lap. He swings my legs around like I'm a rag doll and nuzzles into my neck. "Mmmm..." he draws out. "You smell so good."

"Uh..." I roll my eyes and say, "At least I showered this morning. Or you might not be saying that." Before he can continue a conversation on my potential lack of hygiene, I quickly change the subject. "So, what do you have in mind this evening?" I gesture at my ensemble before adding, "As you can see, I'm living the dream."

Though, if it means being wrapped in Drew's arms, I'm all over that.

Drew's eyes dart away and focus on the floor. Is that... no, it couldn't be. Are Drew's cheeks turning red? This strong, confident man suddenly looks chagrin, and I can't for the life of me figure out why.

Focusing my attention on him, I reach out to brush my thumb across his cheek as I quietly ask, "What's wrong?"

"I... Uh... didn't plan on anything beyond seeing you. Now that I've hijacked your evening, got any ideas?"

My stomach takes that exact moment to gargle and growl furiously, and embarrassment floods through me. A distinct reminder I haven't eaten all afternoon. Crap, how did I lose track of time so easily?

Drew raises an eyebrow and smirks as he asks, "When was the last time you ate?"

Thinking back over my day, I cringe. "Lunch... probably?" It comes out as a question because I remember having a cinnamon roll sometime after breakfast, but I don't remember eating since.

"Angel, it's after eight. Want me to fix you something?"

Shit. I didn't shop for groceries today. There's not much other than breakfast food in the fridge at this point. But there should be plenty for both of us. "Would you be interested in pancakes or eggs for dinner?"

"I ate earlier, but I wouldn't turn down anything. I make a mean pancake, Angel. So be warned." Before I can right myself, Drew leans in and pecks me on the lips before standing to set me on the floor. "Let's get some food in you, and then we'll figure out what else to do."

I shouldn't be surprised when Drew and I work seamlessly together in the kitchen. He insists on making the batter from scratch, while I set in to frying some bacon and eggs. In no time at all, we have plates full of food and are sitting at my kitchen table.

"So," Drew says after he finishes a bite of bacon. "What would you say to a change of plans tomorrow? I'm caught up on all my homework, and if you are, too, I thought we might head out to the beach?"

My eyes widen in disbelief. It's been forever since I've gone to the beach. It's a few hours away, but since I don't have to be anywhere until Monday, I can't imagine why I shouldn't go. "I'm up for it. I got a lot done today and other than an exam I could study for, I'm free until Monday."

Drew's grin spreads wide, making his dimple pop. Damn, the man is sexy. "Good. Bring your homework. My aunt's cabin is in Long Beach. She usually rents it out, but it's free for the weekend. She suggested I take a break since I'm between games and have a rare free weekend."

A weekend away with Drew... Does this mean what I think it means? Or am I reading more into this than he intends? Shit.

Drew must read the shock on my face because he's suddenly back-peddling. "If you don't want to go, it's not a big deal. I'm just extending the invitation. If you'd rather do something else, I'm all game for that, too. There's no pressure, either way, Angel."

The thought of the beach alone has me begging to leave tonight. Giddiness rushes through me, and I practically bounce in my seat as I nod my head and say, "Yes."

Drew's adorable as he cocks his head to the side and raises

an eyebrow. "Yes to what exactly, Angel? You want to go away, or you want to stay here and hang out?"

Gah. I'm such a dork around him.

"Yes." I take a deep breath and try to reel in the million thoughts hurling around like a hurricane in my mind. I nod in reassurance, then fill him in on my thoughts. "As in I want to go away with you."

SINCE DREW and I are eager to get a jump on the day, we're on the road by eight the next morning. He showed up with a sexy smile, coffee, and pastries for the ride. He claims he's packed food for the weekend, and all I need to do is bring a bag of personal belongings and my schoolwork to enjoy the impromptu mini-vacation. I must admit, I'm impressed. I don't even know if I would have thought of the things he's packed for this road trip.

I'm eager as I carry my pillow and a bag of snacks out to the car. My schedule's been just as hectic as Drew's, and the thought of getting away from it all fills me with excitement. Like the gentleman Drew is, he insists on doing the heavy lifting and carries my bags to the car. I'm dying to get away. I haven't been to the beach in years.

Though as we get on the highway, my nerves kick in. I've been on road trips with my girlfriends, but I can't say I've been on an overnight trip with a guy before. Don't get me wrong—I'm not a virgin, but my schedule never lent itself to destination sleepovers, either.

Even though my type A tendencies fly in full force in every other aspect of my life, I've always been a go with the flow type of person when it comes to relationships. The few guys I dated were more out of convenience, rather than chemistry. My focus was on graduation and med school. I didn't have time to tie myself down. And let's face it—the desire for making things long-term wasn't there either. But with Drew... there are so many possibilities.

He's come a long way from the cocky jerk I judged him as that first day. He's somehow managed to worm his way into my heart, and I'm not so sure I want to let it go. I know I shouldn't get attached. Neither of us know where we'll be in mere months from now, but with him—I'm not sure I have a choice. There's no way I want whatever *this* is between us to end, but am I ready to take things further?

Yes, this is beyond physical for me. Just thinking of those lips and that dimple and the way he lights my world on fire with just a simple touch. The answer is quite simple.

Hell yes, I want to take things further. Even if it's only until we graduate. No one can guarantee the future, but I do know I'd be a fool to let this opportunity pass me by.

But how do I let him know I'm ready for more?

I let out a deep sigh as I ponder how to broach this subject.

"Everything okay over there?"

"Yeah," I respond dreamily. I could just tell him, but when I glance to look him in the eye, I completely chicken out. I'm more of a show, don't tell type of person and instead of making this car ride uncomfortable, I think I'll keep this tidbit of information to myself for a while. Besides, I'd rather let things happen naturally than to put awkward expectations out there.

We drive into Long Beach a little before noon. Even in winter, there are people roaming the streets going between shops. It's a clear day, and most are only wearing sweatshirts or light jackets. I'm not much of a shopper, but I wouldn't mind getting a small trinket to remember our trip together.

When I spot an inviting shop, I ask, "Can we go there sometime this weekend?"

"Sure." Drew grins. "Mind if we drop everything off and then come back to town? My aunt's place is just past town on the other side. It's within walking distance from the beach, but it'd be a hike to town."

"Sounds like a plan."

A few minutes later, we pull into a driveway where the most adorable house sits off to one side. The property's lined with trees, so there's no ocean view, but the air still smells like the beach, which is more than enough for me. The cabin, as Drew calls it, is bigger than I expect. It's a two-story modern house, with gray wooden shingles intricately lining the sides. There are flower beds lined with seashells, and a deck wraps around one side. I can't imagine the view at sunset from the floor-to-ceiling windows that face west. If I could live here full time, I'd do so in a heartbeat—and I haven't even made it inside.

Once we get everything inside, I confirm my original assessment. It is simply adorable. There are hard wooden floors, a big fireplace, and cozy leather couches in the living room. An open floor plan makes the kitchen easily accessible, with a large dining room table to separate it. There's a hallway off to one side and a wooden staircase adjacent to it. I can't believe just the two of us are staying here. It could easily house a large family.

Drew interrupts my thoughts. "Let me put the things in the fridge, then we'll head out. Want to head into town to walk around, then drive back up the beach? There's an approach about a half-mile from here."

"Sounds like a plan. Can we stop to walk along the beach? It's such a beautiful day and even though it's a little chilly, I can't come to the beach and not put my toes in the sand."

This earns me a laugh from Drew. "Sure. We can make that happen, Angel."

ANOTHER FUN FACT ABOUT DREW. He may make healthy choices regularly in his food selection, but homemade fudge is his Achilles heel—especially, peanut butter fudge. When we stop in a shop known for ice cream and fudge, Drew's eyes light up like the Fourth of July. After tasting two different kinds, he orders two bricks of plain peanut butter, while I choose peppermint.

As we're walking past another shop on our way to the car, I spot a sweatshirt I'd love to add to my collection. Hoodies are my favorite thing to lounge in, and this gem has my name written all over it. It's CRU's colors, but instead of our school logo, it has Long Beach written on it. This way if I go to another one of Drew's games, I won't have to borrow Sydney's all the time.

"Mind if we stop in here?" I point to the window. "Then we can head to the beach."

When we get inside, I make a bee-line to the display by the window. The fabric is softer than it looked in the window, and I quickly remove my jacket and pull my size from the hanger to try on. It feels like heaven. Soft, cuddly but not too bulky.

"Don't you have enough CRU colors?" Drew teases.

"No, actually. I typically borrow Syd's. I have a sweatshirt or two, but they're bulky, and I bought them when I was in my everything must be oversized phase, my freshman year."

Drew's face clouds with confusion.

So I clarify, "I went through this phase where I bought everything in extra-large. I loved going to football games and since I could layer my clothes under the sweatshirts, I always bought big. Now that I'm going to basketball games, they're too hot and bulky to wear."

"So... you had a thing for football players?" Drew draws out as he cocks an eyebrow in my direction.

Damn, he's cute when he's jealous.

Of everything I've said, that's what he picks up on?

"Uh, can't say I did. I've always thought jocks were a little too into themselves, and never understood why anyone would want to fawn all over them." Drew's eyes widen as my statement catches him off guard. But before he can say anything, I quickly point out one more thing. "I enjoy watching the game. Not necessarily the individual players."

I expect a quick response, but instead, I'm met with silence.

Fuck. Did I say the wrong thing?

Eventually, he puts me out of my misery when he pins me with his teasing eyes. "Maybe I'll have to loan you one of mine."

"Uh... Drew, your jerseys would be a dress on me. I'm not sure they would have the effect I'd be going for."

"Maybe you could wear one for just me?" He shrugs his shoulders and tries to play it off. "I've never had a girl wear only my jersey before. You might ruin me for all others."

Only his jersey? As in... they're naked underneath? Now there's a thought.

But instead of letting my mind wander into the gutter, I bat a hand between us and brush off that thought immediately. "Oh, please... I'm sure plenty of girls have worn your number as they set their hooks in you."

This earns me an eye roll and a loud huff to which I crack up laughing. Drew's adorable when he's frustrated. "They may have tried. But I was never interested... trust me. The only one I'd want wearing my jersey is you, Angel."

Okay, then. Heat rushes to my cheeks, and I know I must change the subject before I embarrass myself. "What do you say we get something in my size, for now?" But I just can't help myself when I suggest, "Maybe I can model your jersey for you in private some time."

Drew's eyes darken, and I swear if we weren't in public, he'd hold me to that promise. We stare at one another with heat building between us, until we're interrupted by a salesman.

"Anything I can get for you?"

My eyes immediately dart to the newcomer, and I quickly stammer, "No. We're good. Thanks. I'm just getting this." I shrug off the hoodie and replace it with the jacket I'd been holding between my knees.

It feels like a million degrees in here, and I don't need either of these coats now. I dart to the register, wanting to put some distance between Drew and myself before I can put my thoughts into action.

What is it about him that lights every nerve on fire with a single look?

By the time I pay, Drew comes up behind me and makes a purchase of his own. Once he's done, he reaches for my hand and leads me to the car we've parked outside. "Ready to hit the beach?"

As we near the approach to the beach, Drew pulls over and puts his SUV into neutral. Then he dials some knobs on the dash. It takes me a minute to realize he's putting it into four-wheel drive. Once a yellow light flashes, he puts the vehicle into drive and heads out onto the beach. The tide is out, and several people and vehicles are scattered along the beach, enjoying their day in the sun. At the end of the distinct driveway, a car is parked on the remains of the gravel.

Drew groans, and I'm instantly on alert.

"What's wrong?"

"I hate it when people park on the approach. Right after where they're parked is the hardest part of the beach to drive on. It makes it more challenging for others to get on and off the beach. I swear more cars get stuck right here than anywhere else in the sand."

My stomach clenches, and my muscles feel rigid as I carefully watch him maneuver his way past the parked vehicle with out-of-state plates. I have no idea how to get a vehicle unstuck in the sand. I've never driven myself on the beach, so It's never been an issue. "Are you sure you want to drive out here?"

As I look around at the other vehicles who have clearly made it past this spot, I put all my faith in Drew to know what he's doing.

Drew's quiet as he guns the engine to pick up speed as he cranks the wheel. I instinctually grab the oh-shit handle, at the top of my door as I brace myself for what's coming. With my legs firmly locking me in place, I ride out the bumps and dips of the uneven sand. The SUV fishtails, but Drew easily corrects our path like he's done this a thousand times. After a few more bumps, the terrain evens out, and Drew no longer guns the engine. The ride becomes smooth, and I easily relax into the soft leather seats.

"Sorry." Drew looks sheepishly in my direction. "Didn't mean to freak you out. But I needed to concentrate through that rough patch." He's maneuvered himself onto the wet sand, and it's like we're riding along a fresh-paved highway.

"No—you do what you need to do. I've never been off-roading, but I can see why they enjoy the rush."

"It is exhilarating," he agrees with an infectious grin. "That's honestly my favorite part. I used to take my dad's truck off-roading and hope I wouldn't get caught each fall when the dirt roads turned to mud."

"Weren't you ever worried you'd get stuck?" Leave it to my practical side to never be far away. Gah. I sound like a nagging mom.

Drew shakes his head and chuckles at my protectiveness. "It's all part of the thrill, but since I didn't like to get into trouble, I'd typically stay on routes I know I could go through with ease, but still get my truck dirty for street cred. I didn't get to do it often, but for some reason, I was proud of washing the mud from my truck before I got caught."

"Seriously?" Who finds it fun to wash muddy vehicles? Uh... That's something we will never have in common. I'm lucky if I run my car through the carwash when it gets so dirty I can't see through the window. "Were you a hick in a past life?" I tease. As I look him over, he doesn't seem like the type —a bit too preppy—but you never know.

"Nope." He pops the p, earning a laugh from me. "I'd never be caught dead wearing cowboy boots, but I did like to have some fun in the mud." He shrugs as if that's all the explanation I should need.

The more I get to know Drew Jacobs, the more I realize he's like an onion. As I peel back each layer, I'm more intrigued. I just hope I don't get too attached and he makes me cry when it ends.

24

DREW

WHEN I FIND a place that's secluded from the crowd, I gun my SUV once again and launch us into the dry sand. I love the slip and slide as I maneuver through the sand and turn us so we will have an easy escape when we leave. Abby's adorable when she grabs the handle and braces herself. Thankfully, instead of fear on her face, it's exhilaration. Her smile lights up my world, and I feel it deep in my soul. To give her a bit more of a ride, I continue down the soft sand longer than I originally intend. I'm not showing off, but I want to keep that smile on her face for as long as I can.

Once I'm parked, I offer, "Want to get out and walk on the beach?"

Abby's eyes sparkle, and her golden-brown eyes shine with excitement. "Duh... why else are we here?"

"Are you the type who likes to get their toes wet in the water?"

"Uh..." She shrugs. "Not really. Maybe in the summer, but

since we're in Washington, and it's never that warm to walk around soaked."

"Summer was the worst when it came to getting wet at the beach. I swear, we could show her a puddle that was only an inch deep, and she'd be up to her neck soaking wet by the time we finished walking. Mom used to make us wait until the very end to go play in the waves because Summer always had to have a full wardrobe change after just supposedly getting her toes wet."

Abby rocks her head back and laughs. "Sounds like me as a kid. My mom would take us to the beach and always had to bring multiple changes of clothing. She finally started bringing a small tent so we could change before returning home. There was no way she'd let me get into her car soaking wet and full of sand."

Now that's an image I can't get out of my head.

I look her over from head to toe, raise my eyebrows, and smirk. "Is this something I should worry about?" I'm only teasing, but the thought alone has me needing to get out of this vehicle and walk around.

"No. Thank you very much. I'm sure I can stay dry and relatively sand free. Besides, we don't have any change of clothes with us. I won't ruin your vehicle. Promise."

Oddly enough, I'm not so sure I'd mind. Sure, sand is a bitch to get out, but if it meant she'd have to strip first...

Abby interrupts my lustful thoughts when she kicks off her shoes and socks and pops open the door. When I hesitate to follow her because my brain is apparently slow on the uptake, Abby chuckles. "Come on, Jacobs. Let's see if we can stay out of trouble." With that, she turns and runs down the beach.

It only takes me a minute to shed my socks and shoes, throw open the door, and sprint to catch up. Abby's got a good start on me, but since my strides double hers, I eat up the distance between us quickly. When I almost catch up, the brat kicks it into high gear and pulls away. Her lead doesn't last long. Within a second or two, I throw out my arms and reach to pull her in. Unfortunately, her legs tangle in mine, and it ends up being more of a tackle. To keep her from getting hurt, I turn us so that I take the brunt of the fall as we land in the soft sand.

"Well, that's one way to win." She smirks when her eyes meet mine, but I can tell she's not bothered by my antics at all. Her face splits in two as she rolls her eyes and giggles. "I'll have to remember you fight dirty."

If she thinks that's playing dirty, she ain't seen nothing yet. My hand reaches under her exposed skin from our tumble and tickles her at the waist. Holy shit. She's ticklish. She twists, turns, and squirms to get out of my reach. But I just can't let that happen. I get lost in the moment and before I know it, she's squealing. "Okay... enough... I can't... breathe."

Instantly, I stop my torment, and she falls onto her back to pant. Since my bottom half is tangled in hers, I lean up on my elbow to look her in the eye as I hold her hip in place. I make no movements to tickle her. But I'm not ready to let her go either.

We stare at each other for an endless moment before she finally breaks our silence with a breathless, "Hi," before biting on her lower lip.

The vixen likely knows that one move alone does it to me every time. Without a second thought, I close the distance between us and press my lips to hers. God. She tastes of peppermint and Abby. Utter perfection. I could die a happy man in this moment. Her tongue darts out and traces the seam of my lips, and I happily invite her in.

Her hand runs through my hair, and I could kiss her like this forever. Her tongue meets mine, and I take control of the kiss until we're both breathless and gasping for air. As I pull back, I realize all good things must come to an end. If I don't put an end to this, I won't want to stop. Ever.

As much as I'd like to continue this train of thought, sex on the beach is better as a drink than reality. There's no way I want sand in places it should never exist, and I'm not much into an exhibitionist either. Hell. I don't even know if Abby's ready for something like that, but there's no way in hell I'd ever turn her down, should she show interest.

I slowly kiss her a few more times, then suggest, "Ready for that walk you wanted?"

She lets out a huff and pouts in the most adorable way. "If you insist." But a smile forms as she rights herself into a standing position, right alongside me. She reaches out her hand and helps me to my feet with ease. Together, we walk hand in hand down the beach, without a care in the world.

We walk in silence, enjoying the seagulls and watching the waves in the distance. Abby points out a large ship in the distance as well as a place to sit off in the distance on a log in the sand. She leads us there, and I gladly follow.

When we reach the log, the wind picks up. Instinctually, I

wrap my arm around her and pull her close. I've always been mesmerized by crashing waves, and I find myself lost in the unique rhythm of the ocean. We're a good thirty feet from the water, so there's no risk in getting wet. Abby takes my hand in hers and leans closer to my chest. Between the steady sound of the water and her warm body on mine, it's so peaceful. Abby runs her fingers along my knuckles, and I relax into her further.

It could be minutes or hours that pass, but I've never been more content than just watching the sunset with the beautiful woman beside me. When she breaks the silence, her voice is barely above a whisper.

Her steady hands never miss a beat as she says, "You know… on the way here, I got a little nervous?"

What? That's the last thing I thought she'd say. Where's she going with this? Shit. Have I done something to offend her? "Why is that?"

She doesn't make eye contact but continues staring out at the ocean and stroking my hand. "I don't want you to get the wrong impression. I'm not a virgin, but I've never gone away with a guy for the night, either."

"Okaaaayyy," I draw out, hoping she'll explain more. I never expected her to be a virgin, but I'm not sure how I feel about thinking of her with other guys. My gut twists as my heart rate spikes.

"Don't get me wrong. I'm completely attracted to you. Because… well…" she sputters, "you're you."

"Glad you think I'm eye candy, Angel," I spit out, though I still don't follow her train of thought.

Instead of laughing, like I expect, Abby looks horrified as her eyes dart to mine. "No... that's not what I meant."

"Well..." I stare at her for a moment before continuing, "what do you mean?" My hackles rise; what else am I supposed to think when someone makes a comment like that? I'm used to being liked for my looks, my status on the team. But I thought Abby was different. I didn't think she gave a shit about any of that.

"Ohmigod. Please don't take that the wrong way. The look on your face says a thousand words." She places a hand on my chest and suddenly, I'm much calmer. "Drew..." She waits until she has my full attention before continuing, "I could be blind, and I'd still be completely attracted to you. You're smart, funny, caring, and more than just a guy with a pretty face. You're the whole package."

I can't help the grin that forms. She just paid me the highest of compliments, and pride soars through me just as much as relief—Abby does see the real me.

"Now, don't let that go to your head." She levels me with a stare. "Your ego is already inflated—as it should be—but that's still not what I'm trying to get at."

"Okay," I say as I try my best to school my features. "What are you getting at?" I prompt.

"I was nervous because of me... and my past. I've never had so much on the line as I'm feeling with you. When I've been with other guys... it was... well, different."

"Different how?"

Abby lets out a long breath I didn't realize she'd been holding and looks back to our hands for a moment. Then takes a deep breath as if she's fortifying herself. She straightens her spine and looks me directly in the eyes. "I didn't have as much to lose with them. I knew they were short-term relationships. I knew things were casual. But with you..." She trails off and glances to the ocean. Suddenly, I'm a bundle of nerves.

I reach out and tenderly lift her chin to force her eyes to meet mine. "With me, what, Angel?" The way her eyes hold mine and raw emotion flows, I feel as if I'm standing on the edge of an airplane ready to take a leap into the great unknown. God. I hope she's about to say what I've been feeling all along.

"With you..." she whispers. "I have so much more to lose."

Shaking my head, I need to put her fears at bay. "You're not out on this ledge alone, Angel. I'm right there with you. If you're not ready to do anything more than what we're doing—I'm completely fine with that. I invited you here this weekend simply to spend time with you. I have *zero* expectations. So, please don't feel any pressure. There are plenty of beds, though I'd never kick you out of mine." I smile to let her know I'm joking. "I'd never expect you to sleep there either."

She sighs heavily. "I know..."

"Abby. I really like you. I'm not going anywhere, and I'll let you take the lead as far as where things go. In the meantime, let's just enjoy this beautiful sunset together."

She reaches to my face and pulls me in for a quick kiss. I feel it from my head to my toes. There's nothing more that I want more than to wake up with her in my arms. But there's no way I will pressure her into anything either.

25

ABBY

OHMIGOD! I am such an idiot. I was simply trying to tell Drew I'm really into him, and now he thinks I want to put the brakes on things. Gah. I'm such a blubbering nitwit. Why oh why couldn't I have just told him I'm falling for him and that the reason I'm afraid is because I've never slept with anyone I've had feelings like this for? Hell. I think I'm on my way to loving him, and I've just squelched any chance I have of showing him what he means to me.

Holy shit. Did I just say *love* him?

Yes—I did. I mean—I do. I've never felt this way for anyone else. I've never given myself the opportunity. Fuck. What should I do now?

Before the sun fully sets, Drew and I walk back hand in hand to his vehicle. It was comfortable but made me feel a little let down. I want to take things further, but how do I let him know—after basically putting my foot in my mouth by stopping it and making things come to a screeching halt.

Since we drove so far down the beach, it doesn't take long to return to the cabin. When we get inside, Drew gets to work on fixing dinner. Well, he pulls a lasagna out of the fridge, pulls a Caesar salad from a bag, and places the loaf of garlic bread on the counter, for when it's ready to go into the oven. He tosses the salad but waits to add the dressing and croutons. I'm a huge pasta fan, so I'm eager for this meal.

When he sets the salad back in the fridge and the lasagna in the oven, he lets me know we still have about an hour before it's ready. He asks if I'd mind if he takes a shower; our little roll in the sand made him feel a bit grimy. I tell him I'll do the same when he gets out.

My mouth waters at the sight of Drew when he returns to the living area. He's got a pair of basketball shorts on and is just pulling his shirt over his head, giving me the best view imaginable. I try not to stare like the complete dork I am, but, God, is it difficult. If I thought I wanted to take things further before—I without a doubt do now. Holy hell, he turns me into a pile of goo just looking at him. I swear I've only seen the likes of him on photoshopped pages of magazines.

Drew pulls me out of my fantasy. "Everything okay, Angel?"

"Uh... Yeah." Just had to unstick my tongue from the roof of my mouth. Thank you very much... but don't mind me. Can you lift your shirt up again?

"Did you get too much sun today? You... uh... look a little flushed," Drew questions as he closes the distance between us. He stops right in front of me and brushes his palm along my cheek. "You feel a little warm. Are you sure you're okay?"

Seriously? This is my life?

How can I tell him I've only got the hots for him and not sound like a nymphomaniac? "Nope," I blurt out. "I'm all good. I think I'll just go hop in that shower now." And take a very cold shower—at that.

I bolt from the room like my ass is on fire, so I can avoid any future embarrassment. I grab my things from the spare bedroom and make my way to the hall bathroom. Just as I'm about to step foot inside, Drew calls out, "If you want to take a bath, there's a jacuzzi tub in the main bathroom. We have plenty of time before dinner."

Cold shower or warm jacuzzi tub? Decisions... decisions. I must hesitate a moment too long because he assures me, "The tub also is attached to the shower, so you're welcome to use both. I've left my shampoo and conditioner in there, should you need it."

Well, that makes my decision easy. I can do both.

"Thanks," I say as I duck into the master bedroom on the other side of the hall.

Maybe this wasn't such a good idea. The room smells entirely of Drew. My senses are already on hyperdrive and having his masculine scent completely envelop me is practically torture. I want nothing more than to march back out there and drag him back in here with me. Maybe I should just do something to take the edge off, so I won't be so hormone driven?

Fuck. What's a girl to do? I know I'd fly off like a rocket if I had my best battery-operated boyfriend. But if I'm being honest, I'd rather not fly on a solo mission. I'd rather it be with

Drew. Maybe I'll just have to figure out a way to get him to 'See the light,' and realize he misunderstood my intentions at the beach.

Decision made. I hop in the shower and set the water to as cold as I can handle. It does nothing to temper my wacked-out libido, but it does make my cheeks less flushed and my body cool down. Maybe I can get through dinner and not have anymore embarrassing moments.

I will neither confirm nor deny that I may have sniffed his body wash. Who wouldn't want to smell it? It does the trick, kind of—but something's missing. Something unique to Drew. Great. Just as I've calmed my body down, I'm worked up again.

God, this is going to be a long and torturous night.

THANKFULLY, dinner goes off without a hitch. I'm able to control my hormones and keep from embarrassing myself even further. I throw on a pair of yoga pants and an oversized t-shirt to lounge in. The conversation flows, and we clean up with ease.

Afterward, Drew and I settle on the couch. He asks if I mind him checking the score as he flips to the sports channel to catch up on the latest college ball stats, and I can't help but smile at how adorable he is. I assure him I'm used to my brother and dad doing the same. I don't care as long as he's not offended if I pull out a book to read.

The sports channel holds my interest for a bit, but when I

realize there's still another quarter left in the game, I reach into my purse and pull out my Kindle. Drew instinctually raises an arm, and I snuggle into his side. There's a sense of comfort as I relax into his arms. It feels as if we've been doing this forever.

When the game finishes, and he's confident about the stats on his opposing teams, he flicks off the television. This gets my attention immediately, and I set my Kindle aside. Glancing at the clock, I see it's already after ten.

Drew stands and stretches as he yawns heavily. "Sorry about that," he says with chagrin written across his face. "I get lost in the stats on the nights I don't have games. It's great to see my opponents and try to get a leg up for next week's practice."

"It's no problem, Drew. Really. I caught up on a book I've been dying to finish. I only have a few chapters left, but I'm sure I know how it'll end as they're just wrapping things up at this point."

"If you want to finish, it won't bother me."

I shake my head. "Nah. It's getting late. What do you say to getting up early, going for a run on the beach, then hang out here some more before heading back to campus?"

"I think that can be arranged."

We spend the next few minutes cleaning up. Before I know it, he's in the master bedroom getting ready for bed, while I use the main hall bathroom. Just as I finish brushing my teeth, a thought hits me for how to rectify my comments from earlier. I just hope my nerves don't fail me now.

26

DREW

I HEAR the water turn off from the hall bathroom just as I shuck off my shirt for bed. As much as I'd love for Abby to sleep with me, I know she's not ready. And let's face it. If she were in my bed, there would be a lot more than sleeping going on.

I'm so turned on by her that just thinking of her makes my dick hard. Why the fuck I changed into basketball shorts is beyond me—they hide nothing. At least the pillow I'd stuffed on my lap lets me keep my errant thoughts about her to myself.

I'm just about to hop into bed when I hear a soft knock on my door.

"Come in," I offer, knowing she's likely just saying good night. I didn't want to make a big deal of saying good night, so I just came in here to distract myself. God knows how uncomfortable I made it in Spokane. That was more than awkward, thank you very much.

When the door opens, Abby steps in and walks slowly

toward me. There's an aura of determination, and I'm puzzled by her expression. It's fierce, yet when I focus on her eyes, there's a hint of vulnerability, making me wonder what's going on in that beautiful head of hers.

She stops at the foot of the bed and stares at me for a moment before stammering, "Uh... did you mean it?"

Dumbfounded, I ask, "Mean what?"

A shy smile forms on her lips, and her features soften. "Did you mean it when you said you wouldn't kick me out of your bed?"

My heart races, and it takes everything in my power not to show her how excited I am over this news. I pretend to think it over, just to give her a hard time. Bringing my hand to my chin, I look to the ceiling. "That depends..." I purposely trail off.

Now it's her turn to clarify. "On what?"

Her cheeks turn pink, and she shuffles on her feet. "On whether or not you snore. You see, I'm a light sleeper," I tease.

My beautiful Angel shakes her head and squints her eyes at me. Then she picks up the pillow I'd thrown to the bottom of the mattress earlier and throws it at me before turning to exit the room.

Her quick retreat causes me to jump into action. Within two strides, I have her wrapped in my arms from behind. "Just where do you think you're going?"

"To sleep in my own room. How the hell am I supposed to know if I snore? I've never shared a bed with anyone. So, I'll just leave you to your beauty sleep, Jacobs." She practically spits out my name like a curse, and I roar with laughter.

"Ohmigod, Angel. I'm kidding. I wouldn't kick you out of

bed if you sounded like a chainsaw. I might invest in some earplugs, but I'd never kick you out!" With that, I turn her in my arms to face her. "I'd be honored if you chose to sleep in my bed, Angel... And I promise..." I wait until I have her full attention, "I'll even act like a gentleman, until you're good and ready."

Abby smirks and pins me with her beautiful golden-brown eyes. "What if I told you I'm ready now, you big Neanderthal?"

Did she say what I think she just said?

Cocking my head to the side, I search every part of her face for something to tell me I hear her incorrectly. "You sure? I'm not here to pressure you."

"Yes... I'm sure... you big doofus. I was trying to tell you earlier, but I fucked it up royally. The reason I'm nervous is because I've never had sex with anyone who has the power to hurt me... I've never had sex with someone I care about so deeply. I'm falling for you, you big, sexy dope of a man."

I stare at her in disbelief. I swear to God, I must be dreaming this.

She's falling for me.

Holy shit. She's fucking falling for me! I inwardly fist pump the air though externally, I remain rooted in place.

As if she can read my mind, she continues, "Yes... you... You're such a gentleman, you wouldn't let me finish earlier. I commend you for backing off, but if I'm being honest, it's taken everything in my power not to jump you since we've been home."

This isn't time for words, but action. As if my mind

suddenly kicks into gear and wills my body to act, I swoop her up in my arms and kiss the fucking daylights out of her. The moment our lips meet, I practically growl, "Next time, just hit me over the head with a frying pan. I've wanted you for so long, but I was waiting for the time to be right. You sexy, sweet, stubborn woman. Don't you see, I'm breaking all my rules for you. I've fallen head over heels, and I'm nowhere ready to let you go."

A wide grin spreads across her face as she cradles mine in her palms. "Neither am I, Drew. Neither am I."

There's no need to respond when she pulls me close and kisses so well. I feel it in my toes. Damn. Where has Abby been all my life? We haven't even done more than make out, yet I'm certain with every fiber of my being, this will be different than anything I've ever experienced. Being with someone you care about is such a treasure, and I intend to let her know just how precious she is.

My hands roam under her shirt, and I'm shocked to find she's removed her bra. She's so fucking responsive as my fingertips trace her nipple. She sucks in a deep breath and breaks our kiss, so I trail kisses along her jawline to her ear.

When Abby writhes into me, from just a simple touch, my lust-filled mind wonders what else she'll do when I touch her other sensitive places. I push up her bulky sweatshirt to get a better view, but it's awkward and gets in the way of me admiring her perfect breasts. I urge her to take it off as I kiss along her rib cage up to the underside of her breast. "Mind if we get rid of this?"

No words are spoken as she quickly sits up and shucks the

sweatshirt onto the floor. Abby half-naked is a glorious view. She has the perfect hour-glass figure that's well hidden under her bulky clothes from day to day.

But I'm the lucky bastard she's sharing this beautiful body with. Her form-fitting yoga pants leave little to the imagination, and I want nothing more than to run my tongue along her body. I waste no time exploring her body with my lips. I lavish her breasts with my tongue as she runs her fingertips along my back and shoulders. Soft moans escape, and her breath quickens as I take in her nipple and suck hard. With my thumb, I flick her other nipple, and she lets out an animalistic noise I've never heard. But it sends a direct message to my cock. She needs more.

If I can get her to be this responsive after only spending a few minutes, I wonder what she'll do when I taste her everywhere. As if I have a new mission, I trail kisses along her rib cage and over her abdomen, while I continue to tease her nipple. Her hips buck, and her hands frantically push at her pants as I reach the soft slope below her belly button. Taking the hint, I remove both her yoga pants and underwear in one fell swoop as I settle between her legs.

Holy. Shit. Abby is a sight to see.

As if it has a mind of its own, my dick thickens and strains against my shorts, dying to be released. I will myself to focus solely on her as I continue kissing down the slope of her abdomen into the promised land.

When she lets her legs fall apart, I'm practically sent a personal invitation to stare at her neatly trimmed perfection. I take in a deep breath to fortify myself from making a fool of myself.

Holy fuck. I'm not prepared for my reaction to her. Her delicious scent fills my senses and somehow, my straining erection gets even thicker. How the fuck is that even possible? It takes everything in my power not to come from the sheer sight of her alone. I want to lick her front to back and milk her until she comes harder than she ever has before.

Without wasting another second, I dip my head to her and devour my first taste. It's even better than I imagined. It's like all my fantasies come true, and I'm living in a wet dream.

Abby's hips spring off the bed, and she's practically speaking in tongues when I hit the spot that's known to make women beg for more. Wanting to give her every bit of satisfaction I can, I dip two fingers into her as I keep up the perfect rhythm to drive her wild. Her muscles instinctually clamp down around my fingers as I feel the need to curl them ever so slightly, to press against her outer wall, causing my Angel to let out a muffled scream as she covers her face with her arms.

"Drew..." she pants then practically purrs, "need you..." loud gasp. "Need you inside me."

"I am inside you," I happily remind her but don't slow my rhythm.

"No..." She shakes her head as her body tightens. "Want to... take you with me."

"They'll be plenty of time for that later," I say as I reach out to focus on her clit with my tongue.

When I glance up, she looks like she wants to protest, but I use this moment to push her over the edge. Doubling down on my efforts, I pull her clit into my mouth and suck for all I'm worth, as I simultaneously press against her inner wall and flick her clit with my tongue.

Abby's body instantly stills and goes stiff as a board for a moment before the room fills with a loud animalistic cry. It's a cross between pleasure and something else entirely. Before another heartbeat can pass, I flick her clit once more, and she forcefully convulses over and over from every muscle within her. Not wanting to leave her alone on that cliff, I lick and suck her with less force, coaxing her down from her high. When she finally stills, all I can hear is her ragged breaths pull in and out through her exhausted lungs.

With a smile on my face, I pull back from her slickness and wipe the back of my hand across my face as I climb up her body to face her. Her eyes practically roll to the back of her head as if she's had an out-of-body experience, and I can't help the pride that flows through me. I did this to her, and I'll do it to her again, any chance I get. I've never had a woman respond to me like that, and the competitive part of me is dying to know if this is something unique to Abby, or if I can make her do it again.

Taking a few moments, I stare at the beauty of Abby as she sucks in breaths of air. Watching her come apart is better than my own release. I get a strange sense of satisfaction in knowing I've had this effect on her. Eventually, her heavy breathing subsides, but her eyes never open.

"Hey, beautiful. Everything okay?"

"I... can die... a satisfied... woman," she sighs. "I think..." another deep breath. "You... just killed me." She's quiet for a moment, as she takes in a deep breath. "But what a way to go." She lets out another heavy sigh as her head flops to the side against a pillow. "Don't mind me. I'll just be over here in my land of bliss, hoping I never return to reality."

I brush back the hair from her face and kiss her cheek softly. "I have plenty more where that comes from. I may make it my new mission to see if I can top that each time we're together."

I can't help but chuckle when I hear her murmur, "Holy shit. He's going to break me."

27

ABBY

AM I DEAD?

Nothing has ever felt so good.

I'm a puddle of goo as I drift down to reality. Drew Jacobs has just completely rocked my world and if I could move, I'd gladly return the favor.

Holy shit. I have *never* experienced an orgasm so intense. Even my toes feel numb and tingly, and my arms... are they even attached to my body? Nothing's ever felt so sublime in my entire existence.

When Drew makes his way back up the bed to face me, I can feel his presence, but my eyelids are glued together as I revel in my orgasmic high. When he asks if everything's okay, I think I respond. But I'm so drunk on Drew, I'm not even sure if I string coherent words together.

I hear him chuckle at whatever my response was, feeling my body drift. I feel Drew shift me so I can rest against him, as if he's the big spoon before everything fades to black.

When I come back to reality, I have no idea how much time has passed. The room is dark, and I can't see the clock that's on the other side of Drew.

His strong arms remain wrapped around me, and his deep, slow breaths tell me he's sound asleep. I take a moment to enjoy the comforts of being in his arms. I never thought I'd like to cuddle in my sleep, but this is something I can get used to. His strong masculine scent is the perfect combination of body wash and all that is Drew.

I shift a little to get closer to him and freeze when I realize my mistake.

I have to pee.

And not just in a—let's just roll over, get comfortable, and it will pass phase. It's an—if I don't get out of this bed this instant, I may have some serious issues scenario. Fuck. Is this seriously happening to me? I don't want to leave this spot, but my body is fucking betraying me at this moment.

I attempt to extricate myself from Drew's long arms, and he's like a friggin' octopus. He snakes a leg over mine to hold me in place as his arms cocoon me tighter. Yeah. There's no way I can move without waking him.

But beggars can't be choosers. When nature calls like this —you answer—or there's hell to pay.

Damn. This is so embarrassing. I've had the most romantic experience of my existence, and I must stop this bliss because my body chooses this time to be over hydrated. Just. My. Luck.

I attempt to slide out from under his strong arms again by sliding away from him one inch at a time. This time, I nearly make it. All I must do is get his legs off mine, and I'm home free. I creep my body further from Drew's warmth, and I manage to get one leg completely out. By the time I get myself free from him, I'm almost at the edge of the king-sized bed. I just need to put my feet on the floor and get myself upright.

Success!

In a ninja-like attempt, my foot hits the floor, and I creep to a standing position. And then the fucking rug literally slips out from under me, and I land with a loud thud on the floor.

"Fuck, that hurt," I moan to myself.

Before I can process how to get up, the light flicks on, and Drew's deep laugh fills the room. "Just where do you think you're going?"

I don't have time to explain. My unexpected fall has made this a dire emergency. Scrambling to my feet, I make a run for the bathroom across the cool wooden floors. "Gotta pee," I pant as I work to regain control of my breathing.

So much for not waking him.

It isn't until I finish my business, and I'm at the sink washing my hands, that reality sets in. Fuck! Drew just witnessed me run stark naked into the bathroom, after falling flat on my very naked ass. The only thing worse would've been if I'd peed myself. What in the world should I say when I return?

Think. Think. Think.

Staring at my reflection in the mirror, even I can see the blush that's covering my body. That certainly won't help matters.

Get it together, Abby. It's not like he doesn't know what just happened, I scold myself as I take steady breaths to calm myself. *If you don't get out there soon, he's likely to come looking for you.*

With that thought, I dry my hands and make my way to the door. But glance back to the mirror once more, with my hand resting on the door handle.

I look myself sternly in the eyes and take a fortifying breath.

I have this, I silently tell my reflection, and I hold my stare until I feel confident.

I've been naked in front of guys before. Sure, they never saw me jump out of bed like I was running away to never come back... but this is Drew. Just go out there and be yourself. What's the worst that could happen?

Before I can think of the thousands of holes in my newfound logic, I twist open the handle and step into the room.

With the bedside lamp on, I can clearly see Drew's still in bed. He's lying on his side, with his head propped up with one hand, while he rests on his elbow. A lazy smile spreads across his perfect lips when I enter the room, and my heart instantly warms.

Apparently, I have nothing to be ashamed of. Drew clearly likes what he sees as his eyes roam every inch of me. Even from this distance, I feel their heat burn into every square inch of my skin.

For a moment, we just stare at one another, but he breaks the silence with, "Everything okay?"

"Yeah," I sigh. "Sorry I woke you. Apparently, I wasn't meant to be stealthy."

"Well, I can't say I've ever witnessed anyone making that

type of exit from my bed." Drew's light chuckle sends shivers up my spine as he continues, "If I didn't know better, I'd say I'd left you unsatisfied. But from the way you passed out earlier, I'm sure that isn't the case."

"Well," I say dramatically as I walk with as much confidence as I can to the bed, "not that your ego needs stroking, but you and I both know you just rocked my world, so what's the point in denying it."

Drew's eyes widen, and a wolfish grin spreads across his face, causing my heart to race with anticipation of what's to come. After all, I'm well rested and ready to pick up where things left off.

I crawl onto the bed, and Drew lifts the covers for me to join him. He's wearing a pair of basketball shorts, and his sexy abs are on full display.

Damn, he is sexy as hell. I must've been distracted before. How the hell did I not notice his hotness?

Instinctively, I run my tongue over my suddenly parched lips and smile in appreciation. If I have any say in the matter, those flimsy shorts leaving little to my wild imagination will be removed in just a matter of time, and I will get to see all the sexy man before me.

As soon as I get close enough for him to reach, he snakes his arm around my waist and pulls me close. Drew practically growls, "Get over here, Angel."

And I happily oblige.

Drew maneuvers us so I'm on my back in an instant, and he hovers over me with a beautiful grin playing at his lips. His blue eyes almost look black in this lighting, and I suddenly feel breathless from their intensity. Shivers run up my spine with anticipation while our gazes lock.

"I'm glad you're back in the land of the living; I'm not done with you."

I reach up to trace his perfect lips with my finger as I challenge, "Same goes for you, mister."

Drew's eyes darken as he stares in disbelief at my boldness. But I can tell he appreciates my train of thought as the bulge in his pants comes to life.

Well, hello there.

His intense expression filled with need makes me bolder. Instinctually, I reach out to feel for myself just how much Drew's affected by me.

As I gently stroke his thick cock through his shorts, it bobs to life on its own. Drew lets out a guttural moan, making my core clench and my determination grow.

These shorts have to go.

As if Drew has the ability to read my mind, the moment my hands reach out to push at the waistline of his shorts, he shifts his body and stands to shed them, taking his underwear off right along with them.

Holy fucking shit. Drew is a sight to be seen.

Once his shorts are pooled on the floor, he grips himself and strokes his shaft almost absent-mindedly as his eyes burrow into my soul. Drew Jacobs, without a doubt, in that one simple move, is the sexiest man I've ever seen.

My core pulses, and I instinctually squirm under his gaze to press my thighs together to give myself some relief. But damn. That's just not enough. I need him. Now. Somehow, I manage to think about the necessities in my urgent state of need. "Condom?"

Before I can say anything else, Drew turns on his heels, and I'm blessed with his chiseled backside quickly retreating into the bathroom. In three quick strides, he disappears, and I hear him unzipping something from the other room. Something drops to the floor and before I can ask, he returns to the bedroom with a strip of condoms in his hands.

Holy shit. There are more condoms than I can count. Does he think we'll use all of those in one night?

A nervous laugh escapes, and I shake my head in disbelief. "Presumptuous much?"

At least he has the gall to look chagrin...sort of. His head shakes slowly as he dips the mattress with the weight of his knee as he crawls back on. "No. Not all at once, but I'm not about to run out either." He moves closer to me on the bed and stops when he's looking me straight in the eye. "God, Angel..." His raspy voice is filled with need. "You have no idea what you do to me. I've been in a constant state of arousal since you showed up at my door on your birthday, and I can't fucking wait to be inside you."

"Well, we can't have that now, can we?" I tease. "What are you waiting for, Drew? I'm right here." Somehow comes out sounding self-assured, which makes the corner of his lips tip into a smirk.

Drew shakes his head playfully, "Oh, Angel. You'd better be careful what you wish for. I'm quickly becoming addicted to you and may not let you go."

Oh. My. Word. Is this what swooning feels like? There's no way he just laid such a claim to me, right?

In an attempt to process his words, I shrug and say the first thing on my mind, "Would that be such a bad thing?"

Drew lets out a deep breath and closes the distance between us with the shake of his head. When he's only centimeters from my lips, I feel his breath wash over me. "What am I going to do with you, Angel?"

I don't even have time to process a response as his body lies flush against me as his lips crash onto mine and devour me for all I'm worth.

His hands roam my body, and my skin erupts into flames. God, he feels amazing. Reaching out to hold him tighter, I run my fingers through his thick hair and along his muscled back. Drew moans into my mouth, as I kiss him back as if my life depends on it. The energy flowing through us is nearly combustible as we nip, lick, and suck at one another.

Without breaking our kiss, Drew shifts his body to the side and traces patterns along my inner thighs with the lightest of touch. Goose bumps erupt from head to toe as his heat rapidly floods me. I can't tell you if I'm hot, cold, content, or burning with need. All I know is I need more of Drew.

His thick cock presses into my thigh and practically begs for my attention. When I reach out to grip it in my hands, Drew moans in appreciation. It's smooth but hard as steel. I only get to stroke him a couple of times before he takes my hand in his and pins it above my head.

Through a series of sensual kisses, Drew's gravelly voice proclaims, "Angel..." kiss. "You're killing me... There'll be plenty of time for that later..." Kiss. "But unless you want me to finish off in your hand, I suggest you let me be in charge... for now." He moves his lips along my jaw and onto my chest as he makes his request.

With the rush of sensations flowing through me, I can hardly think straight. The hunger and need I feel for him makes me complicit to his demands. After all, he's not saying I'll never get my chance. He's only asking for now. When he places his lips over my nipple and draws it in to play with the tip between his teeth, it's all I can do not to beg for him to give me more.

Maybe Drew can read my mind, or perhaps he's becoming a master of my body, because I'm fully convinced he knows exactly what I need. He puts the exact amount of pressure on my clit, long enough to have me hovering on the edge before he dips his fingers into me and reawakens the orgasmic bliss I experienced earlier.

"Drew... Need you now," I pant out as coherent as I can manage because I'm afraid if I go over the edge like before, I may not come back anytime soon. I've never been one to have multiple orgasms in one night, but he has me teetering on the brink of ecstasy. "Need you inside me," I demand more forcefully, so that he understands the severity of my situation.

"Okay, Angel. I'm right here," he pants as he pauses his focus on me to sheath himself with a condom. In record time, he's protected and nudging my legs to spread wider to accommodate space for him.

Slow and determined, Drew reaches down to stroke me a few times, and I instinctually wrap my legs around his waist to pull him closer. My senses are on overload with sensation, and my eyes close as I appreciate how he makes me feel.

"Look at me, Angel," Drew demands, and my eyes spring open to meet his. He takes his time to align our bodies and enter me. It's a tight fit, so he slowly inches inside me, with his eyes locked on mine to ensure I'm right here with him.

Oh, God, I thought what he did to me before was an out of this world experience. That has nothing on what Drew does to me once he's fully seated and begins to move. He swivels his hips in just the perfect rhythm, and I appreciate Drew's awareness and anticipation of every move he makes. It's like he's been given a secret map to my body and knows just how to get the most intense reactions.

As he picks up the pace, I cling to him for dear life. Every nerve ending is like an electric pulse coursing through my body. I feel each inch of him both from the inside and along my skin. I pull myself closer and cling on to every second of reality I can manage. There's no way I want to go over this edge alone. He needs to be there with me.

Drew shifts our bodies and spectacularly hits a spot I've never encountered, and I cry out. "Ohmigod... right there..." I need him to reach it again and again. "Yes... there it is. Holy fucking shit! What are you doing to me?" I pant out as my last coherent thought before I spiral and take Drew right along with me.

My body pulses and spasms harder than I've ever experienced. I feel him thrust his hips a few more times. Then his body stills, and he lets out a sound I can't quite describe before his body goes lax, and he collapses onto me.

"Holy shit, Angel," he pants, breathless. "The better question is what are you doing to me?"

Drew's in impeccable shape, but to know I've knocked the wind out of him brings a smile of satisfaction to my face. Because I did this to him. Well... we've done this together... and it was fucking incredible.

When he pulls back, his expression mirrors my thoughts, and my emotions bubble to the surface. The lopsided grin that plays on his perfect lips makes me a bit bold. So, I tease, "Well, I don't know about you, but I think it's imperative we find out if this is a one-time thing, or just an us thing. I've never experienced anything like *that* before. Have you?"

When his grin grows wider, I push on with as straight of face as I can manage. "You know I'm a firm believer in putting theory into practice..."

I'm cut off before I can say anything more when Drew growls and kisses the sass right off my lips. And, oh, what a kiss it is. I didn't think it was possible, but it's the kind of kiss that I feel deep in my soul all the way to my toes.

When I feel his cock come back to life, he groans and pulls away. "Sorry, Angel. Need to take care of this condom. But hold that thought. When I get back, we're so going to put that theory into practice."

As I stare at his retreating glorious backside, I know without a doubt—This is an us thing.

28
DREW

WAKING up alone is something I've done all my life, but when I wake this morning before practice, my first instinct is to reach out for Abby. Having her in my arms all throughout the day yesterday is something I could get used to. Unfortunately, as I reach out and open my eyes, I find my bed empty. With both of us having early commitments, she thought it best to go to her place when we got back to campus. Knowing she was right, I didn't object. But now as I stretch in my king-sized bed all alone, it feels too big for just me.

I turn off my alarm and toss back the covers to get to the gym on time. I throw on a pair of shorts and head to the kitchen to make a protein shake and pack a snack to scarf between my workout and first class. Between classes then practice this afternoon, my day is full. Maybe Abby can squeeze time in her schedule to have dinner or hang out this evening.

Maybe if I'm lucky, I can convince her to stay the night.

Wait? Since when do I want girls to stay the night?

She's not just any girl, dipshit. With her, there's so much more. I'm just as happy to hear about her day and hang out. We have so much more in common than our chemistry between the sheets. She's beautiful from the inside out. Don't even get me started on the gravitational pull to her I've never experienced before; I sure as hell don't know what to do with it. The timing is shit, with the season in full swing and waiting to hear about med school, but after this weekend, there's no way I'm walking away anytime soon.

My thoughts of Abby are interrupted when DeShawn enters the kitchen and asks, "So where did you take off to this weekend?"

"Abby and I went to my aunt's cabin in Long Beach."

DeShawn's mouth drops as he eyes me suspiciously. "This the same girl you went to Spokane with, right?"

"Yeah," I reply, but he just stares in disbelief. I empty the contents into the blender and am about to press start when I notice DeShawn hesitate at the fridge. When he scratches his nose as he bows his head, I break the silence in the room. "What's your point?"

"It's nothing, man. I just... haven't seen you have a girl around—like *ever*—during the season. I'm just wondering why you're suddenly doing it now." His features cast no judgement, but simple curiosity as he tilts his head in my direction to study me further.

I scoff and try to brush it off. "It's not like I've never had a girlfriend."

"Girlfriend?" DeShawn's brows lift as he turns and closes the door of the fridge. He stares at me almost to the point where it becomes uncomfortable before he finds the words that obviously have been rolling in that thick skull of his, for a while. "That's just it. Yeah, you date, but you've never gone out of your way to spend any amount of time with them afterward. You sure as hell don't invite them to go away for two weekends with the season in full swing."

I let out a huff in frustration. It's none of his damn business what I do or don't do with Abby. But as he's one of my closest friends, I know this is his way of checking to make sure everything's legit. It's still annoying as fuck, but I get it, sort of.

I take a measured breath, determined not to let him ruin my mood for the day. "First of all, you know as well as I do how I feel about hospitals. I was a blundering mess when I heard about my parents' accident. Abby was there for me when I needed her. I'm sure if you'd been there when I got the call, you would've done the same as her."

DeShawn nods in agreement. "You know I would. But what's so different about this girl? There's something I can't quite put my finger on about you lately, and I'm not sure if it's a good or a bad thing."

I square my shoulders and steel my frame to look him in the eye. I don't want him to miss my point, so I simply stare until I have his full attention. "You're right. Something is different. Hell, I'm not even sure I know what it is. What I do know is ever since she showed up to study on her birthday, I can't get her off my mind."

DeShawn's mouth forms the perfect 'O,' and his eyes widen. "Really? You're like... the king of focus. I never thought

I'd see the day that Drew Jacobs willingly admits there's more to life than school or basketball."

I let out a light laugh. "I know, right? Can you believe I freaking thought she was plain and would be a great buffer for distraction when we first met?"

"Seriously?" DeShawn asks in disbelief.

Knowing this is a longer story than I have time for, I press start on the blender and finish my protein shake. The moment I'm done, DeShawn is right on cue and eagerly asks, "So how'd you meet?"

"Well... it all started the day I walked into my chem lab..." I sigh, and DeShawn interrupts.

"You're kidding, right? How did someone catch your eye in class? How'd...you..."

I give him a pointed stare until he stops talking. "You gonna let me finish?" I deadpan.

DeShawn cracks a grin, his eyes roll to the back of his head. He says nothing but nods for me to continue.

I can tell it's hard for him to keep quiet as I explain how I purposely scouted the room. I was sure she was perfect for me because she specifically fit what I was looking for in a lab partner.

DeShawn fists his mouth to keep from interrupting.

But I continue with my criteria of Abby needing to be plain, non-descript, and most of all, studious.

"Damn, I have to meet this girl," DeShawn teases. "How does one go from plain jane to distracting, in such a short time?"

"I'm getting to that," I remind him. "I guess it was the night of her birthday... When she knocked on the door, she took my breath away."

"So..." He waggles his eyebrows. "She's a looker in disguise, eh?"

"It's not like that." My tone's serious and cuts to the chase. I won't let him disrespect her.

DeShawn's hands instantly go up as if he's surrendering to the ill-spoken thoughts.

Before he can say another word, I affirm, "Abby's so much more than a pretty face."

"Obviously." DeShawn smiles. "All the more reason to meet her." Then as if another thought hits him, "Does she have any hot friends?"

Sydney and Chloe are both beautiful. But I got the distinct impression Sydney won't put up with his shit. She appreciates his athleticism, but I'm sure that's where she draws the line. I scratch the tip of my nose as I try to figure out a way to word my response. "Uh. She's got two roommates. I can see if they're available. Maybe we can get Grey to hang out with us, so it doesn't look like such a big deal?"

"Sounds like a plan." DeShawn's smile widens. "But let's not call it a date though. I'd rather just hang—if you know what I mean." Then he glances to the clock on the microwave. "We've gotta get going. See what you can do to set it up."

While DeShawn drives us to the gym, I type out a quick message to Abby.

Me: Good morning, Angel.

Right away, I see those three little bouncing dots telling me she's responding, and my heart picks up the pace in anticipation.

Abby: Morning. How was your night?

I could say a million things, but I'll stick with the truth.

Me: Fine. It's weird to say I missed waking up beside you, right?

Abby: No. I miss sleeping next to you, too.

A grin spreads across my lips, knowing we're on the same page.

Me: Want to come over for dinner after practice? It's my turn to cook, and the guys will be here. Invite your roommates, so you're not stuck with us. There will be plenty to eat—promise.

There. I put it out there. Worst-case scenario, she declines. Best case, I get to spend the evening with her.

Abby: I'll see who's available. But just so we're clear, this isn't a triple date. Syd will automatically decline if that's the case.

I can only imagine how *that* would go over. I look to DeShawn and wonder if Sydney will put him in his place tonight, should he flirt with her. I almost don't want to say anything... to see her fierceness in action. That would be a show on its own.

When I chuckle aloud at the thought, DeShawn side-eyes me but maintains focus on the road.

I ignore him.

Me: Got it. Though I am totally considering this a date for us if I'm going through the trouble of cooking for you.

Abby: Duly noted. What time?

Me: Will seven work?

God bless my mom and her instance of buying an Insta-Pot. It won't take me long at all when I get home from practice to make everything.

"Well... Is she coming?" DeShawn finally asks when he parks outside the gym.

"She'll be there. I've invited her roommates but don't know if they'll make it. Will Grey be home?"

I haven't seen much of him this week, but with him knowing it's my night to cook, I'll bet my best pair of sneakers he'll be there. He'd rather eat a home-cooked meal than in the cafeteria. The man can barely boil water without burning it, so he's always hoping DeShawn or I will cook. The trade-off—he always cleans. Who can beat that?

"He should be." DeShawn lets out a sigh as he gets out of the car and grabs his gym bag from the back. "I was surprised he wasn't home this morning. He hasn't mentioned anything, but knowing him, he couldn't sleep and is already at the gym."

Grey's one of those annoying early birds. He gets up before the crack of dawn on any given day. He was raised on a cattle ranch, and I'd guess he's not looking to change those habits anytime soon. He's often already studying when I enter the kitchen each morning.

"I'll text him," I offer as we make our way down the hall to the locker room.

By the time practice ends, I barely have time to rush home and get the meat browned. I'm just putting everything into the Insta-Pot when I hear a knock at the door. Eager to see Abby, I rush to greet her, but Grey beats me to it. Not wanting to appear over-eager, I slow my stride and wait in the hall.

"You must be Abby," he boisterously announces. "I'm Grey. I've been dying to meet you."

From where I'm standing, I see Abby's cheeks darken, but she manages to stick out her hand. "Nice to officially meet you." She turns and looks behind her before continuing, "This is Sydney and Chloe."

Before either of them can say anything, I step forward and open the door further. "Why don't you let them come in and get settled. Dinner is almost ready. DeShawn will be home anytime. He's picking up some garlic bread."

The girls file in, and I slide close to Abby and pull her in for a chaste kiss. "Glad you could make it, Angel. I've missed you."

Her wide smile makes my heart soar. "Me, too. Need any help?" she asks as she looks around the room.

Shaking my head, I murmur, "Nah, I have it covered. But I won't object to company in the kitchen."

Abby glances to Sydney and Chloe. They both are making themselves at home by settling into the couch and starting a conversation with Grey. When Sydney gives her a nod in our direction letting us know she heard me, Abby follows me into the kitchen.

The moment I get her alone, I pull her in for a hug and inhale slowly. She smells almost edible. The perfect combination of citrus and pear makes my mouth water. She squeezes me tight, then pulls back to look me in the eyes. The way her brown eyes darken instantly fills me with lust.

Now isn't the time, Jacobs, I scold myself. *Especially with a room full of people next door.*

As if she could read my mind, Abby smirks and leans up on her toes to kiss me softly. Though I'm sure it's meant to be an innocent kiss, the vixen Abby is, makes my blood flow hot. Not wanting to get carried away, I try to remember our potential audience.

Why did I invite them again?

After all too short a time, I force myself to pull away and practically pant, "Damn, Angel... if you kiss me like that again, I'm likely to tell everyone to take a hike and have you for dinner instead."

This earns an eye roll as a giggle escapes. "That would be a sure way to piss Sydney and Chloe off. They were both wanting dinner an hour ago, and I made them hold off, insisting you had plenty for them to eat. My friends are amazing, but you don't want to see them hangry."

"Well, we can't have that." I smirk. I'd never be that rude, but if she continued kissing me like that, I might not remember to care.

DeShawn walks in with two loaves of garlic bread. The moment he sees Abby, a Cheshire cat grin spreads across his face. *Ah, shit. What's he up to now?* "Well, well, well. Who do we have here?" He exaggeratedly waggles his eyebrows and places an arm around her shoulder. "You must be the infamous Abby. I've been dying to meet the girl that's got Drew changing his tune."

He looks her over from head to toe and shakes his head. Then he gives a pointed look in my direction. "Dude, you met her in a chem lab?" He takes a step away from Abby and leans against the counter.

"Yes," Abby replies sharper than I expect. "For your information, I was sitting there minding my own business when your boy here," she points a thumb in my direction for emphasis, "came over with his entourage and completely pissed me off."

DeShawn's mouth drops to the floor, and his eyes bug wide. It takes everything in me to keep from bursting with laughter. "Seriously?"

I almost feel like I should sit back and watch this potential show with some popcorn. Abby's eyes laser focus on DeShawn, and I'm not sure what will happen next.

"Seriously," she assures him. "But then I got to know him and thought he might be worth keeping around."

DeShawn slowly looks from her to me, then back to her again. I almost think he's at a loss for words, then he cracks a smile. "I think I like you, Abby." He winks at her then focuses his attention on me. "You know, Drew can be pretty full of himself. If you ever get tired of his crap, I'd be happy to take you out."

"*That* won't be necessary," I interrupt and give him a pointed stare, leaving no room for argument.

What the hell, man?

Abby just laughs and pats me on the shoulder. "Oh, I don't think I'll tire of Drew anytime soon, but thanks for the warning. After that first day, I've never seen that side of him again."

DeShawn rolls his eyes as he shakes his head. "Great answer, Abby. Great answer." Then he turns his attention to me. "You have yourself a keeper, dude. The fact you pissed her off on the first day, and she still comes around, is hilarious."

"Gee, thanks," I mutter. "Whatever did I do to deserve a friend like you?"

DeShawn pats me on the shoulder as he puts the bread on the counter by the stove. "You know you love me, man."

Yeah, I do. But saying that will only inflate his ego further.

Before I can say anything, DeShawn changes the subject. "Were those your roommates in there?"

Abby pulls away and moves toward the living room and of course I follow. "Let me introduce you. I think you may have met Sydney at some point, but I'm sure you haven't met Chloe as she's not as into basketball as Syd."

DeShawn's chin pulls back, and confusion sets in. "Sydney... she isn't by any chance a bartender... is she?"

This stops Abby in her tracks. Her head slowly turns to DeShawn, and she slowly draws out, "Yeah, why?"

Though DeShawn's eyes are wide for the briefest of seconds, he tries to brush it off. "Oh, it's not a big deal. We've met a few times, but it's nothing to worry about."

Shit. I've seen that look before. Something most definitely happened.

But when we walk into the living room and see no reaction from Sydney, I can't help but wonder if I might be wrong. But DeShawn rarely has that look on his face, and I'm certain I didn't imagine it.

My thoughts are interrupted when Abby introduces DeShawn officially to her roommates. Sydney remains stoic, but I'm not sure what to make of it. If I hadn't seen DeShawn's reaction in the kitchen, I'd think they've never met. However, he chooses to sit down on the couch next to Chloe, and any thoughts of him and Sydney disappear.

"So, Chloe." I overhear DeShawn ask while Grey says something to Sydney I don't quite catch. "Weren't you in my psychology class freshman year?"

"More than likely. It's my major so there hasn't been many psych classes I haven't taken at this university." Chloe shrugs as she explains, but I don't think she remembers him being in one of her classes.

DeShawn laughs lightly and shakes his head. "I've only taken the one class since it was a requirement. But I remember you because you sat near the front, and the professor always called on you when you were doodling in your notebook."

This causes a scoff from Chloe. "I listen best when I'm doodling. It's just my thing... as I'm sure you noticed. I always had the answer, didn't I?" She raises an eyebrow in challenge.

DeShawn raises his hands in defense to show he clearly doesn't mean anything by it. "I was just sayin', I noticed you. That's all." Chloe starts to respond, but DeShawn interrupts, "I didn't mean anything negative. I was just saying where I recognized you from, that's all."

"There were literally hundreds of people in that class. How do you remember me?" Chloe asks as if she can't believe what she's hearing. I must admit I'm a little surprised, too.

DeShawn rolls his eyes and sighs heavily. "It's no big deal. I sat behind you a few times and couldn't believe how you could draw such intricate things and still pay attention to what the professor was saying."

"Oh." Chloe appears shocked, but before I can hear what the rest of her response is, the sound of the Insta-Pot has me heading to the kitchen to release the steam.

I gather the plates and utensils we'll need and place everything out along our small kitchen counter so we can all come to dish up. Our kitchen table only seats four, so we'll have to sit at the high countertop with barstools as well. Being bachelors, we usually eat in the living room, but spaghetti is better to be eaten at a table. Besides, we have company.

Once everything's ready, I holler for everyone to come and dish up. It doesn't take long before the kitchen's crowded, and everyone has a plate full of food that I hope tastes as good as it smells. Abby and I end up at the bar, while everyone else sits at the table. It doesn't take long before the once chatty room turns to silence.

Thankfully, as I glance over the room, everyone seems to be engrossed in their food, so the sudden silence isn't my cooking. When I finally take a bite, my mouth waters from the savory sauce. Damn. Not bad, if I do say so myself.

After a few minutes, Grey breaks the silence and stands to get seconds. "Jacobs, this tastes amazing. Thanks for cookin', man." He pats me on the back in appreciation as he walks into the kitchen.

Sydney and Chloe both say how much they appreciate the meal, and I play off their accolades the best I can. "No big deal. Glad everyone could make it."

"I could get used to you cooking." Abby grins, and my heart skips a beat.

Why did I invite everyone again when I could've had this beautiful woman to myself?

Before I let myself get carried away, I shake my head in a vain attempt to clear my thoughts. "I'm happy to cook anytime."

"Be careful what you offer, Drew," Chloe pipes in. "If you cook like this all the time, we might just suddenly appear for dinner every night." Laughter erupts in the room.

"That's always my plan," Grey admits. "I'm more than happy to clean if this man's cooking. In fact, if it weren't for him, I'd be eating at the school cafeteria every night."

Abby looks at me expectantly, to see if Grey's joking and

unfortunately, I must agree with him. "Well, it's a talent to boil water and not burn it," I deadpan.

"Hey, it was one time." Grey shakes his head as he takes his seat at the table again. "You're never going to let me live that down, are you?"

"Can you blame us?" DeShawn chuckles. "The pot had to be thrown away, and the place smelled of smoke for days."

Grey rolls his eyes and sighs heavily. "I know... I know... I deserve it. I totally forgot about it when my brother called. He'd been stationed overseas, and I got so excited to hear his voice, I didn't notice."

"Hey," I interject. "I would've done the same thing... but that doesn't mean I'm not going to give you shit about burning water. You know me better than that."

Grey's grin nearly splits his face in half. "I know... did you ever stop to think that maybe I just pretend I can't cook, because I like yours so much?"

DeShawn and I exchange glances, and for a slight moment, I wonder if he could be speaking some truth because of our visitors, but we decide better of it. "Naw..." we say at once, but I continue, "I'm sure your talent is cleaning, when it comes to meal prep."

"Boy, this is a tough crowd." I hear one of the girls at the table mumble, which earns more laughter.

Grey waves a hand dismissively in the air. "It's all good. The house reeked for weeks, and I can't blame them. I would never let that shit go if it had been one of them, no matter what the reason. I mean—come on—I burned water. Who does that?"

I see DeShawn mumble something to Chloe, but I don't quite catch it. But her reaction has her face turning a darker shade of pink. Whatever it was, I'm not privy to the joke.

After dinner, DeShawn asks, "Did we get dessert?" I eye him in surprise. He typically doesn't have a sweet tooth, and I honestly didn't even think to pick up something.

"Uh, no. I didn't." I shrug.

"I'm stuffed," Sydney says as she stands to take her dish to the sink, but Grey cuts her off.

"I have this. You all can just sit tight." Sydney hands off her plate to Grey. He sets it on his own, then carries them to rinse off before putting them in the dishwasher.

"Would anyone be up to some ice cream?" DeShawn asks the room.

"Who turns down ice cream?" Chloe asks incredulously.

"I can't eat another bite." Sydney pats her stomach. "That garlic bread was the devil."

"I'm full, too." Abby shakes her head as she stands to clear her place.

"I was thinking of heading to the ice cream shop up on campus. Anyone want to join me?" DeShawn offers the room.

"I gotta study for an exam tomorrow, but thanks for the offer," Grey announces as he puts the leftovers into some smaller dishes.

Sydney pipes in, "Me, too. This is my only night off this week, and I need to finish a paper." She glances at her watch then looks to her roommates expectantly.

Chloe looks from Sydney to DeShawn as if she's on the fence.

"I'd be happy to take you to ice cream, Chloe, if you're interested. I can drive you home when we finish."

Did he just ask her out? I look to Abby, who just shrugs. "I had brought my things over here so we could finish our chem assignment. I'm stuffed. Mind giving me a ride home later?"

"Of course," I offer with delight. Any excuse to spend more time with Abby is okay in my book.

Over Abby's shoulder, I notice Sydney eye Chloe and give her a not so subtle look that clearly states she doesn't approve, but it's gone before anyone else is any the wiser. Chloe just shrugs and glances to DeShawn. "Sydney drove. So..." She takes a deep breath as she glances at Sydney one more time, then surprises me with, "If you don't mind dropping me off, I'll take you up on that ice cream."

DeShawn's eyes light up as he hops up from the table. "Sure. Just let me get my keys and wallet."

Sydney thanks me again and says her goodbyes to Abby and Chloe. I swear she gives Chloe a warning about being careful, but I can't be certain. Abby starts a conversation with Grey as he finishes cleaning the kitchen, and my focus is drawn to her instead. I'm not sure what the deal is with DeShawn and Sydney, but at this point, it's not any of my business, so I dismiss it.

When I join the conversation, I realize they're talking about our recent trip to the beach. "So, what did you think of his aunt's cabin?" Grey asks as he wipes down the counter.

"It was a great getaway. I loved being so close to the beach so we could run on it in the morning."

"Yeah." Grey nods in agreement. "Drew takes us down

before the season starts to get away from it all. Being from Colorado, I jump at any chance I can to go to the beach with Drew, even if it does rain a lot here in Washington."

"It doesn't rain *that* often. But sweatshirts are worn all year round at the beach, so there's that." Abby shrugs as if that should explain everything.

"There's nothing like the beach, come rain or shine," Grey adds as he wipes down the last of the counter. "Well... it's been great getting to know you, Abby. I'm sorry to cut this short, but I'm meeting my study group on campus in about twenty minutes. I'm sure I'll see you around."

"It was nice to meet you, too," Abby chimes in. "See ya soon."

Grey nods in agreement, and I add, "Thanks for cleaning up, man."

Grey grins wide as he chortles. "No problem. I'll meet you at the gym tomorrow." There's something about the way he says it makes me think he might be doing more than studying tonight, especially since he hasn't been home much. But when he returns a few minutes later with only his backpack, I dismiss it. Knowing Grey like I do, he would've taken his gym bag to have a sleepover.

The minute the door clicks shut, I close the distance between Abby and myself. Reaching out to her hip, I pull her close. Her scent's been driving me wild all night. I deserve a medal for keeping my distance, but now that we're alone, all bets are off.

She reaches out like the siren she is to cup my face and pulls me toward her. When our soft lips touch, instinctually I open to let her in. When her tongue mingles with mine, I find myself lifting her to close the distance between our heights onto the counter. Here she is the perfect height, and I nestle between her legs to be closer to her. My hand grips the nape of her neck as my fingers run through her soft hair. When she lets out the slightest moan, my dick turns to steel. Fuck, what this woman does to me.

In all too short of time, she pulls away, panting. When her eyes lock onto mine, I can see heat exploding. Her pupils are dilated, and her cheeks flush. Abby is so beautiful, I can barely think.

Eventually, she breaks the silence with, "Do you think we should study?"

Usually, I'm the taskmaster when it comes to studying, but I don't want to think about chemistry that only comes from our textbook. In my lust-filled haze, it takes everything in me to realize she has a point. But maybe if I'm lucky, when we finish studying, I can convince her to pick up where we left off.

29

ABBY

IS it really a walk of shame if you have no regrets?

Sure, I'm in the same clothes as yesterday, but it's the asscrack of dawn and no one cares about it at this hour. Except Drew, of course; he must work out before his first class. But I will never regret the night we shared together.

As I climb the stairs to my apartment and unlock the door, I turn to wave at Drew before he pulls away. Even from here, I can tell he'd rather not leave me. But duty calls.

Yes. I made sure we kept our focus and studied for today. Our diligence over this semester has paid off, and we finished in record time. When we heard DeShawn's vehicle pull up, Drew suggested we finish in his bedroom. Thankfully, we were basically done because with a bed in sight, our chemistry sizzled to epic proportions.

The next thing I knew, clothes were flung everywhere, and I was on the brink of an orgasm of a lifetime. He barely had touched me, and I went off like the Fourth of July. Of course, then I wanted to take the edge off for Drew, and he was more than willing to let me. I'll never forget how his jaw dropped or how dark his eyes turned when I dropped to my knees in full appreciation.

I lost count of the orgasms and drifted off into a dreamless state, feeling both boneless and like I was floating in the air. The last thing I remember was him pulling me close and kissing me one last time.

When his alarm went off at five a.m., I hadn't even realized I'd stayed the night. He woke me in the most memorable way, with that wicked mouth of his. Somehow, we managed leave his house so he could drop me off and still get to the gym on time.

No. This is most definitely *not* a walk of shame.

There's nothing shameful about Drew Jacobs. In fact, with the languid state he has left me in, I'm dying to return.

When I enter my apartment, it's still silent. I make my way to my room and gather what I'll need to take a shower to start my day. Just as I finish my breakfast, my phone vibrates with an incoming text.

Drew: Hey, Angel, just got done with the gym. Have time for breakfast?

Me: I just ate. But I can make you something.

Drew: No worries. I'll grab something on campus.

Me: I really don't mind.

Drew: Nah. It's okay. Are you leaving for campus soon? I can swing by and pick you up.

Me: I'd planned on walking to campus in the next thirty min. If it's not too much trouble, I'll take the ride.

Let's be real. I just want more time with Drew. The thought alone has goose bumps running up my spine.

Drew: See you in five. I'm at the light near your apartment.

Instead of replying, I quickly put my dish in the dishwasher and rush to the bathroom to brush my teeth again. By the time he knocks lightly on my door, I'm grabbing my backpack and ready to leave.

When I open the door, Drew takes my breath away. His hair is wet from the shower, and his masculine scent mixed with his cologne makes my stomach somersault. What does it for me is the way his dark-blue eyes heat when they land on mine. As if he can read my mind, he pulls me in for a searing kiss.

Holy hell, Drew can kiss.

When he pulls back all too soon, he huskily whispers, "How can I miss you already?" Then he shakes his head as if to clear his thoughts. "You ready?"

I step out and pull the door behind me. "Yep. Since you're

driving me, mind if we stop by the coffee shop? Somebody wore me out last night and if I'm going to make it through the day, I need a caffeine fix."

Drew's eyes widen at my accusation, and his grin makes him even sexier. "Um... I didn't hear any complaints."

I shake my head dismissively. "Nope," I draw out. "I certainly am *not* complaining." But I pin him with a stare to show my seriousness. "But I do need caffeine."

This earns me a light chuckle. "Oh, Angel. What am I going to do with you?"

Though I'm sure he meant it as a rhetorical question, I give him a wicked grin and turn on the sass. "Just about anything you damn well please."

When Drew's lips form the perfect 'O,' I quickly run down the stairs to feign waiting patiently by his car.

Though I make it through the day with ease, by the time I get home that evening, I'm exhausted. Living on barely any sleep will do that to you. I still need to finish a paper, but I've worked on it between classes, so it shouldn't take me too long.

When I walk in the door to my apartment, I spot Sydney lounging on the couch watching TV. She's curled up in a blanket, and her hair is pulled in a messy bun. "How was your day?" she asks as I plop down beside her.

"Long," I groan. "I'm glad I don't have much to do before bed, or I'd be screwed."

"I take it you and Drew enjoyed yourself last night," she accuses and instantly, I feel heat in my cheeks.

There's no point in denying it, so I simply nod in agreement.

"I could've sworn you didn't come home until early this morning, but I heard him knock on the door this morning. Was I wrong?"

"No, you heard right. He had to work out with the team this morning, so he dropped me off at the ass-crack of dawn, then he picked me up for class when he was finished."

"Interesting," she draws out.

"What?" I ask, wondering why I feel defensive suddenly.

Syd shakes her head as if she's clearing her thoughts away, "It's nothing... just making an observation, Abs. He seems pretty into you. How do you feel about him?"

I sigh heavily and play with the silver bracelet I was given for high school graduation. "He's pretty special," I admit. "But I'm still concerned about the timing of things. For all I know, we could end up on opposite sides of the country in a mere matter of months. Is it worth the risk to get invested like this?"

Syd pats me on the thigh and shakes her head. "I can't answer that for you. But I will say, more people regret the things they didn't do in life, than the things they have. Do you really want to walk away from a guy you're really connecting with? I saw the way he looks at you. Hell, you even went away for the weekend with him, twice."

"The first time was simply because he needed me," I say in defense. She's making this sound way more serious than it is.

Sydney's eyes roll to the back of her head. "Girl, you're so stubborn. It's perfectly okay to like him. Even if you don't know where you'll be next year. Hell. For all you know, you could end up at the same school, and all this worry will be for nothing."

I level her with a glare. "Syd. The odds are extremely stacked against us that two people from the undergrad program will be selected to the same med school."

"Why don't you just take a page out of my book and enjoy the moment?" Sydney suggests as a consolation. "Drew's one of the good guys."

Yes. He sure is.

"Have you seen Chloe today?" I ask to change the subject. Syd eyes me knowingly, but lets me get away with it.

"No. I think she may be avoiding me. I was studying in my room when she came home last night, and she didn't bother to stop by like usual."

"Well, can you blame her? You all but gave her a flat out warning against DeShawn. What is it you have against him, anyway?"

"He's quite the player off the court. I just don't want her getting hurt."

"Uh, last I checked, I'm sure that decision's up to Chloe. You and I both know she usually has her head screwed on straight, so if DeShawn's interested in her... I say let her be," I warn. "Besides, it's not like he's been known to be a cheater or anything. He's young, virile, and at the top of his game. What single guy wouldn't want to play the field? If you were in his shoes, I'm sure you'd probably do the same."

"I'm not slut shaming him. There's nothing wrong with casual hookups. I just want to make sure Chloe keeps her heart off her sleeve and see him for what he is." Sydney shrugs as if that should explain everything.

But I shake my head, protesting her point. "I still say we

stay out of it. Weren't you just telling me to have fun and let things happen?"

When I raise an eyebrow in her direction, she simply rolls her eyes and states, "You're different."

I pull a face telling her she's crazy—let's face it—she makes zero sense.

Syd lets out an exasperated sigh. "You're always taking the safe bet. You have everything planned out to a T, and never let loose to just let life take you where it may."

"I'm not that predictable," I scoff and of course, Syd raises that damn eyebrow and says nothing in return.

"What?" I ask defensively. "I know how to have fun."

"Come on, Abs. You know I'm right." But then, she pauses as she lifts her finger to her chin and looks to the ceiling as if it has some hidden answer.

I wait to see what's going on in that head of hers.

"Well..." she draws out. "I guess you *could* say going to the beach with Drew was spontaneous. Hell. Most of what you've done since you've met, you've had little control over... Maybe you are loosening up."

Rolling my eyes. "Gee. Thanks. You know I don't have a lot of time, and my track record with guys hasn't been stellar lately. But give me a break. I'm flexible and don't have to have everything planned."

"If you say so..." Syd sing-songs, then recovers. "It's okay, Abs. I love you anyway."

"Gee... I love you, too." Sarcasm drips off my tongue, which only causes her to laugh.

What a brat.

I ignore her, and we return to the program on TV. After a few minutes of watching the hero make a fool of himself to win the girl back, Syd changes the subject. "So now that you and Drew are a thing, you're coming to all the home basketball games with me, right?"

Catching me off guard, I only manage, "Uhhh..." as I contemplate my options. "Sure, I love watching Drew play, but there's no way I can attend *every* home game. Drew must know that, right?"

"Oh, come on, Abs. You can't seriously be contemplating this?"

"We'll see," I commit. But when I think about Drew in his sexy uniform running up and down the court with pure determination spread across his face, I know the answer plain as day. *I'm not going to miss one single game if I can help it.*

30

DREW

IT FEELS like forever since Abby and I spent the weekend at my aunt's cabin. These past few weeks have been extremely hectic, but I wouldn't change them for the world. Having never had to juggle basketball, school, and dating into my already packed schedule, I'm doing my best to find a balance.

Thank God, Abby proved me right when it comes to being studious. We're set to meet after her shift at the library to study in a private room. As I make my way across campus, I pop into the convenience store and pick up some snacks to sneak into the library. I've noticed the few times I've shopped with Abby, she typically picks up a Symphony bar, so I grab one and a bag of Nibs for myself. I'm in the mood for some licorice, and I might as well get her a sugar fix, too.

As usual, I arrive early and wait for Abby in the corridor near the study rooms. She had never returned my text to tell me which room she reserved, so I drop my bag to the floor and lean against the wall to wait.

When a study room opens, a girl I recognize but can't quite place steps out. Her face is in her phone, so she doesn't see me. Before I can say anything to warn her, she bumps into me and nearly falls backward.

"Whoa," I say as I steady her. "You okay?" I offer as I reach out an arm.

"Oh..." she says in surprise. "Drew. I didn't see you."

Shit. I wish I could remember her name. She's a friend of a girl Grey used to date, but I can't for the life of me remember her name. Shelby... Shawna...Cheryl...

I don't know. And it doesn't really matter. It's not like I've talked to her again since Grey asked DeShawn and me to go on a group date with her and her friends our freshman year.

"It's so great to see you again, Drew." She reaches out and places a hand on my arm, but she holds on for much longer than I'm comfortable with. "I was wondering when I'd see you again. It seems like ages ago since we all went out together. What are you up to these days?"

I shrug and politely step back to put some space between us as she eyes me up and down appreciatively. Sure, there was a time I enjoyed my ego being stroked, but now it feels wrong in all sorts of ways. Mainly because she's not Abby. "Oh, you know... basketball and school."

"Yeah, I've watched you play a few times this season. We have a real chance of going to the playoffs again, thanks to you."

I shrug it off. "Yeah. It's a team effort, and we're making every game count."

"So..." She eyes me up and down once more. "Do you still have that rule about not dating during the season?"

Thankfully, before I have the chance to respond, Abby comes around the corner, and I can't help the smile that spreads across my face as I take her in. Her long hair is piled into a knot on the top of her head, and she's wearing the sweatshirt she bought at the beach. She couldn't look sexier if she tried.

"Drew?" the girl before me asks, regaining my attention.

"Sorry." I clear my throat, and it takes everything in me not to eat up the space between Abby and me. "Uh... what did you ask?"

She lets out a huff in exasperation. "I asked," she says a little louder than necessary, "if you still have that rule of no dating during the season."

"Nope," Abby exaggerates from behind the girl, whom I still can't remember the name of, then gives me a devilish smile. "Drew's most certainly given up that rule."

The girl before me gasps then turns to look at Abby. I'm not sure if it's due to being startled or Abby's announcement. But I absolutely love how Abby just stakes her claim on me. Damn, feistiness makes me want to kiss that grin off her beautiful face.

The girl asks in disbelief, "And you are?"

Abby holds out her hand to shake. "I'm Abby," as if that should explain everything. Well, to me it does. The girl between us—not so much.

The girl looks back and forth, and her mouth hangs slightly ajar, not quite jaw dropping, but nowhere near stoic either. If it wouldn't be considered rude, I'd almost laugh at her fish impression. "Uh," she huffs. "I thought you said you didn't date during the season." She looks back and forth between me and Abby.

I just shrug. There's no reason I must explain myself in this situation. Obviously, things have changed, but before I can say so, I'm interrupted, "What's she got that I didn't?" she asks, and I'm not certain she meant to say it aloud.

So that there can be no uncertainty, I reach my hand out to Abby and pull her near me, like the Neanderthal I am and boldly state, "Me."

The girl doesn't say another word but swivels on her heels and storms off in the opposite direction, leaving Abby and me to stare at her retreating back.

"What the hell was that all about?" Abby asks when the girl walks around the corner.

I shake my head in disbelief of the whole scene. "I have no freaking idea. I met her freshman year, and we hung out in a group one time. I honestly don't even remember her name. All we did was talk one night in a restaurant during dinner. I haven't seen her since. Why in the world would she think I would suddenly be interested in her is beyond me."

"I saw the entire thing as I approached. Does this happen to you often?" Abby sounds almost playful, and I'm glad she knows without a doubt nothing was going on.

"Uh, I can't say that experience... or whatever you'd call it... has happened. I'm glad you showed up when you did."

"Awww." Abby pretends to pout like a small child. "Is Drew afraid of a little ole' girl hitting on him?"

Rolling my eyes, I shake my head. "Okay, Angel, that's enough. Are you ready to study, or what?" Having no desire to continue this conversation, I grab my backpack, throw it over my shoulder, and reach for Abby's hand. "Point me to our study room, and let's get to it."

Yeah, I don't miss the exaggerated eye roll, but thankfully, Abby leads us three doors down to the left. Damn, she's adorable. When she's on a mission, it's like her legs move in hyper speed. Once inside, I choose the chair furthest in the room, and Abby sits at the table across from me. She gets right to work on pulling out her material and spreading them out on the desk, so she can be the most productive.

I go through the process of pulling out my laptop and notebook I've been using to conduct my research for my paper that's due later this week. We finished our chem assignment yesterday, but not wanting to lose any time I can spend with her, we've made it a routine to study a few times a week on campus after she gets off work.

Before she gets too into her studies, I reach into my bag and pull out the candy I bought for her. Sliding the bar across the table, I capture Abby's attention. At first, her shocked expression simply stares at my contraband.

"Drew..." she draws out, "you know we're not supposed to eat in here. I'm supposed to enforce these things, not break them myself." Her mortified expression is almost comical.

"Awww... Come on, Angel, I'm not trying to cause trouble. You can save it for later if you like."

Abby lets out a loud huff but quickly snags the Symphony bar and stashes it in her bag. "Thank you for thinking of me.

Let's finish studying, so I can eat it later. No thanks to you, now I'm craving chocolate."

This earns her a laugh from me. "Sorry to be such a bad influence," I tease.

Abby says nothing but blows out an exasperated sigh, making me want to reach across the table and kiss that look off her face.

FUCCKKK! Now that's all I want to do. Does she have to be so sexy?

Somehow, I manage to turn my attention to my paper. I spend the next few minutes reading over my notes. But when Abby reaches up to take her hair out of her messy bun, she completely holds my attention. Even though I've seen her do this a million times while studying, the scent of citrus and pear has my mouth watering. I try not to stare, but it's nearly impossible.

"What?" she asks defensively.

So much for subtlety, Jacobs, I chastise myself. Though let's be honest, I could stare at her all day, if I could get away with it.

Geez, man, get it together.

I shake my head to clear my thoughts. "It's nothing."

Abby squints her eyes as if she's trying to figure out a difficult puzzle. "What were you looking at? Do I have something on my face?"

"No," I draw out on a sigh. "Just enjoying the view."

This earns me a scoff from Abby. "Okay, whatever you say," she deadpans and turns her focus back to her book.

Something feels off.

Does she not know how beautiful she is?

My gut clenches, hoping I'm reading more into this than I should.

"Abby?" I say barely above a whisper, getting her attention. When her eyes find mine, we stare for a long moment at one another. "Have I offended you?"

Confusion morphs across her features. "Why would you ask that?"

"I don't know. I just wanted to make sure you knew back there." I point to the hallway. "You do know you're the only one I'm interested in, right?"

Her jaw drops slightly then quickly returns to its normal position. "Uh, since I'm the one in your bed practically every night, I'd better be."

Damn, I love her sass.

Wait, did I say love?

Instead of making anything of my realization, I play it off. "You can bet your sweet ass you're the only one I'm interested in. You're mine... and mine alone."

"The road goes both ways, Drew. And PS—I wasn't bothered by it at all. It was obvious you weren't interested in her by the way you looked at me when I came around the corner. If anything, you looked annoyed that you had to be talking to her in the first place."

Well, at least that's settled.

I shake my head at the memory. "I still can't believe how possessive she was. We literally bumped into one another in the hall after not speaking for years, and she had the audacity to think she could stake a claim to me?"

"That is kinda weird," Abby admits in a shrug. But then her expression changes to one I recognize well. It's filled with her heated desire and hope. "What do you say we hurry up and finish here, then go back to my place for some dinner? Chloe's working, and Sydney has a date tonight. We should have the place to ourselves." Abby waggles an eyebrow, and I want to say to hell with our studies right now.

"How much more of your assignment do you have to do?" I ask eagerly. I for one could finish this paper tomorrow and still have plenty of time. Knowing I have two out-of-town games later this week, I'd much rather spend some one-on-one time with Abby.

"It won't take me too long. I've worked on it between classes so if I *focus*, I should be able to knock it out sooner."

My lips turn up at her blatant hint. "Okay. I'll be ready when you're done. My paper isn't due until next week. Chop, chop," I tease. "Get to work, lady, so we can grab some dinner."

It isn't even an hour later, and we're walking into Abby's quiet apartment. I'd managed to get a few pages written, but my concentration was complete shit. Every move Abby made, I was acutely aware.

Once inside, she walks to her bedroom to put her bag away, while I stay out in the living room. It takes me all of thirty seconds to see a big envelope propped up on the kitchen table with Abby's name written on a blue sticky note. The moment I recognize what it might be, I call out to Abby. "Hey, Abs, there's something out here you might want to look at."

God, I hope this is what I think it is. If not, our plans for the evening are about to change.

Within seconds, she's by my side. "What is it?" Curiosity evident in her voice.

I point to the large white envelope on the table. "It looks like you have some mail."

It doesn't look too thin, so this is a good thing, right? Please let it be good for Abby's sake. She deserves this.

Abby gasps and lunges for the mail. It takes her less than three seconds to carefully open the envelope and reveal its contents. I wait expectantly as she pulls out a couple of sheets of paper and begins to read them.

Suddenly, she looks to me wide-eyed and screams, "Ohmigod! Ohmigod! Ohmigod! I can't believe it."

Not being able to contain my excitement for her, I pull her in for a hug. Abby climbs me like a tree and wraps her legs around me in the biggest full-body bear hug I've ever received. Then she shouts in my ear, "Ohmigod! Ohmigod!"

"I take it congratulations are in order?" I look expectantly at the letter when she releases the hold around my neck to look me in the eye.

"I got in! I can't believe it, Drew. I fucking got in!"

I proudly grin as I squeeze her once more. "I knew you could do it."

After kissing the hell out of Abby, I set her down, and she does the most adorable happy dance I've ever seen. It's a combination between running in place, like she's on speed, and pumping her fists into the air. Her enthusiasm's so infectious I break out into a happy dance of my own to celebrate with her. Of course, this makes her burst into a fit of laughter.

After a few moments, she takes a deep calming breath.

"Drew, I got into Stanford. I freaking got into Stanford. It's not my first choice, but I'd be happy as hell to go there for med school."

"You and me both, Angel. I'm so proud of you. You've worked your ass off, and you deserve this."

"Wait." She stops abruptly. "Have you heard back from any of the schools you've applied to?"

"Nope, not yet." I shrug dismissively. "But I'm sure I will soon."

Abby chews on her bottom lip for a moment, and I reach out to free it from her teeth with my thumb. "Why the face?"

"I shouldn't be celebrating if you haven't heard yet."

"Uh, I didn't apply to Stanford. But we most certainly should be celebrating. I'm sure we'll hear back from other schools in the coming weeks. Come on," I say as I pull her into the kitchen. "Let's make dinner then I can show you how excited I am for you."

Between the two of us, Abby and I make dinner quickly. Since we have her apartment all to ourselves for a few more hours, we celebrate by watching a movie on the couch. I offer to take her out somewhere, but Abby insists she'd rather stay in and have a brainless night of fun. Just as the opening credits roll, the front door to the apartment flies open, and Sydney comes bursting into the living room and slams the door.

Anger rolls off her in waves. Her breathing's ragged, and her fists are balled at her sides. When she spots us on the couch, she takes a deep breath to calm herself. "Sorry to interrupt, but I'm so pissed right now, I could scream."

"What's wrong?" Abby bolts up from the couch to comfort her friend.

Sydney looks from Abby to me and back again. Shaking her head, she says, "I don't want to ruin your evening. I'll just go hang out in my room."

Clearly something's happened. Sydney's usually calm and carefree. Over the past few weeks, I'd like to think we were all friends. Abby had mentioned she'd been on a date earlier... what if something happened to her?

"That's not necessary," I point out as I reach for the remote to turn off the TV. "You're not interrupting anything. What's going on, Syd? Are you okay?"

Sydney takes in a deep breath and holds it for a while before slowly letting it out. I can see her visibly relax, which makes me less on edge. Though I won't dismiss this completely until I know some asshole didn't hurt her.

"Ohmigod! You aren't going to believe what happened..." Sydney shrugs as she plops down in the oversized chair next to the couch, Abby returns to her place next to me.

"What?" I ask, encouraging her to continue. My nerves are on edge just waiting to react. I take a moment to look her over with care. Nothing seems out of place, but I'll hold off until she explains what's wrong.

"I just had the date from hell!" she practically shouts. "Hell, I tell you... I mean I didn't think it could get any worse, but no... the train wreck kept rolling, and I couldn't get the fuck off the tracks fast enough."

This doesn't sound so bad, so I relax a little into the couch and glance at Abby to take the lead from here. Wait... *Is she covering her face to conceal a laugh?*

I can't give it more thought because Sydney keeps steam rolling the conversation. "First, Brad. Yes, his actual fucking name is Brad... has been asking me out for weeks. I'd kept putting him off because we met when I served him his drink at the bar. You know that's a hard pass. I never date guys who ask me out there. I never know if it's the alcohol talking or if they think I'm an easy mark." She takes a deep breath then continues to ramble. "But fucking Brad was persistent. We ended up seeing one another on campus one day and started talking. We'd bump into each other often, and he kept asking me out. But our schedules never worked. He told me how he wanted to take me to a nice dinner and get to know me better. Finally, we both had tonight free, so I thought, why not take a chance on him..." Sydney stops and stares at the ceiling, taking deep breaths to calm herself.

"Okay..." Abby draws out. "So, what happened?"

"You know those 80s movies I love so much? Well, fucking Brad was like the ultimate douche, times a million, from one of those. He insisted he pick me up, which I thought was a good start. Then he took me to one of the nicest restaurants in town. Once again, I must admit I was impressed. Though I could care less about fancy restaurants, I appreciated his effort. The date starts out typical, and then it takes a freaking nosedive like you wouldn't believe. Apparently, *Brad...*"

Yes, she says his name like an expletive, and I find myself mirroring Abby's expression to keep myself from laughing.

The girl's worked up. I almost feel sorry for Brad. But still... I'd better hold off on judgement.

"Well... how do I put this?" She tilts her head to the ceiling, like it holds all the answers. "Let's see... he's not only notoriously cheap, but he's a deadbeat dad."

"What?" Abby gasps. "Explain."

"Brad apparently has a two-year-old who he never sees because the decent guy that he is, doesn't like to spend the gas money to drive three hours back to his hometown to see said child. He had the audacity to go on for twenty minutes telling me how he thinks the kid is too young to know any better, and all he does is cost money when he gets him anyway. So, why bother to show up at all. Seriously. How can someone say this about their child?"

"Sounds like a winner," Abby deadpans, but I still can't see why this date was so horrible.

"Oh, you're telling me." Sydney's sarcasm's thick by this point. "When we got to the restaurant, he specifically told me to order anything I'd like. I ordered my favorite, chicken marsala and some mixed vegetables, while he ordered some crab puffs as a starter and the shrimp scampi. At first, when he'd mentioned having a kid with his girlfriend from high school, I was okay with it. People don't always stay together. But then when he went on and on about how much of an inconvenience this poor child was, I was done and couldn't wait for the check to come fast enough. I purposely told the waiter I was done as soon as Brad took his last bite to hurry things along."

"God, what a loser," I mumble under my breath, unable to keep my thoughts in.

"Exactly." Sydney pins me with wide eyes. "But, I haven't even gotten to the worst part."

"Seriously?" Abby interrupts. "How can it get any worse?"

"No. When the check comes, fucking Brad gets out his phone to use his calculator. He divided our check by item. He had the audacity to charge me for my meal, my drink, and forty percent of the crab puffs because I ate four of the ten. He was kind enough to split the tax in half and only calculated for a ten percent for a tip."

"You're kidding me," I say in disbelief after picking my jaw up from the floor.

"No." She shakes her head. "I wish I were. Seriously, I can't make this shit up if you paid me."

"How did you get home?" Leave it to Abby to be practical.

Sydney sits up taller, and she smiles wickedly. "Oh, I got up from the table, walked over to the waiter, and handed him sixty bucks, which was more than my portion of the bill, by the way. I told him my date was a total cheapskate and not to let him know how much I'd paid. Stick him with the entire bill and tell him I'll find my own way home. I was out the door and in an Uber within minutes. I'd already ordered one when Brad got out his calculator."

Holy shit. Sydney's a badass through and through.

Still shaking my head in disbelief I chuckle at my next thought. "I'm sure Brad was sweating bullets when he found out he'd been stuck with the bill."

"Serves him right," Abby pipes in. "God, what a dick move! I'm so sorry that happened to you."

Sydney groans loudly as she flops back in her chair. "Uggh, I am so over guys. I am officially on a dick-diet until further notice. Men suck."

"Not all of them." Abby squeezes my hand and smiles apologetically.

Sydney looks over to me. "No offense, Drew, but men are total dicks, and I'm done with them."

"Hey, I'm not a 'fucking Brad.'" I use air quotes to tease. "But I totally get why you'd want a break after that."

"I'm done with trying. Every guy I think I may be interested in is either a liar, cheater, and now a cheapskate. You might be the only decent one left."

Chuckling, I roll my eyes. "We're not all douches. But thanks for the vote of confidence."

Sydney's quiet for a long moment then suddenly jumps out of her chair, catching me off guard. "I think I'll go for a run and let you get back to your evening."

"You sure you don't want to watch a movie with us to get your mind off things?"

"No, I'm gonna hit the gym. I'd rather run outside, but since it's dark, I'll play it safe."

"You sure? You're more than welcome to stay. Or if you need to talk more with Abby, I can head back to my place," I offer, knowing she likely needs Abby more than I do at this point.

Sydney shakes her head. "No, I'm good. I'm just going to

run off my frustration, so I can get some sleep tonight. Seriously though, I'm taking a major break from guys."

Abby laughs. "I don't blame you."

As soon as Sydney's left, Abby snuggles up to me on the couch. Before she presses play on the movie, she looks up to me and says, "Thank you."

"What for?" I ask, having no idea where she's going with her train of thought.

"For being you... For your willingness to leave because you thought she might need a friend, and most important for being nothing like 'fucking Brad.'"

"Angel, that's one thing you'll never have to worry about," I whisper as I close the distance between us and kiss her senseless.

31

ABBY

AS I RUSH through my apartment door, I hear Sydney shout, "Where the hell have you been?"

"Uh, I had to work longer to cover a shift for someone. Don't get your undies in a twist. We still have plenty of time to get there," I rush out as I slip into my bedroom and change into the CRU jersey Drew picked up for me. Thankfully, this one is in my size and happens to have Drew's number on the back, so I feel a sense of pride as I wear it for him.

Drew's been out of town until late last night and has a game that starts in less than an hour. I haven't seen him since the night of Sydney's disaster of a date. When he'd texted earlier, he told me not to make any plans afterward. He has something he can't wait to tell me in person. I'm dying to know what it is.

Sydney storms into my room. "You know this is a playoff game, right? The student section's gonna be packed. If they win this one and both games next week, they'll be strong contenders in the championship tournament."

"I know. I know. Just let me go to the bathroom, and we can get out of here."

The arena is packed when we arrive. Not only is there a long line for students to enter, we're packed into the student seating like sardines. Sydney notices a guy from her class that has two seats next to him, and the next thing I know, we've found ourselves spots for the game.

My eyes immediately find Drew and follow him as he warms up. Even from this distance, his sexy arms get to me. I can see his well-defined muscles and corded veins from here. He's pumped and ready to win this game, by the sheer look of determination on his face. As if he can sense me staring at him, once he makes a lay-in, his eyes find mine in a crowded room, and his face morphs into the most beautiful smile, nearly taking my breath away.

God, Drew is gorgeous.

My thoughts are interrupted by the snarky voice of the girl in front of me. "Ohmigod! Did you see the way Drew Jacobs just looked at me? I swear he was looking right at me and winked."

"No way! You're kidding, right? Wait... Did he just wink at you?"

Sydney must hear her, too. She nudges me with her elbow and rolls her eyes. The way she's biting down on her lip lets me know she wants to burst out laughing. We both know without a doubt where his focus is.

The first girl sighs heavily. "He's seriously one of the

hottest players on the team, besides, well... DeShawn. God, what would it be like to kiss a sexy beast like Drew?"

Sydney looks to me, waggles her eyebrows, and mouths, "Tell her what it's really like."

I emphatically shake my head and whisper shout, "No!"

I'll keep those thoughts to myself, thank you very much.

The girl in front of Syd interrupts my thoughts. "Oh, don't even get me started with DeShawn. I had a friend who dated him last year, and she *always* had something great to say about him."

Seriously? Is she rating him on his sexpertise? Sure, DeShawn's a good-looking guy, but this is a bit much.

The next thing I know, the first girl from in front of us screams as loud as can be, "I love you, Drew!"

What. The. Fuck?

Did she just scream that for the entire arena to hear?

One look at Sydney, and I know I wasn't hearing things. We lose any composure we'd been holding in and burst out laughing so hard, we're gasping for air before forcing ourselves to stop. I've heard Drew tell some crazy stories, but this seriously takes the cake. How complete strangers can have such a reaction to him is beyond me.

The girls in front of us both glance in our direction. When their eyes bug out as if we've lost minds, Syd and I only laugh harder. Yeah, Drew's sexy and hot as hell, but come on, people. Get a life already. He's not God's gift to all womankind. He's just a man, well, my man... and if I have anything to do with it, they won't stand a chance with him.

Thankfully, the game starts, and my attention is quickly

focused on Drew. We score right off the bat. But Utah comes back with a vengeance and scores a three-pointer.

Holy shit. What a shot!

I don't care which team you're rooting for, it was an impressive shot. I just wish it had been our boys to make it. I look to Sydney, whose eyes are wide, and she assures me, "It's okay. Only the first three points. We can do this!"

Within the first five minutes, CRU hits its stride, and they are on fire throughout the game. They outmatch Utah at every turn. We make some amazing defensive plays, which help us take an early lead and hold it through halftime. There's a point in the second half where Utah has a great run. Sydney and I are on our feet screaming with the rest of the fans, but CRU pulls ahead and finishes off with a win.

Whew. I'm exhausted, and I haven't stepped foot on the court.

As I look to Drew, I can clearly see sweat dripping off him. His face is flushed but the grin that splits his face in half is infectious. My smile matches his as he shakes hands with the opposing team. When his teammates congratulate each other with fist bumps and chest bumps, I can't help but wonder if those hurt.

Eventually, Sydney and I make our way out of the arena, and I lose sight of Drew. As much as I'd like to wait for him, I fully agree with his plan. It's easier for him to find me when it's over. He's been called into a press conference and most importantly, must shower before coming to see me. Don't get me wrong. I love Drew sweaty, but I prefer to be the one that helps create it.

I rush to the door when I hear Drew knock a little over an hour later. Drew takes my breath away when he pulls me to him and kisses the living shit out of me. He smells sexy as hell, and my lips naturally part to let him in. His low growl sets my nerves on fire, and I want to climb him like a tree. As if he can read my mind, he lifts me off the floor, and I easily drape my legs around his hips.

Maybe it's the effect of pulling off a big win or the fact that we haven't seen one another in almost a week, but it feels like Drew can't get enough of me. And there's no way I'm denying this man anything. He steps into my apartment, and I think I hear the door close, but do I even care? All that matters is being in his arms.

One hand grips my ass as the other guides our kiss from the base of my neck. Holy fuck. If he keeps this up, I'm going to come from this kiss alone. I think we're moving, but I'm too consumed by all that is Drew to notice. I vaguely hear the click of a door, and I feel Drew lay me on my bed, never breaking our kiss.

I let go of his hips and quickly push my way up the bed, to make room for the both of us. Not wanting there to be anything between us, I quickly grab at the hem of his shirt, and he takes the hint to pull it over his head with one hand, in the sexy way that men do.

While he does that, I sit up, ripping the shirt I'm wearing over my head. Like a magnet drawn to metal, Drew quickly descends over my body, peppering kisses along the way. He starts at my belly button, licking and sucking his way up my rib cage.

God, that feels amazing. My nipples harden, and my hips naturally rise to meet his. In one fluid swoop, he has my bra undone and sighs heavily in appreciation when my boobs are freed. His cool breath creates a breeze across my nipples. If he's not careful, they'll cut steel.

Damn, they're hard. I need relief.

"Drew," I practically pant out. "Need you..."

"I'm right here, Angel." Drew's sexy voice reverberates up my spine, making me desperate. He kisses up my collarbone and along my jawline until he finds my lips again, rendering me speechless.

After all too short of time, he pulls back, nearly breathless. We stare at one another for an immeasurable moment. His large hand caresses the side of my face, brushing my hair back.

"Hi," I whisper, and his dimple pops, making butterflies swarm in my stomach.

Drew's stare is intense, and I've never felt more connected to him as I do in this moment. He closes the distance between our lips and kisses me with more emotion than I can even describe. When he pulls back, his words take my breath away.

"I love you, Abby." He gives me a brief peck then pulls back to look me square in the eyes again. My heart races, and more emotions than I can contain flow through me. "I love you more than I've loved anyone," he whispers, then he closes his eyes to lean his forehead on mine.

Words. Abby. You need words. I think to myself. In this moment, I know without a doubt, I love Drew more than anything as well. But I'm so filled with emotion, it takes me a breath to remember how to speak.

When I finally find my voice, I reach up and caress his beautiful face. When he opens his eyes, I lock mine onto his, so he knows how I feel.

"I love you, too, Drew."

Drew's grin lights up the room. He leans down to kiss me senseless once again. Before I know it, he's removed what's left of my clothes. He's in no hurry as he worships every inch of my body. He takes me higher than I could ever imagine. First time in my life, I find what it means to make love to someone.

32

DREW

I TAKE my time loving Abby the only way I know how. Every nip, lick, and suck puts my body on hyperdrive, making me want to release into her, but I hold off until she climaxes at least twice. Only then do I finally rid myself of my jeans and put on a condom in record time. By the time I bury myself in Abby, she's more than ready for me. I swivel my hips the way I've learned she loves and before too long, we're both falling off the cliff into oblivion. Abby feels incredible as she pulses around me, and her body shifts from stiff to liquid in a matter of heartbeats. Once she's completely come down from her high, I gently remove myself to take care of the condom in the bathroom that adjoins her room.

When I return to the bed, Abby's nearly lifeless body shifts slightly so she can watch me move across the room. Even though her eyes heat, she remains boneless and doesn't move in my direction. I love knowing I've done this to her. When she comes like she just did, I know she's wrecked for the near future.

I quickly adjust the blankets to cover us as I slide between the sheets with her. Propping my head on my elbow, I lie on my side and admire all that is Abby. I run my fingers along her abdomen, tracing along her rib cage, and circle her breasts. "You are so beautiful, Angel. Sorry I attacked you at the door. I had every intention of taking you out to celebrate. But when you climbed me like a spider monkey, I let my body take control."

This earns me a beautiful laugh. Her satisfied smile tells me all I need, but of course, her sass can't stay away. "Uh, did you hear me complaining?"

Of course, this only spurs me on. "No, I don't believe I did. I think if I loved you any harder, we would've broken the bed. Not to mention you'd be passed out, and I wouldn't be able to talk to you coherently for hours."

Abby's only movement is from her eyes rolling sarcastically to the back of her head, though her smile remains wide.

"I'm not so sure I didn't break you," I tease. "I don't think you've moved more than your face since I left you."

"Just blissed out in the best way possible," she says in a heavy sigh. She's quiet for a minute, and I think she might just close her eyes and fall asleep. But her eyes pop open, darting to me, as if she's just remembered something.

She sits up quickly as she says, "Wait. Did you say you wanted to celebrate something?"

She's so adorable, I want to kiss that serious expression right off her face.

"I'm pretty sure what we just did counts as celebration," I tease.

"Is it just the game we're celebrating? You made it sound like more." She eyes me speculatively, and I find myself rolling my eyes at her inability to let things go.

"Well, of course we're celebrating the game, but I also got some news today when I got home."

Her expressive brown eyes light up with delight. "Really, what?"

"Well, I found out I got into Colorado and U Penn." They are in both of our top five schools, so she of all people will appreciate this news.

It takes her a nanosecond to react.

"Ohmigod, Drew!" she squeals. Her arms reach out to hug me as she yells, "That's fantastic! I'm so excited for you!"

I'm distracted for a moment by her beautifully naked body pressed against mine. Her breasts move against my chest, and my dick decides it's time to come back to life.

Not now, buddy, I remind myself as I return my focus to our conversation.

"I'm still holding out for Johns Hopkins, but at least I know I'm going to med school. It takes some pressure off me for the moment; it looks like CRU's a strong contender in the national tournament. All we have to do is win our next game."

"I can't imagine the stress you're under," Abby says as she settles down onto the pillow beneath her and readjusts the blankets to cover her beautiful breasts. "Syd said you had to win the next two games, did something change?"

I feel a smirk form as I recall the news Coach relayed in the locker room. "Yeah, the only team we've lost to got their asses kicked by a no-name team from Indiana, which means if we win next week, we're going in at the top of the brackets. It was sheer luck for us. We were pretty assured we'd return to the tournament based on how we've been playing, but you never know. We're taking it one game at a time, putting that ball through the hoop."

"I seriously don't know how you stay so calm." Abby shakes her head in disbelief. "I'd be a nervous wreck if I were you."

"It doesn't help to stress out over things. I learned that long ago with Summer. I only focus on the things I can control and let the rest work itself out."

Abby sighs heavily. "I wish I had your confidence. It's driving me crazy waiting to hear from the other schools I've applied to."

I bend down and kiss the worried look right off her face. "Just have patience, Angel. Everything will work out."

At first, this is a great distraction to keep her mind from racing, but when I pull back, I'm disappointed to see the worry line between her brows is back. "How can you be so certain? We're both facts and statistics people, Drew. We rely on absolute truths."

How do I explain this without sounding crazy? "I guess..." I start as I try to catch one of the million thoughts racing through my head. "I know I can't control whether or not I get into the schools I've applied. There's not a single doubt I did the best I could. I know I've worked my ass off, but the minute I submitted my application, I realized I can't spend every minute of the day worrying about the results. I don't have the time or energy for it."

I look to the sky to regain control of my thoughts before turning my focus to Abby. "It helps that I also have to focus on my current classes as well as basketball. I want to bring home another championship. We've worked so hard to earn that title last season... And as long as I'm still on the team, I want to hold onto it."

I reach out, pulling her closer to me.

Damn, she smells amazing.

"It also helps that I have this beautiful woman in my arms as a distraction. When she's around, I hardly have time to think about anything else."

"Wow. That wasn't cheesy at all," she deadpans. "You had me... Until you smothered me with compliments. You're the most focused person I know. I know for a fact, I'm not that big of a distraction for you... You wouldn't be able to have the things you do if I were."

Thank God, she has no idea how wrong she is.

Though it's the best distraction imaginable.

"Angel, I'm disciplined. But that doesn't mean I'm not distracted by thinking of you."

THANK God we pull off a win for our next game, and we're guaranteed a spot in the championship tournament. CRU's crushing it with how in sync we've been. I won't jinx us by saying this will be an easy road, but the high we're all riding will lift our spirits as we focus on our next game.

We have to travel to Cali again and currently, I'm waiting in the airport to board the plane. I've been running on pure adrenaline since we took off yesterday. I chose to spend the night with Abby, instead of finishing a paper that was due. I managed to turn it in mere hours before the deadline, which isn't my style at all. But now that I have Abby in my life, I must accept that not turning things in days before the deadline is still acceptable.

I take the lid off my large cup of coffee to let it cool a bit as I settle into the seat next to Grey. Propping my feet up on my carry-on, I do my best to get more comfortable. Being as tall as I am, the airport seating's never comfortable. Grey's buried in his phone, and I'm too tired to care about what has brought a shit-eating grin to his face. If I had to guess, it's likely a girl. I'm sure I have the same expression when I hear from Abby.

When Grey snorts loudly, I bite, "What's so funny?" I ask, peering over his shoulder, but the privacy screen on his phone leaves me nothing to go with.

"It's nothing. Just a funny meme."

Yeah, right. "That's what's been making you wear a shit-eating grin since we've arrived?"

"Yep."

"If that's your story, and you're sticking to it, you might want to tone it down a bit," I deadpan.

I take a breath, contemplating letting him off the hook, but I think better of it. This is Grey after all, and I wouldn't be his best friend if I let it slide. "Just a word to the wise, no one is that into a funny meme."

Grey looks at me impishly. "I'll take that under advisement."

I cock an eyebrow at him. "Come on... this is me you're talking to. Who is she?"

Grey looks around and sighs heavily as he stretches his long legs out in front of him. "I don't know, man. I like this girl, but the timing isn't right. We're going to be on the road for the next few weeks, and I'm not sure I wanna be tied down, if you know what I mean."

"Been there. Done that," I agree wholeheartedly. "If you're not ready to settle down, then it's probably better not to let anything get serious."

"Ha! You're one to talk." Grey smirks. "I'd say you're about as serious as it gets with Abby at the moment."

"I never said I don't want to settle down," I draw out slowly to make it clear I was talking about him and not myself. "You like your single life; there's nothing wrong with that."

"Wait." Grey waits until I've locked eyes on him to continue. "Are you saying this thing with Abby and you is serious?"

I give him a look that clearly says, *No shit, Sherlock.*

"But you've never been tied down. I thought you've just been havin' fun." His slight Southern accent drawls out.

"Being with Abby *is* fun, but there's way more to her than that. I just wish the timing weren't shit."

"What do ya mean?" Grey asks with sudden interest.

I sigh heavily and let the weight of the world roll off my

shoulders. Slowly, I begin to tell him my worries. "Well, for starters, it's been a challenge keeping up with school and the season as you know."

"You're preaching to the choir, man."

Trust me, I know. "Add on the pressure of waiting to see what med school I get into, and that's trouble enough. But I still have this need to be with Abby."

Shocked doesn't begin to describe the look on Grey's face when he pulls in his chin, and his eyes bug out. "You need... to be with her."

"Hell yes, man. I love her. If I could figure out a way to move heaven and earth so we both could follow our dreams and still be together, I'd fucking propose tomorrow. But as it is, we're likely going to end up across the fucking country from each other, so I can't even let myself go there."

"What. The. Fuck." Grey cocks his head to the side and eyes me for a long moment. "You're serious?"

"Do I look like I'm kidding?"

"But you just said you'd propose... as in marry her. You just met this semester. You've had a one-track mind since I met you, and now you're willing to throw it all away for a girl."

Oh my fucking God. Is he listening to a word I'm saying?

"Do you know me at all? I'm *going* to med school. And so is she. Did you miss the point where I likely don't stand a chance in hell of being with her in the long term because I'll never stand in the way of her dreams?"

"Didn't you say you've applied to some of the same schools she has?" Grey asks, filling my heart with hope.

Unfortunately, it's squashed like a bug when I'm forced to

remember reality. "Yeah, but so far, we'll be living on opposite sides of the country." I don't see that working out so well. But I keep those thoughts to myself. Besides, I need to focus on the here and now and what I *can control*. I still have the next six months to be with her, so I plan to make them count.

"Enough about me..." I say, needing to change the subject. The thought of losing Abby isn't something I even want to entertain. "Why isn't this girl you're talking to worthy of being more than a text buddy?"

"I'm just not sure I want to be tied down," Grey quietly admits.

"Enough said. When it's the right person, that won't even be a thought that flits through your mind. You'll be spending every moment trying to be with them, not trying to keep them at arm's length."

"Is that right? Oh, wise one. I seem to recall you saying these exact words last year," Grey reminds me.

"True," I admit. "But that was before I met Abby. My goal of getting into med school has been my primary focus for so long." I take in a deep breath and think about how to phrase this next part. "But now that I've met Abby, I think there's room in my life for more than just one focus..." I trail off quietly.

Grey lets me stay in my own head for a few moments before he breaks the silence. "Aw... man. I'm only twenty-two. The prime of my life. We're gonna go for back-to-back championships. I don't have time to drop my focus for a girl I'm not even sure likes me for anything but being an athlete."

I laugh at the memory of when I first met Abby. "I think

that's what drew me to Abby. I can just be me with her. I've never had to wonder. She had no clue who I was when we met. God, she was adorable when she got frustrated from the constant interruptions in class. Hell, she's called me on my shit from the start." God, those eyes... "I swear, the daggers she threw my way the day we met, were the most adorable thing ever. She even went so far as to call me 'Mr. Blue Eyes' when she tried to get me to focus on our assignment."

Huh. I think I may have started falling for her then.

"Seriously? I thought you'd been joking when you'd said she hated you."

"Naw, man. Totally serious. I was a prick to her, and she totally let me know it."

A grin spreads across Grey's face. "I think I might just like Abby a little more, now."

"Asshole," I grumble and take a long drink of my now room-temperature coffee.

Grey's quiet for a few minutes then he surprises me with, "Hopefully, someday, I'll meet someone I don't have to question."

33

ABBY

WHAT'S THAT SAYING?

March comes in like a lion and out like a lamb?

Whoever said that had no idea what experiencing a championship tournament for basketball was like as a spectator. Hell. I'm not even that big of a fan, but my concentration is shit. I'm on pins and needles as I watch CRU move through the brackets. I had no idea that CRU was competing against sixty-seven other teams. Thankfully, CRU got an automatic bid to the tournament due to their ranking, but that doesn't mean they're getting off easy.

I had no idea what went into these games. According to Drew, CRU's going in as the number one seed of their bracket. The odds are in their favor, with the opponent being the lowest-ranking team, in that group of sixteen. It's crazy, I tell you. Thank God, they pulled off that win. It would've been sad to see the reigning champs go out in the first round.

I've seen little of Drew since it was announced that CRU

is in contention. He spends every waking moment preparing for a game, watching film, or studying to keep up with his coursework. I seriously have no idea how he manages to do everything. But through it all, he still manages to think of me. Every morning when I wake up, I find a text from him, and his voice is the last I hear before I fall asleep. The man is burning the candles at both ends. Thank God this tournament only lasts three weeks.

Luckily, CRU's hosting game two, so Drew doesn't have to add traveling to his already busy schedule. It's on a Friday night, and Sydney's traded shifts to make sure she can attend the game with me. The entire campus is pumped with energy.

How had I been so oblivious last year when we went on to win and become best in the nation? I must've been living under a rock.

If I thought the arena was packed in the playoffs, that's nothing compared to this level of fandom. To guarantee we would have seats, Drew insisted Sydney and I use the tickets he'd been given and sit with his parents. When we arrive, I'm pleased to see his Aunt Kathy has joined them as well. I enjoyed getting to know her while Drew spent time at the hospital.

Kathy squeals with delight as she hugs me in greeting. "It's so great to see you again."

I can't even respond because as soon as she releases me, I'm pulled in for a hug from his mom. "I'm so glad you chose to sit with us, Abby. It'll give us a chance to catch up."

"Of course, Mrs. Jacobs. It's great to see you on the mend."

Drew's mom waves a hand in the air. "Oh, stop with the

Mrs. Jacobs. Please. Call me Karen. I should've corrected you sooner, so I'll blame it on the pain meds."

We all laugh at the expression on her face.

When things settle down, I take the time to introduce Sydney to everyone. Of course, Drew's dad insists on being called Marty as well, and I'm relieved to still feel right at home with them.

It gives me both a sense of ease and longing for a close relationship with Drew's family in the future. I'm thankful to find the bond we'd shared while I visited them in the hospital has stayed intact and if anything, has grown stronger.

"So... have you heard back from any other school than Stanford yet, Abby?" Karen asks casually as we watch CRU warm up on the court.

I know Drew and his parents are close, but I hadn't realized he'd mentioned my acceptance to them. "Not yet," I admit. "But I'm sure we'll find out more in the coming weeks. We're supposed to make our decisions by the middle of next month, so I'll find out soon, if I've been accepted into the others I've applied to."

Holy shit. Is it just a matter of weeks that I'll know? I guess I'd been taking Drew's philosophy to heart and letting the cards fall as they may. But the thought of not being with Drew next year has my stomach plummeting to my feet. Before I can dwell on this, the players are announced, and the National Anthem is played.

Drew looks sexy as hell in his uniform. With his hair a little longer than normal, it curls a bit at the edges. Apparently, he's a bit superstitious, so he hasn't gotten a haircut since they won their league championship. Thank God he decided not to forgo shaving; Drew's beard is scratchy as hell when it starts growing out.

Knowing this is a single-elimination tournament, there's a crackle in the air I can't quite describe. As if the entire crowd's watching history in the making, we're on the edge of our seats waiting for greatness to happen, and we're all hoping our team will pull off this win.

CRU doesn't disappoint. They quickly take possession of the ball and score within the first seconds of the game. But the Bulldogs are just as fierce and want it nearly as much. It's almost like watching a tennis match, the ball keeps traveling at lightning speed to the opposite ends of the court, where baskets are made with each possession. It isn't until nearly the end of the first half, that CRU takes the lead and holds it, which brings a huge relief to his parents and me. I can feel their nervous energy, but they've done their best to not make it too obvious. I have no idea how they've watched him play like this for years and haven't died from a heart attack.

Halftime is over before we know it, and the game is back in full force. Drew, DeShawn, and Grey have played the majority of the game. Their focus and extreme talent take my breath away. It's almost as if they can sense each other because they anticipate each other's moves and direct the ball where it needs to be with minimal opposition from the defense.

Finally, the clock hits zero, and the crowd goes wild. CRU pulls off this win, and we couldn't be more ecstatic. Sydney and I high-five and hug each other, but that isn't nearly enough. When I look to Drew's parents, they're jumping up and down with joy. When they smile down at Drew, I can feel their sense of pride from here.

It isn't until the final buzzer goes off that Drew finds me. The moment he does, an infectious smile lights up his face. He hadn't sought me out the entire game because I was laser focused on him the entire time. It's almost as if he were afraid he'd lose his concentration even for a second, and he'd purposely kept from looking in our direction. Instead of standing to leave like I expect, Drew's parents remain seated and patiently wait as the arena empties. We're in the middle of a row, so there's no need to move until we're good and ready.

"Will you be traveling to their next game in North Carolina?" Karen asks with curiosity.

With them playing on a Thursday night next week, there's no way I can leave town. I have too many classes that I can't miss on Friday. Besides, it's not like I can afford a trip across the country on short notice, anyway. I regretfully say, "No. I'll have to watch it on TV. Will you be going?"

Drew's dad smiles with pride. "We wouldn't miss it for the world."

"We're flying out on Wednesday. If your plans change, you're welcome to stay with us. We've rented a condo from an Airbnb, so there's plenty of room. We learned last year it's better to get a place further away from the crowds, so we can get our rest while they party all night."

"I'm joining them, too," Kathy proudly states. "I just love watching these boys play. We're going to win... I can feel it in my bones. CRU's going to take this championship."

The fact that Drew's family drops everything to support

him pulls at my heartstrings even more. Their love and devotion to one another is unbelievable. As I look at his family, it hits me hard. Not only am I incredibly in love with Drew, but I'm falling for his family, too. My heart tightens in my chest, and the love I feel for them flows through me.

Don't get me wrong, I love my family, but I don't think they would drop everything and traipse across the country to watch me play a sport for a couple of hours. I certainly don't have aunts or uncles who would do this either. Drew's family is special. That's for sure.

After we leave the arena, the plan is for everyone to meet at Drew's. Sydney excuses herself to head back to our place and instead of walking, I ride along with his family. Apparently, when his mother arrived earlier in the day, she cooked up a storm before the game.

When we arrive at his apartment, Drew has yet to arrive, but his parents make themselves right at home. His dad lounges on the couch, while his mom and Kathy get to work in the kitchen. When I offer to help, they shoo me away, claiming that Drew's kitchen is a practically a 'one-butt' kitchen, and there's hardly room for the two of them as it is.

Somehow, I feel Drew's presence before I see him enter the apartment. It's uncanny how my body crackles to life, and my spine zings right before he opens the door. DeShawn and Grey are nowhere to be seen, but I'm sure they'll be here at some point. It's their house after all.

When Drew walks through the door, I stand to greet him. The moment his eyes find mine, his long strides eat up the distance between us in a heartbeat.

"Congratulations! You were amazing!" I exclaim as I reach out to wrap him in a hug.

Well, I thought it would be a hug.

Drew lifts me with ease and spins me around in excitement, causing me to squeal with delight. Then his lips crash onto mine before I have a thought to process that his parents are watching. I gasp in surprise, and the Neanderthal that he is, uses that as an opportunity to slide his tongue in and kiss me for all I'm worth.

Fuck. I could get lost in Drew.

But when I hear his mom yell, "Congratulations, Honey!" as she comes around the corner from the kitchen, I'm quickly brought back to reality.

Drew sets me down but doesn't let me go. I take moment to bury my head in his chest, and he wraps one arm around me in a hug.

Under his breath so that only I can hear, Drew whispers, "Sorry about that. Got carried away."

Drew releases me as his mom approaches to hug him tight. "You were amazing. I know you're gonna kick ass next week, too."

Okay... not expecting that. But she is his biggest fan.

"That's the plan, Mom." When she steps away from his embrace, he eagerly asks, "What'd you make? I'm starving."

His mom laughs, knowingly. "Why don't you come into the kitchen to find out."

We spend the rest of the night hanging out with his family. Grey and DeShawn must've celebrated elsewhere; they never returned home. Drew's family will leave early in the morning to get a jump on traffic, so we say our goodbyes for now.

With a quiet apartment to ourselves, I couldn't be any happier. The way Drew's been looking at me all evening makes me want him desperately. But I am good and keep my thoughts concealed for his family's sake and mine.

The second the door clicks shut, Drew pulls me to him and whispers, "I love you so much, Abby."

"I love you, too, Drew," I whisper as I reach on my tiptoes to close the distance between us.

Drew bends to kiss me. What starts out as an innocent kiss quickly turns into an inferno. Not wanting to put on a show so his roommates can see if they return unexpectedly, I tear my lips apart from his just long enough to say, "Bedroom," and he eagerly complies.

34

ABBY

THE NEXT FEW days pass by in a blur. Drew's more hyper vigilant than ever about staying on top of his studies and working out with his team while he's home. I miss him like crazy, but I know this madness will end when this tournament is over.

The night before he's set to leave, I'm startled by a knock at my door. It's late. Sydney's still at work, Chloe's in her room studying, and I'm reading a book on the couch. Not wanting to disturb Chloe, I quickly make my way to the door and look through the peephole.

The minute I see who it is, I fumble with the lock and fling it open.

"What are you doing here?" I gasp in surprise. Drew's large frame fills up the small space, and his sexy dimple pops when he sees me, making butterflies in my stomach and my heart race. *God, what this man does to me.*

"I couldn't leave without saying goodbye one last time," he

whispers. But instead of kissing me like I expect, he simply places one hand on my hip and slowly drops his forehead to mine. His eyes close, and I hear him inhale slowly. I find myself imitating him with ease. We just stand here for an immeasurable time. My heart rate slows as I match my breathing to his. I feel whatever worries he's brought to my door slip away.

When he pulls his face away from mine, I am met with the most piercing blue eyes. It's as if Drew can see into my soul. "Everything okay?" I whisper.

Drew inhales slowly. "I just needed calm. The guys are back at my place going through every one of their vigilant routines. I totally get why they're doing it, but for some reason tonight, it's driving me insane. I know it's late, and I can't stay, but I just needed to see you."

His honesty nearly brings tears to my eyes. I reach up to brush a lock of his hair from his face. My voice is rough and gravelly when I say, "Wanna come in?"

"If I come in..." Drew shakes his head, and his eyes fill with regret, "I won't leave. We both know it."

Disappointment flows through me but unfortunately, I must agree with him. I know exactly what'll happen if he walks through this door.

Drew takes my hands in his and once again leans forward to press his head to mine. Instantly, I feel peace wash through him, but I need to be certain I'm not misreading things. "Are you *sure* you're okay?"

"Just got a lot on my mind..." He trails off but gives no further explanation.

"I can help carry the burden, if you'll let me," I offer, knowing that whatever it is, he'll likely feel better if he gets it off his chest.

"Naw. I'm fine. It's nothing I can't handle. Just seeing your beautiful face helps."

This earns him a smile, and I reward him by lifting to the tip of my toes to kiss him gently. This kiss isn't rushed or hurried, and it doesn't light the world on fire. But it does manage to sear Drew Jacobs deep within my soul. I wish he'd tell me what's bothering him, but knowing Drew as well as I do, he'll tell when he's good and ready. Not a minute sooner.

Before things get carried away, Drew breaks the kiss. His voice is rough and filled with lust when he says, "I gotta go."

Trying to stay positive, I playfully punch him in the shoulder. "Knock 'em dead, Jacobs. I'm counting on you!"

"Okay," he draws out on a chuckle. "I will."

We're quiet for a moment. Neither of us wanting to be the first to say goodbye.

Drew leans down once again to kiss me chastely on the lips. "Love you, Angel. See you when I get back."

"Love you, too," I whisper in return.

Drew's determination is stronger than mine. Somehow, he manages to kiss me lightly once more, turn, and walk away without another word.

I know he's gone to several away games, so I'm not sure why this feels different. But watching him leave feels like he's taking a piece of me with him.

As soon as he's out of sight, I slowly turn and make my way

back inside. As I twist the deadbolt, I lean my forehead against the door and feel a strange sense of loss.

If he has the power to do this to me now, what will it be like when we part for med school?

Fuck. I'm in so much trouble.

Eventually, I meander my way to the couch, plopping myself down to continue reading my book. But after repeating the same sentence multiple times, I know it's useless. I can't concentrate. My mind's like that octopus ride at the fair. Up and down, round and round. Just when I think I can catch hold of something, it races again, and I lose track of that thought. My stomach twists into knots as I hold on for dear life, trying to wrap my head around my feelings.

That's how Sydney finds me when she gets home from work.

"Since when do you spend time staring at the ceiling?" she asks, breaking me away from my thoughts.

"Uh, when did you get home?" I ask, amazed I didn't hear her come in.

"I just walked in. I thought you might be sleeping, but when I saw your eyes open, I waited a few moments before saying anything."

Seriously? "Huh. I guess I was lost in thought," I offer as an explanation.

Sydney plops down in the chair beside me. "Penny for your thoughts? Though by the way you were zoning out, I may need to offer my tip money for tonight."

"I'm just thinking about Drew," I admit with honesty.

"That can't be a bad thing." Sydney smiles knowingly. "That man is something to think about."

Normally, I'd say something snarky in return to a comment like that but instead, I sigh heavily as I try to explain my whirling thoughts. "He came over to say goodbye, but since he's left... I've... just been... thinking."

"We all know how dangerous your mind is," she teases. "Can you hold off on world domination for a little longer?"

"Ha. Ha. Very funny," I chastise. "I was just thinking about what it meant when he left. I swear he took a part of me with him."

All traces of teasing disappear from Sydney's face. "Aww, Abs. It's okay to like him."

"That's the problem, Syd. I think I like him *too* much. He's only gone for a couple of days, and I already miss him like crazy. Uggh... He hasn't even left town. Why am I already like this?" The shocked expression on Sydney's face would be comical if I weren't so worried now. I take in a quick breath and continue, "What the hell am I going to do next year when we're across the country from one another?"

Syd starts to say something, but I cut her off, "See... this right here is why I probably shouldn't even be dating in the first place. It's why I haven't let myself get attached. I don't know if I can handle it."

"I know it's not easy, but you'll find a way, I'm sure."

"Oh, come on, Syd. You and I both know long distance equals doom. We have four more years of school... and that doesn't even cover residency or if either of us specialize in anything."

Sydney shrugs as she whispers, "True."

"Even if we do manage to get into the same school, we'll still have to balance our schedules." I can't even begin to fathom what our schedules will look like then.

"How have you managed to date him so far?" Sydney asks quietly.

I shrug. "I don't know... we just make it work. But we're in the same city, not across a freaking continent."

This causes Sydney to sigh heavily as she shakes her head, clearly disgusted with my negative-nelly antics. "So, what are your options? You can continue to enjoy being with Drew, or you can cut him loose."

"What. The. Hell?" Caught completely off guard, my jaw hangs open.

As I process her words, my gut clenches, and my chest aches. *Why is it so hard to breathe?*

"Why... why would you say that?" I sputter in disbelief.

Sydney points a finger to my face. "This... right there... Just gave you all the answer you need."

I open my mouth to say something, but words don't come out.

Sydney abruptly stands. "I'd give you a hug, but I'm gonna hop in the shower. Some drunk dude spilled a drink all over me, and I feel sticky as the floor in a frat house. I'll be out in a few minutes if you want to talk some more."

As I look her over, I finally take notice that her once pink shirt is stained reddish brown. "What the hell was he drinking?" I ask as I inspect her further. The entire drink must've landed in her bra because that's where it's concentrated.

Sydney just shakes her head. "Red Rooster."

I have no clue what it is, but from the looks of her shirt, it sure is colorful.

As she walks away, her comment about Drew hits home. I'm not so sure I want to talk about him anymore tonight. I know, I have a major decision to make.

Standing, I stretch to the ceiling in hopes that the weight around my shoulder and back will loosen. No such use. "I think I'm just gonna head to bed. We can talk more tomorrow."

"I'm here for you, Abs." Sydney's voice is filled with sincerity. Until she tacks on, "I just need a shower desperately."

This earns her a chuckle from me. "Go. Shower. We'll talk tomorrow."

As soon as Sydney leaves the room, I grab my Kindle and head to my bedroom.

After brushing my teeth and getting ready for bed, all the while, I weigh my options back and forth. Should I break things off with Drew?

Instantly, my gut clenches, and my stomach feels like lead weights sinking to the bottom of the ocean.

Fuucccck... How can I even think like that?

If I feel this strong after knowing him for such a short time, what will it be like when I'm even more invested?

I could just let things go as they are... and let distance and time let things fizzle out naturally? Let's face it—four years being without him will likely pull us apart on its own. We'll be broke med students who can't afford to traipse across the country on random spare moments of time. Though if I'm being honest with myself, losing him in any way, shape, or form is painful.

Going through my nightly routine, I set my alarm and make sure I have everything ready for class tomorrow. As I'm making sure my phone's on the charger, a text comes through.

Drew: Night, Angel. Sweet dreams.

That's the straw that breaks the camel's back.

Tears pool on my lashes to the point I can't even see the screen. My heart aches at the thought of my worst fear being inevitable. God, I miss him so much.

I take a deep breath to calm my nerves.

Geez, Abby, why am I even thinking like this?

Because you know it will hurt more when I fall harder, my inner voice quietly whispers.

Get it together, Abby, I chastise myself. Drew doesn't need me falling apart right now. He needs to focus on his game.

It's time to put my selfish thoughts aside. I swipe at the tears streaming down my cheeks then quickly type out a reply.

Me: Night. Sweet dreams.

So that I won't type anymore, I do the hardest thing imaginable. I power my phone down and turn off the light.

Slipping between the sheets, I adjust my pillow and attempt to settle my thoughts. But all I end up doing is tossing and turning. Adjusting my pillow and contemplating what I should do about Drew.

I see my clock read each hour as it slowly slips by.

Just when I finally fall asleep—my alarm sounds. I hit

snooze a few times, but when I finally drag myself from my bed, it's only because I can't possibly wait another second in the comforts of my blankets without being late for class.

Not even bothering to shower, I quickly brush my teeth and throw on some deodorant. I may not give a shit about much now, but I do have some standards. Dressing in a pair of black leggings and the first t-shirt I touch, I dress in record time. When I see Drew's oversized hoodie laying on the chair in the corner of my room, my heart clenches.

Wanting to feel closer to him, to help me get through the day, I opt to wear it. He'd left it here while we'd been studying. Though it's been unworn for days, it still smells of him. I inhale deeply, and my chest aches. God, I miss him.

Glancing at my clock, I panic.

Shit! I have less than twenty minutes to have my ass in a seat. My professor is a stickler for punctuality. He even paces for a full five minutes before class begins, so he can start exactly on time. Fuck. I can't be late.

Knowing it takes a good twelve minutes to get to the lecture hall, I grab my phone off the charger and slip it into my bag, slide on the first pair of shoes I can wear without going to the trouble of finding socks, and zip out of my apartment.

I manage to make it to class with three minutes to spare. I take my usual place and do my best to focus on the lecture that starts promptly on time. Of course, my concentration's total shit because with each breath I take, I'm reminded of Drew.

I've never been much of a masochist, but I can't force myself to take off his hoodie. Sure, I probably look like a little girl playing dress up as the sleeves are bunched up, and it hangs long on me, but I gave up long ago worrying about what other people think of my fashion sense, or lack thereof in my case.

I move from class to class throughout the day on auto pilot. I'm physically present in each one, but my mind is nowhere near the walls of any of the classrooms. Nope, my thoughts hopped on the jet plane to North Carolina now. I want so badly to reach out and talk to him, but knowing he's somewhere over the Midwest now, I don't even bother to pull out my phone from my bag.

When I'm finally done with my four classes for the day. I mechanically make my way home. Walking past the mailbox, I remember I haven't checked it in a while. Knowing my key is at home and my roommates are still in class, I climb the stairs to my apartment and retrieve it.

When I open the box, my heart stalls.

There's another large white envelope filling up the space.

Slowly, I reach in to read the name. It could be for Chloe or Sydney. But let's face it, I'm the only one who's been getting mail like this.

When I notice the logo in the return address, my stomach drops.

My legs feel heavy, and my heartrate feels as if it's in slow motion.

No way. No freaking way.

I can't find out today, of all days.

Feeling the weight of the envelope, my heart picks up its pace.

I can't handle another blow today... I just can't. The words written in this letter could be the nail in the coffin for Drew and me.

Somehow, I manage to make it upstairs. Once inside, I go straight to my bedroom to be alone when I receive this news.

Carefully, I lay the envelope on my bed and stare at it as if it's a ticking time bomb.

Should I open it now, or wait?

When I can't take the suspense any longer, I quickly reach for the envelope and rip it open. I'm rewarded with a friggin' paper cut.

"Fuck, that hurts!" I shout as I quickly suck on my finger, hoping to take away the pain. Why in the hell does a minuscule cut hurt like hell?

When I notice the paper falls out into my bed in my haste to get the envelope open, I freeze.

Clear as day, I can see the words, "Congratulations, you've been accepted..."

That's all I need to read before I squeal and jump up and down with joy.

Holy shit! I did it! I got into my number one choice school!

Relief washes through me as my pride soars. I've worked my ass off for this. Everything is finally paying off. Years of sacrifice and dedication all lead to this moment!

"I fucking got into Johns Hopkins!" I shout to my room as I pump my fist in the air.

I rush to the living room to get my phone. There's only one person I want to share this news with. I pick up my phone and realize it's still off from last night. But just as I reach for the button, another thought hits me like a ton of bricks.

Wait...

If I got it, does this mean Drew won't?

Fuck, Fuck, Fuck. He's wanted this for so long. It's one of the best oncology programs in the nation. Remembering Drew's promise to Summer, I quickly stow my phone in my bag once again.

His focus needs to be on his game tomorrow. Not whether he got into med school. No... There's no way I can tell him my news, until this tournament is completely over. If they win tomorrow, they're in the championship round. His focus needs to be on winning this game. Not on me or what school I've gotten into.

I just hope he doesn't hate or resent me when he finds out I didn't tell him right away.

35

DREW

AS I STARE at my phone for the millionth time, I will it to have a text or call from Abby. Hell, I'd settle for a message tapped out in Morse Code at this point. Anything to let me know she's okay. I've lost track of the amount of text messages I've sent to her throughout the day. When I've tried calling, it goes straight to voice mail.

It's been nearly twenty-four hours since she sent her last text. Just a simple "Sweet dreams. Night" is all I've heard from her. Sure, she never responds when she's in class or at work, but this complete radio silence is killing me.

I've even checked her social media accounts, and I can't see any activity there either. It's like she's dropped off the face of the planet. What the hell is going on?

Since we traveled most of yesterday, we have a light practice today, and we play tomorrow night. To distract myself, I go through a light routine at the gym. I try my best not to focus on anything other than the fact that Abby has completely gone off the grid and is AWOL.

As I get ready for bed that night, I'm convinced something must've happened to Abby. We've never gone this long without talking. Knowing we're three hours ahead of the West Coast, I finally give in. Scrolling through my contacts, I pull up Sydney's information. Desperation doesn't look good on me but without a second's hesitation, I hit the call button instead of texting. I don't have time to wait for her to get back to me. I need answers... now.

"Hello?" Sydney answers the phone apprehensively.

"Hey, Syd, it's Drew. Sorry to bother you, but I haven't been able to reach Abby all day. Is everything okay?"

"Oh." Silence fills the air and instantly I'm on hyper alert. Does she know something and not want to tell me?

I hear some rustling in the background. It feels like forever before she finally says something. "Let me check. I haven't seen her since I got home, but her purse is on the counter, so I'm sure she's around."

I hear a light knock on what I assume is Abby's door.

Sydney quietly says Abby's name.

There's a pause.

Then I swear I hear a door shut.

Finally, she puts me out of my misery. "I'm sorry, Drew, but she's sleeping. I tried talking to her, but she didn't even stir."

Relief washes through me. At least she's safe and sound.

"It's no problem, Syd. She must be tired if she's asleep this early." But a new worry lingers. "Has she mentioned anything about being sick?"

"No. Not that I know of. Want me to leave her a message?"

What do I say that won't make me look like a crazed lunatic? "Maybe you can just have her check her phone. It's been off all day."

I hear a light chuckle come through the phone, and I picture Syd shaking her head. "Sure, no problem. Good luck on your game tomorrow. We'll be watching you on TV. Give 'em hell!"

"Thanks, Syd. Please have her call me tomorrow. As weird as this sounds, I've felt like something was off all day, and I just can't explain it. I just want to make sure she's okay."

"Oh..." Sydney's quiet for an unusual length of time. I can't tell if she's distracted, or if she doesn't know what to say. Eventually, she breaks her silence with, "I'll make sure she gets a hold of you tomorrow."

I still don't feel satisfied.

But what can I do?

"Thanks, Syd. I appreciate it," I say before disconnecting the call.

I force myself to turn off my brain and go to sleep. I have a huge game tomorrow night. There's a lot riding on it. I need to be well rested. Besides, Grey's already sleeping in the bed next to me. I don't want to disturb him any further.

I STILL HAVEN'T HEARD from Abby by lunch the next day. I've been going through the motions, preparing the best I can for the game this afternoon. I'm trying not to read anything into her radio silence, but it's proving difficult. Doubt is an evil bitch that gnaws at you until it practically eats you alive.

If I've checked my phone once, I've checked it no less than a million times throughout the day. I'm surprised the button to activate the screen hasn't broken from overuse. Finally, just as I'm about to load the bus to head to the arena, a text comes through.

Relief washes over me as her name fills my screen.

Abby: Good luck tonight. I'll be watching you on TV. Kick some ass.

I want to ask her a million questions, but not wanting to cause any drama before stepping on the court, I stick with simplicity.

Me: Thanks. Will try my best. Love you.

I see those three little dots appear, then disappear, and my heart sinks.

Something's most definitely wrong. If I weren't on a crowded bus, I'd call her to find out what the hell is going on. This is so unlike Abby.

"You okay, man?" Grey asks, breaking my focus on a self-imposed pity party.

"Yeah." I try to sound convincing, but I'm a shit liar.

Thankfully, Grey doesn't call me on it. He can tell something's off, but I don't want to worry him. We have too much at stake to make my problems become his.

Before I can give my phone anymore thought, I stash it in my gym bag, where I refuse to look at it again until this game is over. This isn't the time to have my head out of the game. When the bus stops, I stand, willing my focus to be on the here and now—not at home with Abby.

All through warm-ups, my attention is shit.

I go through the motions, but I'm not connecting with my team.

Thankfully, Coach doesn't notice, or he'd rip me a new asshole.

When we go back into the locker room before the game starts, Grey pulls me aside. So that others don't hear, he harshly whispers, "Drew, whatever shit's going on inside of that head of yours—block it out. We've worked too fucking hard to let it go up in flames."

This knocks the wind out of me.

I look around the locker room at my team and realize he's right. I cannot do this to my team.

Closing my eyes, I take a steadying breath and release it slowly. When I open my eyes, I hope he can see my determination.

Failure isn't an option.

"Okay... let's do this!"

Once the game starts, I manage to keep Abby out of my mind. Thank God, I find my rhythm and easily fall into sync with my team. North Carolina's one hell of a team, and we need every player on deck to pull off a win.

By halftime, we're down by seven points. We head into the locker room, knowing we're down, but not out of this game. Our coaching staff tells us where we're making strides and what our shortcomings are. Coach gives us one last pep talk before we're back out on the court to finish off this game.

Somehow, by the skin of our teeth, we manage to pull off a huge upset. The home crowd is devastated to find CRU will be in the championship game next week instead of them. CRU fans are ecstatic, and their energy sizzles throughout the arena and into the locker room.

By the time we leave the stadium, there's a group ready to go out and celebrate together. But until I hear from Abby, I don't feel much like celebrating. Instead, I say hello to my family since they traveled to watch me play, then I head back to the hotel.

When I pull out my phone, I see one simple text, which gives me hope.

Abby: Congratulations! I'm so proud of you.

My fingers quickly tap out a reply.

Me: Thanks. I still can't believe we're playing in back-to-back championship games.

Abby: You deserve it.

Before I can type anything else, Grey enters the room.

"Thought I'd find you here." Grey plops on his bed and stares at me expectantly. "Spill it. What's going on with you?"

"I don't know what you're talking about," I say dismissively.

"Dude. Your head's been up your ass this entire trip. What is going on?"

"Why aren't you out with the team?" I ask to take the focus from me.

"Because my best friend's holed up in our hotel room when we should be out celebrating. He's been quiet as fuck all day, and now... he's avoiding the subject."

Leave it to Grey to tell it like it is.

I should just tell him. But what the fuck do I say?

My girlfriend hasn't talked to me in two days, and I'm afraid I'm losing her?

Fuck no. I'm not voicing those thoughts aloud. Just thinking them is bad enough.

Instead, I do the last thing I want to do. I pop off my bed and say, "Let's go out. I'm ready to get drunk."

Grey's eyes widen as his mouth drops to the floor.

When I reach the door, I look back over my shoulder. "Are you coming or what? There's a seat at the bar with my name on it."

"Whatever you need, man, I'm here for you."

36

DREW

YEAH, drinking last night probably wasn't my smartest idea. Now both my head and heart hurt. I almost feel bad for Grey as I wasn't the best company. I barely spoke ten words the entire time we sat at the hotel bar. But like the friend he is, he stayed by my side and kept my glass full.

Thank fuck we found a quiet corner where people didn't recognize us. Most of the team was celebrating at local bars where students hang out. After slamming down a few shots, I chased them with a few beers. I wasn't out of control, but for not being a drinker, it was more than my share.

Our flight was early this morning, and it took everything in me to get up when the alarm went off. But it's my own fucking fault I feel this way. I refuse to look at my phone, in fear that Abby remains radio silent. Finding my place on the plane, I pop my earbuds in and will myself to fall back to sleep.

When I wake up as we land, I feel much better. I know better than to drink like I did last night, but at the time, I just couldn't give two fucks about it. I haven't done anything like that since high school, and I feel a bit guilty for resorting to it. This is so unlike me.

It takes forever for the team to get from the airport to our university. I'm dying to see Abby. My only goal is to find her and talk through whatever's wrong. I just hope I'm not too late.

Knowing I skipped a shower this morning, stopping by my apartment first, is a must. Sure, I showered after the game but after drinking, sleeping, and traveling all day, I need to wash the grime off me before seeing her.

As soon as we're back in the apartment, I quickly rush through a shower and change into a pair of jeans and t-shirt. Of course, it's raining in Washington, so I grab a hoodie to offset the weather.

On the way out the door, DeShawn hollers, "Hey, you have some mail!"

When I turn, he's holding two large envelopes and some bills. Immediately, my attention is on the larger envelopes. If their logos are any indication, I'm sure what might be in them. But the way my heart hammers out of my chest with my need to settle things with Abby, I know I can't handle anymore disappointment now, no matter the risk.

"Thanks, man." Snagging the envelopes, I rush to my car. Throwing them on the passenger seat, I hightail it to Abby's.

God only knows what is going through that brilliant mind of hers. But she's gonna talk to me one way or another.

I've purposely kept my phone off all day; I can't handle the possibility of rejection. Her silence is like an axe splitting through my chest and chopping me to pieces bit by bit, as time goes on. I need to see for myself if I'm just imagining things, or if my instincts are right.

God, I don't want to be right in this moment.

Of course, the parking lot's full when I arrive at Abby's apartment. I finally find a spot on the street, about a block away. My long strides eat up the pavement quickly as I close the distance between us. Hell, I'm not even sure she's here, but knowing she doesn't work today, I doubt there's any place else she'd be.

When I knock on her door, I'm forced to impatiently wait for someone to answer. When the door finally cracks open, my heart sinks to find Sydney.

Sydney's face fills with excitement as she pulls me in for a hug. "Congratulations, Drew! You played well yesterday."

Not really, but that's beside the point. Taking a step back, I rub my palm against the back of my neck. "Uh, is Abby around?"

"She's in her room last I checked."

I don't even wait for a response as I push past Sydney and walk to Abby's door. It's open, and she's lying on her bed listening to music with her earbuds in. Instead of rushing in, I take a moment to study her. She's dressed in yoga pants and a hoodie I'd left here the other day. Her hair is stacked on top of her head, and she's staring at the ceiling.

When I look at her beautiful face, I notice dark circles under her eyes, and they seem a bit puffy.

Is it from crying?

Or has she been sick?

God, I hope I haven't been in this funk because she's been sick.

Wait... Sydney would've said something, right?

When I take a step into the room, I startle her.

She jumps, pulling her earbuds out as she goes. "Oh, you scared me. Have you been standing there long?"

"Long enough to notice there's something wrong. Have you been sick?"

Abby shakes her head. "No."

Shit. She has been crying.

"So... What's going on, Angel?" I draw out on a long breath, bracing myself for the worst.

Abby sighs and looks everywhere but at me. There's tension in the room I've never felt before, and I'm certain I'm not going to like what she has to say.

I give her a few moments before I can't handle it any longer. I walk into her room to sit next to her on the bed. When she still doesn't look at me, my chest clenches.

Shit. This is bad.

Knowing I must get this over with one way or another, I reach out and guide her chin, so that she looks me in the eye. The crackle of electricity that's always present when we touch is back in full force.

When her golden-brown eyes find mine, I encourage her to speak her mind. "Abby. You're killing me. Please, just tell me what's going on."

Her beautiful thick lashes blink a few times, and her eyes well up with tears. "I've missed you," she whispers.

Okay... that's not what I expected. Her words don't match the bleak expression on her face.

"I've missed you, too," I say in return, but somehow, I sincerely doubt that's all that's bothering her. "But what's going on? Have I done something to upset you?" Clearly, she's upset. But I have no fucking clue why.

My palms sweat, and my heart races as I prepare for the worst to come.

"When you left the other day, I realized just how much I love you," she says in a small and shaky voice.

Those words bring a smile to my face. "I love you, too, Angel."

Abby shakes her head, and I've clearly misread her message. Her face morphs into an expression that tells me she's on the verge of crying. "No. I really love you. Like I don't think I can possibly love you anymore than I do right now."

"This is a good thing, right?" I ask, not understanding what the fuck is going on. Why is it a problem for her to love me?

"Drew, with that love... You have the power to wreck me. I've missed you so much this week, I physically haven't been able to eat or sleep." Tears pool at her lashes but somehow manage to defy gravity.

What? This makes no sense. "Abby, we've been apart before, and I'm back now. What's wrong?"

Her voice breaks as she explains. "Because I realized that I don't think I can do this anymore. If I can't handle being apart from you for one weekend... How will I handle being all the way across the country from you?"

Fuck.

My worst fear is coming to life.

Her words cut through me like a knife, and it's all I can do to get my next words out. "W... what... are you... saying?"

She looks to the ceiling and pulls in a ragged breath. "Hell, for all I know you're going to resent me on top of all this, too."

What the fuck is she talking about?

"Resent you? Why on earth would I resent you?"

Her voice is small when she whispers, "I got in."

"Got in?" I ask, clearly not connecting the dots. "Got in, where?"

She stands and slowly walks to her desk. There she picks up an envelope I recognize. "I got into Johns Hopkins."

Holy Fuck!

37

ABBY

DREW IMMEDIATELY BOLTS UP from the bed as he yells, "Hold that thought!"

Before I can process anything, Drew sprints out of my bedroom. I can't even get to the hall to follow him before I hear the front door to my apartment slam open and hit the adjacent wall.

Drew's nowhere to be found when I make it to the door. I've never seen anyone run as fast as him. If I hadn't heard his words giving me a sense of hope he'd return, I'd be panicking right now.

Wondering where in the hell he's going, I stand at my front porch to wait.

And wait.

Finally, I see him in the distance, running like he's making a fast break with only seconds left to go in the game. He bounds up my stairs two at a time. He stops abruptly in front of me, panting with the most beautiful smile written across his face.

Bending down to catch his breath, he places his hands on his knees. I don't think I've ever seen him so breathless. For the life of me, I can't figure out what the hell he just bolted off for. When he stands, he holds out a big white envelope.

"Did it..." He takes a deep breath to steady his voice before continuing, "Did it look like this?"

Did what look like this? What the hell is he talking about?

Then I see the logo... and my heart races out of my chest.

No way. It couldn't be.

Have I been worrying for days over nothing?

Please God, let that be the case. I nod frantically, but my voice is stuck in my chest.

Drew rips into the envelope and quickly pulls out his letter. His eyes are laser focused on the message inside, and I've never seen him so unreadable. Eventually, the corners of his lips twitch, but his features remain stoic. Giving me no clue as to what it says.

My heart starts to crumble, and I suddenly can't breathe.

Holy shit, did he not get in?

Drew stares at me for a long moment before words come out of his mouth. "So... if I told you I was accepted into Johns Hopkins, would it change your mind about being with me?"

Oh, God. What's he saying?

I feel my body going weak, and I reach for him to steady myself.

Drew closes the distance between us in an instant, concern written all over his beautiful features. "Abby, are you okay?"

"Did you..." I ask weakly, so I clear my throat to say what needs to be said. "Did you get in?"

Instead of saying anything, Drew reaches to me and pulls me into the tightest hug imaginable and whispers, "Yes."

"Yes?" I ask, needing reassurance. "You got in?"

"Yes!" he shouts loud enough for all my neighbors to hear. "I'm going to Johns Hopkins."

His lips crash down on mine, and it's the greatest feeling I've ever felt.

The weight of this entire week lifts in an instant, and all my self-doubt instantly disappears.

"Are you fucking with me?" I ask in disbelief. The odds of us both being accepted into this school were so slim.

Drew's beautiful face shakes, but his infectious smile spreads. "I got in, Angel."

"Ohmigod, Drew, I've been so stressed. For some reason when you left, it hit me like a ton of bricks how much I love you. I couldn't handle being apart. Then when I got my acceptance letter, I had a whole new worry. I didn't want you to resent me for going to the school of your dreams."

Drew lifts a finger to my lips to stop me from saying more. When he has my full attention, his dark-blue eyes lock onto mine and study me. I'm not sure what he sees, but he still feels the need to ask, "So, this isn't about you not loving me?"

"No... if anything, I love you too much," I whisper in return.

Drew's grin splits his face in half as he picks me up and spins me around on my small porch. "Angel, there's no such thing as loving someone too much. If you'll let me, I'd be glad to prove this to you."

Rolling my eyes, my head tips back and laughs. "God. You're such a Neanderthal... Put me down so we can go inside and talk about this some more."

As soon as my feet hit the floor, Drew steadies me to make sure I'm settled before grasping my hand and pulling me to my room.

When we get inside, he takes his time closing the door.

When he turns, his expression isn't what I expect.

The light, fun-loving man from a moment before is gone.

In his place is a man whose hunger and need are evident. His eyes have darkened as his stance transitions into a predator waiting to pounce.

He stalks toward me like a man on a mission. My heart beats wildly in anticipation. He eats up the distance between us in a matter of one breath. When he stops before me, he stalls for a moment to look me in the eye.

Electricity zings between us, and it's all I can do to keep myself rooted in place.

When Drew speaks, his voice is rough to the point of being raw. "So we're clear..." He pauses for a moment as he places his hand on my hip. With his other hand, he motions between us. "This thing between us isn't going anywhere. If you ever have doubts... You come to me. We talk about it. You don't retreat into your head, and you don't keep your worries to yourself. We. Are. A. Team. Got that?"

Drew stares at me until I nod in agreement, but no words come out.

Then he shocks me again when he reveals what he's been going through. "I've been a fucking wreck since I left, and I have no desire to repeat that ever again. You obviously have no idea what you mean to me, so my new mission is to make sure you never doubt my feelings again."

Holy shit. He's dead serious.

I couldn't love Drew Jacobs more than in this moment. My heart's bursting with emotion as happy tears fill my eyes. "I love you, Drew," I whisper. If I spoke any louder, the words would get stuck in my thick throat.

"Let me love you, Angel," he practically growls as his lips crash onto mine.

Electric pulses sizzle up my spine as Drew deepens our kiss. When his tongue sweeps across my lips, mine part with ease. Needing him closer, my hands roam under his shirt and skim up his back.

Drew breaks our kiss in all too short of time, leaving me disappointed.

However, it's only to step back and rip his shirt over his head in the sexiest of ways. Not wanting to be any further apart from him, I fling off my shirt and push at my leggings and underwear, as if I'm trying for the world record for unclothing myself.

Drew growls appreciatively when he notices my efforts, shucking off his jeans and boxers in one fluid motion. When his cock springs to life, liquid heat flows through me, making me want him more than ever.

Then he closes the distance between us to assist with the removal of my bra. He peppers me with kisses.

How in the hell can he have me on the brink of ecstasy with a few simple kisses?

"I..." kiss. "Love..." followed by another kiss to my neck. "You, Angel," he breathes out on a sigh as he makes his way to my mouth.

"Need you, Drew," is the last coherent thought I have as Drew takes his time loving me, cherishing me, and making sure I know he's mine.

EPILOGUE

Drew
Ten Years Later...

TODAY MARKS another big day for Abby and me. We've been working like crazy, making sure everything goes off without a hitch. We've prepped, planned, and checked over every detail with care. After all, it's no longer just us we must worry about.

Over the years, we've been through many trials and tribulations. I'd never say med school was easy, but with her by my side, it was bearable. She was my rock through it all, and I can honestly say I love her more each day.

I'm pleased to say she kept her promise to never shut me out. There's been several times, I'm sure she wanted to run for the hills because things were too stressful, but somehow, we'd talk through things and work them out. I know I'm not the easiest guy to live with, but she continues to love me, in spite of myself.

Today's the ten-year anniversary of the CRU championship game. Yes, helping my team earn back-to-back national championship titles was out of this world. It was truly a spectacular moment in my life, and I'll never forget the high that came with it. But if I'm being honest, that's not even close to my highlight of that day for me.

No, that honor is directly tied to Abby.

I remember it as if it were yesterday…

I'd insisted on meeting for breakfast early that morning. Wanting to keep as much normalcy as I could manage, I'd asked for breakfast at the diner. She had no idea what was in store for her.

We came in and sat in our usual booth. Vanessa took our order, and I did my best to keep our conversation casual. Abby could clearly tell I was anxious about something, but I was sure she suspected it was likely about the game. So, she prattled on about meaningless things to distract me. God, she was adorable.

As we waited for our food, I noticed my parents and Aunt Kathy slip in behind Abby. But I ignored them, keeping Abby none the wiser. When Sydney and Chloe walked in with two people who I assumed were Abby's parents, I knew it was time.

We'd spoken on the phone, but with the tournament going on, I'd never actually met them. After explaining my plan, they were leery but on board with everything. After all—it wasn't them who needed to agree with me.

It was now or never. My palms began to sweat, and my heart raced out of my chest.

Had I ever been that nervous?

Of course, Abby noticed. "Everything okay, Drew?"

Taking a deep breath to steady myself, I exhaled slowly. Then I began what was likely to be one of the most memorable experiences in my lifetime.

"Abby." I waited until she looked me in the eye, so I knew I had her full attention. "I love you more than anything in this world, you know that, right?"

A beautiful blush spread over her cheeks that I'd never tire of. "Of course. I love you, too. Are you nervous about the game?" Her concern for me was etched across her features.

I reached out to take her hand in mine from across the table. "I'm not nervous about the game..." I drew out. "I'll either win or lose, but I'll leave it all on the court."

Her confidence in me was astounding as she squeezed my hand and nodded silently in understanding.

I looked to my family and hers again, as I gathered up my strength to lay my heart on the line.

"Winning another championship would be amazing, but at the end of the day, it's just a game. I'm actually hoping to have another reason to celebrate this day for many years to come."

Confusion morphed across Abby's features. Her eyebrows pulled together in the most adorable way. I just wanted to kiss that look off her face. But I couldn't let myself get distracted. Instead, I took a stroll down memory lane.

"Abby, when I walked into that classroom, little did I know the partner I scouted for would be the one I'd want in life."

"Okay..." she drew out, clearly not seeing where I was going with this.

"You were strong, independent, and let's be honest—called me on my shit. But you were also the first person besides my family to see the real Drew Jacobs."

"Oh, Drew..." she started to say with tears building up behind her lashes.

God, I hoped she didn't cry before I could finish, or I might be bawling right alongside her.

I stood and came to her side of the booth, where she turned to face me. I was sure she thought I was just coming to comfort her, but when I dropped to one knee, she gasped.

Her beautiful brown eyes were wide and filled with questions.

"Abby Angelos, I think I've loved you from that very first day I annoyed the hell out of you. You're the most kind, loving, and stubborn woman I've ever met. Would you do me the honor of not only being my partner in school, but in life?"

I pulled out the box that had been burning a hole in my pocket since my mother gave it to me the night before.

Immediately, I noticed Abby's hand tremble as she brought it to cover her clearly shocked expression.

"This was my grandmother's wedding ring. And if you don't like it, I'll work hard to get you one you deserve. But in the meantime, will you answer one important question?"

Abby nodded repeatedly. I wasn't sure if it were to get me to keep going, or if it would be the answer to my prayers. But I forced myself to continue.

"Abby, will you make this the happiest day of my life and agree to be my wife? I love you, Abby Angelos. Marry me?"

Abby didn't say anything but jumped into my arms, nearly

knocking me on my ass. I quickly recovered, but instead of staying on one knee, I pulled us into a standing position.

When I was sure she was steady on her feet, I finally looked her in the eyes.

Tears streamed down her face, and her smile could probably be seen from the moon, it was so big. But she still hadn't given me a definite answer. Then I whispered, "Is that a yes?"

"God, Drew!" Abby said on a sob. "Yes... Yes, I'll marry you!"

My heart nearly beat out of my chest as my lips crashed onto hers to show her she'd made me the happiest man alive.

Cheers erupted from the diner, and I could care less we had an audience.

When Abby pulled away breathless, the expression of wonder and beauty would be etched in my memories for as long as I live.

Of course, our friends and family surrounded us by the time we broke free, and each of them congratulated us. When Abby realized the lengths I went through to orchestrate this, she turned to me and said, "You're in so much trouble, Drew Jacobs."

"You can be mad at me after my game this evening. Until then, just continue to love me like you do."

With this, everyone laughed at my smartass antics.

"Dr. Jacobs?" Suzanna, a nurse we've hired to work in our clinic, interrupts my trip down memory lane.

"Your wife is looking for you. You were supposed to meet her out front a few minutes ago. Everyone is waiting."

"Thanks for the reminder," I say as I get up from my desk.

When I reach the lobby of the building Abby and I have leased, I find everyone I know and love standing in there waiting.

Abby still manages to take my breath away when I look into her beautiful golden-brown eyes. I swear she's hardly changed in the last ten years, though she'd wholeheartedly disagree. When Abby spots me, she comes up to take my hand. There's a bounce to her step, and radiant energy flows through her. I love her more now than ever before. She's been my partner in every sense of the word. I'm so thankful I chose her that day when I walked into class. It was by far my best decision. Ever.

I lean in to kiss her, and I'm still mesmerized by her beauty and scent that's uniquely her. She's dressed in a navy-blue wrap dress that accentuates her every curve in the best possible way. Especially, the baby bump that only I can notice.

Abby and I are planners. We plot everything out. Make goals and smash them into oblivion together. Pregnancy wasn't on that list, with opening our practice together, but knowing Abby as well as I do, she's not about to let anything get in her way. I know with every fiber of my being, she'll be the best mom possible.

She steps up to the podium we've set up with pride and confidence. Everyone in the room settles. I stand by her side, never letting go. It's an honor to share this with her.

"Welcome, everyone. Thank you so much for coming." Applause fills the room, and she waits, before continuing.

"Drew and I couldn't be happier to have you experience this journey with us.

"This has been a dream come true for us. For years, we've wanted to return to Spokane and open a practice of our own. Our goal is to provide preventative and routine care to children in this community. We'll be there with you as if you're members of our family. We value you as unique individuals and promise our care and commitment to you. We look forward to working with you and want to welcome you to Jacobs' Pediatrics & Oncology."

Another round of loud applause roars throughout the room, making my heart soar.

I take this moment to step up to the mic and say a few words in honor of this celebration. Sure, we officially opened months ago, but today is the grand opening to welcome the community.

"When my sister Summer was diagnosed with Hodgkin's years ago, my family and I were devastated. But through the strength and support of great health care professionals, we were able to spend many more years with Summer and get through her loss as a family. I know what it's like to have to travel across the state to receive the care you need in this situation. Part of the reason Abby and I wanted to open our practice here, is to provide opportunities for families on this side of the state to get their needs met. We thank you for coming out today to help us celebrate. We couldn't do this without you and want you to know how much your support means to us. Thank you."

Once another round of applause dies down, I remind the crowd, "Please help yourselves to food and refreshments. Abby and I will be around should you have any questions. Thanks again for coming to celebrate this journey with us."

With that, I look to Abby. She reaches up on the tips of her toes and kisses me lightly on the cheek. Seeing that I hadn't forgotten to say anything, she squeezes my hand, and we walk away from the podium to mingle with our guests.

Before we part, she looks to me and caresses my face with her free hand. Then she whispers, "I love you, Dr. Jacobs. We did it. I couldn't have done it without you."

The look on her face makes me wish we were anywhere but in a crowded room. But I'm brought back to my memories at my desk from earlier, and I proudly remind her, "I'm sure glad I chose you, Angel. I'm sure glad I chose you."

She rolls her eyes and smiles. "I won't let you forget it."

THE END

If you want more from this series, be sure to check out Vince: Book Two of the Perfectly Independent Series where Sydney's story continues...

It's funny how one night can change everything.
When Sydney walks into my life she knocks my world off kilter.

She's strong, sexy, independent and possibly more than I can handle. She's everything I've ever wanted, but my reality and the secret I'm harboring, might have her running in the other direction.

Will my perfectly laid out plans go up in flames if I take a chance on her?

Damien: Book Three of the Perfectly Independent Series

When I walk into the diner, all I'm looking for is a decent meal. As a civil engineer for the largest project on campus, I just want to eat in peace. I'm happy to find this hidden gem since students are scarce. Don't get me wrong, co-eds on campus are beautiful, but I was over that scene when I graduated three years ago. I need to finish this job and move onto the next one by the end of the year.

Then Vanessa walks up with a simple smile and takes my breath away. The next thing I know, I'm making every excuse imaginable to dine with this intriguing woman. She's not only smart and sexy; she's completely focused on reaching the goals she has set for herself.

The more I get to know her, the more I know she's the one. I just have to find a way to make her deviate from her perfectly laid plans and take a chance on me.

Grab these stories today!
https://amandashelley.com/books-by-amanda-shelley-2/

ABOUT THE AUTHOR

Amanda Shelley loves falling into a book to experience new worlds. As an avid reader and writer, sharing worlds of her own creation is a passion that has inspired her to become an author. She writes contemporary romance with characters who are strong and sexy with a touch of sass.

When not writing, Amanda enjoys time with her family, playing chauffeur, chef, and being an enthusiastic fan for her children. Keeping up with them keeps her alert and grounded. She enjoys long car rides, chai lattes, and popping her SUV into four-wheel drive for adventures anywhere.

Amanda loves hearing from readers. Be sure sign up for her newsletter and follow her on social media. Join her reader's group *Amanda's Army of Readers* to stay up to date on her latest information.

Readers group: https://www.facebook.com/groups/AmandasArmyofReaders/
Goodreads: https://www.goodreads.com/author/show/19713563.Amanda_Shelley
Newsletter: https://bit.ly/3iyENe6
www.amandashelley.com

facebook.com/authoramandashelley
twitter.com/AmandShelley
instagram.com/authoramandashelley
bookbub.com/profile/amanda-shelley
pinterest.com/authoramandashelley
amazon.com/author/amandashelley

ACKNOWLEDGMENTS

First, I want to thank you, the reader, blogger, and reviewer for reading this book. There are plenty to choose from, and I want you to know I appreciate you choosing mine to spend your time with. Hopefully, you've enjoyed Drew and Abby as much as I have. I'd love to hear from you. You can find me on social media, my reader's group *Amanda's Army of Readers* or at www.amandashelley.com. If you care to share your thoughts on this book with other book lovers, please consider leaving a review at any of the retail sites or on Goodreads and BookBub.

I'd like to thank Amy Queau at Q Design Covers and Premades for creating the incredible cover for this book. You took my vision for this series and brought it to life and with those images, I'm dying to continue writing this series! You're brilliant, and I absolutely love working with you! I see many more books in our future!

This book wouldn't be what it is without my amazing team

of support. To Renita McKinney at A Book A Day Author Services, thank you for helping me make Drew and Abby the best they can be and developing them as characters.

To Susan Soares at SJS Editorial Services, thank you for working with me. I appreciate your time and feedback. You are amazing to work with. This book wouldn't be what it is today without you.

To Julie Deaton at Deaton Author Services, thanks for making my book pretty. I appreciate knowing your proofreading is exquisite, and my worries become less. Your eagle eyes are spectacular, and I don't know what I'd do without you.

To Mickel Yantz, thank you for designing my chapter images. Little did you know as a graphic designer, you'd be talking plot and inadvertently becoming a beta reader. I can't wait to work with you for swag soon.

To the people who have supported me along the way, I'm humbly grateful to have you in my life. Whether you've read my books, asked me about my progress, listened to me talk about my fictional characters as if they're a part of my family, plotted with me or been my cheerleader, I appreciate your continued support. Please know it hasn't gone unnoticed.

Last but certainly not least, to my four beautiful girls, who have had to wait patiently when I said, "Just one more minute," when I obviously meant a lot more than one. I love that you get I have deadlines and will sometimes keep me to task with your not so subtle reminders that "Mom... you should be working" during my designated times. I appreciate your support more than you'll ever know. Even though you can't read these books—because that might be *weird*—for both of us, I love that you keep asking. I love you all more than words can express. You're the reason I continue to strive and reach for my goals each day.

ALSO BY AMANDA SHELLEY

Coming September 28 2021

Fix Your Crown Anthology

Everyone has been affected by cancer in some way or another. We know someone living with cancer or may even have it yourself. I recently joined the Fix Your Crown Anthology where me and 14 other amazing woman authors are taking the proceeds we make and donating to cancer research. For just 99 cents you could help fund badly needed research. Let's stop cancer in its tracks as soon as we can.

Pre-order Fix Your Crown for only 99 cents and immediately receive (7) complimentary books from the authors of the anthology! That's (22) books in total for a buck! Fix Your Crown is available on all major e-retailers!

www.fixyourcrownanthology.com

Participating Authors: Alexi Ferreira, Amanda Shelley, Amaya Black, Angela Sanders, Barb Shuler, Brittany Tarkington, Callie Rae, E.K. Woodcock, Jade Bay, Jami Denise, Jo Richardson, Khloe Summers, Ruby Wolff, Sofia Aves and Tanya Nellestein

What you'll get from me... My story in this anthology is Hoops & Scoops. It features Chloe and DeShawn from the Perfectly Independent series. You won't want to miss their beginning.

Hoops & Scoops

When the one that got away shows up unexpectedly in my living room—I'm shocked.

When she pretends to be a stranger—I'm not having it.

There's no way she doesn't remember.

But I know her weakness—it comes in a pint and best eaten with a spoon.

I need to convince her that hoops aren't my only priority, or I won't stand a chance.

Coming October 26, 2021

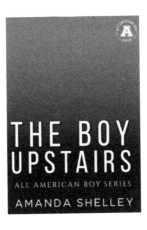

The All-American Boy Series description

Welcome to Bear Creek, Colorado, an idyllic all-American mountain resort town and home of the USA Music Festival. Filled with summer love, country music and unexpected pleasures, this brand-new series of short contemporary stories will bring together a mix of summer fun and music with the backdrop of the Colorado Rocky Mountains.

The All-American Boy Series gives you a taste of 16 new books in a shared world experience. All books are standalone but may include cross-over in characters or scenes.

Series page: https://www.subscribepage.com/all-american-boy-series

The Boy Upstairs

I ran into Derek while trying to escape the neighbor from hell. Instantly, we hit it off. Since he's only here for three months and the microbrewery leaves me little time for commitments, it's the perfect setup for a fling.

He's adventurous, challenges me, and he just gets me from the inside out.

With our expiration date quickly approaching, I'm left to wonder... Will my heart ever be the same without the boy upstairs?

https://amandashelley.com/books-by-amanda-shelley-2/

AVAILABLE AT ALL RETAILERS

https://amandashelley.com/books-by-amanda-shelley-2/

Vince: Book Two of the Perfectly Independent Series

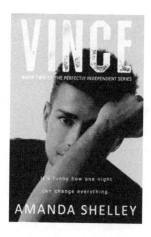

It's funny how one night can change everything.

Family comes first. I knew that. I knew there would be sacrifices and we are so close to having it all. I knew because I had the perfectly laid out plan to make it happen.

That is until she walked in and knocked my world on its ass.

Sydney's strong, sexy, independent – possibly more than I can handle. She's everything I've ever wanted, but my reality and the secret I'm harboring, might have her running in the other direction.

Will it all go up in flames if I take a chance on her?

I guess I'm about to find out.

https://amandashelley.com/books-by-amanda-shelley-2/

Damien: Book Three of the Perfectly Independent Series

Beautiful girls are not hard to find at Columbia River University.

The coeds on campus are great to look at but I was over that scene after graduation three years ago.

These days, outside of being part of the largest civil engineering job on campus, all I'm searching for is a decent meal and some peace and quiet. It's why I'm happy to have found what I consider a hidden gem in the diner I frequent.

All I need to do is finish this job and move on to the next by year's end.

Should be easy enough. Only when Vanessa walks up with a sexy smile and a mouth full of sass, she does more than take my order. She completely takes my breath away.

Next thing I know, I'm here every morning, making every excuse to dine with this intriguing woman. Not only is she smart and sexy, but she's laser focused on reaching the goals she's set for herself.

The more I get to know her, the more I'm convinced she's the one. I just have to find a way to get her to deviate from her perfectly laid plans and take a chance on me.

https://amandashelley.com/books-by-amanda-shelley-2/

Making The Call

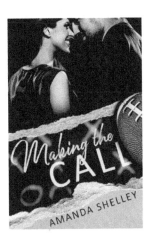

Dani

As a bestselling romance author, most assume my life's glamorous, filled with combustible chemistry, and most of all, romance. Ha! I can only wish. With a deadline looming, I've escaped to my family's cabin on Anderson Island to free myself from distractions. My plan's great, until a man, who could pass as a cover model on one of my books, comes to my rescue. Is there chemistry? Sure. Is he everything I'd look for in a guy? Absolutely. But will my career be at risk if I give into my desire?

Luke

For a player, women line up outside the locker room. For coaches, we're lucky to get in the game. As the youngest NFL coach in the league, I live, eat, breathe, and even sleep football. To gear up for this season, I return to my home on Anderson Island for a much-needed break. When Dani literally crashes into my life, my mind's suddenly on the sexy brunette with a sailors mouth, rather than my team's next play. She has me dusting off another playbook entirely, making me wonder, did I make the right call?

https://amandashelley.com/books-by-amanda-shelley-2/

Resilience: Book One of Resilience Duet

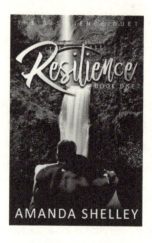

Resolution: Book Two of Resilience Duet

Samantha never saw Enzo coming.

As the dust settles from her divorce, her life is full. She doesn't have time for distractions. She's too busy running her own company and checking off numerous items from her kids' demanding schedule to have a life of her own.

Then he walks into her kitchen with his breathtaking green eyes and a mischievous grin. He's there to surprise his father - her contractor, but his presence makes everything off kilter.

Enzo's perfectly content with his adventurous life as an elite rescue pilot, until a harmless prank turns on him. Instead of surprising his father, he finds his world thrown off course by the beautiful woman with a sexy smile, wicked sass and the mouthwatering ability to keep him on his toes.

With his limited time on leave, is she worth the risk to his heart?

https://amandashelley.com/books-by-amanda-shelley-2/

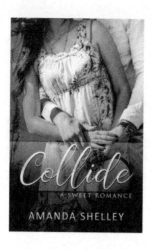

Collide: A Sweet Romance

Falling head over heels was the last thing I expected.

Literally.

Coffee is everywhere – and more than my ego is bruised.

When the handsome stranger I plowed into calls me by name, mortification sinks in.

He rushes off to class. I run home to change, hoping to forget the whole incident.

If only I could be so lucky.

I quickly find it's a small world and Gavin Wallace is completely unavoidable. Everywhere I turn he's there. In my classes. Hanging with my friends.

I've got his full attention and I have to admit, I like it a lot more than I should.

https://amandashelley.com/books-by-amanda-shelley-2/

Made in the USA
Middletown, DE
15 September 2025

13423466R00234